Edmund Kell Blyth

Life of William Ellis

Second Edition

Edmund Kell Blyth

Life of William Ellis
Second Edition

ISBN/EAN: 9783337332730

Printed in Europe, USA, Canada, Australia, Japan

Cover: Foto ©Raphael Reischuk / pixelio.de

More available books at **www.hansebooks.com**

LIFE OF WILLIAM ELLIS

LIFE

OF

WILLIAM ELLIS

(FOUNDER OF THE BIRKBECK SCHOOLS)

WITH SOME ACCOUNT OF HIS WRITINGS,

AND OF HIS LABOURS

FOR THE IMPROVEMENT AND EXTENSION OF EDUCATION.

BY

EDMUND KELL BLYTH.

Second Edition.

TO THE PUPILS OF WILLIAM ELLIS,
FROM THOSE OF IMPERIAL AND ROYAL RANK
TO HUMBLE TOILERS FOR THEIR DAILY BREAD,
WHO HAVE RECEIVED FROM HIM
OR THROUGH HIS LIFE-LONG LABOURS
GUIDANCE AS TO THEIR CONDUCT IN DAILY LIFE:

TO THE FORTUNATE POSSESSORS OF WEALTH
WHO HAVE DERIVED FROM HIS TEACHING
THE KNOWLEDGE OF
THEIR MORAL DUTY IN ITS USE:

AND TO ALL WHO HAVE LEARNED FROM HIM
HOW BEST TO IMPROVE THE CONDITION
OF THEIR LESS FORTUNATE FELLOW-CITIZENS,
AND TO HELP TO DIMINISH DESTITUTION, VICE, AND CRIME,
BY REMOVING THEIR CHIEF CAUSE:

I DEDICATE
THIS RECORD OF HIS LIFE-HISTORY.

PREFACE.

SOME time after the death of William Ellis I undertook the duty of writing an account of his life from the conviction that a record of his character, work, and educational method would be of public advantage. The chief feature of his character—that which controlled his life and acts—was an overmastering, world-wide, practical benevolence. His strong and vivid realization of the mass of misery and destitution which exist in the world, and his personal feeling that it was his duty, as well as that of every other enlightened human being, to try and alleviate it, led him to study its cause; and he found by conclusive evidence that that cause existed mainly, if not entirely, in the character, habits, and conduct of the destitute creatures themselves or their parents. But the effect on his mind was the precise opposite of that produced on Hamlet's when he said,

> "The time is out of joint; O cursed spite,
> "That ever I was born to set it right!"

Ellis felt compelled by his sense of the amount of misery existing in the world not merely to exert himself to set it right, but even to devote his whole life to that mission. He saw that the mere relief of poverty and destitution,

without attacking them at their source, was of little use—
that almsgiving, especially when systemized as by the doles
and gifts in which so much of the benevolent intentions of
testators during the middle ages found its outlet, was worse
than useless—that it demoralized the recipients, and sapped
the foundation of personal energy and self-reliance. He
saw what a difficult and, in many cases, hopeless task it
was to re-form the characters of those who had grown
up to adult age in ignorance, and in whom habits
of indolence, intemperance, and thriftlessness were fixed
and established, and that the only method of doing
permanent good was to seek to form character during
childhood, when the mind is plastic and impressionable.

He, therefore, devoted himself to the working out
of the method by which the character of children
can best be influenced for good or—as we have said—
formed. His old and life-long friend John Stuart Mill has
in his *Logic* (vol. ii., book vi., chap. 5) pointed out that there
may and ought to be a science of the formation of
character, and he gave to such a science (which he said was
still to be created) the name of Ethology. But he did not
proceed to work it out. Ellis, on the other hand, devoted
himself to discover how children can best be influenced
for good and their characters formed, and he found the
solution of the problem in the systematic teaching of right
principles of conduct and training in good habits. His
method of teaching those principles adapted to and in
connection with the phenomena of industrial life as we see
it, is the staple of his work—the great improvement which

he sought to introduce into all schools, high and low. He looked round at existing systems of education and found them all deficient. Schools for the upper classes were one and all wanting in any attempt to form character or to teach lessons of conduct. They were mainly founded upon the teaching of the Greek and Latin classics: and though physical science has during the last half century been introduced in many of them, the chief science of all—the science of self-guidance—is still not systematically taught in any. Schools for the lower classes were, when he began his work, wretchedly inefficient. Since that time—especially since the Education Act of 1870—they have immensely improved. But even in them the real teaching of rules of conduct is hardly attempted. The thought has certainly entered the minds of the superintendents and inspectors of Board Schools. They have expressed their desire that "religion "and morality" should be taught in them. But the actual performance falls sadly short of the intention; no systematic method of teaching them has been adopted, and in only very few schools, the masters of which have seen the advantage of Ellis's method, have they been taught in such a manner as really to form character. In the enormous majority of primary schools such teaching has degenerated into lessons in the ancient history of the Jews and the geography of Palestine, or the reading of chapters in the Bible without any attempt to elucidate the lessons of conduct contained in them, and often without note or comment. How utterly this teaching—admittedly well meant, and prompted by the right thought—falls short of real character-forming education, Ellis has shown in many of his works, especially *Philo-Socrates*, and it was this kind of education, the real and true teaching of self-guidance, which he sought to introduce into all schools as the only effectual method of diminishing destitution, vice, and crime.

When I had done the greater part of my work, I became aware that Miss Ethel E. Ellis, his granddaughter, had undertaken to write a sketch of his life, which, during its progress, expanded into a memoir. I felt at first doubtful whether it was desirable that two biographies should be published; but it appeared to me that her memoir—for she has kindly shown me her work, and has seen mine—was so different in its scope and contents from what I had written, that no harm could arise if both were laid before the public; nay, that if a more extended range of readers were obtained, and the knowledge of the beneficent character we both revered were more widely diffused, good would be the result.

I have gratefully to acknowledge the assistance rendered me by the family of William Ellis, who have placed in my hands all the papers and manuscripts bearing on his life-work which he left behind him. Those papers have, however, been much curtailed by his own act. His extreme modesty led him, within the last three or four years of his life, to destroy a large quantity of his papers, especially letters from men of note, which might have been of public interest; and the records preserved by him are probably smaller in quantity than were ever left behind by a man who had lived so long, so energetic, and so laborious a life.

One series of letters has fortunately been entrusted to me which has proved of the greatest value—those written to the late Professor Hodgson, of Edinburgh, extending from 1846 to June, 1880, and in fact covering the whole period of Ellis's systematic work in the great cause of human improvement. The deep sympathy between the two men and their warm and cordial co-operation in the same objects and by the same methods produced a friendship which lasted through life; and Ellis's letters to Hodgson contain many of his best thoughts, put in perhaps a more friendly and unconstrained manner than we find them in his published works, the latter of which are written in a closely logical style. For this correspondence I desire to express my warmest acknowledgment to Professor Hodgson's widow, who has an earnest sympathy with the common life-work of Ellis and her husband. My thanks are also due to William Mattieu Williams, Esq., the Honorary Secretary of the original Birkbeck School and the Master of George Combe's Secular School at Edinburgh, who was warmly attached to Ellis, for the loan of the letters to him. I hoped to obtain Ellis's letters to the late George Combe himself, another staunch friend and ally in the war against destitution and misery. As all Combe's letters to Ellis were lent to his executors at the time when Combe's biography was written under their direction, I thought I had some claim to a similar courtesy. But I am informed that all his papers are finally put away in such a manner as to be practically inaccessible, and those valuable letters are therefore unavailable.

I must also acknowledge the kind and cordial assistance

of Madame Salis Schwabe, the founder of a school at Naples upon Ellis's system, which has been since taken over by the Government, and has proved eminently successful and beneficial as a model for adoption in Italy. She has addressed to me a letter upon the subject of this memoir, which I am permitted to include in this work, and which will be found in Appendix A. In that letter she has expressed her warm appreciation of the pure and elevating character of Ellis's teaching, of his self-devotion to the cause of the poor and neglected, and his earnest work for the diminution of the vast mass of human misery. I hope that, in the history of his life which I now offer to the public, I may have done something to draw attention to, and excite interest in, labours which in fact attained to the dignity of an apostolate.

Hampstead, July, 1889.

CONTENTS.

LIFE OF WILLIAM ELLIS.

CHAPTER I.

1800—1825.

Introductory—Parentage and Early Years—Entry into Business—The Indemnity Mutual Mariné Assurance Company—Marriage.

THE story of the life of William Ellis is a record of earnest and persevering devotion to the conscientious discharge of the highest duty which a human being can set before himself, namely, the advancement of the well-being of the human race. To that object he devoted every spare moment which he could obtain from the business engagements in which he was occupied from the age of thirteen until he retired from them through failing powers at the age of seventy-eight. To that object, for the attainment of which he believed the most powerful engine to be the education and training of children in those lines of conduct which conduce to well-being, he devoted all the resources of an unusually powerful intellect, a logical faculty of singular clearness and grasp, a fertility of apt illustration derived from varied and extensive reading, and a wide knowledge of men acquired in active life. These were guided by an active benevolence which could not be surpassed. The mere amount of money devoted by him to the cause of human progress would astonish many men—owners of broad lands and large revenues—who think they are performing their duty as leading members of society, and

B

satisfying the claims of charity, by subscribing a few guineas to local schools or hospitals. But the extreme modesty of his nature led him to carry out his plans of beneficence in such a way as to keep as far as possible in the background his own part in the work. The Birkbeck Schools, intended as a practical embodiment of his deeply considered thoughts as to what education should be, were associated with the name of Dr. Birkbeck merely as a memorial to that eminent philanthropist, who died shortly prior to the foundation of the first of them. Many of his most carefully elaborated educational works were published without his name, and some under the auspices, as editors, of other gentlemen whose names he thought might obtain attention for them in quarters where his own might fail to attract. But the story of a long life so entirely and unselfishly devoted to the cause of human advancement ought not to remain untold. James Mill—of whom he always spoke as the person to whom he was most indebted for the direction which his mind received in early life—says,[1] "When a man "has risen to great intellectual or moral eminence, the process "by which his mind was formed is one of the most instructive "circumstances which can be unveiled to mankind. It dis-"plays to their view the means of acquiring excellence, and "suggests the most persuasive motive to employ them." And this life-history is especially one, the knowledge of which may lead some of its readers to realise that they too can do something to advance the welfare of their less fortunate fellow creatures, and may enable others whose energies are already directed to that end, to see more clearly the best way to utilise their powers to the best advantage.

William Ellis was descended from a French Huguenot family, named De Vezian, whose ancestral home was in the mountains of the Cevennes, in the Bishopric of Albi, Languedoc. His grandfather had, at what precise date or

---

[1] *Literary Journal*, 1806, " Review of Millar on Ranks."

under what circumstances is not known, emigrated to England, where he was occupied in commercial pursuits in London. He had one son, to whom he gave the name (after a business friend named Ellis) of Andrew Ellis de Vezian, and who became an underwriter, and for many years carried on business in the city of London, within the limits of which city he also lived. He married about the end of the eighteenth century a lady of Italian extraction, named Sophia Fazio, and of that marriage were born several children, of whom William, born on the 27th January, 1800, was the fourth. It was about three or four years after this that his father ceased to use the name of De Vezian and duplicated the name which preceded it—that of his godfather—being known for the rest of his life as Mr. Andrew Ellis Ellis, or latterly Mr. Ellis Ellis.

William was born in the city of London, but, shortly after his birth, his father, who was then prospering in business, took a house in Devonshire Place, Marylebone, now rather a gloomy town-like street, but then quite on the outskirts of suburban London. Here his children had opportunities of enjoying fresher air than the close and narrow streets of their native city, then without the broad thoroughfares which it now possesses, could provide. It was, doubtless, in the fields and open country which were soon afterwards to become the Regent's Park, and in the neighbourhood of which he was destined to spend the last five-and-twenty years of his life, that he played in early childhood. But his father did not remain many years in Devonshire Place; he moved thence to Kennington, and remained there until about 1820, when he returned to the neighbourhood of the Regent's Park, and settled in Weymouth Street.

When about seven years old, William was sent to school at Bromley, in Kent, then a quiet country village, wholly unconnected with the Metropolis, whose inhabitants would have received with utter disbelief the prophecy that half a century would see them whirled by the powerful magic of steam into the heart of London in the short space of twenty minutes. Of his schoolmaster, and what sort of teaching he received there, no records are in existence. He himself scarcely ever talked about his education at Bromley, and, although he left school at a very early age, I have no doubt he would have spoken of it had it been in any way in advance of the schools of that time. A tradition exists that on one occasion he ran away from school and came home, an escapade which had no other result than a severe punishment; and from this fact we may, doubtless, infer that the school was one of the old-fashioned and severe kind which was too common in those days. He, doubtless, imbibed the rudiments of Latin and Greek, with some Algebra and Mathematics, but the studies which were soon to attract and fascinate his active mind must have been commenced at a later period.

In the year 1813, when only in his fourteenth year, he left school. His father had, some years previously, through the speculations of a partner, been unfortunate in business, but the respect which his high character had earned from his friends and connections in the city bore good fruit in the sympathy and active help of his friends. Five gentlemen, one of whom was Mr. Thomas Tooke, a Russian merchant, and the well-known author of the *History of Prices*, assisted him to re-commence his old business of an underwriter, in which he was afterwards highly successful. But his misfortunes, and the move to Kennington which they rendered necessary, had been followed by further trouble in the loss of his wife, William's mother. And as his expenses, while he was working his way up again, had to be reduced to the lowest possible level, William's school career was terminated as early as possible, and at thirteen he entered his father's office. There he soon acquired the principles of business; his indefatigable energy, his patience, and the clear head and sound cautious judgment which so deeply impressed those who knew him in later life, enabled him to render great and valuable aid to his father in retrieving his position.　So remarkable was his advance in the knowledge and safe practice of the intricate and responsible business of marine insurance, that in the year 1818, when he was only eighteen years of age, his father made a prolonged stay in Paris, entrusting William with the sole charge of his business in London.　That he managed it with care and success may be assumed from the two facts, first, that no subsequent misfortunes ever happened to his father, who retired from business with a competence at an advanced age, and, secondly, that when, in the year 1824, the Indemnity Mutual Marine Assurance Company was formed, he received an offer and accepted the post of assistant manager of that Company.

Prior to that date the only companies which had the power to grant policies of marine insurance were the "Royal Exchange" and the "London Assurance," both old chartered companies, established in the early part of the eighteenth century, and transacting the business of marine assurance only as an adjunct to their other business of life and fire insurance.　But the great bulk of the business of marine insurance was transacted by individual underwriters, a body of separate insurers who had in the infancy of the system met to transact their business at a coffee house in Abchurch Lane, kept by a person named Lloyd, but who had long since deserted the Abchurch Lane coffee house for a large public room, which still bore the name of "Lloyds."　The loss of time, trouble, and expense of negociating policies for large sums in separate risks, often as low as £50 or £100, led a number of merchants to establish marine insurance companies, where an association of underwriters, united as shareholders in one company, should by one operation and one signature transact the same business which at Lloyds' would need a large number of separate negociations and signatures.

The first of these special marine insurance companies which

was established was the Indemnity, and of that Company Ellis became assistant underwriter at the age of twenty-four. The only reason he had for hesitation as to the acceptance of the post was the fact that it would lead to his separation from his father, to whom he was devoted through life; but the far wider sphere for the exercise of his abilities which was opened to him as underwriter to a company led him ultimately to decide upon accepting it. He never regretted the decision. In the year 1826, the chief underwriter to the Company resigned his position, and the able assistant manager succeeded to it. From that date until his final retirement in the year 1878 no further change took place in the quiet current of his professional life, except that at Christmas, 1876, when failing health compelled him to give up the daily attendance involved in the position of underwriter, the directors of the Company, anxious, while relieving him of the drudgery of work, to retain the benefit of his advice and experience upon difficult questions, appointed him to a seat on their Board. During the whole of this period the sound judgment and unvarying caution which he brought to bear upon the Company's work led to its becoming a great and remarkable commercial success. The shares of the Company, with £5 paid thereon, but which at the time of his appointment to the position of chief underwriter stood at a discount, increased from time to time in value until, including additions from time to time made out of profits, they stood so high in public estimation as at one time to command a price of £160 or £170 per share.

Shortly after he joined the Indemnity Company one of the most important events of Mr. Ellis's life took place. In the year 1821 he made the acquaintance (at the house of Sir Martin Archer Shee, P.R.A.) of Miss Mary Turner, daughter of Sharon Turner, a solicitor in London, who is, however, far better known as the author of the history of the Anglo-Saxons, and also of a history of England down to the death of Elizabeth. He became attached to her, and the attachment was reciprocated ; but shortly difficulties arose which bade fair to be fatal to the hopes of the young couple. Mr. Sharon Turner was a member of the Church of England, and strongly orthodox, while Ellis, who had already formed the friendship (of which more will be said later on) of Jeremy Bentham and the Mill family, held more advanced views on religious subjects. This circumstance led to the withdrawal of Mr. Turner's consent to the marriage. Patience, however, and the quiet determination of the young couple ultimately conquered the obstacles in the way of their union, and they were married at Ewell Church, between which place and Epsom Mr. Turner had a cottage, on the 14th May, 1825.

The marriage was a very happy one. Mrs. Ellis was a lady of energy and vigour, with a warm heart and a benevolent disposition, and she also possessed great musical and artistic taste, and considerable literary powers. She thoroughly appreciated and sympathised with the objects to which her husband soon began to devote his time and energy ; and, till her death in 1870, their union was one of mutual and undisturbed affection. Of her mental powers we may judge from a letter which she wrote to Dr. Hodgson, about a year after they made his acquaintance, explaining and defending the principle of Utility.

"Champion Hill, Camberwell, August 8th, 1847.

" My dear Sir,—I am very reluctant to encroach on your "valuable time as it regards others, or on your leisure, so "precious to yourself, by troubling you with another epistle, "and yet I do not think from the tone of your kind long "letter to me you will think me impertinent in doing so, if it "were only to say how impossible it is for me to presume to "discuss the merits of Epicurus' views, or of their relation "with Utilitarianism. In accounting for the faith that is in "me, I attempt nothing beyond. It appears to me that when "Epicurus states we seek our own happiness he only states

"what is a fact: we all endeavour to avoid what gives us
"pain. From earliest childhood this fact is manifested; the
"pleasurable sensations are sought, and the painful avoided.
"The principle of Utility so far combines with this fact as to
"draw from it a principle to regulate conduct, this principle
"being to direct the tendency that every human being has to
"pursue his own happiness so as to make that individual
"happiness coincident with the general happiness—in other
"words, self-control with the least possible sacrifice of indi-
"vidual happiness. On this principle are based all education,
"laws, and government: and the system, so far from being a
"debasing scheme of morality, appears to me the grandest
"ever taught. This idea, as far as regards education, has
"been so much better expressed by a very wise and good
"man,[1] that you must permit me to quote his words: 'The
"'end of education is to render the individual as much as
"'possible an instrument of happiness, first to himself, and
"'next to other beings, for, whether you will or not that the
"'prospect of pain or pleasure has power over the mind,
"'every person's experience teaches him,' &c.

"You speak of self-sacrifice as ennobling: but what is the
"worth of self-sacrifice in itself? Is it not pure Asceticism—
"the flaying of the flesh with a hair shirt, or iron band, with
"no other good obtained than the suffering of the wearer?
"Can also the party for whom such sacrifice is made receive
"anything but discomfort from the act if the mind and heart
"be well regulated? Do not we all feel an increase of
"pleasure when we enjoy without a sacrifice from any one?
"Is not our purest and most complete good attained when
"our wishes and those of our companions are united? Is not
"sympathy (a fellow feeling) Epicurus and Utility combined?
"And, moreover, have we not a standard to refer to as a rule
"of conduct that no storm can uproot? I feel reluctant in
"engaging in a discussion of the doctrines of Epicurus, as I

---

[1] James Mill, in his article on education in the *Encyclopædia Britannica*.

"do not always feel satisfied that I know what may be
"included among them; not so with the principle of Utility
"and the moral rules which may be deduced from it, and I
"only defend the doctrines of Epicurus as far as they coincide
"with that principle. Before I entirely quit this subject, you
"must permit me to say that I read with as much dislike
"and regret such epithets as 'Epicurus' swine or stye' applied
"to this teacher, as I hear from certain religionists 'that the
"'heart of man is desperately wicked' and 'that man is a
"'bundle of filthy rags' as a view of the human race. To such
"as are inclined to be blind, and to act regardless of conse-
"quences, the purest doctrine may be without fruit and forced
"into abomination; and from what I know of Epicurus,
"Christ might as easily be accused of sanctioning intemper-
"ance because he assisted at the feast of Cana, as Epicurus
"of teaching gluttony and mere indulgence of the senses.
"The pretended followers of this great Master may be as
"much degenerated from their exemplar, as Bishops and
"Lord High Cardinals from the humble founder of the
"religion they profess to teach.

"One other point in your letter I must also remark on.
"The longer I live the more deeply I feel the necessity of
"awakening the spirit of content, combined with exertion, in
"order to produce happy results for the individual—to fulfil
"the question Sand asks of '*Pourquoi ne serait on pas à la
"'fois un ouvrier laborieux et un homme instruit?*' The moral
"information is what is wanted to combine with the necessity
"of labour, and to be able to advance this fulfilment even a
"little seems to me a source of gratification where there is
"the power of intellect and physical strength to achieve it.
"Why should we call a man's standard of content *low* if he
"fulfils his share in the duties and demands of this life? or
"why should we suppose his standard is *low*, because he
"makes himself 'satisfied easily with his condition?' This
"letter, if you have patience to read it, will satisfy you that
"you must seek a better correspondent to discuss weighty

"matters with. I only hope you will excuse the trouble I
"give you and not consider yourself bound to answer.—
"Believe me, yours very truly,

"M. ELLIS."

They began their married life at Croydon ; their means
were narrow—his salary being then only £500 a year—but
it is a remarkable evidence how strongly he had practically
imbibed the great principles of forethought and providence
that at the commencement of his married life he only spent
one-half of this limited income. An anecdote of himself
which he related to a lady (Mrs. Fenwick Miller) who saw
much of him during the last few years of his life, is an
additional proof how early and how deeply these principles
had taken root in his mind.

"When I was a boy," he said, "I used to go to the office
"with a companion of my own age. We each had breakfast
"before we started, and dinner on our return home in the
"evening, and we were allowed a penny a day each for lunch.
"We used to buy a small biscuit each, with seeds in it, for the
"penny ; but corn was dear, and it was not much for a
"hungry boy that we could get with a penny. My com-
"panion was very pleased, after some time, to discover that
"he could buy seven of the biscuits for sixpence. He there-
"fore got an advance of his week's money, and bought his
"seven biscuits to last for the week. So far it was all right ;
"that was a good commercial transaction. But on the first
"day he ate two biscuits ; and on the second day he could
"not resist a second and a third biscuit, even ; so that on
"Friday he had none at all left, and I had to give him a
"share of mine."

CHAPTER II.

1820—1824.

IT was about the year 1820 that Ellis made the acquaintance, through the introduction of Mr. Thomas Tooke, of Jeremy Bentham and James Mill, and soon became one of the school of earnest and able young men who derived their inspiration from them, and whose devoted work led to so great progress in many political and social questions. Bentham, the head and central figure of this remarkable group, was then about seventy-two, and lived in Queen's Square Place, Westminster. Of the effect which his writings have had upon the English social progress some idea may be derived from the list of a few of the practical reforms advocated by him which have since that time become law. In the introduction to his works[1] by Mr. John Hill Burton we find a long list of such reforms, of which the following are but a selection, viz.: Reform of the representative system, municipal reform, mitigation of the criminal code, abolition of arrest, abolition of the usury laws, removal of the exclusionary rules of evidence, repeal of the Test and Corporation Acts and Catholic disabilities, abolition of the taxes on knowledge, a uniform system of poor laws under central administration with a system of training pauper children, savings banks and friendly societies, cheap postage, a complete register of births, deaths, and marriages, the

---

[1] *Bentham's Works*, published under the superintendence of his executor, Sir John Bowring. 1843. W. Tait. Edinburgh: Simpkin, Marshall, & Co.

ballot, cheap local courts, free trade, and national education.
As the great advocate of the philosophy which has received
the title of Utilitarian, he based his reforms upon the great
principle of the welfare of the great mass of the community
—in other words, "the greatest happiness of the greatest
number," a phrase which he tells us in one of his letters he
found "in the tail of one of Dr. Priestley's pamphlets,"[1] but
the principles of which he adopted from several earlier
writers, especially Helvetius.[2] Bentham, however, made
them so completely his own, that they are now especially
associated with him, and it was in a great measure from his
powerful influence that the friends who were attracted to
him imbibed his views and exerted themselves in pressing
them forward in various directions of social progress.

How deep was their reverence for him and his power, and
how great was the charm he had for them, we may judge
by what some of his friends say of him. James Mill, his
closest ally and chief literary associate, says[3]:—

"Everything which comes from the pen or from the
"mind of Mr. Bentham is entitled to profound regard.
"Of all the men, in all ages, and in all countries, who
"have made the philosophy of law their study, he has
"made the greatest progress. If the vast additions which
"the science of legislation owes to him be hitherto little
"known to his countrymen, it is owing to the indigence of
"instruction among them, and to the infinite smallness of
"the number who take any interest in the most important
"topics."

Sir Samuel Romilly, whose friendship with Bentham

---

[1] *Bentham's Works* (Memoirs and Correspondence, by Sir John Bowring),
vol. x., page 46.

[2] *Ib.*, vol. x., page 70. "A sort of action is a right one, when the ten-
"dency of it is to augment the mass of happiness in the community. This is
"what we are indebted for to Helvetius." Helvetius' work, *De l'Esprit*, was
condemned to be burned by the Parliament of Paris in 1763.

[3] *Annual Review* for 1808, "Review of Bentham's Pamphlet on Scotch
Reform," quoted in Bain's *Biography of James Mill*, page 95.

lasted until the sad tragedy which deprived the cause of humanity and mercy of his invaluable services, says of him[1]:—

"It is impossible to know Bentham, and to have "witnessed his benevolence, his disinterestedness, and the "zeal with which he has devoted his whole life to the "services of his fellow creatures, without admiring and "revering him."

Sir Francis Burdett (father of Lady Burdett Coutts), a very early advocate of parliamentary reform, who, on 2nd June, 1818, moved a series of resolutions upon that subject, drafted for him by Bentham, writes to the latter in the following language, as to the intended motion[2]:—

"My tongue shall speak as you do prompt mine ear; "and I will venture to promise, knowing so well whom I "promise, that I will refuse attempting no one thing that "you shall say ought to be done. My first reward will "be the hope of doing everlasting good to my country; "my next, and only inferior to it, that of having my name "linked, in immortality, with that of Jeremy Bentham; "and though, to be sure, it is but as a tomtit mounted on "an eagle's wing, the thought delights me. Bentham and "Burdett! The alliteration charms mine ear."

Sir John Bowring, his executor, who was quite a young man when in the year 1820 he made his acquaintance, says of him[3]:—

"Blessings, benefits, benignities, courtesies, in every "shape, I have received at his hands. No son was ever "honoured by an affectionate father with more evidence "of fondness, esteem, and confidence. And to me his "friendship was as that of a guardian angel. It conducted "me with faithful devotion through a period of my exist- "ence in which I was steeped in poverty and overwhelmed

---

[1] *Life of Sir Samuel Romilly*, vol. iii., p. 415.

[2] *Bentham's Works* (Memoirs and Correspondence), vol. x., page 494.

[3] *Ibid.*, vol. x., page 516.

"with slander. His house was an asylum—his purse
"a treasury—his heart an Eden—his mind a fortress
"to me."

And of the quaint and characteristic humour with which
he received his friends, some idea may be formed from the
following letter[1]—a proposition for a symposium—which
also gives an idea of the class of men who gathered round
him during the first two or three years when Ellis obtained
his friendship:—

"Bentham to Henry Brougham.

"13th May, 1822.

"Get together a gang, and bring them to the Hermitage,
"to devour such eatables and drinkables as are to be
"found in it.

    I. From Honourable House.
      1. Brougham, Henry.
      2. Denman.
      3. Hume, Joseph.
      4. Mackintosh, James.
      5. Ricardo, David.
   II. From Lincoln's Inn Fields.
      6. Whishaw, James.
  III. From India House.
      7. Mill, James.

"Hour of attack, half after six.

"Hour of commencement of plunderage, seven.

"Hour of expulsion, with the aid of the adjacent police-
"office, if necessary, quarter before eleven.

"Day of attack to be determined by Universal Suffrage.

"N.B.—To be performed with advantage, all plunderage
"must be regulated.

"Witness, Matchless Constitution."

Next to Jeremy Bentham the most remarkable member
of the circle was James Mill, then aged forty-seven and in the

---

[1] *Bentham's Works* (Memoirs and Correspondence), vol. x., page 533.

zenith of his power. Born in a humble sphere of life in Forfar-
shire, he had by his consummate ability risen to eminence, and
had shortly before been appointed to the post of an assistant
examiner at the India Office, in consequence of the great
knowledge shown by his celebrated *History of British
India*, then recently completed. The Examiner's office
of the Old East India Company was that in which the
despatches to India were drafted and settled, and in
which all the principal measures for Indian administration were framed. It was an office which, while it gave
ample scope for his great powers, left him sufficient leisure
to continue and carry on the political, literary, and economical studies which engrossed his life, and which were
continued by his still more celebrated son, John Stuart Mill,
under the teaching which from his earliest years he received
at his father's hands.

James Mill, though somewhat imperious in his own family,
and deficient in the element of tenderness, did not show
that side of his character to his friends.

"He was sought" (says his son in his *Autobiography*)[1]
"for the vigour and instructiveness of his conversation,
"and used it largely for the diffusion of his opinions. I
"have never known any man who could do such ample
"justice to his best thoughts in colloquial discussions.
"His perfect command over his great mental resources,
"the terseness and expressiveness of his language, and
"the moral earnestness as well as intellectual force of
"his delivery made him one of the most striking of argu-
"mentative conversers; and he was full of anecdote, a
"hearty laugher, and, when with people whom he liked, a
"most lively and amusing companion."

And Lord Brougham, one of his most intimate friends,
says of him[2]:—

"He was a man of extensive and profound learning,

---

[1] *Autobiography of John Stuart Mill*, page 101 (2nd edit.).
[2] Bain's *Biography of James Mill*, page 460.

"thoroughly imbued with the doctrines of metaphysical
"and ethical science; conversant above most men with
"the writings of the ancient philosophers, whose
"language he familiarly knew; and gifted with an
"extraordinary power of application which had made
"entirely natural to him a life of severe and unremitting
"study."

James Mill had, shortly before the date when Ellis
acquired his friendship, written (in the year 1818) his
masterly article on education originally published in the
Encyclopædia Britannica, and subsequently republished in
the collection of his Essays. The general views advocated
in the essay may be gathered from the principle on which it
is based, viz., that "the end of education is to render the
"individual as much as possible an instrument of happiness
"first to himself and next to other beings." And we may
well realise the direction which would be given to
Ellis's mind by so remarkable a man when we read what
John Stuart Mill says of his father's doctrine on this
subject.

"In Psychology," he tells us, in his *Autobiography*,[1] "his
"fundamental doctrine was the formation of all human
"character by circumstances, through the universal prin-
"ciple of association, and the consequent unlimited
"possibility of improving the moral and intellectual
"condition of mankind by education. Of all his doctrines
"none was more important than this, or needs to be more
"insisted on; unfortunately there is none which is more
"contradictory to the prevailing tendencies of speculation,
"both in his time and since."

The great influence exercised by James Mill upon Ellis
was always acknowledged by the latter. In the introduction
to more than one of his works he refers to it; and in a
letter to the *Times*, dated in 1873, which will be found

---

[1] Page 108.

printed later on (chap. vii.), he expresses himself as deeply indebted to the father and son for having set him thinking for himself.

Nearly all the other members of this remarkable knot of men were then or afterwards became earnest workers in the cause of social reform. Brougham, then about forty-two, had been in Parliament for some four years, and had thrown himself earnestly into the advocacy of the great questions, mostly now set at rest, the support of which then seemed to be a forlorn hope. The abolition of slavery, the establishment of a system of national education, and the reform of legal procedure, were subjects of which Brougham had made himself a prominent representative. Denman, a less brilliant advocate, but a better judge, was associated with him in Parliament a year or two later, in the defence of Queen Caroline against the persecution of George IV. Mackintosh, some ten or twelve years their senior, had taken up the mantle of Sir Samuel Romilly, whose noble and brilliant career had been sadly terminated two years previously by a catastrophe resulting from overstrained nerves and overworked brain, and was bravely advocating against the enormous majority of the House of Commons the reform of our then Draconian criminal code. Joseph Hume, who had been for eight years a member of the House, was beginning the career of industrious and careful labour which have made him a model for all future advocates of economy. David Ricardo, who had, under the persuasion of James Mill, conquered his shy and timid nature, had obtained a seat in the House of Commons about two years previously, and we may be sure that the "benevolent countenance and kindliness of manner, very attractive to young persons," which appear to have so strongly impressed John Stuart Mill, were not without their influence upon Ellis. Bickersteth, afterwards Lord Langdale, and Master of the Rolls, was another member of the circle ; he was then known as a warm advocate of Parliamentary Reform, and it was under his advice that

C

Bentham induced Sir Francis Burdett to bring the subject forward in the House of Commons.[1]

The younger members of this circle—to whom, doubtless, the transcendent ability of John Stuart Mill, in years a boy of fifteen, but in literary knowledge and intellectual powers a grown-up man, was a principal attraction—included many young men who have since attained high distinction as advocates of progress. Among them were John Romilly (son of Sir Samuel), who afterwards became Lord Romilly and Master of the Rolls, then a youth of eighteen; and George Grote, the eminent author of the *History of Greece*, and the first prominent advocate of the ballot as a protection of the poor and dependent against the undue influence of the rich, who had been introduced to Mill by Ricardo a year previously, and became one of Bentham's most eminent disciples. Others were John and Charles Austin, Edward Strutt, afterwards Lord Belper; Charles Pelham Villiers, the veteran advocate of Free Trade; and Charles Buller, the pupil of Thomas Carlyle, whose premature death deprived England of one of her most promising politicians. John Arthur Roebuck, who came over from America to join the English Bar, became a member of the circle two or three years later.

From this small knot of earnest men proceeded a series of efforts to advance the principles of civil and religious liberty, to effect progress in legal and social reforms of all kinds, and to elevate the people by education, which have had much influence in bringing about the great changes accomplished in the ensuing half century. Few in number, laughed at as visionaries, arrayed against the interests and prejudices of the time, fighting with the serried mass of untrained and unreasoning Toryism of that day, which defended slavery, resisted the enfranchisement of Catholics and Dissenters, the reform of Parliament, and the

---

[1] *Bentham's Works* (Memoirs and Correspondence), vol. x., page 492.

introduction of Free Trade, they were yet strong in their firm grasp of sound principles of jurisprudence, and the reasons and methods upon and by which legislative reform and sound progress must be based. The effect they have produced has been accomplished by their steady, earnest determination to devote all their powers to the objects which they steadfastly set before themselves; and although the ultimate results have in many cases been obtained many years later, and by the efforts of their successors, yet the original impulse may often be traced to the philosophical Radicals inspired by Bentham and Mill.

This was the circle of which William Ellis, when about twenty years of age, became a member. Of the course of study which his introduction to it led him to adopt, the first information we have is that he joined, about the end of the year 1822, a society of young men which met at Bentham's house to read essays upon, and discuss, social and economical questions. The account given by John Stuart Mill in his *Autobiography* of the formation of this society as well as the adoption of the name Utilitarian, which has since been very generally applied to the philosophy of Bentham, is as follows[1]:—

"It was in the winter of 1822 that I formed the plan of "a little society to be composed of young men agreeing in "fundamental principles—acknowledging utility as their "standard in ethics and politics, and a certain number of "the principal corollaries drawn from it in the philosophy "I had accepted—and meeting once a fortnight to read "essays and discuss questions conformably to the premises "thus agreed on. The fact would hardly be worth men- "tioning but for the circumstance that the name I gave "to the society I had planned was the Utilitarian Society. "It was the first time that any one had taken the title "of Utilitarian; and the term made its way into the

---

"language from this humble source. I did not invent
" the word, but found it in one of Galt's novels, the *Annals
"*of the Parish,* in which the Scotch clergyman, of whom
" the book is a supposed autobiography, is represented as
" warning his parishioners not to leave the gospel and
" become utilitarians. With a boy's fondness for a name
" and a banner I seized on the word, and for some years
" called myself and others by it as a sectarian appellation;
" and it came to be occasionally used by others holding
" the opinions which it was intended to designate. As
" those opinions attracted more notice, the term was
" repeated by strangers and opponents, and got into
" rather common use just about the time when those who
" had originally assumed it laid down that along with
" other sectarian characteristics. The society so called
" consisted at first of no more than three members, one of
" whom, being Mr. Bentham's amanuensis,[1] obtained for us
" permission to hold our meetings in his house. The
" number never, I think, reached ten, and the society was
" broken up in 1826. It had had thus an existence of
" about three years and a half. The chief effect of it as
" regards myself, over and above the benefit of practice in
" oral discussion, was that of bringing me in contact with
" several young men, at that time less advanced than
" myself, among whom, as they professed the same
" opinions, I was for some time a sort of leader, and had
" considerable influence on their mental progress. Any
" young man of education who fell in my way, and whose
" opinions were not incompatible with those of the society,
" I endeavoured to press into its service, and some others
" I probably should never have known, had they not
" joined it. Those of the members who became my
" intimate companions—no one of whom was in any sense
" of the word a disciple, but all of them independent

---

[1] Mr. Walter Coulson, afterwards an eminent conveyancing barrister.

"thinkers on their own basis—were William Eyton
"Tooke, son of the eminent political economist, a young
"man of singular worth, both moral and intellectual, lost
"to the world by an early death; his friend William Ellis,
"an original thinker in the field of political economy, now
"honorably known by his apostolic exertions for the
"improvement of education; George Graham, afterwards
"Official Assignee of the Bankruptcy Court, a thinker of
"originality and power on almost all abstract subjects;
"and (from the time when he came first to England to
"study for the bar in 1824 or 1825) a man who has
"made considerably more noise in the world than any of
"these, John Arthur Roebuck."

It was during this period of his mental development that
Ellis became a co-operator in the establishment of the
Westminster Review, founded by Bentham, mainly for the
advocacy of the principles of which he was the most
prominent exponent, and the reforms which naturally sprang
from them. From its foundation to the present time, the
Review has always been the organ through which the
advanced thinkers of the time have found utterance for their
views. Consequently, it has generally received cordial
support from only a small section of the public, and has not
obtained the wide circle of readers which its senior rivals,
the *Edinburgh* and *Quarterly*, have commanded. But a
curious and convincing proof of the progress which has been
made by public opinion may be obtained by a perusal of
the articles published in the earlier numbers of the *Review*,
bearing in mind that arguments and views which have since
been universally adopted by public opinion were then looked
upon by some as utopian and visionary, by others as
dangerous and revolutionary. It is, from this point of view,
specially interesting to look back more than sixty years afterwards upon the general characteristics of a party and a publication which have had so much influence as pioneers of thought
on the future social and political progress of the country.

CHAPTER III.

1824—1826.

THE *Westminster Review* was a bold attempt on the part of Bentham and the earnest reformers who surrounded·him to bring before the public the arguments for the great reforms they advocated, many of which were then considered hopelessly extreme, though they have since been generally adopted. The *Edinburgh* and *Quarterly*, representing the two chief political parties respectively, were firmly established, and paying well. Bentham saw no reason why a review, advocating the views on which he held such strong opinions, should not be equally successful. So, in January, 1824, the *Review* was commenced under the joint editorship of Mr. (afterwards Sir John) Bowring, as political, and Henry Southern, as literary editor. Among the contributors during the first two or three years, while Ellis wrote for it, we find many names which have since been favourably known as advocates of progress. James Mill's criticism of the *Edinburgh* and *Quarterly Reviews* were brilliant commentaries on the attitude of the Whig and Tory parties, while the younger Mill—as he tells us in his *Autobiography*—wrote several articles during the first three or four years of the existence of the *Review* upon Free Trade and other economical subjects. John Austin, the brilliant writer on Jurisprudence, treated the subject of Primogeniture, while among other names which have since become known to the world are those of Dr. Southwood Smith, William Johnson Fox, Charles Austin, George Grote, Colonel

Perronet Thompson, Albany Fonblanque, and Crabb Robinson, whose close friendship with and devotion to Goethe led to his contributing an interesting review of his works.

The articles which can be identified with certainty as from Ellis's pen are on social subjects, and show the clear and logical style which even at that age he had acquired. Written when he was only twenty-four or twenty-five, we can hardly quote them as expressing matured opinions such as in their entirety he would have confirmed during the latter part of his life. But they are interesting, as showing the development of his mind under the influence due to his friendship with Bentham and James Mill, and also the method in which he treated matters now set at rest, but then the subject of bitter controversy.

The first of his contributions is an article on West India slavery in the second number of the *Westminster Review*, published in April, 1824. The chief characteristic of Ellis's treatment of the question is its eminently practical character. There is not one word of declamation upon the cruelty and wickedness which are inseparable from it. The utter inhumanity of treating human beings as chattels—the impossibility that any prescription, however long, can justify such an institution—are not brought forward. But the whole subject is treated in a practical tone, which shows more than anything what was the then position of the question, and it is a strange sign of the condition of public opinion that even the most advanced proposals of the abolitionists, as contained in the pamphlets reviewed, do not go beyond the "mitigation and gradual abolition of slavery." It will be remembered that it was only a few years before, in 1807, after an opposition supported by the royal dukes and many leading members of both houses—an opposition which even quoted the scriptures as evidence in favour of slavery with all its hideous cruelties—that Fox and Lord Grenville had carried through the great work, the abolition of the slave trade, which is forever associated with their names.

But the abolition of the trade in slaves did not abolish slavery in our West Indian colonies ; and at the time when this article was written Sir Thomas Fowell Buxton had brought the question of emancipation before the House of Commons by moving

"That slavery is repugnant to the British Constitution "and the Christian religion, and ought to be abolished "gradually throughout the British Colonies with as much "expedition as may be found consistent with a due "regard to the well-being of the parties concerned."

Canning, seizing on the weak point, the proposal for gradual abolition, inconsistent with the strong language of the opening words, proposed and carried an amendment merely declaratory of the expediency of ameliorating the condition of the British slave population, and of the hope that such amelioration might fit them for freedom.

It was just after this motion that Ellis wrote his article, at the head of which he placed Wilberforce's appeal, and some half-dozen pamphlets. He begins with a paragraph which might now be deemed more applicable to the cause which he subsequently undertook and made his own— education—than to the question of emancipation.

"They who have the interest of their country really at "heart, and who are actuated by a sincere spirit of "patriotism and philanthropy, do not appear at first sight "to meet with much encouragement."

And a little further on he even criticises the abolitionists for "not attaching sufficient importance to the numerous "obstacles and impediments that were presented in the "short and royal road by which they wished to arrive at "their destined end," and states as the object of his Essay, "to lay before our readers a clear view of the whole "question as it now stands, and to suggest such modifi- "cations and improvements in the present system as might "be adopted without a shadow of injustice to any party."

He at once admits, as the basis of his argument, that

compensation is due to those who have acquired interests under a long sanctioned law.

"The traffic in negroes," he says, "had been permitted "by Parliament for so long a course of years, and en-"couragement had been so repeatedly held out to its "extension, that whatever blame may attach to it on the "ground of humanity must attach to the nation at large, "and not to any individual or body of individuals. The "injustice of depriving our fellow-creatures of their liberty "and reducing them to a state of deplorable misery was "committed by the Government; and it is for the Govern-"ment to atone for its injustice by measuring back its "steps and making all possible reparation to the miserable "sufferers with due and prudent speed, and without "injuring anyone, or making inroads on private property." Having dealt with the cruel wrongs under which the negroes suffered, and having considered what may be done to ameliorate their condition, he proceeds to consider how emancipation could be effected; and the following para-graph contains his conclusion on this point, which, in fact, was somewhat in accordance with the plan ultimately adopted.

"Were the Government of this country," he says, "determined to give the negroes their liberty immediately "at all hazards, without indulging a forethought for the "evil consequences that might ensue to the slaves them-"selves—were they inclined, in short, to act up to the "spirit of the axiom placed so prominently in the fore-"ground by the abolitionists—'that the state of slavery is "'repugnant to the principles of the British Constitution "'and of the Christian religion'—were they to listen to "their feelings alone, and, excluding the voice of reason "from their councils, to come to the conclusion that, since "an act of injustice and barbarity had been committed, "it was the duty of the nation to retrace its steps, hastily "and inadvisedly; the course presenting the fewest

"disadvantages would be, not to invade the property of the
"planters, but to purchase all the negroes in the Colonies
"and give them their liberty at once."

And he expresses his opinion that the value should be
fixed, as in the case of taking land, by arbitration.

One further extract, which is perhaps intended as an
explanation of the extreme moderation of the tone adopted,
shows that the object of the whole article was to effect a
practical solution rather than to rouse the indignation of his
readers.

"The general charge against the abolitionists is," he
says, "that they are blinded by enthusiasm. That charge
"we think will not apply to us. We have purposely
"avoided an appeal to the feelings of our readers by an
"unnecessary mention of, or allusion to, cases of cruelty
"and oppression. Such cases may, or may not, be excep-
"tions to the general mode of treatment. We hope and
"believe that they are exceptions. We have contented
"ourselves with calling attention to the real state of the
"law as it exists at present, and to the mode in which it
"may be improved. Firmly convinced of the justice,
"propriety, and feasibility of all that we have urged, we
"have sought their concurrence and approbation by
"addressing ourselves to their reason alone."

Dealing finally with the attitude of Mr. Canning and the
resolutions which, on his motion, had been passed by the
House of Commons, which merely proposed "effectual and
decisive measures" for ameliorating the condition of the
slave population, he points out that though they were upon
the whole as favourable as could be expected, yet their
defect was vagueness.

"They pledge the Government to nothing. They are
"*vox et prœterea nihil.* . . . The problem is *what are*
"effectual and decisive measures? And here," he continues, "we are met by that which meets us at every turn,
"even when we least expect it—the imperfect represen-

"tation of the people in the House of Commons. A
" Parliament really responsible to the people would neither
" have delayed so long before declaring for emancipation,
" nor·would at last have been satisfied with *such* a decla-
" ration. But what is to be expected from a Parliament
" habitually yielding itself up to the dictation of the
" Ministry, or from a Ministry cramped, even where its
" intentions are good, by the necessity of paying court
" to this or that section of the aristocracy—to the landed
" interest, to the mercantile interest, to the Colonial
" interest, and to we know not how many more squads of
" aristocrats, of which any two or three, sometimes any
" one, by deserting the Ministry could ensure their down-
" fall ! "

How clear was Ellis's foresight may be judged by the
subsequent progress of this measure. In June, 1832, the
Reform Bill passed into law. In the very next year the
Government, finding that the pressure of public opinion was
too strong to be resisted, introduced and carried an Emancipation Bill, framed on the very plan advocated by Ellis,
" not invading the property of the planters, but purchasing
" all the negroes in the Colonies, and giving them their
" liberty at once." Under this plan slavery was abolished
on 1st August, 1834.

The next article which we are able to identify as from
Ellis's pen is one of special interest, for in it we trace the
early stage of the benevolent principles which in a few years
became developed in his mind so strongly as to constitute
the ruling idea of his life. It is an article on Charitable
Institutions, published in the *Review* of July, 1824 ; and in
it he brings to bear upon the right or wrong direction of
benevolence the strong logical grasp which characterises
his treatment of every subject touched by him. Beginning
with a reference to the universal prevalence of benevolent
feelings, he proceeds to put in strong contrast the effect of
charity as guided, or not, by reason and knowledge.

"Of what use," he says, "is the greatest kindness,
"the most profuse liberality, unless the exercise of these
"feelings be followed by beneficial effects?   A person
"may be endowed with a heart 'overflowing with the
"'milk of human kindness,' and be the occasion of much
"more extensive mischief than the most hardened villain.
"The laws in any tolerably governed state limit the
"powers of the latter, but the former unfortunately is
"often encouraged in his career by the approbation of all
"in whose opinion he desires to stand well.   Such a man
"by an indiscriminate almsgiving may be the promoter
"of idleness and beggary, the patron of deception and
"vice, and, so far as he holds out a premium for what is
"bad, an actual diminisher of the sum of good."

He then proceeds, as the basis of his subsequent arguments upon the right or wrong direction of charity, to refer
to the economical conditions which regulate the welfare of
the labouring classes, and to quote the statement of the main
principles of population enumerated by Malthus.   These
principles, which underlie the necessary virtues of prudence
and forethought, especially of parental, or rather of pre-
parental, forethought and prudence, are then applied to
various kinds of charities with careful analysis of their
respective effects, both near and remote.   First comes indiscriminate almsgiving, of which, while admitting that in its
immediate consequences it is beneficial as affording immediate relief, he proceeds to show that the ultimate effect
is to hold out a premium for want of forethought.   He then
contrasts the effects of charity directed to the prevention of
destitution with that merely destined to relieve it.

"The judgment with which a certain sum of money is
"expended for purposes of humanity can only be ascer-
"tained by the sum of good produced.   If A and B each
"lay out £1,000, and A does good and B mischief, or if
"A does twice as much good as B, A is clearly entitled
"to greater credit and estimation than B.   If in a district

"much exposed to storms, where the inhabitants were
"ignorant of the means of defending their habitations
"from the effects of lightning, there were a thousand
"houses, several of which were burnt annually, who would
"do the greatest good, he who laid out his money in
"erecting conductors, or he who confined himself to
"enabling those who were burnt out to rebuild their
"houses, leaving the inhabitants exposed to the same
"annual calamity?"

This leads him to discuss educational charities, and
these he divides into two classes, one which affords
instruction alone, the other support and instruction. With
respect to the latter he shows that the maintenance of
children at schools has a direct tendency to stimulate improvidence.

"If it were possible," he argues, "to supply the requisite
"funds and to provide for the maintenance of all the
"children of the poor, no check would remain upon
"the propensity to early marriage. Their numbers
"would be doubled every twenty or twenty-five years,
"and a rapidly increasing supply of labourers would be
"poured forth from the schools to compete in the market
"of labour. The means of supporting them remaining
"the same, or being increased to a very disproportionate
"extent, they would soon be reduced to the lowest state
"of existence."

With this class of educational charity, he then contrasts
the charities which provide gratuitous education unaccompanied with maintenance. And these, as might be expected
by those who know his subsequent career, meet with his
cordial approval; and he proceeds to demonstrate that
gratuitous education cannot in any way act as an incentive
to population, while unmixed good is produced to society
by the education of children who would otherwise grow up
in ignorance.

"Here, then," he continues, "a fair scope is presented

"to the benevolence of all who wish to confer lasting
"benefits upon the poorer classes. Free schools ought to
"be erected in such abundance that every child in England
"may have an opportunity of learning to read and write.
"Education can now be afforded at so trifling an expense,
"that a village without a school ought henceforward to be
"looked upon as a disgrace to the county in which it is
"situated. Instruction, however, ought not to stop here.
"We are determined, at all events, not to lay ourselves
"open to the imputation of decrying charity. While we
"wish to deter people from a mischievous indulgence
"of their sympathies, we will not be backward in
"showing how it may be indulged with advantage to
"society."
And he proceeds to point out that—
"Reading and writing, which are taught in the free
"schools, are merely the keys to knowledge. The portals
"are yet to be unlocked, and for this purpose the co-
"operation of all is desirable. . . . . The means of
"placing useful knowledge on a large scale within the
"reach of the people are already discovered. Institutions
"for the working classes are fast establishing in every
"town. Glasgow took the lead. London, Liverpool,
"Leeds, Aberdeen, and many others have followed.
"Benevolence need not stop in its career until every town
"in the kingdom is provided with an institution and every
"village has its book society. An occasional course of
"lectures and the distribution of well-chosen books will
"then place knowledge within the reach of all. There is
"one particular kind of knowledge which, in the important
"consequences with which it is fraught to the working
"classes, far surpasses every other. We allude to the
"knowledge of the laws which regulate wages. Their
"happiness is inseparably connected with a knowledge
"of these laws. When the deplorable ignorance of the
"labourers on this subject is removed, our ears will no

"longer be distressed, as they now continually are, with
"accounts of the breaking and burning of agricultural
"and manufacturing machinery. When the poor half-
"starved, half-naked creatures, by whom these acts of
"violence are committed, know how much they are
"indebted to machinery for subsistence, they will refrain
"from those outrages which are not more injurious to
"others than to ourselves. How soon this desirable
"change will be consummated depends, in a great
"measure, upon the exertions of enlightened philan-
"thropists."

We have quoted this passage somewhat fully, because it is the earliest record of the thoughts which grew stronger in the course of years until they absorbed the energies of his later life. They are, it will be seen, somewhat inchoate. The laws which regulate wages are but one branch of the laws of human conduct, the systematic teaching of which, as a means of removing poverty and destitution, was advocated and supported by him during a long life, with the devotion of an apostle.

The rest of the article may be passed over more cursorily. It is the application of the principles already enunciated to other heads of charities. First, he deals with lying-in hospitals, which he shows to be attended with gravely pernicious consequences, while foundling hospitals, as will be supposed, are even more strongly censured, as having a tendency to aggravate the very evils which it was the wish of their founders to mitigate. General hospitals and infirmaries, or charities for the provision of gratuitous medical attendance, are criticised from the same point of view—their effect on the providence and forethought of the people; while, on the other hand, hospitals for the deaf and dumb, and the indigent blind, are exempted from this censure, the good produced by them being unaccompanied with any alloy, because the immediate relief afforded to the unfortunate objects cannot possibly tend to increase their numbers. Hospitals for the cure of wounds, fractures, or serious bodily hurts, are similarly approved, as well as hospitals for highly contagious disorders, which, in addition to their direct benefit to the patients, remove considerable risk of infection from the community. And he concludes this careful and elaborate essay—an essay which may well be recalled at any time, and the clear logical arguments of which ought never to be forgotten—with the following recapitulation :—

"It cannot too often be repeated that the education of "the poor holds out a brilliant object for the exertions of "all who aim at rendering effectual service to mankind. "This attained, every other blessing will follow in its "train. The best remedy for such evils as prudence and "foresight may remove, is to give that education, of "which prudence and foresight cannot fail to be the "consequence."

Two other articles in the *Westminster Review*, from Ellis's pen, are curious, as dealing with a subject which in those days occupied a much larger portion of public attention than now. One, on the exportation of machinery, was published in April, 1825, and another in January, 1826, upon the effect of the employment of machinery upon the happiness of the working classes. They are directed to clearing up mistaken views entertained by very different classes of society. As regards the former question—the exportation of machinery—the view of many leading capitalists and employers of labour at that date was that the exportation of machinery should be vigorously prohibited, on the ground that it would be injurious to our own manufacturers to supply foreign countries with the means of underselling us abroad, and a Committee of the House of Commons, which had during the previous session inquired into the question, had merely reported the conflicting evidence of a number of witnesses, and that "they were of opinion that further "inquiry and a more complete investigation should take

"place before this important subject can be satisfactorily
"decided on."

With respect to the effects of machinery on the welfare of
working classes, the notions entertained by the operatives led
to serious consequences. The Luddite riots were a matter of
recent memory. Throughout Leicestershire and Notting-
hamshire there were organised bands who, under the command of a chief, held the inhabitants in nightly terror,
commanding them to put out their lights and keep within
their houses under penalty of death. Then, in the silence
of night, would houses and factories be broken open, frames
and other machines be demolished, unfinished work be
scattered on the highways, and furniture be wholly destroyed.
Ignorance and want of employment were the causes which
led the Luddites of those days, undeterred by the terrible
penalties of the law—for machine breaking had been made
a capital offence in 1812—to persist year after year in the
course which well nigh drove our lace manufactures from
this country and converted temporary into permanent ruin.
To deal with these errors was the task which Ellis set
himself, and performed with the clearness of perception
and logical power which were the special qualities of his
mind.

The argument of the former article—on the exportation
of machinery—is based on the fact that the benefit derived
from foreign commerce is in the commodities imported.
From this Ellis goes on to show the great advantage to any
country that the foreign nations with which it deals should
be able to produce their commodities with the least possible
labour. The cheaper such foreign commodities can be
produced, the more can be given in exchange for our manufactures ; so that " the wealth of the English is increased by
"every increase in the powers of production which they
"can introduce among their neighbours." " But," he
proceeds, "the principal device by which the prohibitory
"law against the exportation of machinery has been

D

"supported consists in representing two countries not as
"mutual benefactors, but as dangerous rivals. To give
"some colouring to this representation, a third country is
"introduced, which is supposed to be the scene of the
"competition of the other two rival nations."

He then shows that it does not alter the advantage to
each nation that others should possess the best powers of
production of their respective commodities.

"A difference in the relative facility of production is
"essential to interchange. The farmer in Essex and the
"clothier in Yorkshire exchange with one another, because
"one can produce grain and the other cloth with com-
"parative facility."

A similar illustration is brought forward from the superiority of the English in producing cottons, the French in
silk, and the Brazilians in producing sugar and coffee, it
being shown that the greater facilities each nation has in
producing its own commodities, the greater the quantities it
can give in exchange, and the greater the advantage other
nations derive from dealing with it. And so he leads up to
the conclusion that—

"not only would the whole commercial world be benefited
"by an increase in the *general* power of production, but
"the advantages resulting from such an increased power
"in *one* country would be generally diffused."

The other article, on the effects of machinery on the
happiness of the working classes, is a longer and more
elaborate one than that we have just noticed, and though
in these days it may seem to be hardly worth arguing, it
was then a matter which gravely misled large numbers of
the people. At the commencement of his argument, Ellis
gives the easy *reductio ad absurdum* which the subject
admits of.

"If," he says, "the use of machinery is calculated to
"diminish the fund out of which labourers are supported,
"then, by giving up the use of the plough and the harrow,

"and returning to the pastoral state, or by scratching the
"earth with our nails, the produce of the soil would be
"adequate to the maintenance of a much greater number
"of labourers. There are many labourers now in England,
"and the gradations of ingenuity and skill in machinery
"are numerous; but as the number of labourers and the
"funds for their support would be gradually increased in
"proportion as we fell back upon the less perfect machinery;
"so, at last, when we deprived ourselves entirely of its
"assistance, the produce, and hence the population of
"England, would be increased beyond what had ever
"been exhibited in any country on the surface of the
"globe, nay would exceed, perhaps, what the most exalted
"imagination, warmed with the contemplation of ances-
"torial and primitive simplicity, and revelling in dreams
"of a golden age, could dare to conceive."

And in a closely-reasoned essay, which we need not
analyse in detail, he leads gradually to the conclusion that
"the following advantages may be traced to the invention
"and improvement of machinery: First, to the landlords,
"an increase of rent by the cultivation of a lower grada-
"tion of soils; second, to the capitalists, an increase of
"profit, by rendering the same capital more productive;
"third, to the labourers, an increase of wages, by adding
"to the fund which furnishes the means of their employ-
"ment and maintenance."

There is only one other article from the *Westminster Review*
as to which we have definite information that it was in part
from Ellis's pen. It is a short notice published in July, 1825,
of a pamphlet by Mr. J. R. McCulloch, entitled "A Discourse
"on the Rise, Progress, Peculiar Objects, and Importance
"of Political Economy," and was the joint production of
Ellis and John Stuart Mill. It is, in fact, so short and
scanty an outline of an important and interesting work as
to bear internal evidence of having been compressed in
obedience to exigencies of space or some other reason

known to the editors. And this appears to have been the case from the following extract from a letter of James Mill to McCulloch himself[1]:—

"Croydon Common, 18th August, 1825.

" My dear friend,— . . . I suppose you have seen " by this time the review of your discourse in the "*Westminster.* John expresses great dissatisfaction with " the behaviour of the editors. The whole was the joint " production of him and Ellis ; but they say that several " important things were left out, and the article, by that " and other editorial operations, disfigured . .—Yours " faithfully,

"JAMES MILL."

In the article, as published, the reviewers commence with the following optimistic passage:—

" If there is one sign of the times upon which, more " than any other, we should be justified in resting our " hopes of the future progression of the human race in the " career of improvement, that sign undoubtedly is the " demand which is now manifesting itself on the part of " the public for instruction in the science of political " economy."

And then, after remarking upon the great value of political economy as a study, and the importance of teaching it as a method of improving the human race, the writers refer to the foundation in 1824 of a lectureship on Political Economy in honour of the late Mr. Ricardo, to which Mr. McCulloch had been appointed as the first lecturer. And they conclude the essay with the following extract from the pamphlet they are reviewing, which we may well regard as having had its share in influencing Ellis's own future career:—

" Ignorance is the impure and muddy fountain whence " nine-tenths of the vice, misery, and crime to be found " in the world are really derived. Make the body of the

---

[1] Bain's *Biography of James Mill*, page 292.

"people once fully aware of the circumstances which
"really determine their condition, and you may be assured
"that an immense majority will endeavour to turn that
"knowledge to good account. If you once succeed in
"convincing a man that it is for his interest to abandon
"one line of conduct and follow another, the chances are
"ten to one that he will do so."

This was the last article in which we can trace Ellis's hand during the early years of the institution of the *Westminster Review*, to which he then ceased to contribute. But he always retained a friendly relation with it, and upwards of twenty years later, when he was seeking a medium for advocating improved education as a remedy for destitution, vice, and crime, it was to the *Westminster Review* that he offered his contributions, and, as we shall see in a subsequent chapter, wrote in it, between 1848 and 1851, some half-dozen further articles.

CHAPTER IV.

1826—1846.

DURING the whole time that Ellis was working under
the auspices of Bentham and James Mill upon the
Westminster Review, he was continuing the course of study
which he had commenced in conjunction with his friend
John Stuart Mill and the other younger members of the
circle of philosophical Radicals. Before the close of the
Utilitarian Society, which seems to have ceased in 1826,
another series of meetings was commenced for the purpose of
still closer and more continuous study of various sciences.
Beginning with political economy, the students afterwards
took up logic and psychology. They seem not to have
assumed any title, for in both John Stuart Mill's own autobiography and Mrs. Grote's life of her husband,[1] their
meetings are only spoken of as "the readings at Mr. Grote's."
The members must have been almost the same as those of
the Utilitarian Society, as we find that John Stuart Mill,
Ellis, Graham, Eyton Tooke, and W. G. Prescott were
members of both, and the only additional names mentioned
by Mrs. Grote are those of her husband, Charles Buller, and
Mr. Grant. They met twice a week, at half-past eight in the
morning, at the house of Mr. Grote(who lived in the upper part
of the building in Threadneedle Street then and still occupied

---

[1] *Personal Life of George Grote*, by Mrs. Grote.

as a bank by the firm of Prescott, Grote, and Co.), and it is a singular proof of the energy and determination of Ellis that he used to walk up to attend these meetings from Croydon, where he and his newly-married bride were living. The railway, which now makes Croydon almost a suburb of London, was not then dreamed of. The coach (for omnibuses, then called Shillibeers, from the name of their inventor, were only introduced in London in 1829) did not start sufficiently early; so twice a week, winter and summer, Ellis regularly and conscientiously traversed on foot the nine miles from Croydon to the city before half-past eight o'clock. John Stuart Mill's account of the course of studies pursued at their meetings, in which he again refers to Ellis as a leading and original thinker, is as follows[1] :—

"For several years from this period (1825) our social
"studies assumed a shape which contributed very much
"to my mental progress. The idea occurred to us of
"carrying on, by reading and conversation, a joint study
"of several of the branches of science which we wished to
"be masters of. We assembled to the number of a
"dozen or more. Mr. Grote lent a room of his house in
"Threadneedle Street for the purpose, and his partner,
"Prescott, one of the three original members of the
"Utilitarian Society, made one among us. We met two
"mornings in every week, from half-past eight till ten,
"at which hour most of us were called off to our daily
"occupations. Our first subject was political economy.
"We chose some systematic treatise as our text book;
"my father's *Elements* being our first choice. One of us
"read aloud a chapter, or some smaller portion of the
"book. The discussion was then opened, and any one
"who had an objection or other remark to make, made it.
"Our rule was to discuss thoroughly every point raised,
"whether great or small, prolonging the discussion until

---

[1] *Autobiography*, page 119.

"all who took part were satisfied with the conclusion they
"had individually arrived at; and to follow up every topic
"of collateral speculation which the chapter or the conversa-
"tion suggested, never leaving it until we had untied
"every knot which we found. We repeatedly kept up
"the discussion of some one point for several weeks,
"thinking intently on it during the intervals of our
"meetings, and contriving solutions of the new difficulties
"which had risen up in the last morning's discussion.
"When we had finished in this way my father's *Elements*,
"we went in the same manner through Ricardo's *Prin-
"ciples of Political Economy* and Bailey's *Dissertation on
"Value*. These close and vigorous discussions were not
"only improving in a high degree to those who took part
"in them, but brought out new views of some topics of
"abstract political economy. The theory of international
"values, which I afterwards published, emanated from
"these conversations, as did also the modified form of
"Ricardo's theory of profits, laid down in my Essay on
"Profits and Interest. Those among us with whom new
"speculations chiefly originated were Ellis, Graham, and
"I; though others gave valuable aid to the discussions,
"especially Prescott and Roebuck, the one by his know-
"ledge, the other by his dialectical acuteness. . . .

"When we had enough of political economy, we took
"up the syllogistic logic in the same manner, Grote now
"joining us. Our first text book was *Aldrich*, but being
"disgusted with its superficiality, we reprinted one of the
"most finished among the many manuals of the school
"logic which my father, a great collector of such books,
"possessed, the *Manuductio ad Logicam* of the Jesuit Du
"Trieu. After finishing this, we took up Whately's *Logic*,
"then first republished from the *Encyclopædia Metropolitana*,
"and finally the *Computatio Sive Logica* of Hobbes. These
"books, dealt with in our manner, afforded a wide range
"for original metaphysical speculation: and most of

"what has been done in the first book of my *System of*
"*Logic* to rationalise and correct the principles and
"distinctions of the school logicians, and to improve the
"theory of the import of propositions, had its origin in
"these discussions; Graham and I originating most of
"the novelties, while Grote and others furnished an
"excellent tribunal or test. From this time I formed the
"project of writing a book on logic, though on a much
"humbler scale than the one I ultimately executed.

"Having done with logic, we launched into analytic
"psychology, and having chosen *Hartley* for our text
"book, we raised Priestley's edition to an extravagant
"price by searching through London to furnish each of
"us with a copy. When we had finished *Hartley*, we
"suspended our meetings; but my father's *Analysis of*
"*the Mind* being published soon afterwards, we re-
"assembled for the purpose of reading it. With this our
"exercises ended. I have always dated from these con-
"versations my own real inauguration as an original and
"independent thinker. It was also through them that I
"acquired, or very much strengthened, a mental habit to
"which I attribute all that I have ever done, or ever shall
"do, in speculation; that of never accepting half-solutions
"of difficulties as complete; never abandoning a puzzle,
"but again and again returning to it until it was cleared
"up; never allowing obscure corners of a subject to
"remain unexplored because they did not appear im-
"portant; never thinking that I perfectly understood any
"part of a subject until I understood the whole."
Speaking of these meetings to his friend, Mrs. Fenwick
Miller, Ellis said:—

"In those discussions which we used to hold, the
"difference between John Mill and me was brought out
"very often. He was for enquiring into everything, and
"going to the bottom of everybody's theories and ideas;
"I cared only for the practical value of political economy,

"and did not want to think deeply upon points which
"could have no bearing on social affairs and human
"conduct. This difference in mental constitution can be
"found throughout all our works."

While these sterner studies were progressing, the students
did not neglect the practice of debate. Their first
contests were with the Owenites. Roebuck (as we learn
from John Stuart Mill) had discovered a society of Owenites,
called the Co-operative Society, which met for weekly public
discussions in Chancery Lane, and the young and enthusiastic party of economic students were easily induced to
visit these meetings for the purpose of debate. They were
cordially welcomed by the members of the society, and a
number of exciting debates took place. We learn from
John Stuart Mill that Ellis, Roebuck, and he himself were
specially active in these friendly tournaments during the
three or four years that the debates continued, while among
the other friends who joined in them he mentions Charles
Austin, who afterwards attained great eminence at the
Parliamentary bar; Charles Pelham Villiers, the first leader
of the little band which, by its persistent attacks on the pro-
tective system of finance, ultimately secured in the year 1846
the establishment of free trade; and Connop Thirlwall, then a
Chancery barrister, but afterwards celebrated as a historian,
and better known by his subsequent title of Bishop of St.
David's.

But these contests had the effect of causing our young
students to desire a wider field for the cultivation of their
oratorical powers. McCulloch suggested the formation of a
society similar to the Speculative Society at Edinburgh,
where Brougham and others had fought their early battles,
and he helped to form it by introducing the matter to many
other young men of influence to whom he was then giving
private lessons in political economy. This society, which
met once a fortnight, from November to June, was inaugu-
rated about the end of 1825, and the original members

included many young men whose names afterwards became well known in the world. Charles Pelham Villiers brought two of his brothers, one of whom, George, afterwards Earl of Clarendon and Foreign Secretary, took a very active part in the formation of the society, and it soon gained recruits from the debating societies of the two Universities. There were also Macaulay, Praed, Lord Howick (afterwards Earl Grey), Samuel Wilberforce (afterwards Bishop of Oxford), Charles Poulett Thomson (afterwards Lord Sydenham), Edward and Henry Lytton Bulwer (afterwards Lords Lytton and Dalling), Albany Fonblanque, and others. But, like many debating societies, this splendid array of talent did not secure a permanent success. For reasons which John Stuart Mill suggests in his *Autobiography*—of which the most probable seems the difficulty of obtaining a sufficient number of Tory opponents—the enthusiasm which characterised its opening soon died away, and it seems to have been hard work to keep it alive. But other men of mark afterwards joined it. In 1826, we hear of Hayward and Shee (afterwards Justice Shee) as Conservatives, and Charles Buller and Cockburn (afterwards Lord Chief Justice) as regular speakers, and in 1828 Maurice and Sterling joined the society, introducing a new and interesting variety of Radicalism, which strongly disagreed with and vehemently opposed the views of Bentham, thus adding a third and very important party to the contests of political thought.

Of what part Ellis took in this second society there is no record, but the very omission of Mill in his *Autobiography* to mention his name, and the fact that he was now living at Croydon and had become a family man, while his regular occupation at the Indemnity office occupied his whole time during the day, renders it very improbable that he could have taken a prominent part in these debates, which, doubtless, were held in the evening. It seems pretty certain that Ellis gradually withdrew from these youthful exercises and became more and more absorbed in the regular duties of commercial life. In fact, between this date and the year 1846, his literary and educational work seems to have been subordinate to his business and family duties. But he did not wholly abandon it. The thoughts which had taken such strong possession of his mind were expressed in a little work which he published in the year 1829, under the title *Conversations upon Knowledge, Happiness, and Education between a Mechanic and a Patron of the London Mechanics' Institution*, divided into three conversations bearing respectively the names contained in the title. In the preface he tells us that—

> "The substance of these conversations is what was
> "actually conveyed to the author, at different times, by a
> "much valued friend" (doubtless Mr. James Mill). "To the
> "information, for which he is indebted to this friend, he
> "ascribes much of the happiness that he at present enjoys.
> "He offers the following pages to the public in the hope
> "that the lessons contained in them will produce upon
> "others an effect similar to that which they have produced
> "upon himself."

And the style adopted is that of conversation of a kind which at that time was much adopted for treatises of an educational or instructive character, but not so completely Socratic in its method of working out the conclusions aimed at as the conversations of some of Ellis's later writings. But as the general course of thought was that which was clearly taking possession of his mind, and which he afterwards developed in his subsequent works, sometimes in its whole scope, sometimes in the elaboration of portions, it will be interesting to sketch shortly its general outlines. Starting by a few introductory remarks in which the use of knowledge is shown by a few clear illustrations, we are led to consider what kinds of knowledge are most useful ; and our patron, after expressing his doubts whether the knowledge of Chaldee could be productive of any benefits to mankind, and whether the moderns would be much less happy were all the dead languages henceforward unknown, proceeds to state his views as to what ought and what ought not to be included under the head of useful knowledge.

"Everything," he says, "the knowledge of which is "deserving the name of useful, may be comprised under "three heads. Under the first may be placed those "sciences which explain the various phenomena of the "physical world. Under the second, those sciences which "explain the various phenomena of the human mind, and "point out what opinions and what actions are most con- "ducive to the happiness of mankind. Under the third, "those sciences which explain the structure of language, "and point out by what means we may most easily, "pleasantly, and clearly communicate our ideas to one "another." And from that basis he proceeds: "If a "knowledge of the sciences be useful, a knowledge of the "arts must be so also, because the object of the arts is to "reduce to practice that which is learned from the sciences. "The only use of the sciences, in fact, is so to guide us in "our actions that from them we may derive the greatest "possible advantage."

We shall perhaps be surprised to find that the application of these principles leads to a rather different opinion as to some branches of modern education from that generally entertained. Poetry and history—classed together—are only admitted within the precincts of useful knowledge, on the ground that "they may both be made to afford "considerable amusement, and on that ground must be "considered as useful;" but when further analysed, they meet with far from a cordial approval. For as to poetry, our patron continues—

"Whatever may be the subject of which the poet treats, "his principal object, as it appears to me, is to excite "intense feeling, to interest his reader warmly; and to "produce this effect, there is no degree of exaggeration "that poets will not sometimes practice. Exaggeration,

"let it be ever so much disguised, is disregard of truth,
"and a disregard of truth is always mischievous."

And history does not fare very much better. As a record
of facts, the writer shows how little the mere sequence of
events, even when carefully sifted by a writer with powers
of weighing evidence, can teach of cause and effect as
bearing on human action ; while the facts which it is of real
utility to record are to a great extent those of scientific
progress, and comprehended within the other sciences. And
as an illustration of the views of many persons on these
branches of knowledge, he tells how a course of reading
which he had chalked out for a young friend, comprising
Adam Smith's Works, Mill's *Elements of Political Economy*,
Locke on the Human Understanding, and the four first books
of *Euclid*, had been vigorously denounced by an elderly
gentleman, educated at Oxford, who ridiculed the idea of a
person "studying political economy who does not even
"know how many wives Henry the Eighth had!" On the
other hand, the practice of raising up fictitious causes to take
the place of real causes of events is carefully illustrated,
and two of the best known histories of the day—Hume's
History of England and Mitford's *History of Greece*—are
most severely commented on, and the practice of the writers
to introduce false facts, and inferences from facts, in order
to cover and support preconceived opinions, is pointed out.
And the dissertation concludes—

"History and poetry may be separated from everything
"noxious; and then, as sources of amusement they, as
"well as the fine arts, ought to be ranked high. History,
"moreover, *may* be converted into a pleasing means of
"conveying instruction. Good history, it has been said,
"is sound philosophy—that is, general truths illustrated
"by examples drawn from particular actions. In civilised
"life, where abundance of leisure is at the command of
"large classes, if such leisure be not devoted to some
"pursuits, ennui and unhappiness are the consequence.

"Of pursuits for the purpose of mere amusement, those
"are selected with the greatest discrimination, the
"engagement in which is least likely ever to be disturbed.
"History and poetry, as sources of amusement, are
"independent of weather, and in a great measure of
"fortune and health; and it is on this account that a
"taste for reading is more deserving of cultivation than
"a taste for field sports and outdoor amusements in
"general."

The second conversation is connected with the first, and the problem to be solved stated, by our mechanic, now developing more intelligence in the gradual progress of the instructive discussion.

"If I understand you rightly," he says, "the only reason
"for which you value knowledge is because it adds to our
"happiness. But since I last saw you it has occurred to
"me that you have not yet explained what you mean by
"happiness. I have been puzzling myself a good deal
"to find out what it is that really constitutes happiness."
And he states this difficulty a little more fully thus—

"Ideas of what happiness is vary with the country, the
"pursuits, and the habits of each individual. The summit
"of a man's ambition in one country is to drink fermented
"liquor out of the skull of an enemy; in another to pass
"his life in a harem surrounded by houris. One man
"longs to devote the whole of his life to music; another
"to field sports; and of two other men, the first cannot
"bear to be in town, while the second can no more bear
"to be in the country."

The reply to this problem is undertaken by our patron, who, though he declines to give a strict definition in any part of the conversation, defines man as a "rational animal," and states, one by one, the essentials without which happiness is practically impossible to such a being.

"To begin," he says, "happiness, I suppose it will be
"admitted by all, is a state of feeling—feeling of pleasure,

"arising from health and contentment ; as unhappiness is
"a feeling of pain arising from sickness or any other
"source of discontent."
And he continues a little later on—
"Admitting that *all* the things which conduce to
"pleasure cannot be enumerated, *some* of them can; some,
"the absence of which will inevitably produce unhappiness.
"Sufficiency of food, for example, of clothing, of fuel,
"and shelter; protection from violence and fraud, and
"freedom from disease and superstitious terrors; the
"society of some of our own species, of the other sex
"more particularly; the habit of performing actions useful
"to others. No man and no society, in my opinion, can
"enjoy happiness unless these sources of pleasure, these
"securities against pain, be at hand."
This is the outline of the argument, which is worked out
in a careful and elaborate manner, while the possibility of
all classes of society attaining such a condition is affirmed
in strong and hopeful language.
"For my part," our patron says, "I have as little
"hesitation in pronouncing that it is possible for things
"to be so arranged that all classes of society should be
"amply provided with food, clothing, fuel, and shelter, as
"that it is possible to cross the Atlantic in a steamboat,
"the suggestion of doing which a few years ago would
"have met with nothing but ridicule."
The necessity of good laws for securing protection from
violence, and protection of individual members in the owner-
ship of the property they have produced or acquired, is
carefully argued. But the possibility of the co-existence of
poverty and misery with good laws, and the necessity for
individual action by the members of a community to attain
comfort and happiness, are pointed out in a valuable passage
which might be well impressed on many of our prominent
legislators.
"All that we can conclude from such co-existence is,

"that good laws alone will not suffice for happiness,
"although general happiness cannot prevail without good
"laws. Good laws will not cure diseases, to cure diseases
"being the province of physicians. Good laws will not
"enable us to communicate with distant nations, the skill
"of the ship-builder and navigator being requisite for this
"purpose. In like manner, good laws will not guarantee
"to every one a sufficient supply of the necessaries and
"comforts of life, since this is the office of individual
"intelligence and application. Good laws guarantee to
"every one the fruits of his industry ; but good laws do
"not make all equally industrious and frugal ; nor do
"they infuse into any one an equal degree of prudence in
"circumscribing the size of his family within that number
"for which he can secure a comfortable subsistence. And
"it is obvious that, with equal families, the most indus-
"trious and frugal will more probably be well provided
"against want, than the less frugal and industrious ; and
"that, with equal industry and frugality, he who has a
"limited number of children has more means of providing
"for his and their happiness, than his neighbour who has
"chosen to trust to chance, and has been overwhelmed
"with an enormous family."
Freedom from disease, with a rejection of the notion that
ill-health may by inducing repentance be an indirect benefit ;
freedom from superstitious terrors ; and, lastly, the habit of
doing good and wishing well to others, are discussed, and
their necessity for the attainment of happiness on the one
hand, and the certainty on the other that their absence will
lead to unhappiness, shewn ; the conversation terminating
with an appeal by the mechanic for a discussion in the next
conversation of—
    "The means by which you think the great mass of
"mankind may be made to approach as near as possible
"to that of the most perfect happiness."
Education, the subject of the third chapter is the means
  E

proposed ; and the method of educating the young in such a way as to attain this object is carefully elaborated in the conversation. Our patron points out that—

"Life is too short, and the powers of the mind too "limited, to enable any one to master all the sciences—to "become a good moralist and politician, a mathematician, "a chemist, a mechanic, a botanist, a geologist, &c. "Suppose, moreover, that he could master all the sciences, "could he hope to find time or opportunity to reduce "them all to practice?"

Of sciences, therefore, some must be learned by one man, others by others ; the necessary knowledge which the community needs for its well-being being thus provided. And this is done under the stimulus of interest. But he points out that—

"Although a man would do well to confine himself to "a particular profession, it does not follow that he ought "to be equally confined in his knowledge. This capability "of distinguishing is called judgment. A man's judgment "cannot be too extensive ; he may not have the oppor- "tunity of making it so extensive as he could wish."

Discussing then what description of knowledge can least safely be dispensed with, he deals first with religious knowledge, and repeats the special necessity of possessing sound judgment for the purpose of considering religious questions.

"Before you call upon the child to exercise his judg- "ment upon one of the most knotty subjects that can be "submitted to it, something ought to be done towards the "formation of that judgment. Sound judgment may be "defined to be the capability of weighing evidence, of "discriminating between truth and falsehood, and of "deciding upon what is best adapted to bring about any end "which we may have in view. The imparting of a sound "judgment, according to Locke, is the principal business "of education. 'The business of education in respect of "'knowledge, is not, as I think, to perfect a learner in all

"'or any one of the sciences, but to give his mind that
"'freedom, that disposition, and those habits that may
"'enable him to attain any part of knowledge he shall
"'apply himself to, or stand in need of, in the future course
"'of his life.'"

For the development of this judgment, he points out
that the groundwork of the child's education should be to
respect truth, and that when that is done the time is arrived
for teaching it the necessity of guarding against the untruths
of others: the deceptions of history, of the miraculous stories
of Joanna Southcott and those of the Abbé Paris—credited
by the Jansenists of the middle ages—and others are carefully discussed. The qualities that are specially needed to
be inculcated are then referred to, with a special reference
to the duties of parents to consider, before bringing children
into the world, by what means they can educate them and
provide for their happiness. This—the Malthusian doctrine—
is discussed at considerable length, and the arguments in
support of it and of the absolute necessity of parental forethought and prudence elaborately set out. And the conversation closes by a strong recommendation that the
majority of the people should have some acquaintance with
the principles of legislation, so as to be capable of selecting
legislators, of providing adequate securities for the good
conduct of those whom they select to legislate for them, and
of judging of the mode of legislating.

Some further literary work appears to have been a sort of
amusement of his leisure hours during this long interval.
Between 1832 and 1835 he took part, with his wife and a
few other friends, of whom the late Professor Cowper and
his sister, Miss Martha Cowper, afterwards the wife of
Mr. Frederic Hill (the late Secretary to the Post-office, and
brother of Sir Rowland Hill), were the most active, in the
production of a charming little serial work for children,
entitled *The Parents' Cabinet of Amusement and Instruction*,
in which papers on elementary science were alternated with

lively stories, sketches of foreign countries, and interesting biographies. The plan of the work, which was published in thirty-six monthly parts, originated with Miss Cowper, who wrote a number of the articles herself. Some of the stories from the pen of Mrs. Ellis have a wonderful charm, and attest her great literary power. Ellis was the editor, and among his contributions were a series of articles on geography (used in its strict etymological sense, so as to include a description of the solar system) and a biographical sketch of Peter the Great. The series seems to have been successful, for a second edition was shortly afterwards published, and a third in 1859, with the omission of some papers and the addition of a good many more.[1] A fourth edition has just (1889) been issued, which has been edited and re-arranged by Mrs. Hill's daughter.

In 1835 we find Ellis again co-operating with his old friends—James Mill and Lord Brougham—for the spread of economical knowledge. He wrote a series of lectures, which he delivered at the City of London Literary Institution ; and the idea occurred, as we learn from James Mill, to Lord Brougham, that they might usefully be repeated to popular audiences in different parts of the country, if Ellis would lend his manuscripts. This he willingly did, and they were redelivered in many places, and were also printed

---

[1] There is in the *Englishwoman's Review* for October, 1887, a sketch of the life of Mrs. Frederic Hill, which contains an interesting anecdote, showing the relations between the contributors to this work and their editor. Miss Cowper, we are told—

"used to tell a pretty story of how she sent the first tale—'Harry, the "'Shrimper'—to her collaborateur, Mr. Ellis, for approval. She held "him in much reverence, as well as esteem, and his critical fiat was to her "a judgment beyond appeal. 'Well, my dear,' he said, when she saw him, "'I cannot conceive how you could write such a story——' 'There,' "burst in Miss Cowper, 'Mrs. Ellis should not have shown it you. I told "'her to send it back if it was too bad.' 'My dear young lady,' continued "Mr. Ellis, taking her hand, 'you should let me finish my sentence. I "'was going on to say—without your having found out long ago your power "'of story telling.'"

and circulated gratis among various mechanic institutions. Curiously enough, this led to a suggestion of plagiarism against Lord Brougham; but the following extracts from two letters of James Mill to Lord Brougham, the former written when the plan of delivery by other lecturers was being discussed, the latter after they had been delivered in several places, show his opinion of the lectures[1]:—

"India House, 8th July, 1835.

"My dear Lord,— . . . I know well what to expect "from the lectures; and should eagerly give my assent to "whatever may be deemed the best mode of using them. "Is anybody known who could be used as an itinerating "lecturer? .   . —Most faithfully yours,

"J. MILL."

"Mickleham, 5th October, 1835.

"My dear Lord,—Nothing ever was more ridiculous "than this attempt to make a plagiarist of you for the "lectures of Mr. Ellis, which were written for the sole "purpose of being delivered by himself in the City of "London Literary Institution, where my son tells me that "he heard the first lecture; when Mr. Ellis, before begin-"ning to read it, told his hearers that his sole object was "to lay before them the doctrines of the science in the "plainest manner he had been able; that he had aimed "at no originality; that he had taken the doctrines, and "sometimes even the words, as he had found them in the "most approved books. You heard of these lectures for "the first time from me, I having mentioned them "casually in one of our conversations about the time. It "so happened also that a person whom you know had "read your discourse (not then printed) on the study of "the physical sciences to a literary society at Manchester; "and it immediately occurred to you that he might very "usefully read these same lectures to the same society, if

---

[1] Bain's *Biography of James Mill*, pages 389-392.

"Mr. Ellis would part with them for that purpose, which
"he very readily did. They were afterwards lent to Mr.
"Leonard Horner, for the purpose of being read, either
"by himself or somebody else (I forget which), at some
"institution in Edinburgh. And they have been read,
"chiefly through your recommendation, in several other
"places. . . . —Ever truly yours,

" J. MILL."

In his later life Ellis did not think these lectures worth
preserving. No copy or manuscript was found among his
papers, and I have been unable by enquiry to discover
one. Five and twenty years afterwards Lord Brougham
wished to republish them, and wrote Ellis the following
letter :—

"Brougham, 5th December, 1860.

"My dear Mr. Ellis,—Was not the course of lectures
"on political economy which our Useful Knowledge
"Society circulated among different mechanics' institutes
"some years ago written by you? and, if so, would you
"have any objection to their forming, with such additions
"or alterations as you may please to make, a part of the
"unpublished portion of my *Political Philosophy?* I
"have long wished to have that work compleated, and
"although a large portion of the unpublished part (on the
"functions of Government) will appear in my book on
"the British Constitution, about to be published, yet the
"work will still be very imperfect from the omission of
"political economy.

"Pray excuse this trouble, and believe me to be, with
"great esteem, most sincerely yours,

" H. BROUGHAM."

But in five and twenty years Ellis's views and ideas as to
what educational lectures should be had much progressed.
He declined to accede to Lord Brougham's proposal, on the
ground, as he informed the present writer, that he then
thought them of not sufficient value to be worth republishing.

CHAPTER V.

1846.

Commencement of Educational Work—Dr. (afterwards Professor) Hodgson
—George Combe—Reason for long interval—State of Education in 1846—
Infant Schools—Fröbel—Ellis's Method.

IN the year 1846 Ellis commenced the educational labours which, continued through his subsequent life, have rendered him honourably known among the foremost workers in the great cause of the improvement by means of education of the condition of humanity. About the same time, or a few months later, he became acquainted with Dr. William Ballantyne Hodgson, who, till his death in 1880, was one of his closest friends and fellow-workers. Hodgson was a native of Edinburgh, who had for the previous seven years been engaged (first as secretary and afterwards as principal) in the conduct of the Liverpool Mechanics' Institute, which, under his able and energetic management, had very largely increased in efficiency and usefulness. So conspicuous had been his merits that in March, 1846, the University of Glasgow conferred on him—at the early age of thirty—the honorary degree of LL.D. During his management of the institution, a girls' school had been added to it, and when he resigned his post—in 1847—the day pupils numbered 1,650, the High school 250 boys, the girls' school 300 girls, and the evening classes 400 pupils. Dr. Hodgson became, on his resignation of his post at Liverpool, Principal of Chorlton High School—a large private school at Manchester—a position which he occupied for about five years. From that date he was engaged till 1871 in writing and lecturing, chiefly upon economical and educational subjects, on which he became a recognised leader of thought; and in 1858 was appointed one of the assistant commissioners under the Royal Commission, of which the Duke of Newcastle was chairman, to enquire into the state of primary education in England. In July, 1871, he was elected the first Professor of Economic Science (or, as it is called in the foundation deed, of Commercial and Political Economy and Mercantile Law) in the University of Edinburgh, a position which he held until his death in 1880. Dr. Hodgson was a man of great and varied attainments; he possessed a wide acquaintance with ancient and modern literature, which his singularly retentive memory enabled him to utilize in an extraordinary manner. He was a fluent and able speaker and lecturer, a man of brilliant wit, and possessed of a delicate sense of humour, which made him a most charming companion, and a welcome guest in society. The strong convictions which he entertained upon the method by which the improvement of the condition of mankind might be attained, namely, by the general adoption of right methods of education, were the foundation of his friendship with Ellis, and were increased and strengthened by the influence of the latter. The correspondence between them lasted without any break till Hodgson's sudden death from angina pectoris in 1880, and many of Ellis's most earnest thoughts and aspirations are found in that correspondence. The following, the earliest letter from Ellis to Hodgson, relates to the proposed establishment of a school at the National Hall, Holborn, under the management of William Lovett, the Chartist, and gives an interesting picture of Ellis's views at that time:—

"6th August, 1846.

"I have been delighted by the perusal of your two "excellent addresses.[1]   I concur and sympathise most "heartily in all your sentiments.   How happens it that

---

[1] Addresses delivered at the Mechanics' Institute, Liverpool, of which Dr. Hodgson was then principal.

"with such noble and, at the same time, practical views
"you have no normal school attached to your institution?
"Who can estimate the good that might be done by a
"few apostles going forth imbued with your notion of
"duty, and qualified to impart them to others?

"I rise from your discourses dissatisfied with myself.
"I feel that I ought to do more than I have done or am
"doing in the good work in which you are so usefully and
"earnestly engaged. Having stimulated me, therefore,
"pray do not stop short; assist me to bear fruit. We
"both seem to feel that the great work to be now engaged
"in is 'Education,' in other words 'Moral and Intellectual
"'training;' to give knowledge and with knowledge the
"disposition to use it for the benefit of society. I think
"I mentioned to you that the special object which I have
"in view at present is to procure a teacher for a projected
"boys' school, at the National Hall, Holborn. The mem-
"bers of this hall are 'moral force Chartists,' and they have
"been persuaded by some judicious friends not to waste
"their time in mere agitation and speechifying, but to
"attempt the *doing* something; they devote the building,
"in which five or six hundred boys might be taught, and
"the funds for the teacher or teachers, books, implements,
"&c., are to be provided. The school, in fact, is to be
"formed; and I need not ·say that the success of the
"project must depend, in a great measure, upon the
"principal teacher. The boys will, of course, be from
"the working class, and their teacher ought to have the
"feelings of an apostle. I earnestly wish to take a warm
"interest in the school and the teacher, and will cheer-
"fully make myself responsible to him for good treatment,
"and a cordial co-operation in carrying out and, if possible,
"extending the original design.

"I shall gladly receive any hints that you might be
"induced to favour me with on any part of these contem-
"plated proceedings. The salary of the Master it is

"thought should be £70 per annum, and 2d. besides for
"each boy per week. But this is open for consideration,
"and in the inquiry which you so kindly undertake act
"upon your own better judgment and more enlightened
"experience, and be assured you will find in me a not
"very untractable pupil.

"I will only add to what I have said before that in
"offering my name as a guarantee to the teacher (if one
"can be found) I do so merely that he may feel quite
"secure. In other respects I would rather that it did not
"appear, as I am not entitled to claim merit or honour,
"when I am little more than a trustee."

It will be seen from this letter that Ellis was just
beginning the work which absorbed so large a portion of
his subsequent life. The circumstances under which he had
for so many years allowed his energies to remain almost
dormant are best told by himself. We find them given in
two letters to Dr. Hodgson.

"19th August, 1847.

"I am re-reading Combe on the constitution of man.
"You know where I disagree with him, but nevertheless
"I admire—I revere him. Strange it would be if, in a
"world so replete with ignorance and the misery con-
"sequent upon it, men participating in the views of
"Combe, you, and myself could not coincide in some course
"of action to remove that great master evil—Ignorance.
"Combe, I fancy, would find nothing to gainsay in what
"I have written; he would add something more. I, on
"the other hand, might wish to subtract somewhat from
"him. But we all agree in wishing to see man taught
"and trained to place himself in harmony with the laws
"of Nature. Combe dwells more than once upon the im-
"portance of a 'rational restraint upon population,' and
"my conviction of this, more than anything else, led me last
"year to resume actively what I had laid aside for twenty
"years—the teaching of political economy. I abandoned

"it in despair, but am now beginning to hope that ere
"long it will force its way into all the schools of the
"kingdom."

The following letter, besides explaining more in detail
how so long an interval had elapsed in his work, contains
much interesting thought upon the subject of education.
The book to which he refers, called *The Evangel of
Love*, by Henry Sutton,[1] was one which had much charmed
Dr. Hodgson, and had been recommended by him to Ellis
as specially interesting.

" 10th February, 1848.

"I have acted upon your recommendation and have
"procured *The Evangel of Love*, and, although I have not
"read it throughout attentively, I have caught enough of
"its spirit to be induced, while yet fresh from its perusal,
"to venture upon the few remarks that have suggested
"themselves to me.   I quite agree with you in thinking
"it a most extraordinary work for an uneducated lad.
"Stripped of its mysticism and rhapsody, the practical
"conclusions quite surprised me by their soundness.   In
"common with me he would inculcate industry, economy,
"thoughtful anticipation of the future consequences of
"present conduct, particularly as regards parental cares
"and duties and feelings of brotherhood through which
"individual superiorities may diffuse the advantages
"which they possess to those who are less favored.   Not
"being inclined to criticism, I will do no more than advert
"to the few vulgar commonplaces about Mammon, &c.,
"which might have been spared, and go on to what is more
"congenial to my disposition—something practical.

"Many seem to concur in *saying* the right thing.   Who

---

[1] Mr. Sutton was the author of a little volume of poems published at
Nottingham, much admired by Emerson, who met him there in 1848 at the
house of Mr. Joseph Neuberg.   Mr. Sutton also published a volume called
Quinquinergia, or Proposal for a New Practical Theology, 1854.   Mr.
Sutton afterwards went to reside at Manchester.

"is taking steps to secure that the right thing shall
"be *done?* Twenty years ago I laid aside the pen,
"deeming it not to be my vocation, and my exertions
"beyond my business and private circle were cramped by
"want of hope. I have of late been striving to shake off
"this uncomfortable and unsatisfactory state. I wish to
"assist in *doing* something, however trifling. My late
"little books (which will most likely also be my last) were
"meant to be quite subsidiary to the doing department.
"My first has been my reading book for the boys' class
"which I have been teaching for a year and a half. My
"latest is a series of questions framed with a view to
"familiarise schoolmasters with a subject which, on inves-
"tigation, I found was all but *terra incognita* to them.
"A twelvemonth has now nearly elapsed since I com-
"menced my weekly schoolmaster's class. I flatter myself
"that I have thoroughly inoculated six or seven of them
"with the laws of social science. My plan of conducting
"this class has been to propound the question for con-
"sideration ; inadequate or mistaken answers lead to
"other questions, through which I, at last, extract answers,
"unanimously agreed to be satisfactory. I then give my
"answer in my own words, and then proceed on. I can
"assure you we have had some most interesting discussions,
"three or four of my questions having sometimes
"occupied a whole lesson, and the suggested questions
"having been four or five times as numerous as those in
"the book.

"Combe, Hodgson, Sutton, and Ellis, let them differ as
"much as they please on other matters, are all impressed
"with the importance of the population question. It
"formed the subject of your farewell lesson at Liverpool.
"It was the motive force which propelled me to take to
"teaching, for I was not slow to perceive with you that
"writing and lecturing are not to be trusted without teach-
"ing in which repetition is an essential ingredient. In

' executing my task *in extenso,* in handling the population
" question, surrounded as it is with prejudice and difficulty,
" I have been amply repaid by the practical aptitude which
" I cannot but feel that I have acquired as a teacher and
" in impressing myself upon others. In unfolding the
" laws of social life, every step presents the opportunity
" of enforcing the four fundamental duties already
" mentioned, and the investigation of every social evil
" leads inevitably to the tracing its cause to the neglect
" of one or more of those duties. Compare such results
" with what can flow from the wild declamation of those
" who trace the various evils of society to the Currency
" laws, to Competition, to the oppression of Capitalists, to
" Absenteeism, to want of Protection, &c., &c. What a
" unity of Scientific truth! that same forethought which
" will secure one class against low wages will secure
" another against pressure and bankruptcy.

" On 28th February next, a day school for boys will be
" opened at the National Hall, under the superintendence
" of William Lovett, who is quite imbued with all the
" more advanced notions on education. He has engaged
" a master whom I have seen, who appears so far to
" promise well, and who is to join my class. At the end
" of June a day school for boys will also be opened at the
" London Mechanics' Institution, which I expect will be
" conducted by Mr. Runtz, the gentleman whose appear-
" ance pleased you so much here last summer, and whom I
" know to be an earnest and enlightened teacher. From
" his influence and example I expect great things, both as
" regards children and adults.

" Enough of this part of the world. Now let me ask a
" question about Sutton. What is he? How does he earn
" his livelihood? Is he a lecturer or teacher, or has he a
" call that way? His writings would indicate somewhat of
" the apostolic in him. Pray gratify my curiosity on these
" points when you next write. If I am rightly informed there

" is not a town in the kingdom which more urgently requires
" the services of a true schoolmaster than Nottingham. It
" might learn much from its own prophet—but perhaps he
" is not honoured in his own country.

" I will now bring to a close what you must consider
" you have drawn down upon yourself by introducing me
" to Sutton, begging that you will consider yourself quite
" at liberty to leave all this unnoticed and unanswered till
" you are quite at leisure and quite in the humour for
" writing."

It will be seen by the last letter how much Mr. Sutton's
book had impressed Ellis. By a subsequent letter we learn
that he sent him copies of the works which he had then
published, and had written to him in a very friendly spirit,
but had received no answer. Mr. Sutton's name consequently drops out of our narrative: but the response of
George Combe, whose name was also mentioned in both the
above letters, and whose friendship he acquired a year or
two later, was very different. Combe, who was some twelve
years Ellis's senior, had been up to this date known chiefly
as the apostle of phrenology, on which he had published an
elaborate work in 1822, and the author of a valuable book
called *The Constitution of Man*, published in 1828. But
his studies on the philosophy of the human mind had led
him by a different course of thought to the same conclusion
as Ellis on the subject of education. As Mr. William Jolly,
the able editor of his educational works, tells us[1]:

" With him, more perhaps than with most students of
" the Philosophy of Mind, education was ever present to
" his thoughts as the best practical application of its
" principles. From early life he was a diligent worker on
" the subject. It was an all-pervading element in every-
" thing he wrote and did, and it was his constant aim to

---

[1] *Education, its Principles and Practice, as developed by George Combe:*
collated and edited by William Jolly, H.M. Inspector of Schools. Introduction,
p. xvi.

"reduce his philosophy to practice and to help in framing
"a system of Educational Science based on the Science -
"of mind."

Combe published in 1848 a pamphlet entitled "What
should Secular Education embrace?" which naturally
attracted Ellis's interest and attention. His first remarks
on it, written a few days prior to the last letter we have
quoted, are very interesting. He writes to Dr. Hodgson:—

"1st February, 1848.

"I am just fresh from devouring, What should Secular
"Education embrace? How entirely I concur in all
"Combe's practical conclusions! But little is now needed
"to obtain a trial by which his views may be placed before
"the public in active operation. You well know how
"entirely he must have my sympathy in flinging to the
"winds all curricula of study founded upon the notions
"still prevalent in the seventeenth century. Combe
"certainly stands foremost among those who are pointing
"out the right road and urging us to take it. I am
"longing to see the hero who will lead us to action, and I
"am eager to enlist under his banners, feeling, moreover,
"something of a conviction that his advent is not far off.
"But a truce to these rhapsodies!"

With this strong and enthusiastic agreement in Combe's
views, it is not surprising that Ellis sought to know him.
He had six months before mentioned to Hodgson (who
knew Combe) his wish, if possible, to meet him. He had
written Hodgson—

"12th September, 1847.

"I entirely agree with you on the subject of introduc-
"tions, but shall always give a cordial welcome to any-
"body with credentials from you. George Combe requires
"none—honour to the man he deigns to visit, and you
"certainly earn my thanks should you act as the conductor
"to attract such an honour to my house."

But the first communication between them did not arise

through a letter of introduction from Dr. Hodgson, but by Ellis's sending one of his works to Combe. His account of the opening of the correspondence is interesting. He writes to Hodgson :—

"7th March, 1848.

"I desired Smith, Elder, and Co. to send George Combe "a copy of my *Questions and Answers*, and I receive "to-day a most flattering letter of thanks, addressed to "the unknown author. Among other things, he says, 'It "'executes a most valuable idea, and with great success. "'Indeed, I have rarely seen so much sound principle "'communicated so clearly, and in so short a compass. "'It would do great public good were it introduced into "'schools generally. The new Revolution in France, if "'successful, will lead to new social movements here, and "'were our common people instructed from infancy in "'the principles expounded in your work, we should "'stand on a basis of immoveable strength.'"

Combe was, as we might expect, as much impressed by Ellis as the latter had been by him. In a letter to a friend, he described him as "one of the soundest, most "active, and most practical educationists with whom he "had corresponded." Before they met personally, however, many letters passed between them, and Ellis had assisted Combe in the foundation of a school at Edinburgh, and provided him the able master—Mr. W. Mattieu Williams— to whom it owed its success during the five years of its existence. In May, 1849, Ellis wrote to Hodgson :—

"May 6th, 1849.

"Out of the ranks of the poor and the ignorant the "only efficient co-operation that I have as yet met with "has been from that truly earnest working man, George "Combe. Most glad shall I be to learn that others are "beginning to open their eyes to the fact that general "well-being is impossible until instruction in social science "has been made the birth-right of mankind."

It was only in September, 1849, that Combe visited London, and became personally known to Ellis. They visited together some of the schools in which Ellis's methods had recently been introduced, and Combe carefully inspected the teaching which was being given. The result of that inspection, and the impression produced on Combe's mind, is well described in one of Ellis's letters to Hodgson :—

" 15th October, 1849.

" My Saturday voluntary class at the Birkbeck School " has swelled to upwards of fifty boys. Mr. Combe, when " in London, visited and inspected the school," [the first Birkbeck School] "and the one at the National Hall. " He was astonished and delighted at what he heard and " saw. The Williams School, at Edinburgh, numbers " more than one hundred and fifty. Three young men— " self-supporting—are learning under Runtz.' When the " work was begun I hoped for success; I expected it. I " now feel certain of it. The sooner Mr. Morell persuades " his friends to introduce similar instruction into their " schools the better for them. Mr. Combe said that the " answers of the little girls to Mr. Lovett's questions, in " his lesson to them on physiology, would have done " credit to the young surgeons in their first year at " Edinburgh. In my particular branch I invite inspection, " and am ready to assist anybody, regardless of creed or " sect."

From that time the friendship of Ellis and Combe was continued without interruption till Combe's death in 1858; and in his subsequent visits to the metropolis he generally managed to spend a few days at Ellis's charming home at Champion Hill.

Before we proceed to describe the work which Ellis did in the commencement of his campaign against ignorance, poverty, and vice, it will be well to shortly review the position of education at that time. The impulse in the direction of the education of the people which arose, in

F

the sixteenth century, from the Reformation resulted in the foundation of the numerous grammar schools which are found scattered throughout the country, generally associated with the name of Edward VI. or Queen Elizabeth. These grammar schools were mainly founded for the teaching of the grammar of the dead languages—especially Latin ; and at that period there was good reason for the adoption of that method of education, for the Greek and Latin languages contained nearly all the knowledge which mankind then possessed. Science was in its infancy, and the little which was known was to be found in those languages. But the ancient system of these schools had continued with little or no expansion from the sixteenth to the nineteenth century. The only subjects taught were Greek and Latin; the vast majority of the hours devoted by the pupils to study continued to be spent in the tedious grinding of Latin declensions and conjugations by boys who never got beyond this drudgery, and never learned to value the literature of these languages, at a time when the Greek and Latin languages had ceased to contain more than a mere fraction of the knowledge which every boy and girl ought to be taught.

This faulty system had not been overlooked during the three centuries which had elapsed. John Milton wrote in 1644:—

"We do amiss to spend seven or eight years in scraping "together so much miserable Latin and Greek as might "be learned otherwise easily and delightfully in one "year."[1]

Locke, writing in 1692,[2] says:—

"Would not a Chinese, who took notice of our way of "breeding, be apt to imagine that all our young gentle-

---

[1] Milton's *Tractate of Education*.
[2] Locke's *Treatise on Education*.

"men were designed to be teachers and professors of the
"dead languages of foreign countries, and not to be men
"of business in their own?"
But the system remained bound in the fetters of ancient
charters and the wills of "pious founders," which held fast
both the grammar schools and the Universities of Oxford
and Cambridge, and all the efforts of reformers and philosophers failed to put an end to its obsolete methods.
Anthony Trollope in his *Autobiography* bears witness, in
amusingly vivacious language, to the existence of this state
of things in one of the foremost English schools, as well as
a smaller one to which he was sent. He tells us (*Autobiography*, chap. i.):—

"When I left Harrow I was all but nineteen, and I had
"at first gone there at seven." [His school life would
therefore include the years 1822-34.] "During the whole
"of those twelve years no attempt had been made to teach
"me anything but Latin and Greek, and very little attempt
"to teach me those languages. I do not remember any
"lessons either in writing or arithmetic. French and
"German I certainly was not taught. The assertion will
"scarcely be credited, but I do assert that I have no
"recollection of other tuition except that in the dead
"languages. At the school at Sunbury there certainly
"was a writing master and a French master. The latter
"was an extra and I never had extras. I suppose I must
"have been in the writing master's class, but though I can
"call to mind the man, I cannot call to mind his
"ferule. It was by their ferules I always knew them and
"they me. I feel convinced in my mind that I have
"been flogged oftener than any human being alive. It
"was just possible to obtain five scourgings in one day
"at Winchester, and I have often boasted that I obtained
"them all. Looking back over half a century, I am not
"quite sure the boast is true, but, if I did not, nobody
"ever did."

A still more eminent man—Charles Darwin—gives a similar picture of Shrewsbury school under Dr. Butler.[1]

"In the summer of 1818," he says, "I went to Dr. Butler's "great school, in Shrewsbury, and remained there for seven "years, till Midsummer, 1825, when I was sixteen years old.

"Nothing could have been worse for the development "of my mind than Dr. Butler's school, as it was strictly "classical, nothing else being taught except a little ancient "geography and history. The school, as a means of "education to me, was simply a blank. During my whole "life I have been singularly incapable of mastering any "language. Especial attention was paid to verse-making, "and this I could never do well. I had many friends "and got together a good collection of old verses which by "patching together, sometimes aided by other boys, I "could work into any subject. Much attention was paid "to learning by heart the lessons of the previous day. "This I could effect with great facility, learning forty or "fifty lines of Virgil or Homer whilst I was in morning "chapel ; but this exercise was utterly useless, for every "verse was forgotten in forty-eight hours. I was not "idle, and with the exception of versification, generally "worked conscientiously at my classics, not using cribs. "The sole pleasure I ever received from such studies was "from some of the odes of Horace, which I admired "greatly."

And if the education of the upper classes was so wretchedly defective, that of the poor was almost non-existent. The splendid foundations of Edward VI., of which Christ's Hospital is perhaps the most prominent, had been in great measure appropriated for the benefit of the middle classes. Spite of the treatises of learned men pointing out what education ought to be, little effect had been produced in the public mind, and the blind resistance

---

[1] *Life and Letters of Charles Darwin*, by his Son, Francis Darwin. Auto-biography, page 31.

to all change which for thirty years after the French Revolution continued to direct the councils of this country, blocked, in its terror, even the improved education of the people as a danger to society. In 1807 Mr. Whitbread had proposed a large and comprehensive measure of Poor Law Reform, by which he would arrest the progress of pauperism by educating and so raising the character of the labouring classes. But his ideas were treated as visionary: and even so eminent a man as Mr. Windham led the advocates for protecting the people from the dangers of education.

"His friend Dr. Johnson was of opinion," he said,[1] "that it was not right to teach reading beyond a certain "extent in society. The danger was that if the teachers "of the good and propagators of bad principles were "to be candidates for the control of mankind, the latter "would be likely to be too successful. . . . The "increase of this sort of introduction to knowledge would "only tend to make the people study politics, and lay "them open to the arts of designing men."

And even Brougham, when he brought the subject before the House of Lords in 1820 fared little better; his Bill met with no support and had to be dropped.

And yet some progress was being made: but it was not by the help of statesmen and parliaments, but by the patient work of humble labourers in the field, who were showing by their own example what valuable effects might be attained by education. Pestalozzi, whom Ellis, in a review, published in 1851, calls "the father of popular edu-"cation on the continent," had between the years 1775 and 1790 sought to show in his own house, in Switzerland, by a judicious blending of industrial, intellectual, and moral training, what the method of imparting education adapted to the purposes of a national system should be. Poor Pestalozzi ruined himself by his benevolent labours,

---

[1] *Hansard*, vol. ix., p. 548.

but his plans—continued a little later at Hofwyl, near Berne, by his countryman, Von Fellenberg—attracted widespread attention, and laid the foundation of the best schools in Germany. In England the work of Lancaster and Bell had become widely known, and the rivalry which it caused between the Dissenters and the Church had led to the foundation of a large number of schools. Dr. Andrew Bell, who had originated at Madras the system of organising schools by means of monitors, had published an account of it in 1797, in which year it was adopted in the parochial school of St. Botolph's, Aldgate. In the following year Joseph Lancaster, a Quaker, opened a school in the Borough Road, upon the same method. Lancaster's success led to the formation in 1809 of a society for extending schools on the same plan, which, known at first as the Royal Lancasterian Institution, was afterwards called the British and Foreign School Society. The foundation of this society, which was mainly supported by Dissenters, led to the establishment of a rival one by the Church, which assumed the name of the National Society, and was avowedly an institution for extending the principles of the Church of England.

Progress had been made by both these societies, but the method of teaching and the subjects taught were in the early part of the century still lamentably defective. The list of lessons included merely reading, writing, repetition, spelling, and arithmetic, with the addition, in the Church schools, of the catechism, and some Scripture history, and, in other schools, of some selected Bible lessons. Even dictation was unknown. Grammar, geography, and history were not thought of for the common people. Not one of the attractive fields in the wide range of science was opened in the common schools till far on in this century. The laws of health and the principles of social well-being were of course not thought of. Even in the schools founded under the influence of Bell and Lancaster, the teaching of subjects now universal was at first deprecated as " raising "the children above their station in life," though in a few of them some gradual progress took place.

In the meantime, the infant school system of instruction had been introduced in a similar way. About 1780 Oberlin, a pastor in the north-east of France, had originated the idea of schools specially adapted to the capacities of very young children. In this country James Buchanan, one of the teachers engaged by Robert Owen, at New Lanark, in 1815, had introduced into the schools founded by him a separate department, into which he gathered the little children playing about the mill-stream, and by a method suited to their powers, showed how to win their attention and convey to their faculties valuable education while amusing them. His plans were taken up and developed under the auspices of Robert Owen, Brougham, James Mill, and other Liberal reformers. This also led to the formation of a church institution for the purpose of attaining the same object with a due blending of the catechism: in 1836 the Home and Colonial Infant School Society was formed.

In the meantime, a reformer had appeared who had done much to develop the method of education suitable to infants. Friedrich Fröbel, a native of Germany, born in 1772, had adopted the views and become a follower of Pestalozzi. From 1808 to 1810 he taught in Pestalozzi's schools, and in 1816 founded schools of his own, which soon became celebrated throughout Germany, and from that date till his death in 1852 he was engaged, partly in Germany and partly in Switzerland, in school work. He especially devoted his attention to the development of the Pestalozzian system in the teaching of young children; and the Kindergarten, as he calls it, is a school for infants, in which he regulates the length and subject of the lessons in such a way as to engage the attention of the different faculties of each child, and to convey knowledge while training the eyes and ears, as well as the hands and thinking powers, but at the same time never wearying or straining the immature powers of the child. In fact, he regulated children's play in a systematic way, and so as to convert it into the best and truest education.

The improvements which Ellis introduced into education, and upon which he founded his schools, were based upon a careful study of the kinds of knowledge and the individual qualities which children ought to acquire during the years they spend at school. He formed the plan of adapting his lessons to the development of the thinking powers of children who have passed beyond infant schools, instead of merely cultivating their memory. By this he drew out and strengthened every portion of their mental organisation; and he utilised for the purpose of mental training and exercise those particular subjects, the knowledge of which would be most useful to his pupils in the world-education to which the vast majority would pass on quitting the school doors. He advised a method of instruction by which in addition to reading, writing, and arithmetic, which he looked on as merely implements of education, a child should be led by skilful guidance to acquire knowledge—especially knowledge of scientific and physical laws—for himself by investigation and well-directed research, instead of being set to learn it by laborious plodding at text books. And every portion of the school studies was subordinated to the most important knowledge of all—the knowledge of the laws of conduct which affect human well-being, and by obedience to which only can the welfare of the individual and the community be attained.

The name which he gave to the last kind of teaching varied as his work progressed. We have seen him in 1847 speaking of it in his letters to Dr. Hodgson as "the "teaching of political economy." But he soon abandoned this name, as he found that many people failed to under-stand by it the teaching and training of his pupils in the various qualities which lie at the base of all social well-being—such as industry, knowledge, skill, economy, temperance, respect for property, and forethought, especially parental forethought. In the title of the earliest of his works, he called it "social economy." Elsewhere in his books and lectures he calls it "social science," "elementary social science," or "economic science." But even these titles proved unsatisfactory, and we find him twenty years later expressing to Hodgson his difficulty in finding a title which should convey the enormous importance of "lessons on "right conduct." He says:—

"5th July, 1869.

"I wish the word 'economics' could be dropped in "recommending the matters comprehended by it as a "subject for primary schools. The very sound of the "word disinclines nine-tenths of mankind to listen to the "suggestion of granting admission to such instruction in "a primary school. Archbishop Whately adopted the title "of 'money matters' for his lessons—a title by no means "agreeable to me. But I feel the want of a title which "shall, besides not setting people against us, force upon "them the importance of giving a favourable consideration "to the matters in which it is wished to give instruction "to children before they are cast upon the world, first "to take care of themselves, and afterwards of others."

Perhaps the name which pleased him most was the one which he adopted from the celebrated sermon preached by the Rev. James Caird, about 1857, before the Queen, and published by her desire. Mr. Caird had given his sermon the title of "Religion in Common Life," and had defined religion as "the art of being, and of doing, good." Ellis adopted Mr. Caird's title; and in the preface to his book, in which he traced out the right course of conduct in the various conditions of industrial life, he expressed his hope that Mr. Caird, and others similarly engaged, "will "welcome with cordiality this effort of a layman to co-"operate with them in their mission of inculcating the "knowledge and practice of religion in common life."

But it will be well that Ellis's aim in education—the ideal which he sought—should be given in his own language.   In one of his works[1] he says:—

"By education I mean an earnest application of well-
"selected means to impart to all such a knowledge of the
"laws of the universe, especially of their practical bearing
"upon the daily wants and business of life, as that all
"may be clearly convinced that their happiness is only to
"be attained by placing themselves in harmony with
"those laws; to communicate to all such manual, muscu-
"lar, and intellectual dexterity as may qualify them to
"gain, extend, and improve their knowledge, and appro-
"priate and apply it; and also to implant those habits of
"observation, application, and forethought, without which
"the soundest intellectual acquirements are comparatively
"useless.   Such a course of education, persevered in,
"generation after generation, would raise up a people
"knowing and practising the duties of social life, labouring
"and economising for their own present and future main-
"tenance, and struggling and contriving for the benefit of
"all.   A people so educated would be inspired, not with
"the mere vulgar notion of getting on,[2] not with the vain

---

[1] *Questions and Answers suggested by a consideration of some of the Arrangements and Relations of Social Life*, page 178.

[2] It is strange to read in an article in one of our Journals (*The Spectator*, 16th July, 1887), conducted by men of the highest culture, the opinion of the writer that Ellis "was essentially the Evangelist of what has been "irreverently called the 'great gospel of getting on,' and that neither Ellis or "Fröbel saw the whole field of the teacher's work." It is clear that the writer had only a very superficial acquaintance with Ellis's objects and work. One cannot help thinking, from references in the article to "University degrees" and to some unexplained kind of education referred to as "the discipline of "advanced education," that he is a University graduate, and still retains the ancient and obsolete idea of education as necessarily based on Greek and Latin. Of what "the whole field of the teacher's work" is, the writer does not condescend to give us even a hint; but he appears to look down from what he doubtless considers a more exalted platform upon the low aims of those who imagine that the chief object of education is to lead all classes of society to be, and to do, good—to know and practise the conduct which under the varying conditions of life will best conduce to the highest welfare of humanity.

"and illusory desire of rising in the world, but with a
"solemn sense of the sacredness of every duty undertaken,
"of every contract entered into. And thus the desire of
"happiness and gratification, the motive force of our
"conduct and exertions, would be subjugated and regu-
"lated by an all-pervading sense of duty, and thereby be
"rendered more capable of gaining its end."

Upon the relation of the science of conduct to other
scientific knowledge, his views were carefully expressed in
a letter dated 29th May, 1871, and addressed to Mr. Norman
Lockyer, the Secretary to the Royal Commission on
Scientific Instruction and the advancement of Science. In
returning the proof of his evidence he says:—

"Science, as generally understood, occupies itself with
"the structure of the physical world and the forces com-
"prised in it, leading to the capacity in men of dealing
"with those forces and accommodating themselves to
"them."

"Scientific instruction in elementary schools would, I
"conceive, scarcely interest thoughtful and benevolent men
"as it does, did they not hope through its influence to
"promote well-being, or, more humbly, to abate the
"frightful prevalence of destitution, vice, and misery, in
"the midst of which we dwell.

"The scientific instruction which I wish to see introduced
"and which I have been endeavouring to introduce into
"elementary schools, is to supplement all other scientific
"instruction so as to make it more effective in promoting
"well-being.

"The deliberations of the commissioners, the labours
"of the various boards of education, and the legislation
"upon which they are based and to which they may lead,
"all point to the assumption that well-being, individual
"and national, rests upon conduct ; and the practice of
"conduct presupposes a science of conduct.

"It is instruction in this science of conduct which I

"think ought to proceed *pari passu* with all other instruc-
"tion. It is that which teaches how to apply other
"knowledge so as to lead to the general well-being, of
"which each is to receive his share. It is that which
"imparts a knowledge of the essentials of good self-
"guidance, and induces thoughts of self-discipline as a
"necessary preparation for nobility of character and
"goodness of conduct or self-guidance."

It has been contended by some people who only partially
knew what Ellis's methods were, that he cared for no other
teaching than the special subject which he had made his
own. Of such commentators Ellis writes in an amusingly
caustic style to Dr. Hodgson:—

"April 4th, 1852.

"I need scarcely say that I agree with you in the
"necessity of teaching social science, and although I never
"represented this branch of instruction as the whole tree,
"I have never allowed myself to be deterred from my
"purpose by those who, while they charged me with making
"a tree of my branch, omitted to receive it even as a twig,
"hiding their ignorance, ineptitude, and apathy behind the
"plea of disapproval and contempt."

"19th June, 1853.

"I have read Mr. Forster's speech, as reported in the
"*Bradford Observer*, and shall be most happy to welcome
"him here and Mrs. Forster also. I hope you were careful
"to forewarn them of all my unsocial peculiarities. I do
"not by any means improve. I am more and more
"absorbed in one idea; not because, as you have some-
"times supposed, that idea is the only one on which I set
"a value, but because it is the neglected one. In my
"journey through life I have fallen in with a deserted
"child other passers-by would not or could not see. I have
"picked it up and cherished it, and it grows in my
"affections, becoming an object of jealousy to some, and
"exposing me to the ridicule, the pity, and the hatred of

" others, according to their several habits of thought and
" action; but also, and for that I cannot be too grateful,
" attracting to me the friendship and esteem of some
" whom I love to honor.

" I am glad that the impressions from your travels have
" confirmed your preference for our native country.
" Without having quitted it, I think I have been able to
" collect evidence enough to convince me of the justice of
" your appreciation. With all its defects and failings,
" this country is the fountain head of progress. Never
" were we making greater strides than at this moment."

Of the peculiar method of instruction adopted by Ellis—
the Socratic—we must speak later on. But we may well
close this chapter by quoting another letter of Ellis to Dr.
Hodgson, written a year or two earlier, in which he deals
with the object and aims of education. He says:—

" 10th November, 1850.

" Upon the more general matter of education, Mr.
" Combe and myself feel more strongly than you seem to
" do, the insufficiency of the education at present given
" to the rich as well as the poor as a means of well-being.
" We are also keenly alive to the probability of the
" miserable character of the education that would be
" offered to the people if your educational agitation were
" to be shortly brought to a successful close. For these
" reasons we are anxious that the public should be
" enlightened as to the object and aim of education, and
" we know no more efficient means for the purpose than
" the exhibiting, in different neighbourhoods, specimens of
" a much nearer approach to good education than what
" we see around us. Wherever I can find a school into
" which (as with Mr. Holmes' school down here) instruction
" in the conditions of well-being can be introduced, I .
" adopt this method of improving education. A remark-
" able instance of the success of this kind of effort presents
" itself in a Wesleyan school at Limehouse, the master of

"which, with his five pupil teachers, attends my classes
"and teaches social science in his school.   You say that
"in Manchester it is not so much new schools as the
"improvement of the old ones that is wanted.   So say
"we, not only of Manchester, but of the whole country,
"and therefore we urge improvement. While we promote
"extension, and give a preference to secular instruction,
"we contend that the goodness of a school is not to be
"estimated by what it excludes but by what it includes.
"For my own part I would greatly prefer to place my
"child in a school where he was taught the conditions of
"secular well-being with what I considered false religion
"than where he was left to shift for himself in both.

 "Again, while we agree most cordially in the necessity
"of a national system, and consider that nobody is justified
"in attempting to impose additional tasks upon those who
"are already so usefully and laboriously engaged, we
"consider that most probably there is not a member of
"your committee who does not take some interest in the
"school of his own immediate vicinity, and who does not
"consider that education *tant bien que mal* must be
"attended to while you are struggling for something
"better.   To the more intelligent and impressible of
"these I address myself, *in your person*. Make these
"schools I say, where improvable, somewhat more than
"they are—establishments for turning out good and
"useful members of society and not mere readers, writers,
"and cipherers, left to themselves and chance to find out
"what are the conditions of well-being, and to be disposed
"or not to attend to them if found out. Where there are
"no such improvable schools, I say associate to establish
"some in harmony with the more advanced notions of
"the day. You contend, and I am much too hopeful
"to differ with you, that improvement will follow exten-
"sion ; but I affirm that extension *must* follow improve-
"ment. Let us both acquiesce in the conclusion that they

" will aid one another, and give efficacy to our conviction
" by action.

" Look, for example, at what the London Mechanics'
" Institution has accomplished, and what every similar
" institution throughout the kingdom might do. Rather
" more than two years ago they devoted their premises
" during the day time, when they are otherwise unoccupied,
" to the purposes of a day school—secular, of course, in
" accordance with the fundamental principle of their
" establishment. They muster three hundred and forty
" boys, and I am assured by most competent judges that
" no boys in the kingdom are receiving so really efficient
" an education towards enabling themselves to secure a
" fair share of well-being (in the most comprehensive sense
" of the term) by their own conduct. You and some of
" your friends have taken an active interest in such insti-
" tutions. If you could bring them to imitate the parent
" institution they would, while the efforts for the future
" are proceeding, serve to exhibit to the public how good
" moral teaching and training can be given in secular
" schools."

Chapter VI.

1846—1854.

IN the autumn of 1846 Ellis began the practical work of teaching. He proposed to a Mr. Holmes, teacher of some British Schools in Cold Harbour Lane, Camberwell, to give a series of lessons in his school on Social Economy, a proposal which was gladly accepted. His object was to prove by practical experience that the science of social well-being, although by the vast majority of educators looked on as appertaining to political economy, and therefore abstruse and difficult to understand, might be treated in a simple and popular manner, and brought down to the comprehension of children of the ordinary school age. His success was such as to surprise himself, and a very short experience conclusively established that the truths of Social Economy can not only be understood and appreciated by children, but when properly taught prove to be a subject of intense and absorbing interest. He attained this success in spite of the fact that he himself had not then the thorough mastery of the art of conducting a class by questions, which he afterwards attained. Yet so complete was the conviction which this experiment brought to his mind that from this time he devoted himself with a quiet energy and determination peculiarly his own to make this method of teaching known in every possible way; first by the introduction of courses of lessons on Social Economy into existing schools; secondly, by the foundation at his own cost of schools intended to be models of what schools for the working classes should be; thirdly, by the writing and publication of books containing instructions for the use of teachers; fourthly, by drawing public attention, by means of lectures, addresses, and reviews, to the importance of introducing true and real education if the masses of the people were to be raised to a condition of comfort and happiness; and lastly (in default of training colleges) by the personal instruction of classes of teachers with a view to train them in the methods he had originated, so that they might become capable of giving lessons on self-guidance in the various schools which they conducted.

The first work of this kind in which Ellis took a considerable share, though as usual with him he kept himself in the background, was the establishment in conjunction with William Lovett of a school in the National Hall, Holborn. Lovett was a remarkable man, little known and less understood, but one of a class to whom the real greatness of England is due: earnest, self-sacrificing men, actuated by the spirit of Pym and Hampden, who have devoted their lives to the improvement of the condition of the people, but who have never reached the dignity of members of Parliament; who have toiled on in a humble sphere, with no hope of social distinction, and have suffered imprisonment for having remonstrated bravely and publicly against the cruel enforcement of unjust laws against other working men. Lovett, who was the son of the captain of a small trading vessel, was a journeyman carpenter. He had worked hard in 1830 to carry the Reform Bill. He had been the friend of Cobbett and Hunt, and later on became a Chartist, and was the person who, in conjunction with John Arthur Roebuck, framed the Bill which afterwards became so celebrated as the People's Charter, though he always resisted strenuously the proposal advocated by Feargus O'Connor to resort to physical force to obtain its enactment, and was consequently known as one of the leaders of the Moral Force Chartists. He had in 1837 been a member of a society called the

G

London Working Men's Association, which issued an address to the working classes on the subject of education containing some remarkable thoughts which coincided strikingly with the views which Ellis had elaborated. The following two or three passages will be interesting:—

"We assume then, *as a principle*, that all just govern-"ments should seek to prevent the greatest possible evil, "and to promote the greatest amount of good. Now, "if ignorance can be shown to be the most prolific "source of evil, and knowledge the most efficient means "of happiness, it is evidently the duty of Government "to establish *for all classes* the best possible system of "education.

"We further assume that poverty, inequality, and "political injustice are involved in giving to one portion "of society the blessings of education, and leaving the "other in ignorance; and, therefore, the working classes, "who are in general the victims of this system of "oppression and ignorance, have just cause of complaint "against *all partial* systems of education."

And later on the address proceeds—

"Is it consistent with justice that the knowledge "requisite to make a man acquainted with his rights "and duties should be purposely withheld from him, "and that he should be upbraided and despised on the "plea of his ignorance? And is it not equally cruel and "unjust to suffer human beings to be matured in ignorance "and crime, and then to blame and punish them?"

Later on, Lovett became secretary of an association of working men, called the National Association, who in 1842 had opened under the name of the National Hall a large building, formerly a chapel, in Gate Street, Holborn, for lectures, public meetings, concerts, and classes of different kinds. We have already seen in Ellis's letter of 6th August, 1846, to Dr. Hodgson (page 57), that he was taking steps to procure a master for a school which it was proposed to found in that hall; and by another letter of 10th February, 1848, that the same school was to be opened on the 28th of that month. The account of what Ellis did with reference to the foundation of this school, and also the specially characteristic manner of his doing it, are well told by Lovett himself, in an autobiography which he published in 1876. He says[1]:—

"In the beginning of 1846, a kind friend (who, not "liking to be talked of as the doer of good deeds, shall be "designated A. B.) made a proposal to the association, "through Mr. Francis Place, for the establishing of a "day school in the hall, under my superintendence and "management; he agreeing to provide the necessary "desks and apparatus for the opening of the school, as "well as to pay the *fixed salary of the schoolmaster*. Indeed, "the proposal was first made to myself to the effect that I "should conduct it; but having then some distrust of my "own abilities for a teacher, I was fearful of undertaking "the task. I readily agreed, however, to superintend it "as I best could; and hence the proposal was made to the "association in the form stated. The majority of our "members having highly approved of the proposal, "arrangements were speedily made, and certain alterations "effected in the hall for carrying the plan into execu-"tion."

Matters did not, however, progress smoothly; disputes arose in the association as to the choice of a master, an office which Lovett had for the time being declined. These disputes became so embittered that Lovett resigned the position of secretary of the association, and nearly two years elapsed before the plan was carried out. At length, however, on 28th February, 1848, the school was opened, and the following is Lovett's account of the circumstances

---

[1] *Life and Struggles of William Lovett in his pursuit of Bread, Knowledge, and Freedom*, page 319.

attending the opening, and the share which Ellis, still hidden under the letters A. B., had in it[1]:—

"Shortly after this event" (the presentation to Lovett by the hands of W. J. Fox, M.P., of a public testimonial as a mark of respect for his public services[2] by a body of subscribers, of which the late Serjeant Parry acted as chairman) "our day school, so long postponed, was "opened in the hall, our generous friend A. B. not only "furnishing the desks, books, and apparatus required for "the opening, but also the fixed salary of the school- "master. The introduction to our prospectus states that "'the object in forming this school is to provide for the

---

[1] *Life and Struggles of William Lovett*, page 334.

[2] The address presented to Lovett with the testimonial (a tea service and a purse of £140) is from the pen of W. J. Fox, and will be interesting, as showing what Lovett was.

"The testimonial this day presented to William Lovett is intended both "as an expression of gratitude for public services and of respect for private "worth. The subscribers rejoice to feel that they cannot distinguish "between the patriot and the man; but find that the self-same qualities of "integrity, purity, firmness, zeal, and benevolence which have secured to "William Lovett the lasting attachment of those who know him, have also "been the characteristics of his political career. Whether enduring the "loss of his goods, for refusing to be coerced into military service; or that "of his liberty, for protesting against the unconstitutional interference of the "police with the people; whether founding the Working Men's Associa- "tion for the attainment of political rights, or the National Association for "the promotion of social improvement; whether embodying the principles "of democracy, in the memorable document called the People's Charter, or "showing the means of redemption in his work entitled *Chartism, a new* "*organization of the people;* whether cultivating by instruction the intel- "lectual and moral nature of destitute children, or, by numerous addresses "from the above-named associations, recommending peace, temperance, "justice, love, and union to erring multitudes and nations; in labours which "will make themselves known by their results to posterity, or in unrecorded "scenes of friendly and domestic intercourse, William Lovett has ever been "the same; and may this memorial now presented to him serve as an "assurance that the feelings of his friends, admirers, and fellow-labourers in "the cause of humanity are strong and unchanging, like the truth of his "own character, public and private, by which those feelings have been "produced."

"'children of the middle and working classes a sound,
"'secular, useful, and moral education—such as is best
"'calculated to prepare them for the practical business of
"'life—to cause them to understand and perform their
"'duties as members of society—and to enable them to
"'diffuse the greatest amount of happiness among their
"'fellow men.' I may add that it is now" (the year 1857,
when he was penning this chapter of his autobiography),
"upwards of nine years since our school was opened,
"during which time our kind friend A. B. has handsomely
"contributed towards its maintenance, without which
"assistance it could not, I believe, be kept open ; the
"small payment of the children not being sufficient to
"pay the salaries of the teachers and assistants together
"with the rent and outgoings of the place."

The school was opened with nearly one hundred pupils,
and in October of the same year there was a daily attendance
of about two hundred. "The ages of the children," Lovett
wrote to George Combe, "are from six to fourteen, perhaps
"the majority being from eight to eleven. It is opened to
"the public generally, and we have the children of Jews,
"Unitarians, and Christians of various sects as well as those
"of no sect at all—no questions being asked, nor opinions
"taught, calculated to give offence to any."[1]

Of the management of the school, the teaching introduced
into it, and the impression produced by Ellis upon this hard-
headed, able, and honest working man, the following extract
gives an interesting account[2]:—

"For the first eighteen months of the establishment of
"our school I could not devote much time to its superin-
"tendence, being employed, as I have stated, in the service
"of Mr. Howitt. As soon, however, as I was at liberty
"I applied myself to the task of making it as efficient as

---

[1] *Education; its principle and practice, as developed by George Combe:*
collated and edited by William Jolly, page 226.

[2] *Life and Struggles of William Lovett,* page 360.

" possible by the introduction of such subjects as I con-
" ceived indispensable to a good school.   The subject of
" social science, or 'the science of human well-being,' my
" kind friend Mr. William Ellis (the founder of the Birk-
" beck Schools) kindly undertook to introduce into our
" school, in connection with several others in which he
" gave lessons on this very important subject.   I may here
" state that my acquaintance with this clear-headed and
" kind-hearted man formed a new epoch in my life, for my
" attendance at his various lectures and the many interesting
" conversations I had with him gradually dispersed many
" of my social illusions, and opened my mind to the great
" importance of this science, as forming the chief and
" secure basis of morality, of individual prosperity, and
" national happiness.   In fact, the little knowledge I was
" thus enabled to glean regarding social science, was the
" means of enabling me to concentrate and apply my
" previous knowledge in a manner I could never otherwise
" have done.   I may further state that few persons have
" done more for promoting a sound, useful education
" among our people than this earnest good man not only
" by building and supporting a great number of schools,
" but in writing many admirable school books, and by
" personally teaching in various schools the important
" subject of social science or human well-being.   To him,
" in fact, is due the high honour of first introducing the
" teaching of this important subject in our common schools,
" and in simplifying what at one time was considered a very
" abstruse subject, so that children can readily comprehend
" it.   It is, however, to be greatly regretted that this impor-
" tant subject is not yet generally taught, and until it is made
" a most necessary part of education, I fear society will
" have to pay the penalty of this neglect in the social
" wrecks so many of our people become.   For, being
" turned out of their schools without any notion of the
" conditions to be fulfilled for securing well-being, nor any

"knowledge of the duties they owe to society, social or
"political, we need not wonder at the ignorant blunders
"so many of them make. In most of the schools, however,
"established by Mr. Ellis—and known mostly as the
"Birkbeck Schools—this important subject is taught, as
"well as a knowledge of their own nature and the laws of
"health; a knowledge also of the existences around them;
"and a large amount of elementary science—in fact an
"education that will cause them to remember with
"gratitude the lessons received at school."

Lovett himself taught Physiology; he had by patient
industry and devoted labour mastered the subject, and procured an accurate set of diagrams to be prepared by the
draughtsman of University College.

"Having formed a class of boys," he tells us, "and
"another of girls, I commenced my teaching, and was
"gratified, as I proceeded, to find that even the youngest
"in the class took an interest in the lessons, and very
"readily mastered the rather difficult name of the bones,
"muscles, &c. When I had taken my young ones through
"their first course, I was greatly encouraged to persevere
"in my work by Mr. George Combe, of Edinburgh, who,
"in hearing me give a lesson to my class of girls, was
"pleased to make some very complimentary observations
"respecting their knowledge of the subject. At the sug-
"gestion also of Mr. Ellis, and at the request of three of
"the masters of the Birkbeck Schools, I formed classes
"for teaching elementary anatomy and physiology in
"those schools."

The opinion of George Combe with reference to the value
of the teaching in this school was expressed by him in a
letter to the *Scotsman*, dated 17th November, 1849 :—

"The school," he says, "at the time of my visit was
"attended by one hundred and eighty boys and seventy
"girls, under the charge of Mr. John Harris and Miss E.
"Sumter. In this school reading, writing, arithmetic,

"algebra, mechanics, and the several branches of science
"are taught. I heard, for example, Mr. William Ellis
"give a lesson on social economy to a numerous class of
"boys and girls. This was only one of a series of such
"lessons, and the readiness, clearness, and pertinency with
"which the children answered questions showed that their
"knowledge was lodged, not in their memories, but in
"their understandings. I heard also Mr. Lovett give a
"lesson with admirable precision to a class of girls on
"anatomy and physiology. They were taught, by the aid
"of large well-executed drawings, the structure of the
"human body, and they showed a ready knowledge of
"the bones, the superficial muscles, and the circulating,
"respiratory, and digestive organs, with their uses. When
"these girls become wives and mothers, we may hope
"that this instruction will enable them—better than sheer
"ignorance of such subjects would do—to understand and
"obey the laws of health on which their own lives and
"those of their children will greatly depend."

An anecdote of Ellis while teaching at this school is
curiously characteristic of his coolness and tact under trying
circumstances. One Saturday afternoon when he was
giving the boys a lesson in Social Economy a terrific
thunderstorm came on. The National Hall itself was struck
by lightning, and, as they afterwards found, one of the
chimneys of the building was thrown down. As may be
imagined, the thunder was tremendous, and the boys were in
a panic. Ellis stood perfectly calm and collected: and the
moment his voice could be heard he spoke to the frightened
lads, "Now you may be sure you are safe;" he said, "the
"danger is when the lightning is passing: whenever you
"hear the thunder you may know that the danger is over."
But sensible that something was needed to enable the boys
to resume their attention, he at once put his hand in his
pocket, took out half-a-crown, and asked his friend Mr.
Rüntz, who was present and tells the story, to run out and

fetch a plum cake. That was discussed; and the boys' equanimity having been thereby restored, he took up the thread of his lesson.

The school in the National Hall only lasted till 1857. In that year the publican who had taken the adjoining premises and saw the suitability of poor Lovett's school for a music hall, set to work to drive Lovett out of it. By representations of the insecurity of the place he procured a magistrates' order for extensive rebuilding. This was followed by a threat to Lovett to block up an important right of way, which would have materially interfered with the use of the building, while he offered at the same time to buy the lease. Poor Lovett, unable to withstand the threatened litigation and persecution, was advised to sell his lease, and under compulsion he did so. The school was closed, and Lovett's beloved hall, where for fifteen years he had been striving to improve and elevate his fellow men, became a gin palace.

The establishment of this school was followed by the foundation of the series of schools which are more especially associated with Ellis's memory—the Birkbeck Schools. The first of these was founded with the assistance of John Rüntz, a school teacher whom Ellis had two or three years before this met with in a school in Finsbury, and whom, finding him an able and energetic teacher, he had induced to become a fellow-worker in the cause of improved education, and before long adopted as his principal assistant. Rüntz had begun life as a cabinet maker, but had always had an ardent desire for knowledge. He had been a student of music and art at the evening classes founded under the auspices of the Committee of Council. Then, giving up his manual employment, he had studied teaching at the Training School of the British and Foreign School Society, and had been appointed on their nomination to the master-ship of a British School, in Wilson Street, Finsbury. There Ellis looked in one day after leaving his office in Great

Winchester Street, and entered into conversation with him. Rüntz was about to give his boys a moral lesson, in which he intended to treat of wages: a subject which was peculiarly part of the teaching which Ellis had tried to introduce. Ellis waited and listened to it, and was so pleased at what he heard, that he at once offered to send Rüntz a present of Harriet Martineau's *Illustrations of Political Economy*, a work which Ellis much admired. Rüntz willingly accepted it, and this led to their becoming fellow-workers in the pursuit of the object which Ellis had made his own, and to a life-long friendship. Rüntz afterwards became one of the most active and influential members of the Metropolitan Board of Works.

Not long after he first knew Ellis, Rüntz gave up his school in Wilson Street, Finsbury, and, in order to complete his own education in the branches of knowledge in which he felt himself deficient, studied at University College, while he obtained the means for that purpose, and for the support of his family, by giving evening lessons. When he had finished his studies at University College, Ellis had thoroughly satisfied himself by the lessons he had given at Mr. Holmes's school in Camberwell, that the subject of social economy was not only capable of being taught to children, but was the most important addition to the ordinary subjects of instruction, if schools were to be adapted to their true object, the training of boys to be well conducted and useful members of society. His first desire was to get it introduced in Training Colleges. He offered his services as teacher of social economy to the British and Foreign School Society, and also to the Church Training College, at Battersea, but they both declined his offer and refused to take up the subject. It then occurred to him to form a class of schoolmasters and teach them himself, and with the assistance of Rüntz, who had many friends among the teaching fraternity, he induced a number of schoolmasters to come to his office in Great Winchester

Street after office hours on Saturdays. These men he led, in the same earnest spirit with which he and John Stuart Mill had devoted themselves to study twenty years before but with the more definitely developed object of enabling each member of the class to convey the knowledge so acquired to his own boys, to follow under his guidance the laws of conduct which in the present state of social life result in well-being, or its opposite. This class Ellis continued for two or three years, and the number of schoolmasters who attended it was at one time as many as fifty.

But a class of schoolmasters was not sufficient to prove to the world the great principle which it was now Ellis's object to demonstrate: he decided that he would found a school for the purpose. Rüntz was an eminently suitable teacher, and having secured his co-operation, Ellis applied to the Committee of the Mechanics' Institution in Southampton Buildings, Chancery Lane, for leave to use the theatre of their Institution as a school during the day. A School Committee was formed, of which Mr. William Matticu Williams (afterwards teacher of Mr. Combe's Secular School in Edinburgh, and subsequently principal of the Midland Institute at Birmingham) was the honorary secretary. The Earl of Radnor became patron of the school, and with several other gentlemen subscribed to the expenses of founding it. A grant for that purpose was also obtained from the Corporation of London. But the main burthen fell on Ellis, who agreed to guarantee an adequate annual sum to secure expenses for five years. The school, however, was not established without much opposition. The majority of the committee of the Institution actually refused their consent; but a small minority, convinced of the importance of the plan, persisted in pressing it, and called a meeting of the members, who reversed the decision of the committee and resolved to accept the proposal. It was, on the suggestion of Mr. Rüntz, named the Birkbeck School, in memory of Dr. Birkbeck, the distinguished founder of Mechanics' Institutions, by whom the Southampton Buildings Institution had been founded in 1824, and who had died in 1841. The name given to these schools has often led to the supposition that Dr. Birkbeck was the founder, not only of this but of the series of schools of which it was the forerunner. The real founder, Ellis—to whom the recent death of the excellent Dr. Birkbeck was a notorious fact—did not imagine that misapprehension might arise from the adoption of a name, and that thirty or forty years later the school would over and over again be spoken of as founded by Dr. Birkbeck. This, the first Birkbeck School, was opened on the 17th July, 1848, with John Rüntz as head master. The original prospectus contained a clear and able statement of the course of education to be given at it. After stating that the usual rudiments of knowledge, and also the elements of mathematics, mechanics, and the physical sciences are to be taught, it goes on to say that the children—

"are to be made acquainted with the laws of their own
"organisation in order that they may understand how
"much their health, general energy, physical happiness,
"and length of life are dependent on their own conduct,
"also with the laws of social economy, that they may
"properly understand their own position in society, and
"their duties towards it. The system of education
"adopted is that which modern science and experience
"have shown to be most in accordance with the constitu-
"tion of the human mind, and best calculated to strengthen,
"develop, and rightly direct all its faculties, by presenting
"to them the objects naturally adapted to call them into
"varied and healthy activity. The moral training is
"based on the principle that the moral feelings, like the
"physical and intellectual powers, can only be strengthened
"by actual exercise; that the mere teaching of moral pre-
"cepts is not sufficient since they are but intellectual truths
"for the guidance of the feelings and their acquisition an
"intellectual operation; they must be carried into practice."

This school was visited on many occasions by George Combe, who agreed cordially and heartily in the very high opinion entertained by Ellis of Mr. John Rüntz, the master. Combe says:—

"On the day on which I entered it there were two "hundred and eighty boys in attendance. It is very ably "conducted by Mr. J. Rüntz, and several assistant teachers "and monitors. Here, also, I heard Mr. Ellis give a highly "interesting lesson on social economy to a class of boys; "and on another occasion I heard one of the monitors, "Thomas Selby, a boy of twelve years of age, give a lesson "on the same subject to a large class of his schoolfellows, in "a style of distinct efficiency which surprised me, much as "I had anticipated from what I saw of Mr. Ellis's teaching. "The conclusion which I drew was that the great "principles of social economy are so directly referable to "facts with which even children of twelve and fourteen "years of age are conversant, that they may be taught to "individuals of that age with both pleasure and advantage, "provided the teacher himself thoroughly comprehends "them, and be capable of furnishing ready and familiar "illustrations."

Again, three years later—in an article published in the *Westminster Review* of August, 1852—Combe repeated his testimony to the practicability and immense value of such teaching as was given at this Birkbeck School.

"In May last," he says, "we accompanied one of the "most distinguished members of the House of Commons "to Mr. Rüntz's school" [we know from other sources it was Richard Cobden] "and for forty minutes listened to a "lesson on this subject given by a monitor of fourteen "years of age to a class of sixty boys, most of whom were "younger than himself. Our friend remarked on leaving "the room, 'one-half of the House of Commons might "'listen to these lessons with advantage.'"

A very graphic description of Ellis's method of teaching is given by Mr. Mattieu Williams in a paper read to the Social Science Association in 1857. He says:—

"The pupils included the upper classes of the school, "their ages varying from ten to fourteen. The method "adopted by Mr. Ellis was to lay before the class a short "proposition stating the general principle or conclusion "the lesson was intended to demonstrate. This proposition "was written on the blackboard. A series of questions "was then put to the boys, the answers to the first few "being generally pretty obvious, even to the youngest. "Upon these answers other questions were built, each "leading the pupils a step further, then others upon these, "and soon the boys were led by almost invisible degrees "up a sort of intellectual inclined plane, which landed "them at last fairly and firmly upon the principle or "conclusion expressed by the proposition, besides leading "to many collateral facts and conclusions. Mr. Ellis "always made the boys reason for themselves as far as "possible, his questions merely suggesting the course "which their reasoning should follow. Even the defini-"tions used in the science were not given arbitrarily; but "the pupils were led by a series of tentative efforts to "supply them for themselves. They were first asked to "give their own definition. Applications of this definition "were then suggested by the teacher; their definition "perhaps led them into a dilemma. It was amended to "meet the difficulty; tried again in another direction with "a similar result; amended further and so on until the "best and most concise definition was arrived at. Thus "they were not merely taught the definitions dogmatically, "but were led to invent and agree to them and practically "to learn why certain particular limitations or directions "of definition are necessary—a matter of primary impor-"tance in the study of social economy."

Mr. Williams goes on to tell us that the result of his attendance at most of the lessons of the course was to convince him that social science may be successfully taught to children from ten to fourteen years of age; while his subsequent experience as master of the Edinburgh School led him to the still stronger conclusion that it is not only possible to make it a successful branch of juvénile instruction, but that it is much easier to teach it to boys and girls than to adult men. He arranged at Edinburgh a series of meetings to discuss the same subject with a number of most respectable artisans, parents of the, children at his school. He very soon found himself in collision with their prejudices. They could not be induced to investigate economical subjects from the foundation, or to submit to follow any systematic course. The subject which they selected for discussion— "Competition is one of the most efficient agents for diffusing "the benefits of industrial enterprise over the whole world," which is the proposition at the head of one of Ellis's progressive lessons—was pronounced absurd, and he found it practically impossible to get behind the class prejudices of the parents, while on the other hand he found no difficulty in leading the unprejudiced minds of the children to investigate, follow out, and demonstrate similar propositions for themselves.

How hard Ellis worked at the Birkbeck School we learn from a letter to Dr. Hodgson:—

"31st October, 1850.

"I have but little to say of myself. I have not been "absent a single day from this place" (his office in Great Winchester Street). "I give three lessons a week in "the schools, and conduct two adult classes besides, every "Tuesday and Thursday evening."

The Birkbeck School in Southampton Buildings proved a great success. In two years it had three hundred and forty boys in attendance, a number which was about as many as the building would accommodate. About the year 1850 a girls' school was added to it, which was opened in a neighbouring house, No. 9, Southampton Buildings, under the care of a mistress-named Morgan, and numbered about fifty pupils.   During the whole course of its existence, this, the first and chief Birkbeck School, was used as a sort of training college for teachers of similar schools, and it was to this school that Ellis was chiefly indebted for the training of the teachers whom he appointed to the other schools which followed it, as well as to schools the founders of which applied to him for teachers.

As early as May, 1851, he wrote Dr. Hodgson:—

> "23rd May, 1851.

> "Mr. Rüntz is the general director of the Birkbeck "Schools, the established and the projected.   At present "we have masters waiting for schools, and, according to "present appearances, they are likely henceforward to "continue ahead of the schools.   Mr. Rüntz is open to "admit any suitable assistant who is prepared to maintain "himself unpaid from the school, and take his chance of "any opening that may present itself."

Of the work which this school rendered during the first few years of its existence, as well of the high value which Ellis set on Rüntz's work, the following letter to Dr. Hodgson gives an interesting account:—

> "20th December, 1853.

> "I have not taken to amateur teaching myself, because "I think myself qualified for the work.   I have not allied "myself to the lowly born and bred because I think the "absence of learning and refinement a recommendation "in a teacher, but because the learned and the refined are, "unfortunately, behind the requirements of the age, and "are being passed by men who may lack their polish, "but have the vigour and the practical knowledge indis-"pensable to those who would be the apostles of their age.

> "I pity Mr. M." (a gentleman who had sought employ-

ment as a teacher), "but have no idea that Mr. Rüntz
"will be able to give him the one thing needful—an
"income. Mr. Pring received nothing at the Birkbeck
"School, nor did Mr. Pike, Mr. G. Rüntz, Mr. Shields, or
"Mr. Brady, during the first months of their teaching
"there. For anything provided by the school they lived
"in hope—poor nutriment for a man and his wife. Perhaps,
"when the training schools find that masters who can
"teach elementary social science are sought after and
"preferred and come into the receipt of decent incomes,
"they will endeavour to impart such instruction to those
"whom they train. You know whom I recommend as
"the most efficient teacher of social science in the whole
"circle of my acquaintance. Under him any earnest and
"respectable man may receive instruction, and, at the
"same time, gain practice in teaching and managing
"numbers—*gratis:* but there are no funds out of which
"any income can be provided for him."

A further public testimony to the value of Rüntz's work
is contained in a note in the nature of a dedication appended
by Ellis to one of the papers which he collected and published about this time under the title of " Education as a
"means of preventing destitution." In it he expresses "the
"grateful feelings with which he has long watched the
"zeal and ability brought to bear by Mr. Rüntz in his
"efforts to aid in the extension of sound and useful
"education to all classes."

A series of meetings which Ellis arranged and continued
for some time at the first Birkbeck School had specially
interesting associations with it. Not content with conducting classes of teachers, and founding schools for boys,
he instituted a class for adults of which many of his friends
and others interested in education, who wished to learn how
the science of conduct might be taught, availed themselves.
In the autumn of 1847 and throughout 1848, Ellis invited

H

persons of all classes of society to come to the Mechanics'
Institute at four o'clock on Thursdays, and a considerable
number of ladies and gentlemen, including some members of
Parliament, responded to the invitation.   Among those who
came were Richard Cobden and his friends, R. N. Philips,
M.P., and Sir Joshua Walmsley, M.P.; also the Earl of
Radnor, the Countess of Zetland, Miss Caroline Lindley,
Lady Byron, widow of the poet (who brought with her the
master of a school which she supported), and another lady,
whose name is reverenced throughout the world by all
who know what she has done for humanity—Florence
Nightingale.

The following extract from a letter written by her to the
present writer, in reply to one asking her for her recollection of those lessons, will give her impression of the value of
Ellis's teaching.

"October 8th, 1888.

"Yes, some forty years ago I had, indeed, the great
"privilege of attending Mr. William Ellis's classes. It was
"the best and most effective teaching I have ever heard,
"bringing what are called the most difficult subjects in an
"absolutely clear and most *living* way to the understand-
"ing of a child, so as to make them practical and prac-
"ticable.

"A (too) short acquaintance with Mr. Ellis was also my
"privilege.   And I have tried to make many familiar with
"his books. Had I not been called to other work, I
"should probably have pursued education.

"FLORENCE NIGHTINGALE."

The Southampton Buildings School, the first and chief
of the Birkbeck Schools, was finally closed in 1873 as a
consequence of the passing of the Education Act and the
formation of the London School Board. On the inspection
of the schools, in order to ascertain the educational necessities
of the Metropolis, this school was reported by the inspectors

as being "inefficient," and, consequently, for School Board purposes, non-existent. The reason of this condemnation was that the school buildings, which partly consisted of a gallery, were not in accordance with the rules of construction laid down by the Board.

The success of the first Birkbeck School and the thorough demonstration it afforded of the value and importance of oral lessons on conduct—a demonstration which has never failed to be repeated in every school where the lessons have been given by teachers competent and properly educated for their work—led to the foundation of many other schools on the same principle, some of which were established by Ellis himself, others founded by other people and assisted by him, either by providing teachers or subscription of money. With respect to the former class, all of which except the last (the Gospel Oak Schools, founded in 1862) bore the name Birkbeck Schools, Ellis's intention in founding them was at first somewhat different from what it subsequently became. Rüntz, who acted as his chief helper in establishing them, and when they were established became superintendent, was commissioned to purchase disused chapels, halls, or old school buildings, held for short terms of years, and which could be adapted to their purpose at moderate expense. Ellis believed that he had only to show by establishing models in different districts of the Metropolis what schools ought to be, in order to induce all other school managers to adopt and introduce his methods of teaching into their own schools. He did not then contemplate the foundation of schools intended to become permanent institutions. He attached comparatively little importance – either to the attractiveness of the buildings or the prominence of the site of the schools he founded. He thought the immense practical importance of his method could not fail to come home to every educationist who saw it in operation, and that it was certain to be soon adopted generally. He did not realise the extent of resistance to improvement, which would be made by a body of professional teachers trained in what he deemed old and obsolete methods. At the date of the letter we quoted a few pages back (December, 1853), when he had been some years at work, he had become better acquainted with the steady opposition which would be made by University graduates trained on University methods, educated on the principles of making the classical languages the principal subject in their curricula, and whose chief idea was to train their boys so as to obtain University honours. He could not at first imagine that this class of mind would be unable to see as clearly as he saw, that the main and central thought in education ought to be "to form children into well-"disposed and capable men, to help them to a perception "of the line of conduct which they ought to pursue on "quitting school, and to call forth in them a sense of "responsibility perpetually urging them to pursue that line." With this view therefore the first Birkbeck Schools, which he established on the model of the school in Southampton Buildings, were not grand establishments, nor even destined for permanent existence. The Finsbury Birkbeck School, for boys only, was established in an old chapel, leasehold for a term of which about sixteen years was unexpired, which had been known as Bethel Chapel, in Bell Yard, Commercial Place, City Road. This was purchased by Ellis, through Rüntz's agency, adapted for the purpose of a school, and opened on the 16th July, 1849. The master was a Mr. Thomas Wells Cave, a former assistant of the National Hall School, who had also been a short time under Rüntz's training at the Birkbeck School in Southampton Buildings. The bill circulated in the district at the time of opening it describes its objects as follows :—

"The course of instruction includes reading, writing, "arithmetic, English grammar, composition, history, "geography, drawing, and vocal music; also the elements "of algebra, geometry, mensuration, mechanics, and of the "natural sciences.

"The children are likewise instructed in the laws of
"health, and in the principles of social economy, in order
"that they may understand how much their health,
"longevity, and general happiness are dependent on
"themselves, and that they may also the more fully com-
"prehend their position in society and their duties
"towards it.

"Particular attention is paid to moral training."

The fee charged for this extensive curriculum was six
shillings per quarter, or sixpence per week. Of this school,
as well as its predecessors, we have a glimpse in a letter to
Dr. Hodgson:—

"11th August, 1849.

"The schools here are all going on satisfactorily. The
"Finsbury Birkbeck School already musters seventy
"boys, and a very earnest and competent friend of mine
"is giving lessons there twice a week."

A month later we have further news both of this and the
main Birkbeck School. The letter also contains some other
remarks on the educational work of the time, and an interesting statement of the objects which Ellis then set
before himself:—

"14th September, 1849.

"I think I have more than once in former times ex-
"pressed to you my opinion of the College of Preceptors.
"Nothing has since occurred to alter my opinion—not
"even the *Educational Times*. Both College and *Times*
"may be doing good, but as the good is beyond my ken,
"I cannot aid them either with purse or pen, each of them
"being in full requisition for the purpose of pushing my
"own project—the introduction of lessons on economical
"science into schools of primary instruction. This will
"be the main occupation for my surplus funds and time
"for some months, perhaps years. As I proceed I find
"concentration of means more and more necessary. I

"feel that the work to which I am devoting myself is a
"work that must be done by somebody, if education is
"to be well conducted, and that therefore I must be co-
"operating with those who are directing their attention
"principally to other departments. Many are teaching
"the ordinary routine, but I hear of few, excepting your-
"self, who think of teaching political economy. The
"forthcoming number of the *Westminster Review* will
"contain an article on the State of the Nation, in which
"I have entered at large into the question of teaching
"and training; but my chief reliance is upon the practical
"teaching in which a progressively increasing number of
"qualified teachers are engaged with myself.

"The account of the Mechanics' Institutions is very
"much what I should have expected. I have long since
"ceased to expect much from them. The Birkbeck
"School may save the London Mechanics' Institution
"if it is followed up by improved evening classes for
"adults. That school is brim full, and the Finsbury
"Birkbeck musters a hundred and twenty boys."

A few months later we have further news of this school
(in a letter, part of which we have already quoted) showing
its rapid growth. From it we learn the financial system
which Ellis adopted in founding his schools.

"10th November, 1850.

"The standard that we adopt for the Birkbeck Schools
"is threepence per boy,[1] besides a penny per boy to
"pay assistant teachers, guaranteeing twenty-five shillings
"a week at starting. The Finsbury Birkbeck School,
"which was established July last year, contains two

---

[1] That is threepence per boy paid to the master himself for his own salary.
It will be remembered that the fee charged was sixpence per week. The above
payment left twopence per week to pay rates and taxes, cleaning and repairs,
and all other expenses and outgoings. Ellis always sought to make the schools
as nearly as possible self-supporting, with the exception of rent.

"hundred and seventy boys, so that its master has
"upwards of £150 per annum for himself—£50 for assis-
"tants. By some such arrangement the interest of the
"master is bound up in the success of the school, and
"I should advise no attempt to establish a school on any
"other principle."

The Finsbury Birkbeck School remained under the care
of Mr. Cave for about ten years, and its numbers reached the
high total of three hundred and fifty boys. But its success
seems to have stimulated the master to improve his position.
He left the school and opened another in the immediate
neighbourhood as a Collegiate School, where he ultimately
developed into Rev. T. W. Cave, LL.D., and carried away
with him some three hundred of the scholars.

Thus deserted, Ellis found another teacher, a Mr. Foster,
an assistant master from the original Birkbeck School, under
whose management it gradually rose till it again had about
two hundred boys. But Foster unfortunately died about
four years later, and as the lease had then only about two
years of its term remaining, and a suitable opportunity
arose of disposing of the property to a neighbouring manufacturer who needed extension, the school was given up.

The next—the third of the Birkbeck Schools—was a school
for boys in Vincent Square, Westminster, opened in July,
1850. For this, as for the Finsbury School, Ellis purchased,
through Rüntz, the lease of an old chapel with a burial
ground adjoining which had fourteen years to run. He
adapted it for a school and selected as the master Mr. George
Rüntz, a brother of John Rüntz, who had been trained under
him in Southampton Buildings. The school was successful.
In October, 1849, the school numbered sixty-eight pupils;
in two years it had risen to one hundred and ten, and at one
time there was as many as three hundred boys in attendance.
Six years after its foundation George Rüntz left it, being
induced by an offer from the Rev. Newman Hall of an
improved position to accept the head-mastership of Hawk-

stone Hall School. A Mr. Brady, also trained under Mr. John Rüntz, was appointed in his place, and on his death Mr. Foster, whom we have already mentioned as having subsequently succeeded Mr. Cave at Finsbury, became master. But the school had to be given up on the expiry of the lease, as the Dean and Chapter of Westminster refused to renew the lease, although Ellis, understanding that it was their usual custom to grant renewed leases to old tenants, had laid out £800 in adding to and improving the buildings.

The fourth Birkbeck School, the Bethnal Green Schools, in Cambridge Road, Bethnal Green, was founded in January, 1851, for boys and girls. Like two of its predecessors, it was established in an old chapel, this time a freehold, which Ellis bought through Rüntz's agency and converted into a school, putting up, where necessary, partitions, so as to procure separate class-rooms. The master was a Mr. R. W. Pike, who had been also trained under John Rüntz at the parent school, and who was assisted by his sister as mistress of the girls' school. These were also for a long time very successful. A letter of Ellis, written just after their foundation, gives us some news of them, and tells us also something of his doings in another direction, viz., lecturing on the subject; and in this we find his usual modest estimate of his own powers. He says :—

" 1st February, 1851.

" Nature never intended me for a lecturer. Nevertheless,
" I am in hopes that my effort was not altogether vain
" on the 30th. I had a fair sprinkle of the boys' parents
" (considering the hour) and several city eminences, besides
" the Dean of Hereford, Mr. Barham Zincke, Mr. Frederic
" Hill, Dr. Arnott, Mr. and Mrs. Poulett Scrope, Mr.
" Lucas, and Cowper ; and, if they were not satisfied, they
" flattered me into believing them so. They perhaps
" excused the manner out of consideration for the matter.
" It is my intention to repeat this lecture at each of the

"schools in the course of the next three months, and at
"an hour sufficiently late to catch more of the parents.
"The grand news of the day in my little world is the
"success of the Bethnal Green Birkbeck School—fifty-
"eight boys and thirteen girls in three weeks (as good as
"the Birkbeck School at the same age), and in the im-
"mediate vicinity of one of the most vaunted of the B.
"and F. Schools."

The Bethnal Green School rapidly increased in numbers
and attained considerable success. In 1870 there were above
four hundred children in attendance. But the effect of the
Education Act of 1870, and the building of a number of
Board Schools in the neighbourhood, carried on in handsome
buildings, with every modern improvement and with the
right to collect funds from the whole of the Metropolis,
was necessarily to draw away many of the children who
attended them. This effect was recognised by Ellis during
his life. He rejoiced to see the extension of education in
the Metropolis, and did not for a moment regret the consequent falling off of his own schools. He felt they had
done their work: and when, in 1879, the Bethnal Green
Schools had fallen to one hundred and forty boys and
eighty girls, he foresaw that sooner or later they might have
to be given up. The other schools which were then in
existence were converted into middle-class schools, the fees
being raised, and the scope of the education given being somewhat increased. But in Bethnal Green there was no better
class from which the children could be drawn; the schools in
the old chapel contrasted unfavourably with the handsome
buildings of the Board Schools, and the continued falling
away of the numbers led the trustees, on whom the care of
the schools had devolved, to close them a few years after
his death and dispose of the site. Mr. Pike remained the
head master during the whole thirty-five years, from 1851 to
1886, that they remained open.

The fifth Birkbeck School was the Peckham School, in

Willow Brook Road, Peckham, and was the first specially
built by Ellis as a school upon freehold land acquired for
the purpose. It was opened on the 19th April, 1852, for
boys, girls, and infants, under the mastership of Mr. William
Andrew Shields, another of the teachers who had learned
their work under the guidance of John Rüntz, in Southampton Buildings. Shields was a man of remarkable power,
a teacher of great skill and success, and an unusually
enlightened educationist. As a speaker he was clear and
convincing, his language terse and vigorous, and his illustrations singularly apt and vivid. He had been in a small
way of business in early life, which he gave up to adopt the
vocation of a teacher. After being trained under John Rüntz,
he became in February, 1851, head master of the Oddfellows' Secular School, at Manchester, which he left a year
later to undertake the mastership of the Peckham Birkbeck
Schools. The opening announcement was simple and unpre-
tending, it merely says that—

"The course of instruction in these schools will include
"reading, writing, arithmetic, grammar and composition,
"history and geography, drawing, algebra, geometry, vocal
"music, the elements of physiology, natural philosophy,
"and chemistry. The children will also be instructed in
"the moral conditions of human well-being.

"N.B.—The girls will be taught needlework."

The Peckham Birkbeck Schools soon became a model
school of great importance. Shields had all the powers of a
great head master, and had it been his fate to be the master
of a school for the higher classes he would probably have
taken rank with the Arnolds or Thrings of his day. In a
couple of years after he began his work we find him looked
on as a model teacher. In a letter to Hodgson, Ellis tells
him :—

"23rd August, 1854.

"Mr. Shields's lesson last Saturday created such a sensa-
"tion that he has been invited to give another to his boys

"at St. Martin's Hall, Saturday next. I shall stay in town
"in order to be present at it. I do not know whether you
"have formed any engagement to prevent your bearing
"me company."

And again, five years later, Ellis writes to Hodgson:—

"6th November, 1859.

"I cannot resist the temptation of sending you Shields'
"note giving me the account of Mr. Charles Knight's
"visit to Peckham. What a grand thing it is to be able
"to refer talkers and writers to such a worker—to a school
"which exemplifies in the present what teaching *will* do
"in the future. There must be the latent powers, if we
"could but fall in with them, capable of rivalling, if not of
"surpassing, Mr. Shields. A few more such schools would
"soon lead the way to thousands, and extinguish many
"which make some well-disposed men mistrust the
"efficacy of education."

The Peckham Schools, originally built of sufficient size to
accommodate about four hundred children, were soon filled
to overflowing, and in three or four years afterwards they
were enlarged so as to provide school-places for one
thousand children. Even these enormously increased
schools were well filled. The number of children in
attendance was very large for a long series of years, and at
one time reached to about nine hundred. They had a long
career of usefulness, and spite of the establishment of Board
schools throughout London, which took place in three or
four years after the Education Act of 1870, they retained
their reputation as schools where the best education obtainable for the fee charged was given. Unfortunately, Mr.
Shields's health, which was never strong, utterly broke down
in 1877, and he died at Bournemouth in 1878. His death
was a grave blow to the schools and a sorrow to Ellis,
who had then, through increasing infirmity, been compelled to retire from active work. The steady supply of

able trained masters, which had existed during the time of
the original Birkbeck School, was no longer available, and
the masters who were engaged proved unable to support
the mantle of Shields, while Board Schools continued to
increase in the surrounding district.   In the result the last
head master, Mr. Herbert Teather, died of decline in the
beginning of 1887, and the schools were given up at Easter
of that year.

The sixth Birkbeck School was founded in Colvestone
Crescent, Kingsland, in December, 1852, under the master-
ship of Mr. James Rüntz, another brother of John Rüntz.
It was, like Peckham, built specially for the purpose upon
leasehold land, which was some twenty years later converted
into freehold.   The prospectus is rather fuller than that of
the Peckham Schools.   After referring to the ordinary
subjects intended to form its curriculum, it goes on to
specify as an important branch of education the conditions
of human well-being:—

> "So that the children may not go forth to take their
> "part in the work of the world utterly ignorant of any
> "safe guides of conduct; this teaching including, amongst
> "other things, the knowledge of the laws relating to the
> "production and distribution of wealth, the means by
> "which wealth is made to accumulate, the advantage of
> "division of labour and interchange, the laws which
> "regulate wages and profits, the causes of variations in
> "values and prices, the nature of the means adopted to
> "facilitate interchange, but, above all, the courses of con-
> "duct which ought to and must be followed in order to
> "secure future happiness and well-being."

The Kingsland Schools were fortunate in having a very
able master.   James Rüntz shared the ability and possessed
equal earnestness with his brother John, and had his
brother's cordial co-operation in the management of the
schools.   Six months after their opening a letter from Ellis

gives satisfactory news of their progress, and at the same time tells us something of his own work. He says to Dr. Hodgson:—

"19th June, 1853.

"My doings in your absence, which you ask about,
"may be summed up in very few words. I have been with
"little interruption giving five lessons a week. The schools
"prosper, and another Birkbeck was opened at Kingsland
"last December which already musters two hundred boys,
"and a girls' school is to be attached to it next month.
"For want of anything better, I send you by this post a
"number of the *Journal of the Society of Arts*, wherein you
"will see a very condensed report of a speech that I was
"guilty of perpetrating there about six weeks ago.[1]   I
"enclose two reprints from the *Hebrew Observer* which
"will show that my labours among the Jews have not been
"in vain. They have just opened a school for boys and
"girls in Red Lion Square, where a certain proportion of
"non-Jews are admitted, where the instruction is purely
"secular, where the Jewish religion and Hebrew are taught
"separately to the Jewish children, and where my lessons
"in social science are given daily. If fate brings you to
"town, I hope you will be able to trace signs of progress:
"that we have not been idle nor our activity vain."

---

[1] The speech was made in the discussion of a paper read at the Society of Arts by the Dean of Hereford (Rev. Richard Dawes), "On the importance of "giving a self-supporting character as far as possible to schools for the labouring "classes and the means of doing so." In his speech, Ellis gave warm and cordial support to the plans of the Dean, who had established schools at King's Somborne, Hants, in which a superior education had been given to the lower classes on self-supporting principles. He further pointed out the marvellous improvement to be anticipated in our social state by the extensive establishment of such schools as those founded by the Dean, in which the children of these realms should, on leaving school, "have obtained thus much of instruction as "to find themselves acquainted with the general principles on which the "industrial efforts of all must be conducted; and with an outline of the "arrangements which have been adopted and under which they are about to "engage."

The Kingsland Schools continued to thrive. Adapted at first to only some three hundred children, they have been from time to time added to until they now accommodate between five hundred and six hundred. They were originally, like the others, adapted for artizans, and a fee of sixpence per week charged; but in consequence of the Education Act and the foundation of Board Schools in their neighbourhood the fee has been increased, and they are now middle class schools charging £1. 1s. per quarter. They have retained their original reputation as the best schools of the district, and the numbers (boys, girls, and infants) amount at the present date (1889) to over five hundred.

Ten years after the opening of the Kingsland Schools, in October, 1862, Ellis founded another school for boys, girls, and infants, in Allcroft Road, Gospel Oak, Kentish Town, which, though not bearing like its predecessors the name of "Birkbeck," was in fact a Birkbeck School. For the first time he did not avail himself of the services of his friend John Rüntz, either to arrange for the building and equipment of the schools or as superintendent, but invited the writer of these pages, whom he had known for about six years, to assist him in their foundation and management. He had some years previously purchased three or four plots of freehold land on a building estate with the idea that he might some day utilise them for that purpose, and he now built these schools upon them. Like the Peckham and Kingsland Schools, this was designed for a permanent foundation, and the master whom he appointed to them was Mr. Edward Teather, who had been for some years assistant master to Mr. Shields at Peckham. The buildings, as originally founded, were adapted for some five hundred children, but before the expiration of two years from their foundation, they were required by the Midland Railway Company for the purpose of their extension to London, and were re-erected about two hundred yards from the original site on a piece of land adjoining that railway. The success of the schools

having been already secured, they were rebuilt on a somewhat larger scale, so as to be capable of accommodating
some seven or eight hundred pupils. Their success continued. In 1867 the numbers were four hundred and fifty,
and in 1870, when they reached their highest figure, there
were about six hundred and fifty children in attendance.
Like all the schools, they suffered from the passing of the
Education Act of 1870, and the consequent foundation of
several Board Schools in their neighbourhood. As in the
other schools, an increase in the fees charged was made,
and the range of subjects taught somewhat extended so as
to seek for pupils from a somewhat higher stratum of society
than was contemplated in their inception. These schools
are in course of being remodelled (1889) as a more advanced
school with science and technical teaching.

In 1865, the four schools then remaining, viz., the Bethnal
Green, Kingsland, Peckham, and Gospel Oak Schools, were
vested by a deed of foundation in seven trustees, of whom
Ellis reserved to himself the chairmanship during his life ;
since his decease, the number of trustees, which had fallen
to four, has been increased to twelve.

But while these were the schools founded by Ellis himself,
there were many others to which he rendered a helping
hand, sometimes by pecuniary assistance in beginning the
school, sometimes by providing them with masters trained
at one of the schools which he had supported. Even as
early as September 1848, two months after the foundation
of the original Birkbeck School, a Mr. Brooks, who had been
a teacher at Lovett's School, obtained the use of the theatre
of a Mechanics' Institution in John Street, Tottenham Court
Road, capable of accommodating one hundred and fifty boys.
He adopted Ellis's method, and met with cordial and
friendly support from him, though it was not in any sense a
Birkbeck School nor founded by him. It was not permanently successful, though in 1852 it had one hundred and
forty pupils. But shortly after that date Brooks gave it up,

and obtained, probably through Ellis's introduction, an appointment at the Jewish school in Red Lion Square, which was opened about that time. The latter was a school at which (as we have already seen in one of Ellis's letters) non-Jews were admitted, and where—except the separate teaching of the Jewish religion and Hebrew to the Jewish children—the plans and methods were very similar to those of his own schools.

The next school which received his cordial help, though not one of his own, was one founded in Edinburgh by his friend Combe in conjunction with a Mr. James Simpson, and opened under the name of the Edinburgh Secular School, in December, 1848. To the foundation of the school he not only subscribed money, but provided an able master, Mr. W. Mattieu Williams, also trained at the original Birkbeck School, and who had been the honorary secretary of that school from its foundation. Mr. Mattieu Williams, who was a man of great scientific attainments, remained a devoted friend and disciple of Ellis during the whole of his life, and his attachment was warmly reciprocated, continuing after Williams had ceased to be a teacher. The following letter, written to Williams during the time that he was master of the Edinburgh School, will show how Ellis cheered on his pupils and sought to imbue them with his own devotion and self-sacrifice:—

"28th December, 1848.

"I am truly obliged to you for your very interesting "letter. The difficulties which you have to grapple with "are unquestionably great, and so it was anticipated they "would be. Hitherto they have been no more formidable "than to stimulate an earnest man to increased vigour.

"There is advantage as well as disadvantage in the "smallness of your numbers at starting. You will the "more readily organise a small nucleus round which the "new comers will form themselves almost automatically.

"What you say of the intelligence and efficiency of the

"teachers in the Heriot and other schools is no doubt true,
"and should force us to have this question constantly present
"to our minds: Why have we made our present attempt?
"Because all existing schools leave out what we consider
"*vital.* Your course is therefore plain: to give as good an
"education as the other schools in respect of all the useful
"matter which they teach, and to teach what you consider
"vital besides, and use every effort to convince parents of
"the *vital* importance of what you offer to teach. Your
"success as a teacher entirely depends upon the character
"of your teaching and your ability to diffuse a conviction of
"the excellence of your purpose. I am most sanguine
"that we shall all have reason to rejoice in what we are
"doing. The great, the pressing want of the day is the
"means of diffusing among all classes that knowledge
"which is in the world, but possessed only by a few, and
"therefore comparatively *unproductive.* But God will
"speed the plough which is held by such zealous
"husbandmen as Mr. Combe and yourself, and if the
"first crops should not be encouraging, toiling in one
"another's company will be a labour of love, and you
"will not easily let go your faith in the necessary though
"deferred consequence of what you have undertaken."

The Edinburgh School lasted for ten years, but was
closed in 1854, partly in consequence of Williams being
appointed to the position of lecturer on chemistry and
physics at the Midland Institute, Birmingham, and partly in
consequence of the death of Mr. Simpson and the infirm
health of Mr. Combe, who was unable to obtain a suitable
teacher in Williams's place. The average attendance while
the school lasted was over one hundred and fifty.

While Williams was in Edinburgh, however, he assisted
Mr. Combe and Mr. Simpson in the formation of a school
on similar principles, which was called the "Leith Secular
School." A Mr. Hay granted a room free of cost, and
the first master was a teacher who bore the name of

I

William Ellis.   Its formation, as Williams wrote, "was first
"suggested by a working man, whose son had died from the
"effects of a brutal flogging at one of the common schools."
It was announced by a circular in November, 1852, and was
actually opened on 7th March, 1853.   Before the end of the
month it had one hundred and forty pupils in attendance,
the full number which the room would hold.   In reference
to this Ellis wrote to Williams the following letter:—

"22nd November, 1852.

"I cannot allow Mrs. Ellis's dispatches to depart with-
"out adding a few lines to thank you for your interest-
"ing communications in regard to what you have been
"doing at Leith.   The benefit to the people there will be
"inestimable, and their school, when established, will
"accustom them to look for their own up-raising and
"that of their children through *work* done by themselves,
"rather than through *words* of complaint and anger
"directed against the works or neglected works of others.
"Foundations or institutions may fail or be misused, but
"the knowledge and habits given to the young cannot fail
"to fructify.

"It cheers and fortifies me to know that I have such an
"associate, as it must Mr. Combe to know that he has
"such a disciple.   As Leith is now following Glasgow, so,
"I feel assured, will other places shortly in their turn look
"to the Williams School at Edinburgh for light and
"guidance in their attempts to keep pace with the age
"and not to be bye-words in the land.   I hope you will
"be able to provide your Leith friends, who must naturally
"look up to you, with an inoculated master."

The Leith School was carried on in its original form for
about five years.   Then Mr. Hay adopted it as his own and
changed its name to "Hay's Mechanics' School."   It was
frequently visited by George Combe and other friends of
broader education, and was a great success.   It was carried

on till about 1874, at which date the effect of the Scotch Education Act, 1872, securing for national education many of the improvements sought for by the promoters of these schools, began to be felt; and the Leith School, which had done good work, was given up.

Another school opened in October, 1849, in Lower Road, Islington, though not a Birkbeck School, nor on Ellis's responsibility, was cordially helped by him. It was first opened in a single large room, in October, 1849, by a Mr. Wells, a teacher, who had been brought up in Mr. Holmes's School at Camberwell, and who had afterwards been an assistant teacher at the original Birkbeck School. Wells, however, did not make it a success and left it about the close of 1851. It was taken up, on his quitting it, by a Mr. J. Howard, who had been a teacher at the Finsbury Birkbeck School. Howard was specially a science teacher, and held several certificates for the teaching of science, for which he became known. He took the school on his own responsibility and made it a success, and it still exists and has a high reputation as a science school. But it would have been given up on the expiration of the lease but for timely help given by Ellis. He ascertained that the freehold might be had, sent his faithful assistant Rüntz to secure it, and when asked in whose name the conveyance should be taken, directed that Mr. Howard's name should be inserted.

Another school which adopted Ellis's plans, though not founded by him, was one in Carlisle Street, Edgware Road, opened about Midsummer, 1850. It was opened in a Mechanics' Institution, which was hired for use as a school during the day and fitted up with moveable desks, so that they might be put on one side in the evening. The master was a Mr. Curtis, a British School master who had been for a time at Southampton Buildings. It was only temporary; the occupation was only on an annual tenancy, and after being carried on for three or four years it was given up and the desks removed.

Other schools founded for the purpose of giving a broader education were two in Glasgow, established by the Glasgow Secular School Society in 1850 and 1853 respectively, and to which Ellis gave substantial help, and a school founded by the Oddfellows at Manchester, under the name of the National Independent Oddfellows' Secular School. To the last, which was founded in February, 1851, Ellis not only rendered pecuniary help, but sent them to start the school one of his best teachers, Mr. Shields. Shields organised the school, and taught it for a year, when he returned to London to take charge of the Peckham Birkbeck Schools, being succeeded by a Mr. John Angell, who had been a friend and fellow student of Mr. Mattieu Williams. The school, however, was given up some years later, after Mr. Angell had left it. Another Manchester school of more importance was founded in 1854, under the title of the Manchester Model Secular School, by a society called the National Public School Association, which included Richard Cobden, Sir Thomas Bazley, Dr. Hodgson, and other prominent men. The head master of the school was Mr. Benjamin Templar, an able and enthusiastic educationist, who worked hard and wrote many papers on the subject of improved education. Ellis subscribed largely to the school, and it was carried on for about ten years by Mr. Templar. About that time Mr. Templar resigned, and opened a school at Holly Bank, Cheetham Hill, in premises bought for him by Ellis, at which he continued to carry on the work on his own behalf as a private middle class school. Templar carried on this school for about eight or ten years, when his health failed and he moved to Southport.

Another school may be mentioned in which Ellis took a warm interest, and the founder of which was one of his most intimate friends—Mr. Thomas Horlock Bastard, of Charlton Marshall, near Blandford, Dorset, a gentleman of considerable property there, who had been introduced to him by George Combe, and entered warmly into his views. Mr.

Bastard's first work was the establishment of a Labourers' Club, at the opening of which, in October, 1855, Ellis presided. A little later, Mr. Bastard founded a middle class school in the town of Blandford, called the Milldown School, on the plan of the Birkbeck Schools. His announcement at the opening of this school states that " Physiology

"in connection with the laws of heath, and economic
"science in connection with the laws of industry and
"wealth, are special subjects to be taught; the donor
"trusting that the last part of this instruction clause will
"receive marked attention from the managers and
"teachers, and that labour and work of all kinds will be
"set before the children in a true light, as estimable in
"themselves and as the source and means whereby *self-*
"*help* or *independence* is attained." Mr. Bastard's school
is still in existence, and, for a small country school, thriving.

Another school was established about 1855 at Hethersett, Norfolk, which adopted Ellis's plans and to which he rendered material help. The most active agent in founding it was Miss Caroline Lindley; and the following letter was written by Ellis to the local committee which was engaged in the work:—

"Champion Hill, 30th January, 1855.
" My dear friends,—Your letter of the 13th, only
" forwarded to me yesterday, was most welcome. It seems
" to give me a foretaste of the harvest that I am hoping to
" see gathered in from the seed which it has been my
" happiness to commit to such intelligent and industrious
" husbandmen.

" Never were men toiling in the field under more
" favorable auspices. At your head is one of those
" individuals" (Miss Caroline Lindley) "rarely to be met
" with, possessing feeling ever ready to melt at the sight
" of misery, and an intelligence prepared to examine the
" various means suggested for its relief, and to seize and
' apply the real ones. To her be the attachment, the

"gratitude, and the respect due to one who moved us to
"action.   To us be the delight of aiding her in her labour
"of love.   As King's Sombourne was made famous among
"villages in Hampshire through Richard Dawes, so may
"Hethersett be made famous in Norfolk through Caroline
"Lindley.

   "Among the evils to which society is liable, two large
"classes are distinguishable.   One is of those which it is
"beyond the compass of human power to do more than
"alleviate.   The other is of those which by kindly and
"judicious effort may be averted.   But evils of this latter
"kind must be anticipated to be guarded against.   If not
"anticipated and guarded against, they become incurable.
"I need not tell you that adult suffering and privation
"originating in ignorance and bad habits are of this
"latter kind, and that they are only to be prevented by
"the judicious teaching and training of childhood and youth.
"You have shown your earnest appreciation of this truth
"by the zeal with which you superintend your school and
"second the head master in the performance of his duty.

   "In spite of the din of war and the strife of party, be
"assured that you are engaged in the most pressing work
"of the day—in that which has hitherto been most
"neglected.   Our naval and military organisation may
"be far from perfect, but our educational organisation,
"considered as a means of preventing destitution, vice,
"and crime, is barbarous in the extreme."

One other school may be mentioned to which Ellis gave
considerable help, and this was a school in connection with
the Church of England.   It was the school of St. Thomas,
Charterhouse, founded by Rev. William Rogers (now rector
of St. Botolph, Bishopsgate), in Golden Lane and Goswell
Street, whose acquaintance Ellis made about the year 1858.
Mr. Rogers had been appointed in 1845 to the incumbency
of one of the poorest and most destitute districts in London,
consisting mainly of courts and alleys and with a population

of which costermongers were the largest contingent. He was a man of indomitable vigour and at once set himself to work, with the energy and power of a Hercules cleansing an Augean stable, to battle with the poverty and destitution of the district by removing its cause. He founded, built, and established schools in which some two thousand children were taught at prices varying from £1 per quarter in the upper school down to threepence per week. Such courageous and philanthropic energy, engaged in battling with destitution in one of its strongholds, which had obtained for Rogers the friendship and support of the late Prince Consort, also won Ellis's heart, and he and Rogers became warm friends. Ellis not only subscribed considerable sums of money to his schools, but helped him to improve the character of the education in them, and himself gave lessons on social economy there. A letter which Ellis wrote to him in 1859 is specially interesting. He says :—

"May, 1859.

"My thoughts are partly looking back upon works "done and left undone in the past, and partly looking "forwards to the work to be done, and, if possible, not left "undone in the future. My intercourse with you for "these last two years has given me a much more "favourable balance to look back upon, and I am antici-"pating that the partnership into which you have admitted "me will yield to us both a handsome division of profits. "You, who understand me, will excuse my treating of "things sacred in mercantile language. Before I drop it "I beg most earnestly that you will use, without reserve, "all the authority that you are rightfully entitled to as "senior partner. Make what calls you please for "additional capital and additional services. Don't fear to "make more than I can meet, for I shall not fail to call "'enough' and to satisfy you that I ought to do so, in case "you should outrun my expectations, although my fears "do not point in that direction."

CHAPTER VII.

1846—1854.

THE success of his experiment in teaching social economy to the boys of Mr. Holmes' school led Ellis to undertake other work, in addition to founding schools, for the purpose of obtaining what he then sanguinely hoped for, the early and general adoption of his new method. He at once began to write the series of elementary works for the use of teachers, which we have already seen referred to in his letters. The first of these was the *Outlines of Social Economy*, published in 1846, which, as he tells us in the advertisement of them affixed to his subsequent books, was

"written specially with a view to inculcate upon the rising "generation the three great duties of social life:—

"1st.—To strive to be self supporting, and not to be a "burden on society.

"2nd.—To avoid making any engagements, explicit or "implied, with persons now living or yet to be born, for "the due performance of which there is no reasonable "prospect.

"3rd.—To make such use of all superior advantages, "whether of knowledge, skill, or wealth, as to promote to "the utmost the general happiness of mankind."

And the leading thought which actuated him in undertaking this work, and the others which followed it, is well told in the preface.

"The writer of this little work," he says, "has long been
"impressed with a feeling of the necessity which exists for
"some more definite and systematic instruction than has
"yet been provided for boys in the higher class of schools,
"to give a direction to their thoughts, and to guide and
"stimulate them in their efforts to increase their know-
"ledge, when they shall have entered into the active
"business of life.

"Well does he remember the chaotic state of his own
"understanding, when, at an unusually early age, he
"was transported from the school to the counting-house.
"Vivid is his recollection, also, of what he owes, deep his
"feeling of gratitude, to those thoughtful and gifted men
"into whose society he was thrown at a later period.
"The little cultivation and exercise of his reason and
"judgment that he can pretend to—a useful direction to
"his studies, and an impulse to his exertions—are what he
"traces to this happy master-circumstance of his life.

"In his wish to do for others, however imperfectly,
"what has been done for himself, he wrote the following
"pages, which have furnished him with texts for a series
"of lessons given by himself to a class of thirty boys, out of
"a school of one hundred and eighty, in his own neigh-
"bourhood."

With these objects before him, he published in 1846 the
Outlines of Social Economy, in which the series of lessons
which he had been giving to children was placed in consecutive order and in a form suitable for teachers. The *Outlines*
attracted a good deal of attention. They reached a third
edition, and were translated into French by M. C. Terrien,
and published with an introduction by M. Barthélémy St.
Hilaire. They were followed in 1847 by a work intended
for the enlightenment of schoolmasters as to the nature of
the mind, entitled *Outlines of the History and Formation of
the Understanding* (which will be further referred to a little
later), and in the ensuing year by a further work, described

in the title page as *A Sequel to the Outlines of Social Economy*, which was, in fact, a similar course of lessons thrown into the form of dialogue, and called *Questions and Answers suggested by a consideration of some of the arrangements and relations of social life*. In two letters to Dr. Hodgson he refers to these books as follows:—

" 19th August, 1847.

" Your opinion of my last little book (too flattering, I "fear) is very encouraging to me. The order of the *Social* "*Economy* was adopted with the notion (mistaken, per- "haps) that it presented better than any other a striking "and succinct view of some of the arrangements and "relations of social life. I have awakened some school- "masters to a sense of their importance, and live in the "expectation of awakening more. The order is the "synthetical. I am busy preparing some *Questions and* "*Answers* in a different order—the analytical. Together "they may help to qualify masters to teach. My experi- "ence does not lead me to anticipate much good from "books alone to the boys themselves. You expressed "your dislike, in which I concur, to prepared questions "and answers as catechisms, but mine are not intended to "be of this kind. I am not, however, entirely without "misgivings about them, and I wish very much to have "your critical as well as experimental judgment upon "them. With this view Mrs. Ellis has taken down with "her" [to Tunbridge Wells] "the first part of my MS. She "has undertaken to copy it, and if you will not consider it "too great a bore, she will send you her copy as she gets "on from week to week. Say no, if you would rather be "without it. If you agree to have it and don't like it "when you have got it, put it in the fire. If you like it and "will try it with your classes, it would be an essential "service if I could be made acquainted with your observa- "tions and discoveries of deficiencies, obscurities, and "redundancies."

"5th September, 1847.

"Inclosed you will find the first ten sheets of my MS.
"My object, you will understand, is not to put a string of
"questions into the hands of a teacher, supplying the
"answers in the form of a catechism agreeably to which
"he may examine his scholars, but rather a series of
"questions such as might be put by one enquiring into the
"arrangements and relations of social life as they actually
"present themselves.   The erroneous and insufficient
"answers of the pupils would of course, with a qualified
"teacher, suggest other questions.   I offer what I deem to
"be true and sufficient answers.   My obligation to you
"will be great if you can supply me with any important
"questions that may have been omitted, and with correc-
"tions to answers that appear to you erroneous or
"incomplete."

In 1849 he published a further little work entitled
Introduction to the Study of the Social Sciences, containing
an explanation, suitable for all who should take an interest
in education, of the scientific principles under which moral
science should be disseminated, and the best method of
teaching it.   A fifth book, specially intended for the practical
assistance of teachers, was published in 1850 under the title
of *Progressive Lessons in Social Science*.   This was a series
of sixty lessons (increased in the second edition a few years
later to a hundred) in which the course to be taken by the
teacher who has mastered his subject is suggested.   No
answers, however, are given in the book, as Ellis had
discovered that the *Questions and Answers*, already
mentioned, were in some schools used as lesson books and
learned by rote—a misuse of his work which he specially
objected to, one main object of the lessons, the training of
the thinking and logical powers of the pupil, being thereby
utterly lost.   The *Progressive Lessons* have been twice translated into French, the first edition in 1851 by M. C. Terrien,
the second in 1873 by Ellis's son-in-law, M. Albin Ducamp.

All these books were published anonymously, those sub-sequent to the first being merely described as " by the author of *Outlines of Social Economy.*"   In 1851 he first published a work under his own name, which was entitled *Education as a means of preventing destitution: with exemplifica-tions from the teaching of the conditions of well-being and the principles and applications of economical science at the Birkbeck Schools, prefaced by a letter to Lord John Russell, M.P.* This work comprised six separate essays: two of them being interesting investigations of the method by which education, rightly applied, might be made the means of preventing or diminishing des-titution, with a demonstration that under-education, not over-population, was the cause of destitution; two others explaining the method of teaching adopted in the Birkbeck Schools; another on the important subject of the morality of expenditure; and the book concluded with an eloquent appeal for the admission of instruction in economical science to all our schools. This book for the first time made Ellis's name known as the leader of the campaign against poverty and destitution. Like some of his other works, it found its way abroad; a Dutch translation by Heer J. P. Bredius was published in 1852, with a preface and concluding address by the translator.

The experience of a few years' teaching in schools, however, led him to see many points in his work which were susceptible of improvement. After the third edition of the *Outlines of Social Economy* he ceased to reprint it; and in 1854 he published a new work which in some measure was a repetition of the *Outlines* but varied and re-written in the light of his acquired experience. This was published not only without the author's own name, but with that, as editor, of a friend who had been doing good work in the improvement of education, the Rev. Richard Dawes, Dean of Hereford. It was entitled *Lessons on the Phenomena of Industrial Life and the Conditions of*

Industrial Success; and a comparison of the method of development of the consecutive propositions which constitute the work with those of the *Outlines* will show how greatly he had benefited by the teaching which he had in the intervening eight years been unceasingly carrying on.

His reason for publishing this work anonymously is characteristically told in a letter to Dr. Hodgson:—

"30th April, 1854.

" Although you do not mention the fact, I suppose you "received the note which I wrote last week, announcing "that I had despatched the concluding portion of my "MS. to Chapman, in compliance with your request. " Pray be careful not to connect my name with the work, · "which I expect will be out in a fortnight. The Dean "hopes to obtain admission for it into the Church Train- ¶ing Schools, and if such an Ogre as I am were known "to be its author, the circulation of the work might be "narrowed, and the Dean's influence weakened, both of "which it is desirable to avoid. Will you not bestow a "word of pity upon a disconsolate parent thus driven to "separation from his offspring, or to see it perish before "his eyes? You may think—lucky fellow to be thus "relieved of an ill-favored bantling!—but remember that " I have the affections of a father, and I love and admire "what I have given life to, with all its faults. In fact, "some of my more sagacious friends have charged me "with an incapacity either to discover blemishes in my "own children, or beauties in other people's."

After the publication of this work, Ellis ceased to take much interest in the circulation of the *Outlines*. He felt that the *Lessons on the Phenomena of Industrial Life* were so much more complete and better adapted for their chief purpose, viz., as a treatise by which teachers might qualify themselves for giving oral lessons to their pupils, that to those of his friends who wished to study his method he always recommended it as his most matured work on the subject.

The following letter to Dr. Hodgson, written a few years subsequently, when the third edition of the *Outlines* had just been published, and the third edition of the *Lessons of the Phenomena of Industrial Life* was just called for, gives Ellis's own criticism on the two:—

"22nd November, 1860.

"You are labouring under some mistake in regard to
"the Dean's book.   I did not even see the proof sheets of
"the second edition, and hope not to be asked to revise
"those of the projected third edition.   Mr. Shields may
"have been talking to you about the third edition of my
"*Outlines of Social Economy*, published last spring.   At
"one time I had determined not to reprint it, but to allow
"it to die with my *Questions and Answers*, now out of
"print.   I thought the *Phenomena* in conjunction with
"my *Religion in Common Life*[1] might supersede both.   But
"as it has a steady sale and treats the subject from a some-
"what different point of view and was my first bantling, I
"consented to the prolongation of its existence, and treated
"it to a third suit of clothes in compliance with a few
"improved notions of cut and fit.   The young into whose
"hands it may fall may be led to look into, and pursue
"the line of study pointed out by, my *Progressive Lessons.*
"Otherwise it is nothing worth."

The *Lessons in the Phenomena of Industrial Life* had a considerable circulation.   In 1871, as we learn from a statement of Ellis to the Royal Commission of that year, ten thousand copies had been sold, and in all probability a far larger number would have been circulated had the great merits of this book and its excellent method been known to teachers.

---

[1] See *post*, chap. viii.

This will be a convenient opportunity for pointing out the special differences between other treatises on political economy and the social economy of Ellis. All of them, of course, include an inquiry into the laws regulating wealth, wages, rent, value, price, money, and taxation; but the order in which these subjects are arranged is widely different, while in Ellis's works alone are the consequences of individual conduct and the importance of cultivating the personal qualities upon which both individual and social well-being rest, introduced in such a manner as to be brought vividly home to the mind of the student. The very thought of influencing human beings in favour of obedience to economical laws is not found, even in the treatises of the most eminent of earlier writers ; with Ellis the pervading idea which guides and animates every page of his works is to elicit from those laws the strongest possible stimulus to right conduct. Viewed as a means of directing and guiding learners—whether they be youthful pupils or persons of maturer age seeking for economical knowledge— other treatises seem merely the dry bones of learning, compared with the vivid life-like coherent system which Ellis places before his pupils. In his works alone do we find the philosophy of human conduct—the art of right living under the conditions of civilised life—built up, step by step, from the foundation of the qualities which lie at the base of all human well-being. As developed by Ellis, social economy is a union of the principles of political economy as understood by his predecessors, with those of morals and religion. Its purpose is to instil motives of action, adapted to the phenomena of existing society, such as can alone effect permanent improvement in the welfare of the people.

This difference in the arrangement of the various branches of the subject which Ellis introduced, or, as we may call it, his new method of teaching economics, is so important, that it will be desirable to trace the sequence of thought in one or two of the great writers on political economy, and then contrast it with the manner in which Ellis treats the subject. Adam Smith's great work, entitled *An Inquiry into the Nature and Causes of the Wealth of Nations*, starts (book i.) by investigating the " causes of improvement in the produc- " tive powers of labour, and of the order according to which " its produce is naturally distributed among the different " ranks of the people." Under this head the laws of division of labour, money, price, wages, and rent are discussed ; while the subsequent books treat of the nature, accumulation, and employment of stock (*i.e.* wealth), (book ii.); of the different progress of opulence in different nations (book iii.); of different systems of political economy (book iv.); and lastly, of the revenue of the sovereign or commonwealth (book v.)

But the work does not profess to discuss the welfare or well-being of the wealth-producing members of the community; it deals rather with the commodities produced. In one part we have a short chapter of five pages (book iii., chapter i.) upon the "natural progress of opulence," but it does not contain a single sentence dealing with those causes of more or less rapid progress which exist in the individual qualities and conduct of the members of the society. Towards the end of the work (book v., chapter i.), the author points out that "the education of the common people requires " the attention of the public," but the chapter on this subject is in reference to the propriety of defraying the expense of education out of the funds belonging to the public, and the thought that the action of its individual members may be guided so as to make or mar the welfare of a community does not find place in Adam Smith's treatise.

Take next James Mill's *Elements of Political Economy*, a most valuable work, of which Ellis had a profound admiration. The author divides his work into four chapters, in which he deals with the laws regulating, first, production; secondly, distribution; thirdly, exchange; and fourthly, consumption. But even James Mill, thoroughly as he grasped the importance, as a method of elevating the human race, of education, a subject on which he wrote a most masterly treatise, does not seem to have connected the laws of political economy with education, as being knowledge which should be so taught as to stimulate to right or prevent wrong action. He treats rather of wealth as the thing to be produced, distributed, and consumed, than of the living producers and consumers whose lives are to be guided. The single exception perhaps is the paragraph (chapter ii., sec. 2, § 2) in which he states the great principle which has become permanently associated with the name of his friend Malthus, that the tendency of population to increase unduly may be checked by two methods, viz., by poverty—involving premature destruction of the beings born into the world—or by prudence on the part of the parents. The principle, however, is merely stated, but not commented on or treated as if he had present to his mind the use of the principle educationally for the purpose of influencing human conduct.

John Stuart Mill, the lifelong friend of Ellis, and his fellow pupil in the philosophy of Bentham and James Mill, might have been expected to have introduced into his writings some of the ideas which absorbed Ellis's thoughts. He was composing his great work on the *Principles of Political Economy* at the same time as Ellis was writing his much more modest *Outlines of Social Economy.* John Stuart Mill's treatise was, as he tells us in his *Autobiography*, begun in 1845, and finished and published in 1847. But throughout the whole of that wonderful composition, we only find one passage suggesting the thought that the work he was engaged upon should, by suitable teaching, be used as an engine for human progress and advancement. Even then it is only cursorily mentioned and then left. This passage is in his chapter on the probable future of the labouring classes (book iv., chapter vii.), when he says:—

" With these resources " (newspapers, political tracts, lectures, and discussions) " it cannot be doubted that they "

J

(the people) "will increase in intelligence even by their "own unaided efforts; while there is reason to hope that "great improvements, both in the quality and quantity of "school education, will be effected by the exertions either "of government or of individuals, and that the progress of "the mass of the people in mental cultivation, and in the "virtues which are dependent on it, will take place more "rapidly and with fewer intermittences and aberrations "than if left to itself."

On the other hand, we find that Ellis in all his works bases the whole superstructure of his system upon the individual qualities necessary for human well-being. Taking as a representative work his *Lessons on the Phenomena of Industrial Life* we find that he starts with the self-evident fact that food, clothing, shelter, and fuel are necessary to human life, but are not produced without labour. From this he demonstrates the necessity for *industry*.

The necessity for the right direction and beneficial employment of industry leads on to the requirement of *knowledge and skill*. The alternation of summer and winter; the liability of human beings, both to temporary incapacity through illness, and to the ultimate loss of power due to old age; and the length of time which must elapse between the commencement of a railway, canal, or dock, before it becomes of use, are the steps which prove the need of *economy*, that is, habits of saving and self-denial, without which industry, knowledge, and skill would be comparatively useless. All these fundamental qualities are impressed on his pupils most earnestly, and the way in which they can be acquired, diffused, and cultivated is shown. The prevalence in civilised nations of the habit of making and preserving commodities and things needed for comfortable existence, some perishable or rapidly consumable, others more permanent in their character, necessitates a designation of these things—*wealth*. For here, as throughout Ellis's works, we find the facts observed and classified, and then named.

Out of wealth is carved the idea of *capital*, namely, the portion of wealth which is employed in the production of fresh wealth to replace that consumed. The necessity for abstention by other individual members of a community from interference with the products of the labours of the industrious, and the need for protection, by the joint action of society, of those who produce wealth in the enjoyment of what they have produced and saved, form the next step, leading to the idea of *property* and *respect for property* as a necessary quality of social life; it being self-evident that no one would labour and save if liable to be deprived of the fruits of his industry and economy by fraud, robbery, or outrage.

Upon these necessary qualities, viewed as fundamental principles of individual action, and which are not even treated of as factors in social well-being by his predecessors, Ellis builds up the more advanced propositions of political or social economy. He proceeds to develop and explain the various social phenomena which are also treated of by Adam Smith and the Mills, though perhaps in a somewhat more consecutive order; for one special feature of all Ellis's works is that each chapter has, like the propositions of Euclid, been led up to by the immediately preceding or some other earlier chapter. The next chapters after that on *property* are those on *wages, profit, rent, division of labour*, and *interchange*, subjects in the treatment of which he follows the lines of thought of his old friend and master, James Mill. Interchange leads by a natural sequence to *value, measures*, and *weights* of commodities, and the equally necessary measure of value called *money*. The various methods of using money by which commerce is facilitated—*credit, bills, rates of exchange, banks* and *banking*, and *paper money*, form the next group of lessons, after which various subjects which have been led up to in previous chapters are taken up and explained. *Insurance* against unforeseen misfortune; *price* and its fluctuations, with their causes, and a special explanation of *interest* and *annuities*, the means by which a nation borrows money for national necessities, lead up to two or three chapters of a somewhat broader scope. *Industrial progress*, a subject which was very shortly discussed by Adam Smith as "the progress of opulence," is treated by Ellis very fully in proportion to the extent of his book. His object is thoroughly practical—namely, to show how individual members of society should be prepared for great industrial changes, such as the supplanting of coach traffic by railways, which, though causing injury to particular classes of the community, are clearly of the greatest advantage to society as a whole, so that the individuals affected should, by a capacity for self-adaptation, coupled with economy, be prepared, as far as possible, to resist the immediate evil consequences, and to avail themselves of the subsequent greater benefit of the change.   Other chapters follow dealing with *emigration, restrictions on trade, industrial derangement*, and the true method of investigating its causes, of *strikes* and *lockouts*, and the various kinds of *taxation* by which the expenditure needful for national purposes is raised.

Here other writers on political economy generally conclude their treatises. But Ellis goes on in several of his books to deal with the inferences as to human conduct which are to be drawn from the propositions which have hitherto been developed. In the *Outlines of Social Economy* he concludes with a singularly interesting chapter on the right principles of *individual expenditure*, that is, of unproductive consumption, or the use of wealth otherwise than as capital. James Mill has a most useful chapter upon productive and unproductive consumption, the former being described as a means to production, and the commodities consumed being in fact capital, while in the latter case they are lost without being replaced in the process of consumption and enjoyment, the only result being the pleasure and satisfaction thereby yielded. But

James Mill does not pursue his researches into the true principles by which unproductive expenditure should be guided. Ellis, on the other hand, takes up this enquiry. He points out that expenditure (*i.e.*, expenditure of the surplus acquired by each individual beyond suitable maintenance) must take place in one of three ways—mischievously, uselessly, or usefully to society. The first method is that of idleness, riot, and debauchery, injurious to the individual who spends, to his companions, and to society. Instances of the second method are the building and maintaining of many unoccupied houses, the shutting up of a tract of beautiful country within park palings which no one is allowed to enter, and the purchase of works of art which are secluded from human eyes. Under the third are included the laying out of a park or public ground for the healthful recreation of the inhabitants of large towns, the founding of schools, universities and hospitals, the buying of works of art and genius for the instruction and refinement of the community, and "the " noblest of all charities, the assisting to raise his suffering "brethren above the need of charity," the final inference being that "the noble satisfaction of doing good is to be "earned through the judgment and devotion by which "expenditure is made the means of attaining useful results " for society."

In another of Ellis's books (*Education as a means of preventing destitution*, p. 93), the morality of expenditure is still more fully treated. He analyses the respective careers of Lord Mereacres, a peer who expends his £20,000 per annum in stylish and fashionable living, performing the ordinary social duties of a nobleman but no more; of Lord Care-nought, another peer who spends, first his own money and then that of his creditors, in gambling, betting, riot, and debauchery ; of John Save-all, the head of a large manufacturing establishment, who, having made a large fortune by industry, frugality, and integrity, continues to live on £500 a year and accumulates the remainder of his £20,000 per annum, and who, although he seeks for and selects efficient workmen and managers, and pays them adequate salaries, does not seek to employ his great means for the benefit of others ; and lastly, of Robert Steerwell, whose rise has been similar to Save-all's, who spends on his own needs as much as but not more than he requires, but who has acted and continues in his great prosperity to act upon the principle that wealth is only a means to an end :—

"A most efficient and indispensable means for ulterior "purposes ; for self-support in the first place ; secondly, "to qualify for the undertaking and performing the nearer "and dearer duties of domestic life ; and lastly, to aid in "the performance of some of the wider and nobler duties "of social life."

The discussion of these types of character and conduct is singularly interesting and merits careful study. Thoughtless social comment will point at Robert Steerwell as deficient in spirit for not living in a style as good as his fellows— will sneer at Save-all as a mean, despicable fellow—will pity Lord Care-nought as after all more the enemy of himself than any one else—and will praise Lord Mereacres as an exemplary and highly respectable nobleman. But the careful examination of each of these four methods of expending an income will show that the expenditure of Lord Care-nought is in the highest degree mischievous—that Lord Mereacres is a useless, if ornamental, member of society, whose expenditure consists in devoting to his own personal enjoyment the income of the wealth handed down to him by his ancestors without attempting to benefit his fellow-countrymen and the world—that John Save-all does a considerable amount of good by the use, as capital, of the wealth which he does not care to spend on himself—but that Robert Steerwell's principle is the true one, namely, that of spending upon his own comfort as much of his income as and not more than he reasonably needs, of making adequate provision by saving for the future of himself and those dependent on him, and of utilising the remainder in the best method which he can discover for the improvement of the well-being of humanity.

In the second edition of the *Progressive Lessons*, published in 1862, twelve years after the first, the course of study laid down in these earlier works is further expanded, and a series of lessons on individual conduct, derived as corollaries from the truths of political economy, is added, the questions by which teachers can bring them home to the minds of the pupils being pointed out. The sixteen concluding lessons are entirely on this subject. In the first edition of this work, he had concluded his series (then only sixty in number) by lessons in which he shows by what questions pupils may be led how to judge of a people's civilisation by the way in which wealth is consumed, and to see how a deficiency of the fundamental qualities needful for well-being is the cause of the sufferings of a people, rather than the much misunderstood over-population; to understand the consequent necessity for education of a right kind, and to estimate the importance of right conduct, and the morals and habits of a people as well as its laws and courts of justice, as a means to its well-being and happiness. But in the second edition this point is only a stage from which the additional lessons start, constituting a closely reasoned code of ethics in the form of a suggested series of questions. In these lessons his teachers are shown how they may teach their pupils to form correct judgments on different kinds of conduct, how to classify them as good or bad, right or wrong, the ultimate test of conduct being its tendency to produce results favourable or unfavourable to general well-being. Then its consequences are discussed, and the tendency, as civilisation progresses, to take into account those consequences in judging of it, while the effect of this judgment as a cause of conduct is the next step in this course of lessons. Individual attainments, the capacity of judging between good and evil, and the formation of right habits and dispositions, are next discussed, the soundness of public opinion and the goodness or badness of government being then considered. Then follows an enquiry into the relationship between acts which are immoral as being contrary to general well-being, and acts which are criminal as being contrary to laws, the difference between the two being fully illustrated; and the series closes with an explanation of the distinction between what government can do and what can only be effected by intelligence in the community to appreciate good conduct, and the disposition to prefer good to bad conduct, which can only be supplied by education.

It is this teaching of the practical lessons derived from the study of the phenomena of social life for the purpose of individual self-guidance, which is the special feature introduced into education by Ellis. It is somewhat strange to find that so valuable a thought has not been adopted by subsequent writers, and that educators have been content to send forth their pupils on their voyage through life with no attempt to provide them with any chart for their guidance except natural instinct. But dismissing from consideration for the present this special portion of his method, and limiting ourselves to the portion which is more strictly included within the limits of political economy, we think that any intelligent reader who has had experience in the study or teaching of a scientific subject to the young will realise the immense superiority of Ellis's arrangement for educational purposes. The various thoughts grow out of those which precede them like the trunk of a tree from the root—the branches from the trunk. He starts in a closely deductive manner from a few indisputable axioms. Each proposition is evolved from its predecessors in a natural sequence. In his actual teaching it will be remembered the lessons were oral, and the pupils were guided by skilfully directed questions to find out the answers for themselves. A careful study of Ellis's works will show that each of the technical terms of political economy is only used when the idea to be expressed by it has been developed and the necessity for a word to express that idea becomes apparent.

Herbert Spencer has put in clear strong language the thought which should be ever present to teachers and writers of books for the use of teachers. He tells us[1] that the education of the child must accord both in mode and arrangement with the education of mankind considered historically, since both, being processes of evolution, must conform to the general laws of evolution. And, as one of the inferences from this principle, he points out that "the "process of self-development should be encouraged to the "uttermost. Children should be led to make their own "investigations and to draw their own inferences. They "should be told as little as possible and induced to discover "as much as possible." This method was precisely that which Ellis had adopted several years before Herbert Spencer published his essay. It was the thought which was one of the vital principles of his system. On the other hand, nearly every other writer of books for the study of political economy, except those who have followed Ellis, fail to understand this vital principle of educational method. We will take the first that comes; it is not necessary to mention it by name, as it is only a specimen of the general fault— defective arrangement. The work from which we quote has been adopted as a class-book in several schools sufficiently advanced to include political economy in their curricula. It shows careful study of prior works on the subject—especially of John Stuart Mill—and a conscientious working out of details. But the author follows the antiquated lines, and the development of the subject, viewed educationally, is singularly confused; ideas and even technical words are from time to time introduced, even

---

[1] *Education—Intellectual, Moral, and Physical, pages* 75, 77.

at the very beginning of the work, which presuppose, for clear comprehension of the proposition expressed, considerable knowledge of the subject.

This confusion and want of systematic development will be seen from a few examples. At the outset of the book (page 1) wealth is defined as "anything which has an "exchange value,". while "exchange" is first treated of at page 39, and "value" is not defined until page 44. When we contrast this definition with Ellis's simpler and truer explanation of wealth as "commodities which are the "produce of labour," the confusion as well as want of arrangement in the sequence of thought becomes apparent. "Exchange" and "value" are technical words expressing ideas which are subsidiary to, and which ought in a beginner's mind to follow, not to precede that of wealth—ideas which cannot be grasped until that of wealth is understood. Again, wealth may be possessed by the solitary denizen of an island—a Robinson Crusoe—where exchange and value are non-existent, while, on the other hand, this definition would include land,[1] which is known to be constantly exchanged, bought, and sold, although the very next step in the book is the proposition that "wealth is "produced by land, labour, and capital."

Then, although this last proposition is laid before the mind of our "beginners" at page 5 of the book from which we quote, the explanation of the meaning of the word "capital" is only given twenty pages later. Money and its functions are not defined and explained until page 49, while we have a discussion of the difference between wealth and money at

---

[1] John Stuart Mill, not following his eminent father, falls into this inaccuracy in the beginning of his work, and defines wealth as including land (*Political Economy*, fourth edition, vol. i., page 10), and even the skill, energy, and perseverance of the artizans of a country (page 59). But he never treats of it in his book in accordance with this definition. Production and consumption of wealth, which are the very titles of his chapters, are inconsistent with the use of the word in such a sense.

page 2, and between capital and money at page 25. Again, at an early part of the book (page 34), we are told that capital (why not all wealth) is the result of saving, and that the desire to save, which differs in intensity in different ages and countries, "is produced by two motives—first, a "prudent foresight for the future; secondly, the desire to "acquire wealth by investments." And yet the ideas which are intended to be conveyed by the word "investments" only appear much later in the book. Interest as a payment for the use of capital is only elucidated at page 137, and the custom of owners of capital to entrust it to the management of others in the form of shares in joint-stock companies is explained still later, at page 157.

We have quoted these few instances not for the purpose of criticising any particular author, but in order to explain the defective arrangement of the subject in all writers who base their compilations on earlier works, as compared with the clearly progressive and perfectly evolutional method of Ellis, and so to make clear the special excellence of plan and arrangement, and the great accuracy of definition which characterise Ellis's writings, and make his works upon economics so superior for educational purposes to others on the same subject—even to those of his valued friend and fellow-student, John Stuart Mill. But his treatment of political economy in the limited sense, that is, considered separately from human conduct, is the only portion of the subject in which any comparison can be instituted between Ellis and other writers. In the inferences which arise from it, the demonstrations which evolve themselves at each step in his progress through social life of what acts of the members of a community will lead to well-being, and what to disaster and misery, Ellis's works stand alone. Although it seems a self-evident proposition that economic science—like every other science—is only useful in so far as it conduces to human well-being, no other writer on the subject, except his own pupils and followers, has joined to it the life-like teaching from which alone practical benefit is to be obtained.

It was evidently the comprehension of this merit of Ellis, which induced a writer in the *Times*, when reviewing the *Autobiography of John Stuart Mill* (*Times*, 10th November, 1873), to speak of Ellis as "the founder, as he "may be called, of social science." But Ellis—with the extreme modesty which had led him to publish his valuable little works anonymously—at once wrote the following letter to the editor, disclaiming the well-deserved epithet:—

"Sir,—May I ask the favour of a small space in your "columns to enable me to correct a slight misrepresentation "in your notice of the *Autobiography of John S. Mill*, a mis-"representation quite unimportant to anybody but myself?

"The clever writer of that notice refers to me as 'the "'founder of social science,' a designation of which I "might well be proud, did I but deserve it.

"My connexion with 'social science' is very simple and "very humble. Fifty years ago it was my good fortune "to be introduced to Mr. James Mill, and through him to "his son, John Stuart Mill, to both of whom I am indebted "for more than I can find words to express. They set me "thinking for myself. I trust I profited a little by their "uniform kindness and by the assistance which no willing "student, however dull, could fail to derive from men of "such distinguished attainments.

"One result of my studies and reflections has been the "deep conviction that the elementary truths of Social "Science—founded long before I was born—ought to be "taught in all our schools; and for more than twenty-five "years I have employed the greater part of the time which "I could spare from business to promote such teaching, "both as a teacher and a writer of little books intended "chiefly for children and their teachers.

"I am, Sir, yours most truly,
"November 10th, 1873." "WILLIAM ELLIS.

One of the books which we have mentioned, the *Outlines of the History and Formation of the Understanding*, the second of the series, is a sort of complemental work to the *Outlines of Social Economy*, and requires further special notice. Its object was the enlightenment of teachers with respect to the nature and qualities of the human mind, which was the raw material on which they had to work. He explained it thus in a conversation with his friend, John Rüntz—

"If I go into a carpenter's shop, I am sure that the "carpenter knows what he is employed on. With a "schoolmaster, I am not sure that he understands the "material upon which he has to do his work. So I must "construct a treatise which will enlighten him."

It was with a view, therefore, of placing this knowledge within easy reach of schoolmasters that Ellis wrote this little book. Teachers in primary schools, whom Ellis sought to attract to his special subject of teaching, were not likely to have access to, or the leisure to study, James Mill's *Analysis of the Human Mind*, in which he had taken up and developed Hartley's method of explaining mental phenomena, nor John Stuart Mill's exhaustive work upon *Logic, ratiocinative and inductive.* But both of these were part of the groundwork on which Ellis had founded his system. He and John Stuart Mill had studied Hartley side by side at their early morning meetings at Mr. Grote's house in Threadneedle Street; they had renewed those meetings for the purpose of studying James Mill's work; while John Stuart Mill's *Logic*, published about 1844, had been, as he himself tells us, commenced in 1830 as the outcome of the same morning conversations. This knowledge Ellis wished to bring home to the humblest schoolmaster who cared to spend a sixpence in procuring it, and in this little work we find abstracted and epitomised the leading propositions of these two great works. The work was published at two shillings, but a note at the commencement of the book—

similar to one at the beginning of the *Outlines of Social Economy*—announced that "the publishers have instructions
"to supply a single copy for sixpence to any schoolmaster
"making a written application."

There is no formal preface, but in lieu of one we have a dedication "To all earnest schoolmasters," in which, after drawing attention to the new thoughts on education which he had recently introduced, he concludes with the following eloquent appeal to parents :—

"Yes, my friends, talk to your children freely and
"perpetually on all subjects—on the 'nature,' not only of
"some things, but of all things; and among them, of that
"most curious and interesting of all things, a specimen of
"which they always have about them, the human under-
"standing.   Above all, as they progressively become
"under your parental guidance more and more acquainted
"with the nature or laws of things, let them learn how
"necessary it is for their happiness that their own conduct
"should be regulated by these laws.   Teach them to
"observe for themselves how misery, suffering, and dis-
"comfort, are almost always traceable to a disregard of
"these laws—a disregard sometimes arising from igno-
"rance, sometimes from inattention, sometimes from
"inertness.   Point out to them, that as fire warms or
"burns, water supports or destroys life, medicinal agents
"cure or kill, according to the manner of using them, so
"also will the understanding guide to happiness or hurry
"to destruction according to the pains taken to exercise
"and form it.   Let nothing induce you to suffer them to
"be blinded to the 'nature' of their duties.   The laws of
"creation are what must 'rub against them at every step.'
"Neither sanction nor tolerate any attempt to prevent
"their learning thoroughly that their duties consist in a
"steady attention and adaptation to these laws, under
"whatever system of classification they may be arranged
"by whatever names designated—physical, intellectual

" moral, or social.   According to their steady performance
" of the duties corresponding to these laws will they find
" the laws themselves, uniform and undeviating as they
" are, 'rub against them,' so as to promote their happiness
" or to make them miserable.

 " Yes, my friends, talk to your children—talk fervently,
" affectionately, and truthfully, and, unappreciated as you
" yet may be for a time, chilled by faint praise, and
" thwarted by meddling ignorance, they will love you and
" hang upon you while children, and bless and revere you
" when grown into men.".

The book—a little handbook of some hundred and twenty
pages—contains a complete but compressed summary, first,
of the formation, development, and nature of the intellectual
powers of civilised human beings ; secondly, of the method
in which those powers work for the acquisition and application of knowledge ; and thirdly, by way of practical
inference from the preceding portion of the work, of
the method in which the faculties therein elucidated
should be moulded by education so as to increase the
well-being of humanity through the improvement of human
conduct.   The writer does not claim originality for his
propositions, but freely acknowledges his indebtedness
to others.   " Whatever of good, and useful, and true is
 "in them," he tells us in his preface, " has been freely
 "borrowed from the great lights and leaders of the
 "world—in spirit still with us though departed in body—
 "and from one mightier than all,[1] inasmuch as he has added
 "to his ample inheritance the results of his own successful
 "researches and happy combinations, who still lives labour-
 "ing like a giant to enlighten and improve us, whom for me
 "to attempt to eulogize would be as arrogant as it would
 "be impertinent."
The book may be said to be an epitome of Hartley's

---

[1] John Stuart Mill.

method of explaining mental phenomena as elaborated and illustrated by James Mill in his *Analysis of the Human Mind*, combined with an explanation of the method by which knowledge is sought for and acquired as worked out in John Stuart Mill's great work on *Logic*. But the arrangement, the method in which the two are combined, and the practical application for the use of teachers, are Ellis's own. From the sensations which lie at the base of the very idea of mind, he leads up to ideas—the memory of sensations. The association of ideas, Hartley's great principle, follows, with the instruments by which ideas are expressed, conveyed, and preserved—language and its subdivision, names and propositions. Memory, leading to the anticipation of future results based on past experience, brings us to volition or human will, prompting to action. This is the point to which James Mill's work conducts his readers. But at this point Ellis passes to "a survey of what these faculties have to work upon," and deals with knowledge and the method of acquiring it. Chapters on cause and effect, observation and experiment, the inductive and deductive methods, and the doctrine of chance, or probabilities, are explained upon the lines which Ellis had thought out in John Stuart Mill's company, and which the latter had (in his work on *Logic*) examined in the detail needed by philosophers, while Ellis was content with the humbler office of placing the salient principles within the reach of schoolmasters. At this point, however, the theoretical and practical methods of treatment somewhat diverge. John Stuart Mill proceeds[1] to examine in the abstract what he names Ethology, or the Science of Character—the science which determines the kind of character produced in conformity to general laws by any set of circumstances, physical and moral; the science upon which is based the art of education. He describes it[2] as a deductive science,

---

[1] *System of Logic*, vol. ii., page 441.　　　[2] *Ib.*, page 446.

which is a system of corollaries from Psychology, the experimental science, previously defined as the science of the elementary laws of mind; and he goes on to describe what might be accomplished by the science of Ethology in language which may almost be looked on as a theoretical outline of the work which Ellis had undertaken and was actually doing.

On the other hand, Ellis, taking the practical course, proceeds at this stage to discuss the true principles which should be adopted by those who seek to acquire sound judgment and to practice consistency. Then, returning to the analysis of mind, he explains, in a chapter on pleasures and pains, the various kinds of motive which actuate human action; on the one hand, the cruelty and revenge of the savage, the brutal and debasing pleasures and amusements of the half-civilised, and the pomp, display, and ambition of the selfish and worldly; and, on the other hand, the acquisition of knowledge, the cultivation of science and art, and, highest of all, devotion to the improvement of others, to the enlightenment and elevation of the human race, and to the diffusion of knowledge so that its blessings may be extended to all. And he concludes with a chapter peculiarly his own, which is the practical application of the entire treatise and the working out in detail of John Stuart Mill's science of Ethology. In this he explains the manner by which, adopting a right method of teaching and training, character may be formed and the human mind guided and influenced so as to produce the desire to perform the duties of social life which we have already quoted at the beginning of this chapter. This definition of the duties of social life, as we have seen, he adopted and introduced in the advertisement of the *Outlines of Social Economy.*

Another work, scarcely exceeding the limits of a pamphlet, published in 1852, with a similarly anonymous title, viz., "by the author of the *Outlines of Social Economy,*" was intended to explain to the young the reasons why knowledge

K

should be acquired, and what kind of knowledge should be communicated. It is entitled *What am I? Where am I? What ought I to do? How am I to become qualified and disposed to do what I ought?* It is a simple, interesting, and consecutive argument, starting by an explanation of the nature and needs of human beings, then giving a description of the earth and the various powers and agencies which pervade it, the knowledge of and power of utilising which has been vastly increased within the last century. These are followed by a sketch of the conduct needed to utilise these powers and agencies so as to produce the degree of comfort and well-being sought in civilised life, from which premises the knowledge and training which ought to be given to children in order to bring about the habits and dispositions conducing to this conduct are shown. And the treatise shows in conclusion that these may be summed up under the following names of recognised branches of study, viz.:—

Natural history.

Physical Science in all its branches.

Vegetable and Animal Physiology.

The arrangements and relations of social life.

Of course the power of reading, of writing, of drawing, and of calculating, is the means for acquiring proficiency in these studies. But the deepest interest in their work can easily be excited, as the author shows, in children who understand and appreciate the object of sending them to school.

A little *brochure* which Ellis published about the same time (1852), at the price of threepence, was apparently intended for circulation among the working classes, as it discusses the questions which then, as now, have the deepest interest for them and most affect their welfare. It was entitled *Reminiscences and Reflections of an Old Operative,* and was, of course, absolutely anonymous. The writer introduces himself as follows :—

" I am a retired operative engineer, and am an old man.

" My life has had its vicissitudes. At times I have been
" out of work, and at other times I have seemed to myself
" to be compelled to work harder and longer than was
" good for my health, or, at all events, I have been
" tempted by extra pay, or have feared to damage my
" position by declining, to over-exert myself. Between
" these two extremes of no work and over-work, I have
" often had too little to do, and have been obliged to put
" up with too little wages for the little I could get to do."
He then proceeds to consider the relation of workmen and
capitalists and the battles between them known as strikes and
combinations. Considering the effect of a general strike, that
is, not in a single trade, but generally in all trades, he shows it
would be "a contest between those who are in need of the
" means of present subsistence and those who, possessing the
" means of present subsistence, are anxious to secure the
" means of future subsistence." The fruitlessness of such a
strike is apparent, and the more careful investigation of the
direct and indirect operation of more limited strikes enables
him to show their utter inutility. Co-operative societies are
next considered, and in reference to these the distinction
between what capitalists receive as owners of their capital
and what they receive as administrators, a distinction very
often overlooked or misapprehended, is clearly shown, the
rest of the pamphlet being devoted to a sketch of the
conduct which had enabled him to save sufficient to maintain
his old age without being a burden to any one, beginning by
the resolute putting aside of threepence a week out of the
sixpence pocket money which his father allowed him to
retain from the small weekly wages received by him as a
boy at the factory where he had been placed. But so far
from advocating the mere accumulation of money, he shows
that it is but a means to an end, and concludes:—

     " I have never been ambitious to accumulate property
     " beyond what was necessary to secure to you" (his
children) " the possession of the knowledge and disposition

"essential to your own happy self-guidance in life, or to
"soften the suffering that the premature death of your
"parents might have exposed you to. Wealth and well-
"being, individual and national, are the results of right
"conduct, as right conduct is the result of knowledge and
"good habits. To pour out wealth upon those of whose
"capacity to use it we know nothing, is about as insane
"as to pour forth fuel, careless whether it should serve to
"warm an apartment, feed an engine, or add fury to the
"flames that are destroying a city."

Another method by which Ellis sought to attract the attention of the higher classes to the importance of his method, and its bearing on the question of improving the condition of the people, was by articles in reviews. Between October, 1848, and May, 1851, he wrote, in addition to the series of books which we have already mentioned, no less than eight articles, of which seven were published in the *Westminster Review*, and one in the *British Quarterly Review*. In one of these he dealt with the causes of poverty and pointed out the importance of parental forethought as a factor in the well-being of society. In another he enquired into the problem of how to deal with distressed needle-women. The singularly interesting novel, *Mary Barton*, which had just been published, and produced a deep impression upon the public mind, while it placed its authoress at once among the first rank of our novelists, was the subject of the third review and gave him ample scope for discussing the state of the working classes and the best method of improving it. A fourth on "The State "of the Nation" pointed out the neglect of the study of industrial science and the importance of remedying that neglect. This review is specially interesting as containing a preliminary sketch of the *Progressive Lessons*, which he published two or three years later. A fifth review was entitled "Relief Measures," and dealt with the then state of the country, a large part being devoted to the question of Ireland. The Irish famine of 1844 was then fresh in the national memory, and politicians were even then proposing to remedy poverty and destitution by legislation. Encumbered estates courts were then much favoured just as, since then, the reform of the land laws and a change in the governing body have been advocated as means to make Ireland thriving and prosperous. Ellis, in a few of the telling interrogative enquiries which he knew so well how to frame, discusses who are the destitute, what are the qualities which have made them poor and destitute, what are the qualities by which the self-supporting are enabled to support not only themselves but others, and how these qualities can be implanted in that portion of a people—the young—who have not yet formed bad habits. Education itself was dealt with in two articles—one on classical education, in which he urged the importance of substituting instruction of the upper classes in real knowledge for the mere routine of Greek and Latin classics, by which degrees were in those days obtained; the other upon the progress of the movement for popular education, in which the growth and development of national education were traced from the time of Pestalozzi, whom Ellis calls "the father of popular education on the "Continent," to the date of the article in January, 1851. The last of these interesting essays was entitled "The "European Difficulty," in which the relation of popular education to social well-being was well shown; and which concluded with a plea for the introduction into such education of a higher and more real quality than it had then reached.

Of these essays the one on *Mary Barton* led to Ellis's seeking to acquire, and ultimately making, the acquaintance of the authoress. He writes Dr. Hodgson as to this:—

"14th January, 1849.

"I enclose a copy of each of my late contributions to "the *Westminster Review* for your acceptance, unworthy "as they are of that honour. I also enclose a copy of the

"last as well as of my late pamphlet for Mrs. Gaskell. It
"will be a prodigious gratification to me if I can succeed
"in drawing and fixing her attention upon the causes of
"that misery which she has so powerfully and pathetically
"described. At all events, assure her of the deep interest
"with which I listened to the good reading of her well-
"written narrative."

It was after this that Ellis undertook, at Hodgson's
request and with the co-operation of Mrs. Ellis, to review
the work. He writes Hodgson again, a couple of months
later:—

"4th March, 1849.
"I am in daily expectation of the proof of the article
"on *Mary Barton*, written by Mrs. Ellis and myself, at
"your solicitation, for the forthcoming number of the
"*Westminster Review*. I write this note while I have
"leisure, that it may be in readiness to accompany the
"proof the moment I receive it. There will be no time to
"waste, because the *Review* ought to be in the hands of
"the public on the first of April. I wish you to read the
"proof for two reasons: first, that I may have the benefit
"of any suggestions for its improvement; and, second, to
"learn from you whether a few copies of the article,
"printed in the same form as my previous articles, would
"be agreeable to the author, useful to the book, and, above
"all, would aid in the improvement and enlightenment of
"anybody in Manchester.

"I beg that you will bear in mind that I have no preten-
"sions to literary merit. Literature is not my vocation.
"My only excuse for handling the pen is the earnest
"desire to see done and to aid in doing what so few see
"the importance of and so few have the inclination to
"engage in. How I wish I had your talent and readiness
"and versatility as a superstructure on what I conceive to
"be my own solid foundation! You allude in your last
"note to '*my* favorite subjects.' Are they not *yours*

"also? I am anxious to see all human beings impressed
"with the knowledge that this world must be the abode
"of misery instead of happiness unless industry, skill,
"economy,and parental forethought prevail universally,and
"trained to the practice of the virtues which this know-
"ledge points out to be indispensable. Is this a frivolous
"anxiety or a whimsical conceit? Or is it an anxiety
"which challenges the concurrence and sympathy of all
"who earnestly wish for the improvement of their fellow
"citizens? If the latter, the subjects alluded to are not
"mine—they are the world's—they are Dr. Hodgson's."

The review when published led to the Ellis family making
Mrs. Gaskell's acquaintance. She visited them at Champion
Hill, and the following letter from Mrs. Ellis to Dr.
Hodgson gives a pleasant memory of their acquaintance
with the charming novelist :—

"Champion Hill, May 6th, 1849.
"I do not know whether Mrs. Gaskell has returned
"home. I called the Saturday of last week and unfor-
"tunately found her out, and have not been able to leave
"home since. We have seen but little of her, our living
"out of town being a great obstacle, and requiring more
"time than her numerous engagements could well spare.
"But we have been delighted and gratified with her, and
"both wish we had the good fortune to have her for our
"neighbour. Her gentle modesty and unaffected manners
"are most attractive."

In the year 1853 Ellis obtained the audience of a different
class of the community. We have seen that he had friends
among the managers of the Jewish schools, and was in that
year giving lessons upon social economy at a Jewish school
in Red Lion Square. He also wrote in a Jewish weekly
newspaper, called the *Hebrew Observer*, a series of thirteen
articles on secular education, which appeared between
February and June of that year, in which, pointing out

the lack of education in the country and the inevitable result of ignorance in misery and crime, he criticised severely Lord John Russell's action in supporting denominational schools and in merely advocating the continuance and extension of existing schools without improvement.

Another method by which he tried to advance the work he had at heart was by securing the co-operation in his work of eminent reformers. Richard Cobden was one of these. He was the friend of Combe; he had in 1846, as a glorious result of several years' hard and continuous toil, converted the majority of the House of Commons to the principles of free trade ; and he was looked upon as the man most competent to carry out any great social reform which would be of advantage to the people. Ellis made Cobden's acquaintance and sought to secure his co-operation in the work of national education. Early in 1848 he published a small pamphlet containing an appeal to Cobden and the members of the Anti-Corn-Law League to take up the question, and concluding with a few questions and answers on "Secular education, what it is and what it ought "to be." In these he points out the object to be sought by education, viz., "to form such habits, to impart such know-
"ledge, and develop such a disposition, as will fit the
"future man to take his share in the business of life with
"comfort to himself and usefulness to others;" and comments severely upon the singular defect in the then education code, which, stamped with the authority of the Committee of Council, admitted a knowledge of Latin and Greek among its "optional" subjects, but excluded a knowledge of the arrangements and relations of social life from both its "essential" and "optional" list. The appeal to the Council of the League concludes : "Form from among yourselves a
"National Board to promote and watch over the diffusion
"and improvement of secular education. Let the efforts
"of this board be directed to organising new schools, im-
"proving old ones, and giving a useful direction to the

"education which is attempted. This is no season for
"hesitation or delay. Never were activity and determi-
"nation more called for. Push forward, then, to victory—
"to the most glorious victory that man ever won for his
"kind, a victory over folly, vice, crime, and misery. Devote
"yourselves vigorously to the work, and co-operation,
"sympathy, and money in abundance will be forthcoming."

Before publishing this pamphlet, Ellis showed the manuscript of the questions on secular education to Cobden himself. The following letter to Dr. Hodgson tells us of his first
interview with Cobden, and the impression produced on his
mind. It has much of interest in it besides the reference to
Cobden.

"9th April, 1848.

"It was the very Tuesday of the prohibited dinners[1]
"that I had my first interview with Mr. Cobden. I had
"previously written those few questions on secular educa-
"tion for the instruction and exercise of some young
"friends. My lengthened conversation with Mr. Cobden
"left upon my mind the impression that he did not feel
"so deeply as could be wished the *paramount* importance
"of such teaching and training as I advocate, a feeling
"likely to be shared by numbers whom he influences;
"and this led me on the spur of the moment to write the
"'Appeal.' I sent the MS. to him, and received verbally
"and in writing the expression of his hearty concurrence,
"accompanied, I regret to say, by the statement that
"except by the aid of his name no co-operation was to be
"expected from him on account of the already too
"numerous claims on his time and strength. When the
"MS. was returned to me, not wishing to rely entirely on
"my own judgment, I requested my friend John Mill to
"give me the benefit of his opinion and criticism, which

---

[1] The public dinners at Paris, the prohibition of which by Louis Philippe
was the exciting cause which led to the French Revolution of 1848.

"he did very obligingly, and suggested several amend-
"ments which I adopted, but expressing his most hearty
"concurrence in my expositions. Even now I am by no
"means so vain as to fancy that I have put down my
"thoughts in the best shape or expressed them in the
"most appropriate terms. Of this I am confident, that
"the matter attempted to be expressed is that to which
"the larger part of mankind, and of the instructors of
"youth in particular, are *practically* blind, and it is of
"unspeakable importance that they should cease to be so.

"I cannot say that I am very partial to the form of
"questions and answers or of catechisms. I was asked
"for them and was induced to write them as a sequel to
"the *Outlines* to aid teachers in a branch of science to
"which hitherto they have been total strangers. And as
"it is forced upon me by painful experience every day
"how men as at present educated can express their
"assent and approbation to what they *merely* read, and
"afterwards assent to and approve something, smartly
"put and antithetically expressed, of a completely opposite
"tendency, I thought it would be worth some little pains
"to traverse the same ground in a different direction in
"order to confirm truths previously expounded. Would
"that I could have better performed my appointed task.

"I had already noticed the extract from Chevalier.[1]
"Very good, and quite true; and I am happy to say there
"are others besides striving hard to enlighten French
"darkness, and they will succeed, too. The Revolution,
"which has transferred power to the masses, is quickening
"the well informed to a sense of their duty, and this,
"among the dangers and disasters, is the blessing of the
"Revolution. Happy will it be for us if the enlightened
"and powerful will be roused to the performance of their

---

[1] Michel Chevalier was the leading advocate of free trade in France, the friend and ally of Cobden.

"duties by something short of a revolution. This is no
"time for Dilettante legislation, Dilettante literature, or
" Dilettante teaching.

 "Lovett's school at the National Hall numbers, I am
" told, two hundred boys. I have not yet seen it, but have
"undertaken to go up there soon and give voluntary
"class lessons in social science once a week. I received
"the annual report of the Liverpool Mechanics' Institute,
"and about the same time that of the London University.
"They made me melancholy. I saw the forms and frag-
"ments of éducation; the clothes and the body, but the
"slightest conceivable symptom of a soul within. I could
"fancy in perusing them that these establishments, to
"borrow Combe's illustration, teach six names for a horse,
"and leave their pupils quite in the dark as to its nature
"and qualities. If I were asked 'What are these people
"'aiming at?' charity would induce me to answer that
"probably they had never put that question to themselves.
"There was one thing, I might add, that they certainly
"never had aimed at, viz., 'to fit the beings whose
"'education was entrusted to them to live in this world
"'with comfort to themselves and usefulness to others.'

 "I had written thus far in the morning when I was
"interrupted by two visitors—one my neighbour, Mr.
"Ricardo, a magistrate; the other Lovett, the moral-force
"Chartist. They both seem a little uneasy about to-
"morrow's proceedings.[1] The latter, as you may well
"suppose, is vehemently opposed to all O'Connor's pro-
"ceedings. How miserable it is that a man so low in all
"the qualities that ought to command respect should, by
"the defects in our institutions, and by the want of earnest-
"ness and judgment in our rulers, be enabled to wield
"such extensive influence over the uneasy classes? Must

-----

[1] The Chartist demonstration on Kennington Common, led by Feargus
O'Connor.

"what Bentham said be always true, that the oppressed
"many can only expect relief by making the ruling few
"uncomfortable?   There is truly in what is passing among
"and around us much to induce a spirit of mournful solici-
"tude, and yet not of despair, for, as I wrote to George
"Combe, 'Aristocracies may pass away, but the people
"'will remain.'"

Cobden's views on education seem to have progressed
under the influence of Ellis and Combe, and he began to
see the importance of thoroughly good secular schools—
a term which would be better expressed by the name
"character-forming unsectarian schools."   During the next
few years he was much occupied both in and out of Parliament upon the subject; and the letter from George Combe
to Mattieu Williams which follows gives interesting information upon what he and Ellis were trying to accomplish
in 1853.   He says :—

"London, 1st July, 1853.

"W. Mattieu Williams, Esq.

"My dear sir,—Mr. Ellis has offered through me to
"furnish £5,000 to Mr. Cobden to found a normal train-
"ing school for secular education in Manchester, if he,
"Mr. Cobden, will place himself at the head of it   I have
"seen Mr. Cobden repeatedly, and he is greatly advanced
"from his position last year in our direction.   He says
"that Lord John's Bill will be withdrawn.   He considers
"it to have given Baines a fresh handle for his opposition,
"and thus to have done positive mischief.   He now
"considers Mr. Ellis as in the right, and will use all
"his influence to induce the Manchester Educational
"Association to institute a first-rate secular school there,
"and to point to it as showing what such an education
"is.   He will defend secular education in the House of
"Commons, and insist that the same allowances shall be
"made to secular schools as are made to sectarian schools.
"His chief difficulty in regard to a training school is that it

"would require a large annual subscription to maintain it,
"and he doubts if this could be relied on in Manchester;
"but he will consult with the Manchester educationists
"and see Mr. Ellis on the subject.—Yours sincerely,

"GEO. COMBE."

Another prominent politician whom Ellis tried about this time to interest in his plans was the Right Honourable W. E. Gladstone. But, as might be expected from Mr. Gladstone's strongly orthodox predilections, his mind was not one which proved accessible to Ellis's appeal. The letter from Mr. Gladstone is lost; Ellis's letter to Combe enclosing it for Combe's perusal cannot be obtained; but we can imagine from the appeal to Cobden and the League what they were, and the following extract from a letter from Combe to Ellis shows what the answer was :—

"20th April, 1848.

"Mr. Gladstone's letter is an exponent of the state of
"mind of a large portion of estimable persons in this
"country whose errors form the grand bulwark to
"educational progress. It has greatly puzzled me how to
"deal with them. I see by your letter that you treat him,
"and I presume others of his class, as if they were in the
"right in their own high and holy position, and try and
"soften their prejudices and induce them by gentle treat-
"ment to consider your principles, under the assurance
"that there is nothing in them that really conflicts with
"their own.—Yours sincerely,   "GEO. COMBE."

A few quotations from letters written during these years (1846-1853) to Hodgson will be interesting as containing Ellis's opinions on various matters of interest in relation to political and other questions of the day. The first two refer to a newspaper controversy between the *Manchester Examiner* and the *Manchester Times* (two Manchester papers which afterwards amalgamated) upon the ethics of mercantile speculation, one of them having commented severely on the

conduct of merchants who held stocks of corn or other
commodities in the hope of profit.

"1st September, 1847.

"A merchant is essentially a speculator (the latter
"being what Bentham would call a dyslogistic expression).
"He is neither a good nor a bad man for buying corn in
"the month of May, whether he buy at forty shillings or
"a hundred shillings a quarter—whether the approach-
"ing harvest prove abundant or deficient. The result of
"a harvest is always a matter of conjecture at that time,
"and miserable would the country be which was unprovided
"with speculators. If the harvest prove abundant the
"speculator loses; but that no more makes him a bad
"man than his gain from a bad harvest would make him
"a good one. Has he been upright, truthful, and *reasonably*
"*prepared to meet unfavourable contingencies?* The
"answer to this question will be furnished by an
"investigation in each individual case, and I fear but too
"frequently it will be found that love of vain expenditure
"leading to greediness of gain and accompanied by an
"almost total ignorance of the *principles of commerce* cause
"that ruin in which so many are involved. Our merchants
"are practical coasting navigators who venture on voyages
"to the Pacific and Indian seas without chronometers and
"not knowing how to work lunars; and yet they fearlessly
"carry on, despising those who would warn them of their
"danger."

"5th September, 1847.

"A question of political economy is a question of
"morals. The conclusions of political economy (rightly
"understood) are conclusions in morals or no conclusions
"at all. Political economy, being subordinate, can never
"be in antagonism to morals. But in newspaper contro-
"versies, as elsewhere, there seems to be more satisfaction
"in exposing an adversary than in expounding a truth."

The following letters relate to the commercial panic of

1847 and to a book of Blanqui's which Hodgson lent him about this time :—

> "19th September, 1847.

"More failures in the city, and more, I fear, still to "come! Silly babblers attribute them, some to Peel's "currency or bank bill, some to free trade! The occur-"rences are nearly simultaneous, say they. Not more "simultaneous, I answered to one of these wiseacres, than "the discovery of Leverrier's planet. Harmer's great "declaration of insolvency had been ripening for years, "and the same may be said of others that have lately "occurred. Of course there are others not chargeable either "with imprudence or greediness who become involved. As, "when a reckless man burns down his own house, he may "also burn his immediate neighbour's or a whole district. "I am somewhat of an economist, and have also some "little experience in business, and I volunteer my opinion "to you on these matters, because *practical* men will wish "to persuade you that the widespread ruin around us, so "much to be deplored, is attributable to Peel rather than to "their own blindness in neglecting, as Combe would say, "to place themselves in harmony with the laws of nature, "and particularly in their neglecting to establish the "supremacy of the moral law.

"I have read Blanqui. I must give my opinion upon "his work dogmatically, for reasons would occupy more "space and time than I have at command. A translation "would not do. A person competent to translate it ought "to be able to write a better book. He is an enlightened "man and his views are generally correct. There is nothing "original in the work; his illustrations are adapted for "France, not for England, his arrangement might be "greatly improved, his style is frequently florid and "diffuse, and his reasoning not always conclusive. Upon "many of the more difficult questions, of interest particu-"larly, he has not yet, as the sailors would say, found

"bottom, but yet unconsciously talks away quite at his
"ease. With all this, so far ahead is he of the prevailing
"public opinion that I should always be glad to hear of
"his book being in anybody's hand either here or in
"France, although I cannot recommend anybody to
"venture upon publishing a translation."

"3rd January, 1848.

"We had another large failure in London to close the
"old year, and there must be much loss, difficult to endure,
"which does not meet the public eye. There would be
"some consolation in the midst of all this suffering had
"we but reason to think that mankind were at this moment
"reading their lesson right. Some, I doubt not, are
"profiting, but for the mass future lessons in suffering
"will be required and will consequently come.

"The Rev. Mr. Dawes sent me some weeks ago his
"*Suggestive Hints towards Improved Secular Instruction*
"(Groombridge and Sons, Paternoster Row). If strange
"to you, I would venture to recommend it for your pre-
"paratory section. The spirit that reigns throughout this
"truly practical work is excellent."

The following letters give interesting glimpses of the work
he was doing during this period :—

"22nd May, 1848.

"I am glad to hear that you found my pamphlet (the
"appeal to Cobden and the League) transferred into a
"Welsh paper; still more glad should I be to hear of my
"*Outlines* being in a Welsh school. I begin to see that
"my labours during the last two years will not have been
"thrown away. Economical science is destined (and that
"soon) to be taught in all our primary schools. George
"Combe has taken me by the hand most cordially. A
"German friend has translated my *Outlines*, with some
"additions that I gave him, and sent it to an influential
"quarter in Berlin, through which he expects it will be
"introduced into the Prussian primary schools.

" Mill, I am proud to say, honoured me with a copy
"of his magnificent work" (*The Principles of Political
Economy*), "worthy of its predecessor" (his work on *Logic*).
" Read what he thinks of the popular question, and what
" George Grote says in the *Spectator* of 13th in reviewing
" Mill. What a disgrace it is that such knowledge, so
"capable of being expounded and diffused, should be,
"as it were, ignored and disregarded. This must be
"endured no longer."

" 13th February, 1850.

" An expression in your present note conveys to my
"mind the impression (not for the first time) that I
"appear to you rather to turn my back upon or shut
"myself out from much useful assistance that otherwise
"would readily come to me from others. If I really do
"appear to you in this light, some unfortunate lights and
"shades must, I think, have placed me to disadvantage
"in your field of vision. I am now far advanced in the
"fourth year of my attempt to introduce the systematic
"teaching of social science into all schools of primary
"instruction. I have reaped many indirect gratifications
"that I did not calculate upon, and principally through
"my wish to avail myself of any assistance that was
"obtainable. Among the first was that of becoming
"acquainted with you, and afterwards with Mr. Combe,
"who has co-operated so cordially with me. Two most
"excellent friends here, upon whom I have made a deep
"impression, are actively engaged in teaching in the same
"manner as myself, and others are forming themselves. I
"have also formed a very intimate *liaison* with a most
"talented French gentleman who went back to Paris about
"ten days ago for the purpose of pushing the subject at
"head-quarters there. I have a letter from him this very
"day. He has been conferring with M. Barthélémy St.
"Hilaire, a man of some celebrity, keenly alive to the
"importance of what I am doing, and enthusiastically

L

" desirous of urging on something similar for France. He
" has also been most favourably received at the very foun-
" tain head of power, and has made arrangements for the
" translation and publication of the elementary works, as
" well as some of the articles, which I have written. I
" have taken some pains, besides, to put myself in commu-
" nication with schoolmasters, and seldom lose an oppor-
" tunity of producing an impression when I think I may
" do so without becoming a bore.

" I teach three times a week in the schools, and I am
" about to teach an adult class of working men. I am
" also on the point of publishing my *Progressive Lessons*,
" of which I gave a sketch in the *Westminster Review*,
" and a second edition of the *Outlines of Social Economy*,
" considerably enlarged, and I hope improved. I may
" mention besides that I have been in correspondence
" with the Rev. R. Dawes and the Rev. H. Moseley, the
" latter of whom has been at one of my lessons, and
" the former intends to come when next in town. I
" hope this will prove that I do not foolishly cut myself
" off either from opportunities of self-improvement or of
" external assistance, and also that my time is too well
" and too fully employed to admit of my running after
" vain talkers or writers who, instead of helping me with
" useful work, would distract me with idle professions.

" In fact, I have now arrived at that crisis in my
" engagements that henceforward all who think that my
" co-operation with them, or theirs with me, will be useful,
" must come to me. My time is no longer my own to go
" anywhere, but I am not inaccessible, neither am I in-
" sensible to the value of every new recruit in the cause
" of improved secular education, and will gladly welcome
" any that you can send me. Much I might add of the
" good things that seem to me to be coming, but I will
" cherish no sanguine anticipations beyond what are
" necessary to keep me in good cheer for my work."

CHAPTER VIII

1854—1858.

Overwork—University College School—Lessons to the Royal Children—
Religion in Common Life—Where must we look for the Prevention of Crime—
Letters of Tom Brown—Visit to Dr. Hodgson—Death of George Combe.

THE eight years which followed Ellis's commencement
of the work of introducing systematic teaching of
social economy into schools was a period of constant and
unremitting labour. How much he had accomplished in that
period we have seen; how hard and close his toil must have
been may be gathered from the fact that after a visit of three
weeks which Mrs. Ellis made to the Isle of Wight in July,
1854, in consequence of the health of her younger daughter,
during which her husband joined her, first for five days and
subsequently for a further four days, she wrote to Dr.
Hodgson that it was "the first year since our marriage of
his ever having had a holiday." From the same letter we
learn that, in consequence of his not being so well as could
be wished, she persuaded him to take medical advice; and
what that advice was may be gathered from the following
letter, written a few months later to Dr. Hodgson, in which
he says:—

"25th December, 1854.

"With the exception of an adult class on Saturday
"afternoon, I have nearly abandoned teaching, and am
"warned not to think of resuming it for some time. At
"the office I am, if possible, busier than ever" (it will be
remembered the Crimean War had broken out in the previous
autumn, and the Allies were then besieging Sebastopol,

causing great anxiety and responsibility in the underwriting world), "but in the evenings I am indulging in ease,
"and shall be glad of your company to assist me in that
"unusual and laborious work. I have been amusing myself
"since I last saw you, writing a paper upon (I would give
"you a hundred trials at guessing what, and as you could
"not succeed I will tell you at once) the Mormons !!!   I
"was first led to think of it by an atrocious article in the
"*Times* of 15th September last, my object being to
"point out what are the duties of society towards the
"Mormons and to itself, and of the Mormons to society.
"It will, I think, be too long and not shaped for a review,
"but you may judge if you like when you come here
"whether in whole or in part you can make it available.

"I have been dreadfully remiss of late in my corre-
"spondence with our invaluable friend Mr. Combe—rather
"a slave to idleness and Mormonism.   If you think he
"will care for this and there is nothing in it that you do
"not wish him to know, forward it to him.   He will learn
"that he is not absent from my thoughts."

It was in the autumn of 1854, and probably in consequence of the warning which he had received against too
continuous mental exertion, that Ellis commenced the custom
of a change of scene in the autumn, which he continued
for many years. He also began to take occasional short
excursions.   In 1854 he hired a furnished house at Rose
Hill, Dorking, for six weeks; in the ensuing year he
occupied another house called "The Orchard," also at
Dorking, and paid a visit about the end of September to
his friend Mr. Bastard, at Charlton Marshall, Dorsetshire;
while in August, 1856, he went with Mrs. Ellis for a fortnight's excursion to Westmoreland and Cumberland.   In
subsequent years he obtained change of scene by taking a
house for a couple of months in some country suburb.
Twice he visited Esher; once Addington, near Croydon,
and in June, 1858, he and Mrs. Ellis paid Dr. Hodgson a

visit at Fronfelen, near Machynlleth, which he repeated in July for a fortnight with Mr. Shields as his companion. On all these occasions he specially enjoyed rambling about the country. The habit of taking long walks, which had been continued from his early married life, when he used to walk up from Croydon to the morning meetings in Threadneedle Street, lasted for many years after this, and his long rambles were only reduced or discontinued when his powers began to grow weaker. Throughout life it was his habit to walk one way to or from the City, and some of his friends used to drop in on him at the closing of the office for the pleasure of accompanying him in his southward or westward walk.

The following further extracts from his correspondence with Dr. Hodgson tell us something of his movements during the succeeding three or four years:—

"23rd February, 1855.

"Your note of yesterday, confirming all that I had "heard from our incomparable friend, Mr. Combe, and "announcing, besides, your projected lectures on economic "science, is most gratifying to me. You are at work "again, and, as a consequence, are brushing off the rust, "recruiting strength and vigour, and becoming happier.

"The very little value that I attach to classical litera- "ture and to the knowledge contained in it would not "have prevented me, had I been in your place and pos- "sessed of your attainments, from undertaking what you "have just completed,[1] and I rejoice that your attachment

---

[1] Dr. Hodgson had written an article on "Classical Instruction: its use and abuse," in the *Westminster Review* of October, 1853, which he re-published, with elaborate notes, as one of the parts of Chapman's Library for the people, in the ensuing year. It was a review of a book by his old master, Professor Pillans, entitled *The Rationale of Discipline*, in which, while advocating the teaching of the classics as part of the literary culture of a gentleman, he pointed out the number and importance of the subjects which the excessive amount of time devoted in most schools to the teaching of classics excluded from their curricula.

"to the relics of a once useful article does not blind you
"to the greater utility of more modern articles containing
"all that is worth preserving in the old, and that in addi-
"tion which, if suffered to go to decay, would throw us
"back upon Greek and Roman civilisation—a civilisation,
"I take it, that you would not prefer to our own. But
"whatever our individual views and prepossessions may
"be, if we would be employed or even listened to, we
"must conform in some respects to prevailing demand
"and opinion. We can then turn to account the power
"which we gain by doing well what is asked of us, in
"promoting what we think right, but which others are
"unprepared for.

"In this spirit I sat down to write my letter to the
"Quakers. They put forth opinions on morals with which
"I disagree. They say that theirs are founded on
"Scripture. My opinions are of course drawn from the
"consideration of what is conducive to general well-being.
"But to convict them in the eyes of the public I follow
"them to their own ground, and so long as the right of
"interpretation is conceded to us I would undertake to
"show other sects as well as Quakers that any tenets
"professed by them incompatible with general well-being
"were necessarily unwarranted by Scripture.

"Your hatred of the Quakers, however, appears to be
"somewhat unreasonable. They contradict themselves—
"talk one way and act another. They are unconscious of
"their inconsistency—they are hardened to it. Their
"whole teaching from their infancy has made confusion
"and contradiction orderly and harmonious to them. But
"in this respect, they suffer in common with nearly the
"whole world, and we must avoid hating the human race.
"Classically expressed, we must avoid misanthropy.

"I can think of no illustrations wherewith to help you.
"You have of course noticed the bread-disturbances at
"Liverpool; there are others in the Eastern parts of London

" recorded in the papers to-day. It might be worth your
" while to refer to the speech delivered at the opening of
" the Seaham Institution some weeks ago by the great
" historian Alison. What a refreshing spectacle to see a
" man of great historical reputation condescending to teach
" the people in reference to strikes, &c.!!"

25th April, 1855.

" It has been a great delight to me to hear both from
" our friend Mr. Combe and yourself, how usefully you
" have been employed at Edinburgh" (this refers to his
course of lectures on economic science). " I have no doubt
" that the enjoyment which awaits you at the Pyrenees
" will be heightened by the recollection of past work
" faithfully done during the winter.

" I shall be very glad to have some chat with you
" about the best method of introducing instruction on
" economic subjects to people who are mastered by
" prejudices and misconceptions in regard to the science
" of political economy. Interrogative lessons on physio-
" logy not only afford an opportunity of inviting attention
" to all the fundamental and more important parts of the
" science, but can scarcely be well given without doing so.
" It would appear almost like trifling with the children of
" the poor to get them to understand and tell us that good
" food, clothing, and shelter, cleanliness and ventilation,
" &c., are essential to the preservation of health, and not to
" show them that all these things are obtainable by them
" when they arrive at manhood, in spite of appearances to
" the contrary in their parents' dwellings, provided they
" take the pains to qualify themselves while young, and
" make a good use of their qualifications when the time
" arrives for their providing for themselves."

" 7th December, 1856.

" It has given me much pleasure to hear the details of
" your summer tour and the enjoyment that you seem to

"have drawn from it, and it rejoices me equally to learn
"the plan of your educational campaign. If the enjoy-
"ment from this is not quite so intense as the other, the
"deficiency will, I trust, be more than made up by the
"agreeable retrospection of labor well bestowed and
"success achieved in store for you.

   "My own doings just now towards helping the good
"cause are of the slenderest. I am presiding at the
"Saturday teachers' class, and am teaching once a week
"at the Foundling Hospital, where a young teacher from
"Mr. Shields' has been at work for a year and already in
"that time operated a marked improvement. The Rev. C.
"Mackenzie has just completed his annual examination of
"the school, and reported most favorably on its state.
"At the invitation of that reverend gentleman I have
"consented to conduct a large class of young men, at
"Crosby Hall, on Social Science. We are to begin soon
"after Christmas. The clergy, no longer able to shut out
"social science, are beginning to discover that it is per-
"fectly scriptural. The great educational triumph of the
"day, however, is Mr. Shields' class at University College
"School. Upwards of sixty boys always in attendance,
"and Mr. Key himself never absent from it. He has
"altered one of his days from Friday to Thursday, at
"the urgent request of several Jewish parents, who do
"not wish their boys to lose the lesson through its inter-
"ference with their Sabbath.

   "All these are little things to dwell upon, but they are
"little seeds which will unfold into large plants and over-
"shadow the earth."

The fact referred to in this last letter, the introduction of
the teaching of social science into University College School,
had caused Ellis great satisfaction. It was the first school
for the wealthier classes in which he had achieved this
success. Mr. Key, the then head master, was a valued
friend of his; and it was through Key's influence that the

consent of the Council was obtained. The following extract from the report of the Council of University College gives the opinion of that body on the innovation:—

"The Council had been apprised by the head master of
"a novelty in the course of instruction given in the school
"by the formation of a class in the elementary doctrines
"of Political Economy or of Industrial and Social Science,
"conducted by Mr. Shields. The Committee paid special
"attention to this subject, and report that Mr. Shields
"explains to his class the elementary doctrines of Political
"Economy in the widest sense of the word, as it bears not
"only on the production and distribution of wealth, but
"also on the conditions of industrial success and social
"happiness, and on the practical duties of each individual
"towards others; that the class is conducted without long
"and continuous expositions, in a conversational manner,
"so as to excite the interest and mental activity of the
"pupils and to impress on them the general principles
"of economical science, not as simple generalities, but
"illustrated copiously by familiar fact and usage; that it
"appears likely to impart a powerful stimulus to the
"intellect of pupils, and to form in them a habit of apply-
"ing sound and rational theory to the practical economy
"of society, and to prove a valuable addition to the
"course of instruction in the school."

Unfortunately the teaching of social science on Ellis's method was discontinued a few years later, Mr. Shields being compelled at that time to devote himself more closely to his own school at Peckham, and it has never been renewed. Mr. Key's successor has not become aware of the immense value of social economy, taught as a character-forming subject and an incentive to right conduct, and although he has had classes on political economy at University College School, they have not been conducted by masters qualified to teach it orally, but on the anti-quated plan—by the use of elementary treatises of the old type, read as text books by the pupils and examined on by the teachers. Unfortunately this method of teaching it too often leads to the mere acquisition of verbal propositions without the thorough comprehension and assimilation of the principles contained in them. Many who have studied it in this way have said that the subject thus taught was almost always felt to be dry, tedious, and uninteresting; while from pupils who have learned the subject as taught at the Birkbeck Schools there is but one report, namely, that it became one of the most interesting and absorbing of all their school lessons.

It was during this period—in the year 1855—that Ellis was requested to give a course of lessons to a class of pupils of far higher rank than any whom he had yet taught. Hitherto his lessons had been given either to children of the working classes at primary schools, or to teachers of similar schools who assembled on Saturday afternoons; he was now invited to teach the subject to a class of Royal rank. The great pains taken by the late Prince Consort in the education of the Royal children are well known, and that he devoted his utmost energies to secure them the best preparation possible to prepare them for the high stations which they were destined to fill. Some years before this, His Royal Highness had consulted George Combe upon the subject of their education, and subsequently from time to time invited his advice. Combe had lent him Ellis's book on education, which had much interested him. It led him to invite Ellis to wait upon him at Buckingham Palace, and, after a full explanation of the method of teaching the science of conduct which Ellis adopted, to request him to give some lessons in it to the Royal children. Ellis willingly complied with the Prince's request and gave them two courses, the former to the eldest four, viz., the Princess Royal (now Empress Victoria of Germany), the Prince of Wales, Princess Alice (afterwards Grand Duchess of Hesse Darmstadt), and Prince Alfred, Duke of Edinburgh; and the latter to the two princes only. For upwards of a year (except when the Court was absent from London) he attended at Buckingham Palace on Saturday afternoons, and led his youthful pupils to understand what they might otherwise never have mastered—the constitution and working of the complicated social and economic life of a nation, and the laws which ought to direct the actions of the individuals constituting it, in the guidance of which they might in future life have so great an influence. The princes and princesses whom he taught never forgot his lessons; the Princess Royal especially has never missed an opportunity of expressing her deep and grateful acknowledgments to him. She communicated with him long after she had quitted England for the land of her adoption, over which she was destined to reign for, alas, so short a period. Within the last two or three years of Ellis's life, when he had withdrawn from active work, she availed herself of the occasion of a visit to England to write him personally and ask him to pay her a visit and drink a cup of afternoon tea with her at Marlborough House, where she was staying with the Prince of Wales. Ellis wrote and apologised for his inability through infirmity to attend Her Imperial Highness, but expressed the great pleasure he should have in seeing her again if she would visit him. This suggestion she promptly complied with by calling on him at his residence near the Regent's Park, and spending an hour or two with him. Ellis derived the liveliest pleasure from this visit, for his lessons had led him to understand the great powers and noble disposition of the Princess, which in the sorrows and anxieties of her later life have been so fully manifested.

The giving of this course of lessons led Ellis to reduce them to writing, and to publish them for general use in a somewhat different form from any of his previous books. The original manuscript is merely headed "Conversational "Lessons introductory to the Study of Moral Philosophy."

But, some time after he had commenced his lessons, the sermon delivered at Crathie Church, by Rev. John Caird, was published by the special command of the Queen, who had been much delighted by it, under the title of *Religion in Common Life.* Ellis was much struck by the coincidence of the views expressed theoretically by Mr. Caird, as to the principles which should guide conduct in every day life, with those which he was trying to introduce into school education, in connection with clear and definite knowledge of the social conditions under which those principles were to be applied. Caird says: "To be religious

"in the world—to be pious, and holy, and earnest minded
"in the counting house, the manufactory, the market place,
"the field, the farm—to carry out our good and solemn
"thoughts and feelings into the throng and thoroughfare
"of daily life—this is the great difficulty of our Christian
"calling." And afterwards, considering religion in the light of an art, he defines it to be "the art of being and of "doing good." But, as Ellis points out in his preface, Caird's sermon is not even an attempted or intended exposition of the duties of common life, but rather an exhortation to the proper performance of those duties, whatever they may be, and a solemn warning that no attention, however regular, to rites and ceremonies can be taken as a substitute for good works. The knowledge of the duties of common life, the performance of which is justly stated by him to be the "art" of religion, constitutes what he appropriately calls its "science." But what are these duties? What is this science? This was the enquiry to which Ellis's lessons to the Royal children had been devoted, and it was from this view of the subject that he afterwards, when sending his work to the press, decided to alter the original title by prefixing to it the words "A Layman's "Contribution to the Knowledge and Practice of Religion "in Common Life."

In this book Ellis traverses much the same course as

in his previous works. But on a careful perusal of the work it will be found that the pervading thought is still more intensely that of personal duty. Every chapter leads up to the thought of what ought to be done under the social circumstances explained in it. The thought of individual conduct, which is conspicuously absent from most other works on economics, is the pervading thought in this work. One or two quotations will illustrate this. In the very first chapter, as an outline of what he proposes to teach, he tells his Royal pupils (page 17):—

" Before we enter upon the consideration of these ques-
"tions, at the risk even of some repetition, I will ask you to
"examine a little more at length what is comprised under
"the word 'conduct.' It furnishes us with a name, in fact, for
"the subject that I am inviting you to study—our actions—
"the consequences that flow from them—the causes that
"lead to them. Where is the individual deserving to be
"classed among rational beings, who has not meditated,
"and does not perpetually meditate upon the subject?
"who does not, whatever may be his convictions of duty,
"moral, social, and religious, on some occasions, in some
"emergencies, say to himself—Ought I to do this?—Ought
"I to do that? or in one question,—What ought to be my
"conduct? The thoughtful, conscientious man is anxious
"about his own conduct. Why is he anxious? Because
"he knows that certain lines of conduct are followed by
"certain consequences, and other lines of conduct by other
"consequences."

And again and again he recurs to the duty of those who are placed above the rest of mankind in station, position and wealth, to use their advantages for the benefit of mankind, and the responsibility of those that neglect to do so, but waste their wealth extravagantly. These lessons are rather more fully elaborated in this book than in the previous ones, where the pupils were chiefly from the humbler classes. Pointing out the benefits which all classes of society derive from the

able and intelligent conduct of capitalists, he continues
(page 167):—

"While it is impossible to conceive how employers,
"whose whole energy and intelligence are devoted to the
"maintenance and increase of wealth by distributing wages
"among labourers according to their respective producing
"capacities, can be chargeable with the miserable con-
"dition of the destitute, it is scarcely possible to avoid
"charging upon the great consumers of wealth some
"connivance at that misery, seeing how small a part of
"their enjoyment of wealth consists in the alleviation of
"misery, and how much smaller a part, if any, is found by
"them in well directed efforts at its diminution or
"prevention."

And the conclusion to which, in the last chapter, he leads
his pupils, is a noble exposition of the objects which the
highborn and wealthy who desire to do their duty should
strive to attain (page 455):—

"To ask of people, as we see them, to forego all luxury
"and enjoyment for the sake of doing good may be sublime,
"but it is the sublime of folly.   To aim, by improved
"teaching and training, to lead the young to look upon
"doing good as the height of luxury and enjoyment, if it
"be sublime, is the sublime of wisdom.   With our present
"educational experience, it would be premature to express
"an opinion as to the extent of the change that may come
"over men's minds in regard to the employment of their
"wealth as a means of procuring the higher enjoyments
"and refinements of life.   Greater changes are noted in
"the world's history even than the one which you and I
"may think not very far distant.   That the contemplation
"of a high state of well-being among our fellow creatures,
"especially if coupled with a consciousness of having done
"one's utmost to promote it, is destined to be looked upon
"as the most refined, as well as the most secure, of all
"enjoyments in the holding, and therefore the wisest

"object of every man's ambition. As a means of self-
"discipline and improvement, what holier and better
"purpose can young people place before themselves than
"the attainment of habits and talents, with a view to
"devote them to the service of our common humanity!"

The *Religion in Common Life* is an elaboration of the series
of lessons which had been more concisely sketched in previous
works, and as such is of the highest value to teachers who
wish to prepare themselves, by careful study of the line of
thought to be followed, for conveying the important knowledge contained in it to their pupils. The close and consecutive logical building up of the fabric of social life is
found in this as in Ellis's other works. The illustrations,
the arguments, and, above all, the constant practical and
personal bearing of those arguments upon the duties of
common life which are required to be performed by the
individual members of a community, are more full and
complete in this work than in its predecessors. But as a
literary composition it can hardly be called interesting.
The reviewers, looking upon it from the literary side, criticised it unfavourably. Most of them failed to realise its
great object and meaning, or to gather from it the central
thought which actuated the author. By readers and educationists, who have imbibed that thought, it has always
been highly valued. But by the critics, who form their
impression of a book by its attractiveness to the general
public, it was not favourably received. The *Economist* and
Athenæum noticed it, but very coldly ; the book was scarcely
understood by those organs of opinion in its true character
of a carefully arranged storehouse, in which teachers might
learn how to teach the practical ethics of social life. And
they criticised it accordingly. This Ellis was prepared for.
In a letter to Dr. Hodgson, he says :—

" 12th January, 1858.

"Mrs. Hodgson's remarks upon the contents of my book
"are most gratifying to me. I seem to have no fear of

"the impression likely to be made upon anybody who
"will be at the pains to study it. Difference of opinion
"and objection to parts may be elicited, but acknowledg-
"ment of the importance of the subjects expounded and
"discussed will not be withheld. I have not seen the
"*Athenæum*, but with that or any other literary periodical
"I would bet large odds that the sentiments expressed
"would be such as would indicate that the writer either
"had not been at the pains to read the work, or was
"incapable of understanding what he had read."

In the same year in which Ellis wrote the *Religion in
Common Life* he also published a short treatise investigating
a problem of social life which he had not hitherto dealt with
except incidentally. It is entitled *Where must we look for
the further prevention of crime?* and in treating this important question he first examines in his usual thorough manner
the conditions of social well-being and the kind of conduct
which, from their tendency to destroy or prevent well-being,
must be prevented by united social action, that is, declared
to be criminal.

Classifying the means of promoting good and preventing
bad conduct into two heads—the governmental and the
educational—he first deals with the former—the criminal
law of the state. He investigates the various circumstances
under which different crimes are committed and the tempta-
tions which have led the culprits to violate laws of which
they are perfectly aware, and by which they will necessarily
subject themselves to the risk of punishment. He then
shows that the mitigation of the cruel and vindictive punishments which formerly prevailed, coupled with the greater
certainty that crime will meet with detection and punishment,
has largely conduced to its diminution. But after reviewing
the possible improvements which may be hoped from
further progress in criminal legislation, the conclusion cannot
be resisted that existing punishments are insufficient to
counterbalance temptation. But, if they can neither be

dispensed with or further reduced on the one hand, nor added to on the other, our principal hope for the further diminution of crime must be in subtracting from the temptation.

This leads to the educational method of preventing crime. The proximate cause of crime is the state of feeling in the person tempted which induces him to perpetrate it when others abstain or even recoil from it. Is it or is it not possible to carry out the precept "Train up a child in "the way he should go?"—a maxim which may be said to include the converse, viz., "Neglect to train him and "he will go in some one of the ways in which he should "not go."

"Active measures," he says (page 42), "are taken by "society to prevent the exposure, the starving and the "killing of children. And who will say that they ought "not to be taken? But if there be anything really to "admire in the life of a good mother—if it be true that "an ill-trained child is almost sure to go wrong—which "is the greatest act of cruelty: to leave a child unfed or "untrained? to kill the child or condemn it to a life of "infamy and suffering?"

We need not analyse at length the method and subject of teaching and training needed for this purpose, in which Ellis repeats the explanations of his former books, and works out the science of forming character upon the same lines as his purely educational writings. Few will in these days disagree with the conclusion that great, though gradual, social amelioration will result from the more general and systematic application of these principles. But in spite of this, there must be much infirmity and mal-tendency of character to deplore ; and in the concluding chapter, Ellis proceeds to consider what he had not dealt with in previous writings, namely, how criminal dispositions unguarded against by early education, and developing themselves in criminal conduct, are to be dealt with so as to relieve

M

society from some portion of its suffering—or, in other words, the best reformatory methods.

In discussing this subject, he first considers the cases where the offenders are young and have fallen into crime through neglect, or where, in the case of older criminals, the circumstances betoken no deep-seated depravity or no incurable weakness. In those cases, duty to society necessitates the confinement of the criminal, and that his fare, while he is maintained out of others' earnings, should be of the humblest. But in cases of this sort, and also where the predisposing cause of crime is idleness, that is, a distaste for industrial employment, or extravagance, that is, a hankering after expense unmindful of the future, it seems clear that these habits may be in some measure counteracted by judicious training.

The prisoner's discipline admits of being so conducted as that each step made by him in producing power shall be accompanied by additional indulgence, of his own earning, being placed at his disposal; of thought for the future, and present exertion or sacrifice with a view to the future being voluntarily adopted by him, so that habits of industry and forethought may be implanted or strengthened. And the practice of inflicting hard labour in the nature of a penance is strongly commented on.

"There has been—" he says (page 83), "must it not be "confessed that there still is?—a practice of condemning "prisoners to hard labour as a punishment. Which of the "two methods of treatment is better calculated to exercise "a favourable influence over men who have been led into "crime through a distaste for labour—and who are to be "once more returned to society—imprisonment with "hard labour, or imprisonment with the opportunity of "mitigating the suffering under it, and of shortening its "term, by labour ever growing less and less hard as the "new habit gains strength? Whether to form or reform "characters, is it not desirable that a taste for industrial

"employment should be induced, as well as the application
"through which knowledge and skill may be brought to
"aid industrial effort? Ought we not to suspect that
"some of our want of school success may be owing
"to the practice of imposing tasks upon idle boys;
"and that some of our want of reformatory success may
"be attributed to the practice of punishing by hard
"labour?"

Upon criminals who are less susceptible to reformation
Ellis's views are similarly based upon a consideration of the
disposition of the criminal, both when imprisoned, and as a
condition for setting him free. He comments in very strong
language upon the practice of condemning convicts to terms
of imprisonment, at the end of which they are to be let loose
on society without the least regard to the state of mind in
which they quit prison; a practice which he thinks has led
to deplorable consequences.

" The exclusion from society," he says (page 88), "of the
" elder criminals—in other words, their confinement—must
" be cared for. Tests of reformation which no hardened
" convict can possibly stand must be adopted. To over-
" look such obvious rules of common sense—to sentence
" convicts to terms of imprisonment of shorter or longer
" duration, as punishments for different kinds of offences,
" and at the expiration of these terms to turn them loose
" upon society without any regard to the disposition in
" which they return to their old haunts and companions—
" surely there can be no such method of dealing with
" criminals still prevalent amongst us, or, if there be, it
" cannot be endured much longer! What! sentence
" drunken, lazy, dissipated, brutal men, who have beaten
" their wives and children, embezzled the property of
" their employers, committed frauds and assaults, and
" resisted the police, to a few months' or years' imprison-
" ment ; and then, without more ado, set them at large, to
" assault, plunder, and harass all who come near them, to

"occupy over and over again the time of the police and
"administrators of justice, and add expense to outrage!
"Incredible!　If to do that which is opposed to the general
"well-being constitute a criminal or an ignorant act, what
"must we say of the legislators who enact such laws or
"leave them unrepealed or unimproved?　Is it easy to
"acquit them of both ignorance and criminality, or to
"refrain from invoking them to purge themselves from
"the disgrace which the charge of either must fix upon
"them?

"Let the reformable be reformed, and let unerring tests
"of reform be used for the sake both of the convicts
"about to be released and of society.　Let the unreform-
"able be retained in confinement.　But the expense will
"be enormous, and it will be difficult to meet the demand
"for increased prison room!　This may be.　Nevertheless
"one advantage will be obtained from the concentration
"into groups of the expense and inconvenience entailed
"upon society by a large criminal population.　Collected
"in masses it is more likely to meet the attention which
"it deserves, and to draw forth efforts to obtain relief
"from it.　Whereas the larger expense and inconvenience
"arising out of repetitions of crime, recaptures, recom-
"mittals, and repeated trials may pass unheeded.

"When society has once recognised the fact—to which
"it has not as yet opened its eyes—that there are criminals,
"as there are lunatics, so confirmed as to make their cure
"hopeless, and their restoration to liberty almost criminal
"in those who sanction it, attention will be turned to the
"best methods for the maintenance and discipline of
"those whom it is impossible to shake off.　Perchance
"it may be found that criminals, although incapable on
"entering jail, will, after a few months' judicious discipline,
"become capable of earning wherewithal to relieve society
"from the expense or from a large part of the expense of
"maintaining them."

And even when the convict has proved his reformation by the strongest tests, Ellis, in the plans which he recommends, does not forget the grave difficulty which a released criminal, even when reformed, has in gaining an honest living; he claims our sympathy for such a man, struggling against criminal courses and perhaps eventually relapsing into crime, and claims that something ought to be done to remove so glaring a social iniquity as that of almost compelling a penitent and reformed convict to resume his criminal career. To this end he proposes the establishment of industrial houses of refuge to which discharged criminals (and no unreformed criminals ought, he says, to be discharged) should have access, where employment under proper discipline would be provided for them, where they might stay till through the interference of their friends and relations, or their own energy, more remunerative employment is obtained for them. And, in conclusion, he concisely repeats his views as follows (page 92):—

"The cry that may be raised with advantage should
" be, ' Discharge no criminals who have once been convicted
" 'till you have taken the proper means to reform them,
" 'and to test the success of your application of these means.
" 'Organise, also, your reformatory establishments and
" 'your industrial houses of refuge, so as to make them as
" 'nearly as possible self-supporting. Do these things
" 'earnestly and intelligently, and, making every allowance
" 'for want of expertness in the officials available for the
" 'services required of them, you will at least accomplish
" 'this much:—there will be fewer criminals at large to
" 'terrify and corrupt society, and a great saving in the
" 'outlay at present occasioned by the necessity of re-
" 'capturing, recommitting, reconvicting, and reimprisoning
" 'the same individual.'"

But these proposals are for the protection of society against the crime which even in the most advanced state of society must be provided for. He again returns to the more hopeful—the preventive—method, and concludes this interesting investigation as follows (page 99):—

"There is, however, much room for hope in another
"direction. An education vastly superior to any-
"thing hitherto attempted and made universal, specially
"aiming at teaching what good conduct is and how it is
"to be attained, and at training so as to inspire a desire
"and love for good conduct—at teaching what bad con-
"duct is, and how it is to be avoided—and at training so
"as to induce a horror of bad conduct, is the means on
"which all intelligent and well-disposed men must fix
"their thoughts if they would effect any further sensible
"diminution in the number of criminals.

"Considerable time must elapse before education, let it
"be ever so much improved and extended, can be expected
"to prevent moral malformations. Such malformations
"will perhaps never be prevented. The solution of that
"problem must be bequeathed to future ages. Mean-
"while criminals and the criminally disposed are not to be
"endured at large, terrifying, distressing, and contami-
"nating society. Criminals must be hunted out, seized upon,
"tried, convicted, and placed in confinement. Further
"than this, all the criminally disposed, who have thwarted
"the efforts of education in their behalf, are not to be
"abandoned in despair as utterly irreclaimable. Some,
"perhaps most, of them ought to be subjected to reforma-
"tory discipline. The expectation, however, of a large
"measure of success in this latter and more difficult
"department of effort is hardly warranted. Where
"partial success has been attained, relapses are to be
"feared. To reform a character is surely a more arduous
"task than to form one; and how can we look for success
"in a difficult undertaking from those who are unequal to
"the easier? This consolation is in store for mankind.
"In proportion as they approach excellence in the per-
"formance of the easier duty, so will the strain upon

" them for the performance of the more difficult be lessened.
" Let them engage, then, in that holiest of duties, knowing
" no rest till child-neglect is become as obsolete as the
" slave trade—till institutions abound for educating the
" young so efficaciously that, when sent forth into the world,
" they may need no relief from the rates, fear no inter-
" ference from the police, nor overtax the capabilities of
" criminal reformers."

It was during the same year, 1857, that Ellis's attention
was strongly attracted to a book which had been recently
published, and had been extremely popular—having soon
run through several editions—named *Tom Brown's Schooldays*. The book is a very cleverly drawn picture of school
life at Rugby, between 1830 and 1837. It is written in a
charming style ; the descriptions of scenery are vivid and
interesting, and there is much dramatic power in the narrative of the various episodes of a boy's school life as he
gradually progresses from the lower school to the rank of a
sixth-form boy, captain of the eleven. But with this the
author shows the most remarkable failure to understand
the wretchedly bad moral tone of the state of things he is
describing, still less to realise the wonderful effects which
may be produced by judicious teaching and training, or the
method in which a schoolmaster can and ought to set about
a work of so vast importance to his pupils and society.
Ellis found in this sketch of Rugby life in William the
Fourth's reign, the description of a school where fagging in
its worst form was sanctioned by the authorities; where
there was scarcely an attempt to protect the little boys from
the tyranny of the bigger ones ; where stealing, running in
debt, bullying, gambling, drinking, cruelty carried almost to
death, lying and cheating, prevailed, sometimes known to,
sometimes even winked at by, Dr. Arnold, while on the
other hand he found the author telling his readers that "his
eye was everywhere," again and again indulging in fulsome
praises of his remarkable qualities as a teacher, and of the

wonderful effects produced by his government, and becoming almost rhapsodical over the effect of his sermons.

Yet this model teacher is elsewhere described as so utterly carried away by his anger in examining the lower fourth class, as to recompense a poor nervous lad suddenly called on to construe a piece of Latin, and making a comic mistake in his translation, by a box on'the ear which knocked him down over a form. On another occasion, he is described as knowing no better how to deal with a gross case of bullying than to pretend not to observe it, while he made private arrangements with a steady and strong præpostor to thrash the bully privately, that is, not in the master's presence but before the boys. Of such schools as Ellis longed to see existing the author seemed to have no idea. "Vulgus" (that is a daily eight lines of Latin composition), the grinding of Latin or Greek verses, the learning by rote of lines, and the cramming of other classics were all the lessons of which we hear. And even as to these, the description of Tom Brown's preparation of his "Vulgus" by the "traditionary" method (as the author facetiously terms the deception of the master by the fraudulent appropriation of previous boys' compositions) was met by the author with no stronger comment than "when did risk hinder boys from short cuts or pleasant paths." It is true that some two or three years later Tom (whose prominent characteristic is throughout represented to be his straightforwardness and honesty) is at last shown the folly and dishonesty of such a method of preparing his lessons, and persuaded to give it up by a young weak lad of his own age who is described as being Tom's good angel, and converting him into a noble, true, and earnest lad. But this is after the influence of Dr. Arnold and all his masters, during the first year or two of his stay, had not prevented his falling so low that an author tells us of Tom and his chief companion that "partly by their own fault—partly "from circumstances—partly from faults of others, they "found themselves outlaws, ticket-of-leave men, or what

"you will in that line—in short, dangerous parties, and
"lived the sort of hand-to-mouth, wild, reckless life, which
"such parties generally have to put up with."
Upon this book Ellis was prompted to publish three letters
purporting to be written in the name of Tom Brown to
Rev. Frederick Temple, M.A. (now Bishop of London), who
was then the head master of Rugby School. In these letters
he quoted passage after passage showing conduct of the
kind mentioned above with palliations, justifications, and
even expressions of approbation interspersed and even for
the worst stories no stronger comment than "I am writing
"of schools in our time and must give the evil with the
"good." How little idea the author had of what a school
should be, or what a good schoolmaster can and ought to do
is shown by quoting such passages as this:—"Boys follow
"each other in herds like sheep for good or evil; they
"hate thinking, and have rarely any settled principles.
"Every school indeed has its own traditionary standard
"of right and wrong, which cannot be transgressed with
"impunity, making certain things as low and blackguard
"and certain others as lawful and right."
And while showing vividly the grave faults of the book and
the deficiencies in moral perception shown by the writer, Ellis
explains for Mr. Temple's information his views as to the
objects to be aimed at, and the methods which should be
adopted, in a school really constituted and managed so as to
bring about the development of young plastic-natured boys
into good and noble men and citizens, knowing their duty,
trained to judge of the difficult problems of right and wrong
which will come before them in future life, and disposed by
that training to select and follow the right course. Ellis's main
object in writing the letter was not so much the wish to be
severe on the well-intentioned, though not clear-minded,
author, but to draw public attention to the defects of our
public schools, and to bring about their improvement. He
writes to Dr. Hodgson (who arranged for the publication

of his letters in the paper in which they appeared) as
follows:—

" 21st December, 1857.

" As you have read the book on which I am comment-
"ing, you will at once catch the drift of my remarks.
" My reason for putting them in the form which I have
"chosen is the belief that Mr. Temple is prepared to
"introduce considerable reforms into Rugby. A friend
"of mine has given him a copy of my book" (*Religion
in Common Life*) "and is trying to influence him in the
"right direction, with some prospect of success."

And, again, a day or two later:—

" 24th December, 1857.

" It is high time that men of sense should unite to put
"down the system of fagging, flogging, and cramming,
"still persevered in, under the pretence of education, in
"our public schools."

Incidentally (though it is not the chief object of the
letters) Ellis cannot help. pointing out the author's
vague undisciplined ideas about social matters generally,
and his disposition to indulge in somewhat virulent abuse of
everybody who happens not to meet with his special
approval. He quotes and shows the folly of such passages
as this:—

" I have been credibly informed and am inclined to
"believe that the various boards of directors—those
"gigantic jobbers and bribers—while quarrelling about
"everything else, agreed together, some ten years back, to
"buy up the learned profession of medicine, body and
"soul;"

and the author's comments on village feasts, about which he
remarks that gentlefolk and farmers have left off subscribing
to them by reason of "the further separation of classes
"consequent on twenty years of buying cheap and selling
"dear, and its accompanying overwork," from which it

would seem that the author supposed that the mercantile
practice of purchasing commodities where they are plentiful
and therefore in excess, and transporting them to where
they are scarce and therefore needed, tended to diminish
the quantity of commodities obtainable by the working
classes for their labour.

Very differently was Ellis impressed by the life of George
Stephenson, which came out about this time and which he
made the subject of a lecture delivered in several places.
This, with notices of other interesting events of the time,
will be found in the following letter to Hodgson during the
ensuing year:—

17th February, 1858.

"We are reading the life of George Stephenson. I am
"struck with the copiousness of the materials afforded to
"one inclined to speculate or write a lecture upon edu-
"cation. What an opportunity for contrasting the really
"efficient teaching and training received by Stephenson,
"while his education, in the ordinary acceptation of the
"term, appeared to be neglected, and that neglected or
"mis-directed in the case of too many others whose
"literary attainments are laboriously cared for.

"Buckle's *History of Civilization* has also come into
"my hands. Have you seen it? or do you know anything
"of the author? It is a wonderful production. His range
"of reading is prodigious, and his proficiency in academi-
"cal knowledge great and varied. With all this he thinks
"for himself and cannot fail to set others thinking
"also."

Ellis did not, however, after finishing his great work,
continue to hold quite so high an opinion of Buckle. He
found his great merit was in the collection and arrangement
of historical facts, but that his powers of generalization and
the inferences he drew from those facts were often materially
at fault. From a subsequent letter, we learn that he con-

sidered him "a lilliputian among philosophers—a giant
"among historians." A few days later he returns to
Stephenson.

22nd February, 1858.

"You know well enough, without my repeating it, how
"ready I am to echo your sentiment that our hopes are
"in the young, and yet I would not discourage attempts
"to enlighten and guide adults. George Stephenson,
"who was not easily daunted by difficulties, said that he
"could engineer materials, but could not engineer men.
"Those who have paid attention to the subject, see that
"the difficulty in engineering men will continue so long
"as the work is not entered upon while men are yet
"children. Pains are taken to select material of the right
"sort. Decayed timber and inferior metal are rejected as
"unusable, and yet surprise is expressed and disappoint-
"ment experienced because workmen who have been
"suffered to grow up uninformed and ill-disciplined
"cannot be turned to the best account."

About the beginning of 1858 a movement arose in the
city of London for commemorating the valuable work of
Mr. Thomas Tooke, who had recently died. It will be
remembered that Mr. Tooke had not only been the valued
friend of Ellis's father, but had in his own early life rendered
him great service, and had introduced him to Bentham and
the Mills. It will not be surprising that he gave his cordial
support to the proposal. It was thought by some people
that the foundation of a professorship of economic science at
King's College would be a suitable method of commemorating the author of the *History of Prices,* and as Dr. Hodgson
was at that time without any permanent occupation, it
occurred to Ellis that he might be a suitable professor if he
would accept the post.

The following letters to Hodgson show what was Ellis's
position in regard to it, but, as will be seen, Dr. Hodgson

was indisposed to accept the professorship at King's College, and nothing came of it:—

14th March, 1858.

" There is a disposition among the friends of the late Mr. " Thomas Tooke to raise a fund for the purpose of com- " memorating his services in promoting the acknow- " ledgment and application of economic truths. I shall " certainly take part in it, although a subordinate part. " One suggestion is to endow a professorship of economic " science at King's College. Our late friend, Mr. Cowper, " was, as you know, a professor there. Should this idea " be carried out, would the appointment be worth your " thinking of or would the fundamental principles of the " college be an insuperable bar to your acceptance of a " chair there? I mention the matter thus early so that " you may consider this among other projects that will " be placed before you, and, if you do not reject it *in* " *limine*, I can keep you advised of the proceedings " towards accomplishing the object proposed and its " probable issue. At present it has not gone beyond the " talk of a few friends, preparatory to a more formal " meeting."

" 21st March, 1858.

" My sentiments are sufficiently in accordance with " yours to preclude me from entertaining a wish to found " and endow a professorship at King's College, but as an " old friend to Mr. Tooke, one whose family has been " deeply indebted to him, and who is personally under " great obligations to him, I could not refuse to concur in " a testimonial to him, such as is acceptable to his other " friends and is supposed to be in consonance with his " own views. I shall not fail to use all my influence to make " a testimonial to my late respected friend contribute to " that advancement, the contemplation of which charms " my vacant hours and the promotion of which is the " principal aim of my efforts.

"The prevailing educational disorder is little understood
"by the professor race, and not likely to be mitigated by
"them even when they enjoy freedom under 'really
"'liberal institutions.' There is no great difficulty in
"founding colleges and schools or in engaging professors
"and teachers. The difficulty is to get common sense
"into the heads of professors and teachers in combination
"with the capacity of imparting it."

In June, 1858, Ellis, accompanied by Mrs. Ellis and his
daughters, paid the visit, which we have already mentioned,
to Dr. Hodgson at Fronfelen, a beautiful mountain residence
which Hodgson had taken for twelve months in Merioneth-
shire, between Machynlleth and Dolgelly. It was for only a
fortnight: but the walks which they took over the hills and
through the valleys of that charming country were so
healthful and enjoyable that Ellis repeated his visit for
another fortnight, with Mr. Shields as a companion, about
the end of July. On his return from the latter visit (which
he made *viâ* Aberystwith and Hereford) he had a pleasant
meeting with his old friend the Dean of Hereford. One or
two extracts from letters during this period (one of which
tells of his journey home) are interesting and characteristic.
Hodgson, whose first wife was then suffering from the
permanent ill-health which resulted in her death a couple of
years later, was in very low spirits. Ellis writes to him:—

"8th July, 1858.

"I sympathise with your sufferings from depression of
"spirits. I cannot always keep aloof from them, and am
"obliged to aggravate them by self-reproaches when I
"compare my own happy circumstances with the miserable
"lot of thousands around me, in whose behalf I do not
"exert myself nearly as much as I ought."

"2nd August, 1858.

"I have plunged out of pleasure into business, but it is
"satisfactory to feel that the holiday, which has been so

"thoroughly enjoyed, has also made one more vigorous
"and intent upon following up duties relinquished for a
"time.

"Our run to the coach did us no harm. We soon
"recovered our breath outside the coach, and only felt
"disappointed at not being able to exchange parting
"recognitions with Mrs. Hodgson. A tinge of sorrow is
"inseparable from the closing scenes of a pleasure excur-
"sion : but for that, nothing could be more charming than
"our last days in Wales. I am able to indulge in the
"hope that our rapid transit over the country may have
"left some permanently beneficial results behind. We
"had some useful talk with the foreman of the lead works
"which we visited. He invited us to lunch at his cottage,
"and I gave him the Dean's book" (the *Lessons on the
Phenomena of Industrial Life*) "with an accompanying
"*vivâ voce* exhortation on school matters.

"On the coach top from Aberystwith to Kington I sat
"beside a clergyman, who did anything but turn aside
"from the animated observations on education as a means
"of improving the condition of the people with which
"Shields and I peppered and perplexed him. He was
"bound to Newport. On the platform at the Hereford
"station whom should we see but the Dean, waiting to
"receive the Judges momentarily expected to open the
"Assizes. While he and I were exchanging a few hasty
"and friendly recognitions, our clerical companion was
"learning with some surprise that it was the Dean of
"Hereford who was thus familiarly conversing with the
"strange man at whose side he had been seated. He told
"Mr. Shields that he should certainly get the Dean's
"book, and I believe that he will study it."

"6th August, 1858.
"I have read the address of Mr. Y.'s workmen" (a con-
tractor who had lately failed). "There is much in it that

"engages one's sympathy, while one is led to suspect that
"prejudice and misapprehensions common to their class
"prevail among them. Mr. Y.'s doings and his difficulties
"had escaped my notice. Like many other ambitious
"contractors, has he fallen a sacrifice to an indiscreet use
"of credit? Has the loss of £14,000 sufficed to ruin one
"who had given employment to so large a number of
"workmen? I am of course writing in the dark, but the
"merit of a man who draws around him from other parts
"six thousand human beings, and then turns them adrift
"to seek employment from other capitalists who have
"fortunately known how to manage their business so as
"to provide wages for their own workmen and some of
"these displaced elsewhere, is not to pass unquestioned.
"My eye seldom rests on a case of this kind but a host
"of thoughts crowd in upon me, uppermost among which
"is the mighty change destined to be wrought when
"principles shall have been sought for and learned to
"guide opinion on industrial conduct. According to our
"most advanced university and school notions, education
"is perfect which omits consideration of these principles
"altogether.

"Wonderful as is that wire which we hope is hencefor-
"ward to link together all the nations of the earth, it is a
"bauble in comparison with the latent powers of judgment
"that may be called into action to secure dispositions and
"conduct favourable to well-being."

It was in August, 1858, that an event occurred which was
the cause of deep grief to Ellis—the death of his friend,
George Combe. He had seen him at Kingston-on-Thames
at the beginning of July, and then wrote Hodgson that he
found him "looking uncommonly well" and "himself in all
"respects." Combe had gone a few days afterwards to
Moor Park, Farnham, a hydropathic establishment belonging
to Dr. E. W. Lane, intending to stay a month and then go

on a visit to his friend Mr. Bastard at Charlton Marshall. But, unfortunately, he there caught a cold which resulted in inflammation of the lungs, of which he died on the 14th August. Mrs. Ellis, who had visited Mrs. Combe at Farnham after the sad event, wrote Dr. Hodgson with full particulars, and the information induced Hodgson, who was at that time without any permanent occupation, to decide to go to Edinburgh and carry on the educational work which Combe had then commenced.

His letter announcing this intention was answered by Ellis in the following long and interesting letter:—

"22nd August, 1858.

" I was cowardly enough to leave Mrs. Ellis the melan-"choly task of breaking to you the intelligence of our "revered friend's death. Last year we should have been "better prepared to part with him, but his apparently "improved health during the winter led us to flatter our-"selves that he might yet be spared awhile to his friends "and the world. He has run his course nobly, has done "great and good work, encouraged and assisted all who "were disposed to improve themselves and others, and "left a bright example behind him. His work of love "and usefulness was relinquished only with his life, for "on the Saturday preceding his death he gave a lesson "to some children at an adjoining poor school. With "you, I say all honour to his memory, and may we prove "that he was not mistaken in honouring us with his "friendship, by following in his steps!

" I rejoice at your decision to resume work. It matters "little whether it be at Edinburgh or elsewhere. We "must, each of us, seize the openings presented and "buckle to some employment that we can feel to be "useful to others and improving to ourselves. Striving "in a right spirit to accomplish what it will be cheering "or consoling to look back upon, we cannot fail to make "our daily life endurable, if not happy, and to experience

N

"a growing affection for the work undertaken and for our
" fellow workmen.

"You must not suppose, because I direct my own
" thoughts and efforts principally to improving the edu-
" cation of the young, that I cannot sympathise warmly
"in the efforts of others to introduce improvements
" among existing adults. There is a wide field for useful-
" ness presented to all who are disposed and qualified to
" lead people to think—as Mr. Combe happily expressed
" it, to attend to moral causation. It is impossible to shut
" one's eyes to the evidences of the progress that is being
" made day by day. Each step, at the same time, makes
" one more sensible of what remains to be done, and
" wherein we may contribute towards accomplishing and
" hastening future progress.

"In teaching or lecturing upon economic science or
" any other branch of the social sciences, an opening
" offers itself which is certainly not presented to a teacher
" of physical science. He is summoned to expound the
" effects produced by bodies upon one another according
" to the circumstances in which they are placed. He
" may, and frequently does, travel beyond this and take
" human agency into his account, but, as human agency
" has generally formed no part of his scientific studies,
" he is perpetually committing himself to the most
" contradictory and puerile statements when he ventures
" beyond the immediate operations of man upon the
" bodies of whose qualities he is teaching.

" The position of a teacher of social science is very different.
" If he understand his mission and be up to what is required
" of him, he will never wander, nor allow his pupils or
" audience to wander, from the main subject, to throw
" light upon which is the end of all his arguments,
" evidence, and illustrations—and that subject is, of course,
" 'human conduct.' Teachers of economic science have
" hitherto scarcely done justice to their theme. They

"ought not to stop at expositions of what constitutes
"good and bad conduct, and the test by which one may
"be distinguished by the other. They should proceed to
"show how it may be hoped to secure the one and
"prevent the other. Beyond referring to 'protection
"'of property' and the governmental means of enforcing
"'conduct,' that branch of their subject is wholly omitted.

"Since I resumed the economic studies of my youth in
"later life, I have been more and more attracted to the
"question which follows to the thoughtful man upon the
"solution of the first difficulty of what constitutes good
"conduct, 'how is this conduct to be hoped for?' If one
"might hazard the attempt to sum up, in a few short
"expressions, all the resources at our disposal for bringing
"about the conduct to be desired, I would say the *dis-*
"*position* to right conduct must be cultivated, which
"involves instruction to distinguish what good conduct is,
"and training to raise up the desire and implant the
"habit of practising what is known to be good. These
"are my notions in brief of the expanded field open to
"the modern teacher of economic science, whether his
"mission be among children in a school or among adults
"in the lecture-room.

"In addressing adults, as you are proposing to do, it
"would be a great mistake not to consider their state of
"mind, and how they will best receive the instruction
"intended for them—how they may be taught while
"averse to listen to what should be presented in the form
"of a lesson. If the 'historic development of economic
"'science' is the mode of presenting your subject best
"calculated to gain a hearing and to command attention
"from an Edinburgh audience, that would quite reconcile
"me—nay, would induce me to concur in its adoption.
"It leaves the lecturer plenty of scope, while reviewing
"the changes of opinion and in our laws as they have
"occurred, to insist upon justice being done to the

"opinions which have been made to give way to those
"now adopted.　For example, 'free trade' has superseded
"'protection.'　It is not right for that reason—ought it to
"have done so? and why?　The punishment of death
"has been abandoned as a means of protecting property.
"Has that been an improvement? and why?　It is urged
"by some that the punishment of death as a means of
"protecting life should also be abandoned?　Would that
"be an improvement or not? and why?

"These seem to me to be the kind of questions which
"admit of being interspersed in your historic course, and
"of infusing vitality and vigour into it.　The skill of the
"lecturer will be so to blend the reminiscences of the past
"with instruction for the future as to call forth a lively
"interest for the hour."

CHAPTER IX.

1858—1864.

THE Royal Commission appointed 30th June, 1858, to enquire into the state of popular education in England, and generally known as the Duke of Newcastle's Commission, from the name of its chairman, naturally excited the deepest interest in Ellis's mind, and he exerted himself to bring such influence to bear on it as should draw the attention of the Commissioners to the grave defects in the existing systems. The Duke was known to be an earnest, painstaking, and conscientious man, and one who would spare no exertion to thoroughly complete the work he undertook. The Rev. William Rogers, whose energetic labours in the cause of education have been already referred to, was a member of the Commission, and it included Mr. Goldwin Smith, Mr. Nassau Senior, and other earnest advocates of educational progress. The first step taken by the Commission was to nominate ten sub-commissioners, whose duties were to make personal enquiries in certain selected districts, and to supply the fullest information as to the character of the education which was available to the working classes, and statistically as to the quantity in proportion to the population. Five different pairs of districts were selected as samples of the various populations of the country, two being metropolitan, two selected from agricultural parts of the kingdom, two from manufacturing, two from mining, and two from maritime districts. A sub-commissioner was appointed to each district, and, as Dr. Hodgson had then no permanent engagement, Ellis thought that his great talents would be well employed in this work. Through his friend, Mr. Rogers, he secured Hodgson's nomination to one of the metropolitan districts; and the following letters announced to him the appointment he had received (which was willingly undertaken) and contain some further interesting discussion of the work to be done, with passing sketches of what Ellis himself was then doing:—

.   "25th September, 1858.

"I am going off early to-morrow morning to see my "father at Folkestone. I shall try and post this letter at "Reigate, so that it may reach you on Monday, and "anticipate, or at all events be up with, the official "communication which is to be sent to you.

"You are appointed one of ten sub-commissioners "under the Commission of which the Duke of Newcastle "is president and Mr. Rogers one of the Board. The "object of it is to enquire into and report upon the state of "education throughout the kingdom. Your acceptance of "it will, of course, necessitate the suspension of your pro-"jected course of lectures. The mention of your name "originated with me, but you were proposed by Mr. "Rogers. I felt so doubtful of success that I would not "subject you to unnecessary agitation. Hence the appa-"rent surprise and unavoidable absence of notice, which is "to be regretted.

"I need not tell you that my motive in making this "move is the belief that a wide field of utility is opened. "The Duke of Newcastle is most assiduous, and I expect "that you will be the star among the sub-commissioners. "If you accept you may have an opportunity of exchanging "the metropolitan district for another, but I hope you "will prefer headquarters.

"The emoluments will, I believe, be a secondary con-

"sideration with you, but if they do not come up to your
"standard of what they ought to be, the fund which I set
"apart for educational purposes is equal to meet any
"demand that you can make upon it. As far as I can under-
"stand, the salary is £600 per annum, with an allowance
"of 15s. per diem for expenses, the appointment being
"for six months certain with the expectation of lasting
"longer.

"I earnestly hope that it will fall in with your views to
"accept this appointment, and that an early letter will
"announce your intention to take up your quarters at 6,
"Lancaster Terrace, so that I may arrange for a meeting
"betweeen Rogers, Hodgson, and Ellis previous to the 7th
"October. I have told my reverend friend that he will
"be no more disturbed by your theology than he has
"been by mine. He seems satisfied with this assurance,
"and you will be at ease."

"12th October, 1858.

"Be of good cheer! I do not say be sanguine! I am
"no more sanguine of seeing recognizable results from the
"labour that you are entering upon than I am from what
"I have been working at for more than ten years. Never-
"theless, I have great faith in the abundant crops that
"must follow from seed intelligently and faithfully sown,
"and in the happier frame of mind that will abide by the
"husbandman. We are, if I am not mistaken, steadily
"though slowly rising to something better, and it would
"be as foolish to despair as to boast beforehand of
"immediate success following on the report for which you
"are to supply some of the material.

"I am to read my lecture on the early years of George
"Stephenson, at Mr. Rogers' school, in Golden Lane,
"Thursday evening, 28th October, and he invites you
"and me to dine with him on that day.

"To-night, I read it at Peckham, and this day week
"at Bethnal Green.

"To-morrow I resume my weekly lesson at Mr. Rogers'
"school, Goswell Street, and on Monday next I return,
"after a lapse of three years, to the Jews' Free School, it
"being arranged by the committee and the head-master
"that all the junior masters and pupil teachers are to be
"present. I am in hopes that this school will come
"within your division of the East London Union, and, if
"it do, it will merit special mention. The head-master,
"to whom I can introduce you, is an able and energetic
"man, and the school is under the inspection of Mr.
"Arnold, who cares more for poetry than social science."

By the month of November, Hodgson was hard at work
in his district, which included parts of east and south
London; and the two following letters, written to him
about the end of November, show the support that Ellis
was giving him in his arduous duties.

"23rd November, 1858.
"I am glad to learn that you are finding an opening
"through which I may be turned to some useful account.
"Don't spare me, if you can make the present small
"aperture introducer to some wider space, which you can
"fill to advantage with a disposable reservoir at your
"command. The enclosed account will explain to you
"what you ought to have received this morning, or what
"you may find to-morrow, at 17, Great Queen Street.[1]
"May the persuasive tones that accompany each book as
"it is presented to the teacher deemed worthy of it,
"penetrate his soul, clear his vision, and direct his aim!
"Allow me to urge upon you the banishment from
"your mind of all uneasiness in regard to suspicions on
"theological grounds. Mr. Rogers and I are on the best
"of terms. Since we met, he has placed one of his pupil

---

[1] A dozen copies of the *Lessons on the Phenomena of Industrial Life*,
presented by Ellis for distribution among teachers.

"teachers at Mr. Shields' school, to pick up, if he can,
"under him, the knowledge and aptitude to give lessons
"similar to his, in Goswell Street. All that you need
"trouble yourself about is so to apply your superior talents
"and intelligence as to do well the work which you have in
"hand, and to let a thorough practical acquaintance with
"the wants of the people, and the excellencies and
"deficiencies of the means for supplying them shine
"through all the reports that issue from your pen. If
"any unpleasant rumblings should reach my ear, I will give
"you warning.

"While we are steadily pursuing our own path of duty
"as seen by our own light, we must not be surprised that
"others who differ from us should pursue their paths
"guided by their lights. If they are more in earnest than
"we are, less given to vain talking and scribbling, might
"we not imitate them with advantage? We may regret
"that they are in error, but to reproach them for being in
"earnest as intolerant and bigots does not add much to
"our lustre. For myself, I plead guilty to having a
"*bigotted* dislike to see the time of children wasted or
"misapplied in school, and am very intolerant of all who
"assist or connive at it. The fact is that intelligent,
"genteel, and well-to-do people, as a rule, have been put
"to shame by the zeal of less instructed and less thriving
"people, and have found it pleasanter to abuse them than
"to raise their own zeal and industry to a level with those
"of their more benighted brethren."

"26th November, 1858.

"Are you aware that Mr. Rogers' house, Charterhouse
"Square, is situated in your district on this side of the
"Thames? This was new to me when mentioned by him
"in the course of our conversation as we walked together
"from Goswell Street to Saint Pancras Church last
"Wednesday.

"I gather from him that he expects, as a consequence,
"to have a visit from you officially when you enter upon
"your examination into the northern part of your district.
"He seems much in earnest both for the improvement
"and efficiency of his own schools and for the useful
"working of the Commission.　He tells me that so far he
"is well pleased with the reports received from the pro-
"vincial assistant commissioners—the agricultural more
"particularly, who are far above indulging in indiscriminate
"praise of the schools which they have visited.

"I had given Mr. Rogers one of the printed papers
"which you sent to me.[1]　He was very friendly in his
"enquiries about you, and would apparently have been
"glad to know more than I could tell him.　I am begin-
"ning to think that I shall be disappointed if your united
"labours do not yield good fruits."

Upon the general question of education for the poor, and
the information he had obtained during the work he had
done, Ellis was invited to lay his views, in answer to a
number of questions prepared by the Commissioners, before
them; and he also had a preliminary interview with the
Duke of Newcastle.　His account of that, and his opinion
of an eminent statesman of the last generation, will be
interesting.　He writes thus to Hodgson:—

"25th March, 1859.

"I am glad to learn that here and there a gleam of
"sunshine lightens the educational darkness around you.
"I have had a long interview this very morning, by
"appointment, with the Duke of Newcastle, in Portman
"Square.　He questioned me a great deal and did not
"seem to dissent from any of the views I put forth.　I
"found him far above the average of those with whom I
"have conversed on the subject of education.　I am greatly

---

[1] The paper of questions distributed by the sub-commissioners for the purpose of obtaining information from schoolmasters.

"mistaken if he do not welcome whatever of enlightened
"and practical you can suggest in your report. The
"movement may be small and imperceptible, but it is in
"the direction that we wish, and ought to encourage us to
"work zealously. Results beyond our expectation, and
"at an early day, may be our reward."

Ellis's own views on the subject which the Commissioners
had before them, was conveyed, not in a series of formal
answers to questions, but in a letter addressed to the secretary of the Commissioners, in which, after referring to the
social calamities which he considered might be cured or
largely ameliorated by suitable teaching, such as poverty
and destitution, the miseries consequent on commercial
panics and industrial convulsions, as well as on strikes and
combinations, he gives his own views as follows:—

"14th April, 1859.

"F. Stephen, Esq.,—In describing to you the current
"of my own thoughts, I beg you will understand that I
"am laying claim to no originality. I wish to make a
"plain statement of my views in reply to your questions.
"Indeed, I believe that something like unanimity of
"acquiescence, quite independent of any exposition from
"me, would welcome my preliminary averment, that
"ignorance and ill-conduct in some of their many forms
"are the causes of much of the human misery generally
"admitted and deplored, and that ignorance and ill-
"conduct may be largely prevented by education.

"It is at this point that I would humbly and yet
"earnestly solicit attention, not to ignorance and ill-
"conduct in general, but to the *special kinds* of ignorance
"and ill-conduct which have to be prevented and to the
"*special kinds* of instruction and discipline which can
"alone efficiently cope with them.

"To begin with ill-conduct. Can anybody doubt, if the
"prevailing improvidence, drunkenness, dishonesty, idle-

"ness, and recklessness could be materially diminished,
"that the prevailing misery would not also be greatly
"diminished? Training, judiciously adapted to its purpose,
"must, of course, be mainly relied upon for guarding
"against the bad habits which lead to ill-conduct; but
"such training will hardly be forthcoming unless accom-
"panied by instruction in (to use the title of the Dean of
"Hereford's little elementary work) 'the phenomena of
"'industrial life and the conditions of industrial success.'
"This instruction, if conducted merely as well as our
"present limited experience has shown it may be, will so far
"prevent ignorance as to make all children thoroughly
"acquainted with—

"1. The sources of wealth; industry, knowledge, skill,
  "and economy.

"2. The connexion between capital and labour, the
  "reciprocal duties of employer and employed,
  "master and servant, and the circumstances which
  "determine the rates of wages and profits.

"3. The importance of respect for property, and the
  "necessity of government and laws for enforcing
  "this respect where not otherwise sufficiently felt.

"4 The advantages of division of labour and the new
  "responsibilities incurred by its adoption, the
  "causes and consequences of fluctuations of value,
  "and the more urgent call for integrity, per-
  "severance, punctuality, order, and forbearance to
  "allow all the operations of interchange to be
  "satisfactorily conducted.

"5. The uses of money; the causes and consequences
  "of fluctuations of prices and wages; the suicidal
  "folly of opposing prices in harmony with sup-
  "plies, actual and contingent; of organising com-
  "binations, strikes, and turn-outs; of impeding the
  "introduction of machinery and of other improved
  "methods of production, and the free flow of

"capital and labour from one trade, district, and
"country to others where a more profitable em-
"ployment for them is expected.

" 6. The use of credit in distributing capital and placing
"it under the control of those most competent to
"employ it; the functions of banks and bankers;
"the new responsibilities incurred by the use of
"credit; the causes of bankruptcies, commercial
"panics, and stoppage of works; and the precau-
"tions through which the suffering from these
"calamities may be mitigated.

" Did I not fear to exhaust your patience, and thereby
"to lose all chance of being favourably listened to, I
"might amplify under each of these heads as well as add
"to their number. But I abstain, remarking only that
"my experience of life has convinced me that ignorance
"upon the matters above enumerated prevails widely
"among all classes, and that much of the ill-conduct and
"of the misery consequent upon it is attributable to this
"ignorance.

"If I am right in my estimate of the causes of the
"destitution and crime that afflict society, the educational
"question which suggests itself is: What is being done in
"our schools to prevent the continuance of like ignorance
"and ill-conduct, and of the misery consequent among
"them?

"I hope I may be mistaken; but I fear that the in-
"struction, of which I have endeavoured to give an out-
"line, and the discipline corresponding to it, are rarely to
"be met with in our schools, and that the teachers, with
"all the exemplary devotion shown by so many of them
"to their arduous duties, are not possessed of the informa-
"tion which I contend ought to be imparted to the young,
"and, of course, cannot have acquired the expertness
"requisite for communicating it efficiently. I also fear
"that, at this very moment, the principals of training

"schools are not alive to the necessity of sending forth
"their new teachers, year by year, imbued with the in-
"formation essential for keeping destitution at bay, prac-
"tised in teaching it, and deeply impressed with a sense
"of the duty towards themselves and their pupils of
"exemplifying in their lives and conduct the advantage
"of a steady compliance with the rules of conduct de-
"ducible from the information daily expounded, illustrated,
"and enforced by them in their schools.

" The Commissioners will, of course, have ample oppor-
"tunities of judging from the reports of their Assistant
"Commissioners whether my fears are well grounded.

"Should it appear that the kind of instruction which
"must be incorporated with the other kinds of instruction
"ordinarily provided in our schools, to make them
"thoroughly reliable places of education, is seldom or
"never to be found in them, and should it also appear that
"it is no part of the aim of training schools to supply the
"omission in future, where are we to look for the *further*
"diminution of misery and crime, unless it be to the
"recognition and exposure of these fatal defects in our
"educational machinery, as the first steps to their
"rectification ? "

The Duke of Newcastle appears to have been much
impressed by Ellis's views, and acknowledged it by the very
next post in the following letter:—

"Clumber, 15th April, 1859.
" Dear Sir,—Although I have only had time this morn-
"ing for a very hasty perusal of the remarks you have
"sent me in answer to the questions from the Education
"Commission, I will not delay a post in thanking you for
"them. They place in a succinct and clear form the
"opinions which I had so much pleasure in hearing from
"you when you called upon me in London. I shall
"certainly examine the reports of the Assistant Com-

"missioners with a view to ascertaining whether their
"thoughts have been turned in the same interesting
"direction as your observations."

Another letter which Ellis wrote to the Duke of Newcastle, two or three months later, will be of interest. He had
received from Mr. Moses Angel, master of the Jews' Free
School in Spitalfields, an interesting report on the teaching
of social science in his school, which included some of the
poorest children at the East End of London, and sent it on
to the Duke, with the following letter:—

"2nd June, 1859.

"The note and papers enclosed will, I think, appear to
"you sufficiently interesting to make it unnecessary for
"me to offer any apology for what I am doing. But I
"beg your Grace will not be at the trouble of acknow-
"ledging the receipt of them.

"One subject touched upon in our late conversation
"was the difficulty of introducing into our common schools
"instruction such as is set forth in the Dean of Hereford's
"*Lessons on the Phenomena of Industrial Life and Condi-*
"*tions of Industrial Success.*

"I may mention that the Jews' Free School is situated
"in one of the poorest districts of London, and that the
"scholars who attend it are of the kind likely to be drawn
"from such a district.

"Surely, if the proper means be but taken, the work
"accomplished there might be attempted with some hope
"of success in districts less unfavourably circumstanced.

"I trust that one of your Assistant Commissioners will
"take some notice in his report of the commendable
"exertions both of the master and of the promoters of the
"school."

The report of the Commissioners was an important and
valuable document, and, with the reports of the sub-commissioners, it laid the foundation of the system of national

education which was carried through Parliament in 1870 by the late W. E. Forster.

Of the special defect in existing systems which Ellis sought to remedy by the introduction of lessons adapted to guide the pupils in future life, the Commissioners say as follows (*Report*, p. 127):—

"But we feel bound to state that the omission of one "subject from the syllabus and from the examination "papers has left on our minds a painful impression. "Next to religion, the knowledge most important to a "labouring man is that of the causes which regulate the "amount of his wages, the hours of his work, the regularity "of his employment, and the prices of what he consumes. "The want of such knowledge leads him constantly into "error and violence, destructive to himself and to his "family, oppressive to his fellow workman, ruinous to his "employers, and mischievous to society. Of the elements "of such knowledge we see no traces in the syllabus, "except the words 'Savings Banks and the nature of "'interest,' in the female syllabus. If some of the time "now devoted to the geography of Palestine, the succes- "sion of the kings of Israel, the wars of the Roses, or the "heresies in the Early Church, were given to political "economy, much valuable instruction might be acquired, "and little that is worth having would be lost."

This reference to the great want in all educational institutions, the only one in a report of several hundred pages, though it recognises the defect, was not sufficiently distinct and outspoken to satisfy Ellis. In an article from his pen, which appeared in the *Museum and English Journal of Education* of February, 1865, on "Middle Class Education, "what to aim at, as well as how to aim," he says, referring to the Duke of Newcastle's Commission and another which had been appointed to enquire into public schools:—

"Searching and laborious as these enquiries were and "able as were the reports, it has always appeared to us

"that they would have been much more effective and useful
"had there been an introductory exposition of the pur-
"poses for which education is desirable. We will not say
"that these purposes were not perceived and admitted by
"the Commissioners; but if they were, the avowal of
"them was repressed, and the reports might have been
"just what they were, had the Commissioners never
"bestowed a thought upon what we conceive to be the
"reason of our being at any pains about education at all."

And in a letter to Dr. Hodgson we find a further statement of his view of the result of the Commission. He
says :—

"20th January, 1865.

"You know the trouble which I took to help the Com-
"mission of 58-9 to a useful result. Its report, in spite of
"your exertions as well as my own, was a disappointment,
"and its treatment by the Government a greater. Never-
"theless, I should be sorry to do it scant justice, which is
"near akin to injustice. The impression left by it on my
"mind was that 'how to aim' was more thought of than
"what to aim at."

Dr. Hodgson's own report as sub-commissioner seems to
have been very satisfactory to Ellis. One or two letters to
Hodgson, written in the latter part of the year 1859, give us
some information of this and also of renewed communications
with his old friend Lord Brougham, with a view to obtain
his assistance at the meeting of the Social Science Association, and also mention a course of six lectures to teachers
which Ellis delivered in October and November of that year
at South Kensington, under the auspices of the Science and
Art Department. He says :—

"22nd September, 1859.

"I will not lose a day in acknowledging your note of
"yesterday.

"Let me tell you, in the first place, that I am more

o

"than satisfied with your report, which I read with great
"interest, and the critical portions more than once. What
"is of more consequence, it has made a strong and favour-
"able impression upon Mr. Rogers. Mrs. Ellis and my
"daughter, who were allowed to share in the treat, were
"also enthusiastic in their commendation and expressions
"of delight.

"You mention the possibility of your going to Brad-
"ford" [the meeting of the Social Science Association
in October]. "I hope you will, and I may induce you to
"agree with me. If I did not misunderstand what Mrs.
"Ellis communicated to me, Mrs. Hodgson mentioned in
"a note to her that six copies of your report had been
"placed at your disposal. Now, what I beg to suggest is,
"that you will send one *in confidence* to Lord Brougham
"*at my request.* You will judge from his two notes to
"me, which I enclose for your perusal, whether he is in a
"favourable state of mind to profit by its perusal, and
"then to give his support to anything that you will under-
"take at Bradford. The moment I hear from you that
"you fall in with the suggestion, I will write to his lordship
"and tell him what I have earnestly begged of you to do.

"It is all but fixed that I give a course of six lectures
"on 'Social Science as a branch of school instruction' at
"Kensington. I am going there on Saturday to adjust
"preliminaries with the officials in company with Mr.
"Rogers. He regrets with me not to have had the
"opportunity of some chat with you on your return from
"the Continent. He goes next week with Mr. Lake to
"visit some of the training colleges in the country. I
"don't hear that any visits of inspection have yet been
"made to the London training colleges."

"25th September, 1859.
"I wrote to Lord Brougham from the city yesterday,
"giving him all the particulars suggested by you, and

"adding besides some considerations of my own. It is
"right that I should mention that the present interchange
"of most friendly communications between his Lordship
"and myself originated in an application of his to me.[1] It
"would have been uncourteous in me not to respond to it,
"inexcusable not to turn it if possible to useful account.

" Mr. Rogers and I settled with Mr. Cole definitively the
"programme of my lectures yesterday. The course has
"the hearty concurrence of Lord Granville. I expect in
"a few days to send you a syllabus, the proof of which
"has been approved by the illustrious Cole. It now only
"remains for me not to spoil the opportunity bestowed
"upon me, discredit my subject, and disappoint my
"friends. I shall read my introductory lecture and im-
"provise the others, and the stiffness of the first and the
"halting colloquiousness of the last may prevent my pro-
"pitiating my audience sufficiently to induce them to
"attend to my expositions and exhortations. But the
"work is to be done, and in the absence of those who,
"with the qualifications of lecturers, which I do not possess,
"combine the knowledge and the desire to impart it, which
" I feel I really do possess, I must undertake it and execute
"the task to the best of my ability."

The course of lectures at South Kensington drew good
audiences, and excited much interest in those who attended
them. It was a course of six lectures, the first delivered on
11th October, and the last on the 15th November. The
first—the only one which was written out and read by Ellis
from the manuscript—was on the necessity of social science
as a branch of school education; the other five took the
hearers shortly over a similar outline of the framework and
constitution of a modern industrial society to that of his
previous works. The reason for this difference in his method
of delivering his lectures may be easily explained. On the

---

[1] See Lord Brougham's letter, *supra*, p. 54.

one hand, he was painfully short-sighted, and could hardly see to read his lecture without holding the manuscript so close to his eyes as to interfere with the delivery. On the other, he considered that he did not possess the gift of extempore oratory. The fact was that his thoughts took so closely reasoned and logical a form that it was hardly possible to be fluent. Consequently, he had to choose between two difficulties. When the subject of his lecture was somewhat special, he would write it; when he was going over ground with which he was by long habit familiar, he would trust himself to lecture extempore.

There is one passage in the first lecture, the only one which was printed, which is interesting, as it puts in a concise form the national folly and wrong of allowing children to grow up in ignorance. He says :—

"Fixing our attention upon the condition and number
"of the inhabitants of this island, and tracing the course
"of improvement in the first, and of increase in the second,
"from the past to our own times, is it not undeniable
"that our progress in knowledge has been one of the
"causes of our progress in wealth and numbers? Con-
"ditions are attached to the sustained, and still more to
"the increased, well-being of our dense population. An
"ignorant man among us is unavoidably a nuisance. He
"must be wholly or partially maintained by those who
"are not ignorant. Twenty millions of ignorant people
"could not exist in Great Britain. If this be the case a
"wrong is done, an act of cruelty is committed, every time
"that a child is suffered to grow up into an ignorant man."

There are two other letters of this year which contain some specially interesting remarks upon the comparative influence of natural organisation and education in the formation of character. Hodgson thought that in a lecture which Ellis had delivered he had not attached sufficient importance to the former, and had spoken in a derogatory way of Combe's views as a Phrenologist. He seems, from

the reply, to have written strongly on the subject.   Ellis
answers :—

" 22nd April, 1859.

"The amazement with which your note has filled me
"calls to my mind that which was expressed by a French
"general while contemplating the Balaklava cavalry
"charge, '*C'est magnifique, mais ce n'est pas la guerre.*'"

"I am, as you know, an indifferent writer and spokes-
"man, besides being untrained as a logician. I will not,
"therefore, in opposition to your interpretation of what
"I wrote and said, venture to set up my own, but I must
"maintain that I intended to write and say nothing like
"that which you have exercised your combativeness
"against.

"My want of respect for Mr. Combe, with which you
"charge me, is based upon the same use of evidence by
"which a certain quoter of scripture once maintained
"that suicide was enjoined by Christ.

"The sentiments contained in my lecture had often
"been expressed conversationally to Mr. Combe. Our
"mutual regard had sprung up in spite of our acknow-
"ledged phrenological differences, and his for me con-
"tinued unshaken to the end; witness the mention of
"my name in his will.[1]

"In treating of Education as conduct bearing upon
"attainments and dispositions, themselves in their turn the
"causes of conduct, I could not avoid adverting to the
"influences of organisation in conjunction with those of
"education for the purpose of assigning its due weight to
"each of them. I may have been led into error, although
"unconsciously, in my estimate of the comparative
"influence of each. Certainly, I had not the slightest
"notion of denying the influence of either. I am not

---

[1] Combe bequeathed to Ellis a legacy of nineteen guineas, expressed to be
"as a mark of his esteem."

"aware that I ever said or did anything to induce
"inattention to organic peculiarities. I have condemned
"and will continue to condemn, as the opportunity arises,
"any attempt to justify neglect of education by despond-
"ing allusions to those organic peculiarities which demand
"peculiar treatment, and need not daunt us nor distract us
"from our efforts to educate the masses.

"When George Stephenson attributed his success to
"'perseverance,' not to 'original genius,' it never occurred
"to him that he was making a 'gratuitous attack' on
"organisation. I was no less innocent in my attempt to
"direct attention to the proximate proportions of the
"influences of external and internal circumstances over
"disposition and conduct. I readily confess my ignorance
"of phrenology. The little acquaintance that I have with
"it is derived from Mr. Combe and yourself, and I fear
"that my mental calibre appeared quite unequal to the
"digestion of the phrenological aliment supplied by my
"able instructors."

"24th April, 1859.

" I could subscribe your 'Confession of Faith' without
"altering a word. Till I received your letter I could
"have imagined, in my simplicity, that you would have
"concurred in all the sentiments that I uttered the other
"night.

"In commenting upon various kinds of ill-conduct, I
"had, as you may suppose, no thought of passing over
"'child neglect.' That subject is yet to be gone into
"more fully in my next lecture. But to make that kind
"of ill-conduct stand out in all its hideous deformity, it
"was necessary to claim recognition for the all but omni-
"potent influence of education upon the great majority of
"mankind, and to sweep from my path all objections
"drawn from 'natural depravity,' 'original differences,'
"and the like, which, however applicable they may be to
"a small minority, ought not to be allowed to obstruct

"our efforts, or to damp our energies in doing our duty
"by the young generally.

"Among the numerous criticisms and improvements
"which Mr. Combe contributed to my 'Where must we
"'look for the further prevention of crime?' he did not
"make a single objection to the doctrines set forth—
"identical, as I believe, with those of my lecture.

"In my lecture to the schoolmasters last December, you
"may remember that I had to disencumber my path from
"the influences of climate, the aspects of nature, &c., none
"of which I deny, although I cannot consent to their being
"pleaded against education. They may modify, but they
"must not prevent education. And if intruded where
"education is being insisted upon, urged forward, or begged
"for, they must be ejected. Inferior cerebral developments
"must be treated after the same fashion.

"My strictures, if I am not mistaken, left your doctrines
"and those of Mr. Combe, properly understood, untouched
"and respected. The distortions of them which float in
"the public mind, among the influences of moons and
"comets, of paper-issues, prayer and fasting, saints and
"devils, were what I was intent upon gibbetting. Nobody
"would regret more than myself to have acted, even
"unintentionally, as executioner of the virtuous and
"innocent in company with the vicious and guilty."

The lectures delivered at South Kensington in November
led to Ellis being requested, about the end of the year, to
conduct a class of teachers in training, at St. Mark's College,
Chelsea. The following two letters to Hodgson contain
his account of the invitation and the first lecture:—

"13th December, 1859.

"Curiously enough your letter announcing the spread
"of economic science-teaching through you comes to me
"when I am about to go up (at the sacrifice of an
"afternoon in business), in compliance with an invitation

"from the Rev. Derwent Coleridge, to make arrange-
"ments for conducting a class at St. Mark's Training
"College, Chelsea.   This is the first fruits of my lectures
"at South Kensington.

                              " 13th March, 1860.

"I sent you a pennyworth of copies of the paper on
"education" (a paper contributed by Ellis to the March
number of the *Friend of the People*) "by yesterday's
"post.   It is not worth reprinting, although I hope, from
"the quarters to which it has penetrated, that it will
"contribute somewhat to the advancement of the good
"cause.   We may meet with rebuffs, but faint heart will
"no more win a good cause than it will a fair lady.   I
"put off writing till to-day, because I thought you would
"like to have some report of what took place yesterday
"evening at St. Mark's.

"Scene, the Music Hall—time, 5-30 p.m.—a hundred
"and twenty boys in voluntary attendance, by circular invi-
"tation to them and explanation to their parents of the
"object of the course of proposed lessons.   These boys
"were flanked at each side by the students in training, a
"hundred in number, and the principal, vice-principal,
"and Mr. Daymond (the excellent training master who
"has set all this in motion), were present to hear my
"lesson to the boys.   I had a friend with me—a semi-
"worshipper, who begged hard to be allowed to come—
"and he says that he never heard me give so good a
"lesson.   Of course, I did little more than break ground,
"and as you are well acquainted with the length of my
"tether, I will not pour forth upon you a deluge of
"matter with the composition of which you are already
"familiar.

"If my place had been occupied by Shields, and I had
"been a spectator like my friend, I could have gloried in
"the sight, and reckoned up the thousands of future
"men and women saved from destitution and crime by

"the inauguration of such an improvement in our training
"colleges. As it was, I was deeply impressed with the
"grandeur of the opportunity, not unmixed with fear
"lest I should spoil it by my inability to turn it to
"account."

The lessons at St. Mark's College lasted through the
summer. They were highly appreciated by the pupils and
by the principal, the Rev. Derwent Coleridge, who, in a few
impressive words addressed to the class at the close of the
course, expressed his strong opinion in favour of special
attention to the subject matter of the lectures.

"Your religious training here," he said, "prepares and
"disposes you, it may be hoped, to benefit your fellow
"creatures, especially the children whose teaching and
"training you are about to undertake. But the best
"intentions, the best dispositions, must be accompanied
"by intelligence, if they are to produce the best fruit; and
"you must be as sensible as I am that the kind of instruc-
"tion which you have been receiving is indispensable
"towards enabling you to give effect to the good inten-
"tions with which religion inspires you."

The autumn of that year was spent at Shirley—a place
between Croydon and Bromley, where his walks in the
surrounding country were of special interest to Ellis, as
they recalled the scenes of his school days, as well as of his
early married life. In the winter of 1860-1, he arranged a
course of lectures to teachers at University College, by his
faithful henchman, Mr. Shields, whose great teaching powers
had made him a man of mark in the educational world.
How highly Ellis valued him is shown by a letter to Dr.
Hodgson shortly after the commencement of this course:—

"22nd November, 1860.

"I return you Mr. Jones'[1] letter. He has on the whole
"painted for you a faithful picture of Mr. Shields' intro-

---

[1] A teacher who was attending Mr. Shields' class.

"ductory lecture and the impression produced by it. I
"propose attending the whole course; it is an intellectual
"treat to me, to say nothing of the satisfaction I derive
"from watching the signs of progress among persons en-
"gaged in the *lower* walks of education. My pen jibs
"whenever I attempt to describe or narrate; it is not in
"my style. I will not, therefore, interfere with Mr. Jones'
"report. Mr. Shields' grand work is his school; without
"that his other efforts, excellent as they are, would be
"nothing in my eyes. That is at the back of all his
"influence, and that it is which induces the public to lend
"him their ear. He is again, I fear, allowing himself to
"be carried away by his ardour, and undertaking more
"than I dare hope he will carry through with impunity."

During the ensuing three years—1861 to 1863—Ellis was
mainly occupied in writing and publishing a work to
which he gave the name of *Philo-Socrates*, and in which he
has embodied in their most matured form his deepest
thoughts, not only upon the principles which should govern
the education of the young, but also upon morals generally.
It is in fact a complete system of ethics, including a
fuller development of the science of the formation of
character—the science to which John Stuart Mill had given
the name of Ethology. The form of the work and the
selection of the name were due to the recent publication of
the translation of Plato's dialogues of Socrates by Dr.
Whewell, which had deeply interested Ellis. The style of
investigating moral problems adopted by Socrates, and the
gradual elucidation of truth by means of argumentative
dialogue were specially in harmony with his own method,
and by their means he was enabled to frame and answer
the objections and errors which were likely to be put forward
by students more effectively than he could do in the ordinary
form of a monologue. It will be remembered that as early
as 1829 he published a short treatise upon *Knowledge*,

Happiness, and Education, in the form of a conversation, and
during the fifteen years which had elapsed since he began
conducting classes of boys and teachers he had been
specially accustomed to the method of investigating economical and moral subjects by oral lessons. He had become
accustomed to lead his classes by means of the interrogative
method, first to approach and examine the subjects proposed
for their consideration, then to state and put into shape the
difficulties arising at each stage, and ultimately to discover
the solution of those difficulties by the guidance involved in
suitable questions. He had in fact been practising the
Socratic method long before he came to know Socrates
himself as he is depicted for us by his pupil Plato in the
celebrated conversations; and when he became acquainted
with that work he saw how clearly and vividly he could
bring out and elucidate in the form of Socratic dialogues
the principles of the important kind of knowledge for which
he desired to gain publicity—the science of conduct or self-
guidance.

And in addition to the similarity of method, the subjects
which Socrates is recorded by Plato to have mainly sought
to investigate were practically the same which formed a
large part of Ellis's own thoughts and conversations with
his friends and pupils. Dr. Whewell gives the following
epitome[1] of the problems the solution of which is attempted
in these dialogues:—

"What then were these cardinal Socratic questions?
"What was this knowledge which Socrates sought in vain
"and which Plato thought he had found? What could
"the questions be which stimulated so long, so anxious,
"so persevering an enquiry? Do these questions possess
"the same interest still?

"What is right? What is wrong? What is good?

---

[1] *The Platonic Dialogues for English Readers*, by William Whewell, D.D.,
"Introduction to the Laches," vol. i., pages 9, 10.

"or what is bad? What advantage has right over wrong?
"good over bad?"

And Dr. Whewell goes on to point out that these
questions were only preliminary in Socrates' mind to the
further and more practical ones—

"How are we to teach men—men, young men, young
"women, children—what is right and what is wrong?
"How are we to make them good? Prevent their being
"bad?

"And it was in point of fact with especial reference to
"these practical questions that Plato and that Socrates
"asked the previous more abstract questions. They
"wanted—Socrates especially wanted—to establish a
"better basis for the education of the young people of his
"time than then existed. He was a great educational
"reformer. Plato was a still bolder reformer in the same
"department."

But, although Socrates (or Plato in his name) adopted as
the test of right conduct the same rule as has been in
modern times advocated by Bentham and his pupils, viz.,
"that each man in the state must so live as most to promote
"not his own good, but the good of the state,"[1] yet his idea
of education falls curiously short of what is required in
modern times.

"What then, asks Socrates,[2] is the education to be?
"Perhaps, he goes on, we could hardly find a better than
"that which the experience of the past has already dis-
"covered; which consists in gymnastic for the body, and
"music (afterwards defined to include poetry) for the
"mind. And we shall begin our course of education with
"music rather than with gymnastic."

Dr. Whewell, although he has given us this most interesting
contribution to the knowledge of the greatest philosopher of

---

[1] *Ib.*, vol. iii., page 302; "Republic," book vii., sec. 5.
[2] *Ib.*, vol. iii., page 174; "Republic," book ii., sec. 16.

ancient Greece, does not seem to realise from it the thoughts to which his epitome of Socrates' teaching quoted above naturally lead. Living amid the university life of a past generation, which could not understand any education except that founded on the teaching of languages, he seems to have been entirely ignorant of what was then being done to develop it into a true character-forming art—the art of implanting in the pupils' minds the most necessary of all sciences, the science of self-guidance. He shows this very clearly in his remarks on education in another part of the book. He says[1] :—

"The account given of the Greek education is in"teresting; nor can it be denied that it represents what "has in all cultured nations been deemed, and would still "be deemed among ourselves, a good education: modi"fying, of course, some of the subjects taught; for instance, "omitting music and introducing certain foreign languages, "ancient and modern. That it was not a moral education "founded on making morality a science, which was what "Socrates and Plato alleged against it, was a defect which "has not yet been remedied in education, and which no "one now, I think, aspires to remedy."

From these quotations we shall see very clearly why Ellis, fresh from a perusal of these Platonic dialogues, gave his book the name of *Philo-Socrates.* And the explanation which he gives on the title page, as part of the title, makes his purpose still more clear. He there describes his book as—

"A series of papers wherein subjects are investigated "which, there is reason to believe, would have interested "Socrates, and in a manner that he would not disapprove, "were he among us now, gifted with the knowledge, and "familiar with the habits and doings, of our times."

Philo-Socrates is considered by those who know Ellis's

---

[1] *Ib.,* vol. ii., page 37; "Protagoras," sec. 41—44.

works as the most complete and comprehensive of all his writings. It bears traces of even more careful and elaborate thought than any other of his works. It includes not only the consecutive course of lessons upon social science which he had dealt with, first in the *Outlines of Social Economy*, and afterwards in his *Lessons on the Phenomena of Industrial Life* and his *Religion in Common Life*, but also much of the teaching upon the mental constitution of humanity which he had investigated in the *Outlines of the History and Formation of the Understanding.* We find in it, further, a number of papers on the principles on which all education intended to influence conduct should be based. And finally a series of conversational essays upon purely ethical subjects such as Right and Wrong—Laws, Morals, and Religion—Duty and Conscience—and the respective values of the Reasoning Faculties and of Supernatural Inspiration or Intuition as affecting the actions and consequent welfare of the human race. It will not, therefore, be thought superfluous to give some account of this work, or at all events of those portions of it which are either a variation from or an addition to his previous writings.

Philo-Socrates is divided into eight parts (forming four volumes), the first of which was published about April, 1861, the eighth in the beginning of 1864. Of these vols. i. and iii. (parts 1, 2, 5, and 6) are " Among the Boys," and are in fact a repetition, in the form of Socratic dialogue, of the lessons which he had so often given, sometimes to boys, sometimes to teachers, and once to his Royal pupils. They are, however, so framed as to avoid the misuse to which his old *Questions and Answers* had been put; they could not be placed in boys' hands to be learned as a catechism. The special remark which occurs to us in considering his treatment of the subject is that the old, dry, political economy of his predecessors, dealing with the phenomena of the " Wealth of Nations " merely as wealth, has, even more than in his previous works, developed into the life-like social economy which deals with the well-being and happiness of the human beings who produce it, and their acts, conduct, and character, as bearing on their welfare. The same gradual opening out of the subject is adopted as in his previous works, but in *Philo-Socrates* there is prefixed to the series of lessons—before commencing upon the fundamental qualities of industry and intelligence—a most careful lesson "On Conduct" leading the pupils to realise how the well-being and happiness of the members of a community, as well as of the community itself as a social body, is mainly due to the conduct and actions of the individuals in their separate capacity, and in the aggregate as members of the social body. And this series is closed (vol. iii., p. 284) by a lesson "On Self-discipline," in which the conclusion to be drawn from the series of previous conversational papers is again summed up and brought home to the pupils in such a way as to impress upon them still more deeply the necessity of acting in accordance with the lessons of self-guidance which they had received, so as to promote the general well-being. The following short extracts from the latter part of the paper "On Conduct," in which the relative importance of other studies is compared with that of the science of conduct, sums up the arguments which have been elicited from the boys in the preceding conversation (vol. i., p. 23):—

"PHILO-SOCRATES: Which science may I conclude is "in your estimation the more important for you to "master—the science of astronomy, which deals with "the movements of the heavenly bodies, or the science of "conduct, which, besides dealing with the movements, "that is, with the dispositions and actions of men, "individually and collectively, explains how you may "assist in moulding your own characters?

"BOYS: We can give but one answer. The science of "conduct must be the more important. It would be "disgraceful in us to omit any opportunity that was "presented to us for acquiring a knowledge of it.

"P.: The capacity to distinguish between good and bad
"conduct is more than important—it is indispensable;
"but because precedence is given to acquirements which
"impart this capacity, other acquirements are not the
"less to be cherished and sought for. One can scarcely
"imagine how students of astronomy can fail to acquire,
"with their science, elevation of sentiment, expansion of
"intellect, and a distaste for things mean and vicious.
"You will probably, in the course of our conversations, have
"occasion to admit that you must be resigned to remain
"in ignorance of many branches of knowledge, and to
"acquire no more than a smattering of others. It can
"scarcely be said that there is any kind of knowledge
"the possession of which ought to be despised; but we
"are driven to confess that it is beyond the compass of
"any one human being to make himself master of the
"whole. Some, each individual must manage to dispense
"with, leaving others to learn what he is obliged to omit;
"while there are other branches which no one can omit to
"learn without danger to his own happiness. Can you
"fancy yourself able to steer your course happily and
"respectably through life with a very slight knowledge of
"chemistry, navigation, and architecture?

"B.: Yes, for others could be found to help us, as we
"might help them, when each wanted assistance.

"P.: And also with a very slight knowledge of the
"science of conduct?

"B.: No; and our ignorance here would disqualify us
"for judging rightly of the assistance that might be
"tendered to us by those who had the special knowledge
"which we were deficient in."

Of the other papers of this series, special attention may
be drawn to that "On Intelligence" (vol. i., page 51), the conclusion of which is an earnest appeal to the boys to cultivate .
the habit of thinking beforehand of the consequence of their
acts and the avoidance of those which are unfavourable to

general well-being—"On Character" (vol. i., page 129)—"On Borrowing and Lending" (vol. iii., page 24), which comprises a careful investigation of the morals of credit—and "On Expenditure" (vol. iii., page 153), which contains some of Ellis's most scathing censures upon rich men who live in luxury without devoting any part of their wealth to the prevention and relief of human misery. "Under happier influences," say his boys, answering a guiding question, "it may be "hoped that profuse expenditure in the midst of destitution "and child-neglect will pass into the rank of crimes and "vices, with heretic and witch burning, slave catching and "holding, privateering and duelling; and be only known to "future generations as gathered from the historical records "of bygone superstitions and barbarisms." But the most remarkable of these papers is the concluding one "On Self-discipline" (vol. iii., page 284). It is, of course, impossible to epitomise closely-reasoned thoughts and interrogations by which the boys are led up to the following conclusions as to the objects of their education or preparation for life. It is a course of teaching which any schoolmaster may follow after an adequate study of Ellis's method, and it is difficult to imagine any schoolmaster failing to realise the importance of it; and, it may be added, the conclusions as well as the arguments leading to them may be studied with advantage by all, both old and young (p. 307).

"BOYS: First, we must bend our minds to persevere in "forming the habits and acquiring the knowledge possible "at our age, and the aptitude for acquiring what more "will be necessary to enable us to become self-supporting "and capable of performing all our duties and fulfilling all "our obligations.

"Secondly, knowing as we do that many individuals "are addicted to plunder and harass their neighbours, and "that many more give proofs of a propensity to obtain "their living by violence and fraud, rather than by steady "labour and upright dealing, we must prepare ourselves

P

"to be able to co-operate with other well-disposed indi-
"viduals so as to organise protection against all who would
"disturb the general well-being.

 "Thirdly, we must be preparing to take our share in the
"performance of another work. The maimed, the imper-
"fectly organised, and others overtaken by unavoidable
"calamities, are dependent upon contributions from the
"earnings of others, among whom we ought to hope to be.
"There are, besides, many destitute and helpless who might
"be otherwise had they been well cared for in infancy
"and childhood; and sad to say there are thousands of
"neglected children around us growing up to lives of
"shame, of misery, and of crime. We must take our part
"in contributing to the relief of the former and to the
"salvation of the latter.

 "Fourthly, being aware of the vast range of knowledge,
"the capacity for long-sustained attention, and the sagacity
"and forbearance required to judge of the fittest means
"for securing the execution of all this work, what laws to
"enact, how to administer them, and how to assist in
"selecting the legislators and functionaries best adapted,
"each for the special duty confided to him, we must be
"doing our utmost to master all those attainments and
"form all those habits which will enable us to do the
"lighter work, at all events, and to bring no discredit
"upon the choice, if we should be selected to perform the
"more arduous."

Of the frame of mind which Ellis suggests should, and
may by judicious training, be produced in boys of the
wealthier classes, the following passage is a sufficient
explanation (p. 310):—

 "Boys: We must bear in mind that men's views in
"regard to what constitutes the enjoyment or indulgence
"desirable from abundance of wealth have undergone,
"and are undergoing, great changes—changes, too, indi-
"cative of growing intelligence and goodness. A time

"may come when rich men will take as much pleasure,
"and devote as great pains, to provide that all the
"children around them shall be receiving a good edu-
"cation, as that their mansions shall be sumptuously
"furnished and their equipages well-appointed. All that is
"required is that objects to be sought for should be prized
"in proportion to their glory and loveliness. The efforts to
"attain them can scarcely fail to follow in the same order.

"P. : Will not some new or greatly improved machinery
"be required to bring about the great change in moral
"sentiments which you are contemplating?

"B.: No other improved machinery, as far as we can
"see, than that improved education which you are insisting
"upon—an education the very essence of which is to form
"the understandings and dispositions of the young, so as
"to bring them to estimate conduct by its tendency to
"promote the general well-being, and to aim at the
"practice of that self-discipline which will lead them to
"the further knowledge, and strengthen them in the
"habits desirable for enabling them to contribute as
"largely as possible to that well-being."

Volume ii. (parts 3 and 4) is "Among the Teachers," and
contains in their most matured form the thoughts upon
education—especially on religious education—which he
wished to bring to the minds of teachers of all classes.
The severest opposition which he had met with was from
the clergy of all orthodox denominations, especially the
evangelical party, who excluded his teaching from their
schools, designated those which he had himself founded
as "irreligious" because the Bible was not read in them, and
some even went so far as to denounce him as an "enemy
"of religion." It was from this view of religious teaching
that the Department of Education imposed, as a condition
of recognising schools, that there should be Scripture
teaching of some kind, or as a minimum (resulting as a
compromise from the conflicts of different sects) that

selections from the Bible should be read "without note or "comment." The object of these papers is to show what a truly religious education ought to be, what were the essentials of it, and why the Bible, so far from being used to teach from, ought to be preceded by education fitted to enable the children to understand the real meaning of the lessons contained in it. Upon professions of religion— upon those "professing Christians" who live in luxurious ease, attend church and conform to its outward ordinances, while doing nothing for the benefit of the poor and destitute, and especially of neglected children, Ellis was singularly severe, and denounced such sham religion in strong terms as "a passive depravity which can enjoy itself while the seeds "of misery, vice, and crime are being sown broadcast." He concludes an interesting chapter "On professing Christians," with the following eloquent denunciation of such conduct (vol. ii., p. 48):—

"In the midst of crowds of neglected children, numerous "enough almost to dishearten the humane, with all their "devotion, energy, and powers of endurance, two classes of "adults are observable—one of professing Christians who "look on, pitying children much in the same way as they "acknowledge Christ: that is, with their lips, not stirring "a finger, not contributing a mite, not subtracting a luxury "from their enjoyments in order to provide that children "shall cease to be objects of pity—the other of men who, "making no professions, stretch forth both their hands, "shrink from the pollution of luxurious enjoyment, while "children lack the bread of life, and not only contribute "largely from their means, but work for the purpose of "being able to contribute more. Which is the religious, "which the irreligious class? In which shall we look for "the enemies of religion ?"

We shall find that Ellis's idea of religion and a religious education was practical:—

"We are bound," he says (vol. ii., page 60), "to reject,

"as irreligious, all professions of religion which do not
"correspond with the conduct habitually practised and
"approved; and also to accept no conduct as religious
"which is not good, however much it may be upheld by
"the self-constituted interpreters of religion. We must
"give no quarter to 'religious bandits.'"[1]
And the converse statement of a truly religious character
is equally interesting.

"The foundation on which you rely," he says, addressing
his class of teachers (vol. ii., page 190), "for the superstructure
"of a religious character is—habits of good conduct formed
"by imitation and example, and strengthened by feelings
"of love, gratitude, and respect; and intelligence, day by
"day awakening to a wider and juster appreciation of the
"distinctions between right and wrong, good and bad,
"just and unjust. You cannot conceive any better pre-
"paration whereon to form a mind capable of contem-
"plating and appreciating the perfection of goodness and
"wisdom."
The following quotation (vol. ii., page 63) shows more
fully the practical view of religion adopted by Ellis in all
his works:—

"PHILO-SOCRATES: Who is a good Christian?

"TEACHERS: He must, at least, be one who does good
"works. 'By their fruits shall ye know them.'

"P.: You would hardly object to the quaint expression
"of one of the early fathers, 'He who does good is a
"'Christian, though he be an atheist.' May I add, 'and
"'who does not connive at good works left undone?'

"T.: Of course. To connive at good works left undone
"is not very far removed from doing bad works.

"P.: Is any kind of conduct specially enjoined by the
"Christian religion?

---

[1] This refers to an anecdote previously related of a bandit of the middle
ages, who assumed to be religious, and proclaimed himself to be a "Friend
"to God and enemy to all mankind."

"T.: Love to God and love to man, as nearly as possible
"the words of the Saviour, will suffice to convey to you
"our notions of the conduct enjoined to Christians.

"P.: Quite.　And of which conduct can we judge more
"readily—that towards God or that towards man?

"T.: Of conduct towards man.　We can scarcely judge
"of conduct towards God, except through conduct towards
"man.　Conduct towards God is not otherwise cognizable,
"beyond each individual's consciousness.

"P.: Is 'Love one another,' then, the Divine precept by
"which love to God may most readily be judged?

"T.: More readily than by any other known to us."

With these views of what a really religious character
and religious education are, Ellis shows in other parts of
these papers how entirely existing views of duty have been
attained by the application of modern intelligence, and how
different those views, as exemplified in modern conduct, are
from the interpretation and exemplification of Christianity
in the past.　He shows how the Christian scriptures and the
doctrines of Christianity have been the same—so far as words
written, translated, and printed are concerned—for eighteen
hundred years, while during that period we have seen, on
the one hand, the Crusades, when united Christendom was
leagued together to expel the Mahomedans from Palestine;
and on the other, during the present century, a Christian
force sent to Palestine to co-operate with the Mahomedan
Government, first in preventing the barbarous massacre of a
Christian by a Mahomedan population, and afterwards in
saving the disarmed Mahomedans from massacre by the
Christians when they became the stronger party.　The bitter
persecution of heretics in the name of Christianity during the
middle ages, and, even in very recent times, the infliction of
disabilities and penalties for differences of belief, stigmatised
as heresy or infidelity by a legislation controlled by a Protestant Christian Church; the defence of slavery and the slave
trade by the British Church till far into the nineteenth century,

and by American Christian ministers at the very time (1862) when he was writing; and the ferocious revenge, inflicted in the name of punishment, are all shown to have either been done in the very name and under the sanction of so-called Christianity, or defended and vindicated by the highest members of a Christian Church. And yet the most modern development of moral thought has led most Christian ministers in the present day to denounce these practices in the name of religion as strongly as their predecessors defended them. It was easy to demonstrate the proposition that though Christianity is supposed to be the same and unaltered, it had been interpreted differently at different times, and that, in fact, " People bring to the Bible a great part of what they find in " it." The conclusion established as to the conduct of those who insisted on Bible lessons in schools as the sole basis of religion and education, was that it was neglecting the cultivation of that intelligence which would cause the Bible to be sought for, and when found to be rightly interpreted and so read to advantage; that, instead of education being based on the Bible, the study of the Bible should be based on education; and that children should be prepared by intelligent cultivation of their moral faculties for deriving the full benefit of it and avoiding the misdirection which has during a long period of history been derived from it.

The question of the suitability of the Bible as a school book is carefully and reverently discussed, and the prominent passages of the Old and New Testament which are most frequently selected as lessons are brought forward for consideration in reference to their effect on children, and the guidance which children are likely to derive from them. The common object of all teachers is assumed to be to ascertain how schoolwork may be made most efficient in sending forth into the world religious and well-conducted men and women.

Taking then the Old Testament first, our attention is drawn to the narrative of the command given by God to

Adam and Eve, "Of the tree of the knowledge of good and
" evil, thou shall not eat of it: for in the day that thou eatest
" thereof thou shalt surely die"—followed by the expulsion
of man by the following Divine decree, " And the Lord God
" said, Behold, the man is become as one of us, to know
" good and evil: and now, lest he put forth his hand, and take
" also of the tree of life, and eat, and live for ever: Therefore
" the Lord God sent him forth from the garden of Eden, to
" till the ground from whence he was taken."   And the question presents itself irresistibly how this extract can help the
teacher who is striving to teach his boys to know right from
wrong, to distinguish between good and evil, and to incline
to cleave to the good and eschew the evil.

In the same way the attention of the teachers is drawn
to the account of the murder of Abel; to the history of
Noah, who was selected for preservation as a righteous man
with his family when the Deluge was sent for the purpose
of putting an end to wickedness, and was immediately afterwards led to curse his own son for conduct arising out of
his own drunkenness; to the history of Abraham and Sarah,
and their conduct to Ishmael and Hagar; to the account of
Esau and Jacob, and to the singular fraud recorded (Genesis
xxvii.) to have been practised on Isaac, a fraud which led to
Jacob's becoming the founder of the chosen people, and
with respect to which a halo of sanctity seems to be
attached to a transaction which in these days would be
described as a conspiracy between a mother and one child
to defraud another child and cozen the father.

The earnest and reverent consideration of these narratives
leads irresistibly to the conclusion that a medley of good and
evil ought not to be placed before children till they are capable
of discriminating one from the other, and drawing the right
lessons from the entire history.

"What moral nature and intellectual cultivation," says
Philo-Socrates (vol. ii., p. 87), "can children bring to bear upon
" a scene of adult life thus spread before them ?   Are not

"children the germs of good or bad, civilised or barbarous,
"intelligent or ignorant men, to become either according
"to the state of society into which they are born—to the
"teaching and training of which they are to be the
"recipients? Will not the good, the civilised, the in-
"telligent, form a very different judgment of the actors
"in the scene which you have presented to us to that
"which will be formed by the bad, the barbarous, and the
"ignorant? Will it not be a matter of uncertainty what
"impressions will be made upon children—upon those
"who are unformed both as to their habits and intellects?"

We are further led to consider the histories of Jacob and
Rachel—of Joseph and his brethren—of the plagues of
Egypt—of the Divine command alleged to be given by the
Lord to borrow of the Egyptians jewels of silver and jewels
of gold without any intention of returning them, whereby
they "spoiled the Egyptians." All are treated in the same
earnest and calm method. All are shown to be unsuitable
for children without the necessary intelligence and preparation to understand and draw the proper lessons from
them.

These remarks upon the teaching of the Scriptures of the
Old Testament are followed by a similar inquiry into the use
of the New Testament in schools; and the chapters taken
for consideration are the fifth and sixth chapters of St.
Matthew's Gospel, including the sermon on the Mount—
the object being (vol. ii., p. 106) "to ascertain whether the
"Gospels, used as reading-lessons, are adapted to help
"children to a perception of the line of conduct which they
"ought to pursue on quitting school, and to call forth in
"them a sense of responsibility perpetually urging them
"to pursue that line." One or two specimens will suffice.
Even the very first verse, "Blessed are the poor in spirit:
"for theirs is the kingdom of heaven," needs careful inquiry
to find its meaning.

"Who are the poor in spirit," asks Philo-Socrates (p.

"107), among your relations, friends and acquaintances,
"the people whom you see and of whom you hear? The
"firemen, who mount the fire escapes; the boatmen, who
"launch the lifeboat; the sister of charity, who cou-
"rageously visits the abode of sickness and contagion;
"the boy, who takes up the quarrel of the injured and
"helpless, who boldly acknowledges a fault to meet its
"consequences, and avows an opinion however unaccept-
"able? Or the man, who shrinks from the dangers to
"which he is summoned by the call of duty; leans upon
"the opinions of others and forms none of his own; and
"the boy who hides his faults at the risk of seeing the
"consequences of them fastened upon another? And to
"which of these is the kingdom of heaven reserved?
"What is the meaning of being 'blessed?' Happy,
"cheerful, contented at the moment? or looking forward
"to such a state of feeling at a future time, in compen-
"sation for present privation, suffering, or afflictions
"courageously and unrepiningly endured?"

It is not necessary to do more than show the number of
inquiries needed at every point to enable the deep meaning
of these two celebrated chapters to be brought to the minds
of children. It is curious to trace how many verses need
such investigation as this. Some are even incomprehensible,
and apparently in conflict with the simplest lessons of duty.
How can a teacher, desirous to impress on his pupils the
most important fundamental lessons of industry, intelligence,
self-denial, and forethought, expect that they will be competent to reconcile with such teaching the ideas which will
be conveyed to their minds by the well-known verses:—

"Behold the fowls of the air: for they sow not, neither
"do they reap, nor gather into barns; yet your heavenly
"Father feedeth them. Are ye not much better than
"they?

"Which of you by taking thought can add one cubit to
"his stature?

" And why take ye thought for raiment?   Consider the
" lilies of the field, how they grow; they toil not, neither
" do they spin;

" And yet I say unto you, that even Solomon in all his
" glory was not arrayed like one of these.

" Wherefore, if God clothe the grass of the field, which
" to-day is, and to-morrow is cast into the oven, shall he
" not much more clothe you, O ye of little faith?

" Take therefore no thought for the morrow: for the
" morrow shall take thought for the things of itself.
" Sufficient unto the day is the evil thereof."

It will be evident from these extracts that the practice of
reading "without note or comment," which was then being
imposed as a condition by the Department of Education, was
strongly disapproved of. To boast and stipulate that the
reading of the Bible should be unaccompanied by any
attempt to ascertain in what sense passages bearing upon
varieties of conduct are received, or to exercise the memories
of the children upon the subject matter of the reading beyond
the words, the dates, and the places mentioned, was in Ellis's
view injurious to the highest object of education, and treating
the Bible itself with disrespect.

But those opponents of Ellis's method who drew the
inference from his views on this subject that his teaching
was not in the truest sense religious were gravely misled.
In a most interesting paper on the subject of truthfulness in
investigation he tells us further (vol. ii., page 166):—

" Supposing you to concur in my views of the in-
" expediency of attempting to introduce Bible lessons
" into your schools, your lessons in religion, or, more
" properly, your preparations for them, will be to lead
" your pupils, throughout the whole course of their
" instruction, to distinguish the true from the false, the
" good from the bad, with the conviction that an earnest
" desire to seek and act up to the good and the true, and
" to shun the bad and the false, can never be opposed to

"any religion or interpretation of religion that ought to
" be held to."

A short further extract from the same paper (vol. ii.,
page 171) puts in a fuller way the conclusions drawn by
Ellis from his careful and elaborate study of the Bible as a
means of education.

" I do not see how a religious use can be made of the
" Bible in schools. Mature minds alone are competent
" to master its contents. None but immature minds con-
" gregate in schools. The utmost that can be done for
" them there before they take their departure is so to
" prepare, and bud, or graft them, as that they may give
" promise of bursting into a happy maturity. Most
" people will admit that the minds of children are too
" immature to be capable of understanding what are
" classed among the higher branches of knowledge, upon
" which all who study them are found to come to a common
" agreement. Nevertheless, few will be found to assent
" to our deduction from this acknowledged immaturity,
" that it is inexpedient and irreligious to thrust upon
" children 'the Book,' replete though it be with subli-
" mities, to the height of which the greatest minds can
" hardly soar; with ambiguities which the acutest
" intellects can rarely clear up; with apparent contra-
" dictions not easy to explain; and with records of acts
" and sentiments difficult to reconcile with an unfaltering
" faith in the goodness and wisdom of God. Our interest
" lies, however, rather with what we would introduce and
" keep in our schools, for the purpose of rearing up
" intelligent and well-conducted men, than with what we
" would exclude; and we will examine the ground already
" gone over to make sure that nothing has been omitted
" which is requisite for producing that state of under-
" standing and that tone of feeling on which hopes of
" the religious character may reasonably rest."

.   .   .   .   .   .

"TEACHERS (p. 175): Will it not be objected that we "show ourselves more indifferent or less particular about "the conduct of man to God than about the conduct of "man to man?

"P.: And may we not answer that the only sure mode "of judging of man's conduct towards God is through "his conduct to his fellow-men? And in striving to judge "of the comparative results of teaching morality and "religion through the Bible, instead of teaching the "Bible through morality and religion, will it not be "appropriate to put some such question as this: Out of "which school will men take the clearest perception of "the distinctions between good and bad in the conduct of "man to man throughout all the relations of life?"

The second volume is closed by some interesting papers upon the intelligence and morality of that portion of the clergy who were opposing the search after truth by setting up the claim of authority to bar its progress. It will be remembered that the well-known collection of writings by the Rev. Frederick Temple (afterwards Bishop of London) and other clergymen, known as *Essays and Reviews*, had recently been published, and had attracted great attention from its courage and earnestness. A collection of essays in reply was published, introduced by a preface by the Bishop of Oxford (Wilberforce), in which the strongest language of reprobation was used and charges of "infidelity," "atheism," "irreligiousness," "violation of professional fitness," "criminal "levity," were flung wholesale at the truth-seekers. The Bishop of Oxford in his preface had demanded "the "distinct, solemn, and, if need be, *severe decision of authority* "that assertions such as these cannot be put forward as "possibly true, or even advanced as admitting of question"— an attitude which, as may be imagined, roused Ellis's indignation; and he could not refrain from dealing with such a pretence as that of barring the search for truth in strong terms.

In a previous paper "On Tolerance and Intolerance" he had shown the limits of what society ought and ought not to tolerate. Obedience to the laws framed for the protection of the community must be insisted on. Society could not exist unless such obedience were enforced, and acts injurious to the general welfare prevented or punished. The man who objects to the laws in existence for the time being is not and cannot be allowed to disobey them, even though he alleges that he objects to them on conscientious grounds. On the other hand, those who desire the reform or alteration of laws must rely upon persuasion to procure their amendment, and such persuasion involves and includes liberty of discussion and remonstrance in the fullest sense of those terms. Experience has shown not only that laws once existing and defended by a majority of the community have become discredited and repealed, with such general satisfaction that after their repeal it has become a wonder that they can ever have been borne. Nay, history has even recorded how opinions now universally received on questions of natural science, such as the shape of the earth, the causes of day and night and eclipses and the like, have been met by charges of infidelity and enmity to religion, and sought to be suppressed by the exercise of the "authority" of the Church. It may well be imagined, then, with what indignant scorn Ellis would treat a proposal by a leader of a Protestant Christian Church so able and prominent as Bishop Wilberforce, to put down by authority the earnest and devoted search by men of the standing and attainments of Temple, Jowett, and their colleagues, after improved interpretation of Christian doctrines and the truth upon the discovery of which human well-being is so largely dependent. He expresses his unbounded contempt for an ecclesiastic guilty of using the intolerant language of Bishop Wilberforce's preface to "other ecclesiastics as much morally and intellectually his "superiors as they are conventionally his inferiors," and

after pointing out (vol. ii., p. 304) that "it is one of the most
" important of moral duties to encourage not merely the tole-
" rance, but the cultivation of habits of freedom of thought
" and expression as the mainstays of integrity and candour,
" the conservators of knowledge, the correctors of error, and
" the pioneers of improvement and progress," he asks—in the
light of the then attitude of Bishop Wilberforce and his
colleagues, in which the majority of the chief dignitaries of
the Church supported them—" how the clergy of all denomi-
" nations stand before the world as promoters of openness
" of disposition, non-concealment of thought, ardour in the
" search after truth, confession of doubt and difficulty of
" belief, and even of dissent ? Are they as tolerant of freedom
" of thought and expression as they are of conduct which is
" adverse to well-being, and which ought, accordingly, to be
" regarded by them as irreligious and unchristian ?"

Volume iv. (parts 7 and 8) is described as "Among the
" Hindoos," and is an interesting series of papers devoted to
an inquiry into the principles by which human conduct may
be judged, and to a consideration of the comparative value
of free truth-seeking investigation and argument by the use
of the reasoning faculties on the one hand, and of supernatural authority, inspiration, and intuition on the other; in
discovering what acts are, or are not, conducive to general
well-being, and in persuading mankind to adopt them.
Although the site of the discussions is imagined to be in
Hindostan, the consideration of these questions is applicable
to any community in the whole world: and the reason for
adopting the Hindoos as the other parties to the dialogue is
evidently for the sake of obtaining a point of view external
to and above the social system investigated, and from which
the supernatural records which have descended from remote
antiquity might be more freely and impartially discussed.

Early in this series we find an interesting paper on the
general subject of Laws, Morals, and Religion, in which the
outlines of the subject to be discussed are sketched. The

distinction between morals and laws is carefully explained;
morals being defined as " rules in general for the guidance
" of human conduct as a means of promoting the general
" happiness," and laws as " those rules in particular which
" are laid down and enjoined by the governing power."   In
contrast with these are stated by the Hindoos some of the
rules inculcated by the ancient sacred writings of the
Hindoos as well as of the Mahomedans and Christians: as,
for example, penance or fasting, that is, self-inflicted pain or
abstention of some kind for the sole purpose of earning the
Divine favour or averting the Divine wrath.   The discussion
goes on to trace how the sacred writings have remained
unaltered from remote antiquity, while the interpretation of
them and the acts and conduct consequent on such interpretation have materially varied and are now very different
from what they were in past times.   That the Vedas have
not rendered any assistance in forwarding works of steam
transport or telegraphic communication, in developing the
skill of the surgeon or in bringing about that wonderful
discovery, chloroform, is unquestionable; while the frightful
persecutions, cruelties, and other wrongs, which have been
practised in past times by the believers in the Vedas, as
well as in the Bible and Koran, lead to the conclusion that
the altered interpretation placed on them has proceeded
from some source external to them.   In these preliminary
papers the teaching of the missionaries, who have visited
India and sought to implant Christian doctrines there, is
also discussed and commented on.   From this basis the
conversations proceed to investigate the question, what
conduct is moral and what immoral—in other words, what
conduct will promote the general well-being of mankind,
and conduce to human happiness; what conduct will disturb
it, and conduce to human misery or diminish human
happiness.

Here the writer takes up the subject which he had before
discussed in his *Outlines of the History and Formation of*

the Understanding. The sensations of the infant are explained—the first pleasures and pains which it is capable of feeling—the gradual development of those pleasures into those of the adult human being ; and the classification of those pleasures follows, in which the act of giving, or sharing, or resigning the means of gratification is specially included, and in mature life the pleasures made up of the contemplation of future pleasures to be secured, or of future pains to be averted, sometimes by abstinence from present enjoyment, sometimes by endurance of pain in undergoing severe labour and in encountering danger. From this the various lines of conduct are pointed out which will conduce to well-being or the reverse ; and the inference is easily led up to (vol. iv., page 78), that the chief difficulty in training the young is "to apply that treatment and discipline to them "which will dispose them to seek enjoyment, or pleasure, "or happiness, in that exercise of their faculties which is "most likely to lead to future happiness ; and that method "of imparting knowledge which will bring the young to "acquire their knowledge by rediscovering for themselves "that which has already been discovered, so that their "faculties shall be trained to acquire for themselves, on "leaving school, all the further knowledge which it will be "desirable for them to possess and apply."

Things good and evil, and the various circumstances affecting them—droughts and the consequent famines; wars; pestilences and their causes; with the methods by which each may be prevented, lead on to the consideration of what is right and wrong—what will conduce to bring about the good and avert the evil. The history of the past is inquired into as a basis of hope for the rapid progress of mankind in the future in intelligence, conduct, and consequent well-being. Of the two kinds of knowledge, which are sought by human beings, a careful distinction is made (vol. iv., page 143).

"A pupil who can repeat long passages from the Vedas,

Q

"the Koran, or the Bible, and who can name the date of
"every remarkable event that has occurred within the
"historic period, and every town and river on the earth, is
"said to *know*; and the man who can construct or drive
"a locomotive, build or navigate a ship, irrigate a hill
"district with water drawn from the valley, extract gas
"from the coal, and distribute it appropriately to supply
"light to a distant city, and contrive the means of trans-
"mitting intelligence with the rapidity of thought over
"hundreds of miles of desert, and under hundreds of
"miles of sea, is also said to *know*. But the knowledge
"of one is not to be confounded with that of the other."

This distinction brings out prominently to what methods
the great acquisition of knowledge and capacity in the past
is due, and how further knowledge and capacity may be
looked for in the future.

It is impossible to do more than very shortly refer to the
three papers of the series which deal with human ideas of
the supernatural, and the practical effect of posthumous
rewards and punishments on the one hand, and the true use
of the reasoning faculties on the other. The Hindoos, in
the course of these dialogues, elicit the characteristics by
which any writings purporting to be of Divine origin must
be tested. Any alleged revelation which is derogatory to the
character of the Deity or Deities, if more than one, is agreed
to be necessarily spurious,[1] though possibly not a fabrica-
tion, but the work of enthusiasts who had deluded them-

---

[1] Socrates leads up to and proves the same proposition. "But we shall
"have to repudiate," he says, "a large part of those fables which are now in
"vogue, and especially of what I call the greater fables, the stories which
"Hesiod and Homer and the other poets tell us. They told, and tell, their
"stories to men. But in these stories there is a fault which deserves the
"gravest condemnation; namely when an author gives a bad representation of
"the character of gods and heroes. We must condemn such a poet as we
"should condemn a painter whose picture should bear no resemblance to the
"objects which he tries to imitate."—Whewell's *Platonic Dialogues*, vol. iii.,
page 174, "Republic," book ii., § 16.

selves into the notion that they had been made vehicles of inspiration for communicating the Divine commands to mankind. They reject as incredible the idea of a cruel and vindictive God—a God who has predestined the greater part of mankind to an eternity of torment. They reject, as impossible and contrary to reason, the conception of a God or Being of infinite goodness and wisdom who so dooms those whom He has himself created. They dismiss from their minds their old belief in the transmigration of souls as one into which their ignorance and credulity had led them; as well as other doctrines of their country once sacred to them. They point out in the Christian religion the singular contradiction of a doctrine of future rewards and punishments for earthly conduct, without belief in which witnesses were rejected in courts of law, and on the other hand the doctrine of salvation by faith, so that without faith in Jesus there is no hope of posthumous reward for conduct, however meritorious, and with faith in Jesus, no fear of posthumous punishment for conduct, however culpable. And they are led to see that they cannot but reject these ideas as being such as their reasoning faculties in the present day cannot tolerate or receive. And yet the practice of testing the truth of these ancient doctrines by the reasoning faculties is of slow growth, and has been the result of the gradual development of intelligence, knowledge, and power of judgment of the human mind, and its application to these subjects. We may quote one interesting passage as to this (vol. iv., page 180):—

"HINDOOS: We think it must be conceded that every "step in man's progress is marked by the wider range "taken by his reasoning faculties, while he has greatly "reduced the range within which he gives play to his "intuitive faculties.

"P.: Does he place less reliance than formerly on "charms, omens, prayers, fasts, and penances, on the "presence of good and evil spirits hovering around in-

"visible, on angels with or without wings, on the images
"of gods, whether of wood, stone, or metal; and more
"upon knowledge and the application of its resources for
"the securing of his own well-being?

"H.: Less upon prayer, penance, and omens, and more
"upon his acquaintance with the physical forces around
"him and his skill in applying them.

"P.: We have a proverb current among us which
"expresses that 'God helps those that help themselves.'

"H.: And if He also refuse to help those who will not
"help themselves, the inference is inevitable, that His only
"way of helping anybody is through the operation of
"those general laws by which the universe is governed,
"and which all who would obtain help must study and
"learn and afterwards apply.

"P.: An ancient fable current among the Greeks em-
"bodies the same thought. The carman who prayed to
"Hercules to extricate his cart out of the ruts in which it
"was fixed, was told by a voice from heaven to put his
"shoulder to the wheel."

Three interesting papers on "Duty and Conscience," on
"Public Spirit," and on the "Desirable and the Practicable,"
conclude this volume. We can only give one or two extracts
from them. The main principle of duty—what each man
ought to do—having been previously defined, conscience, the
feeling which tells each person what he ought to do, is thus
explained (vol. iv., page 238):—

"H.: If there are persons to be found who can combine
"indulgence with a total disregard of the comfort and
"feelings of others, and yet give signs of as much intelli-
"gence as is implied in the question, 'why should we
"'sacrifice our indulgence to a sense of duty?' we could
"only class them as we do the blind, the deaf and dumb,
"and the imbecile, and those who have lost a limb, and
"admit them to be short of something which the perfectly
"organized possess—to be without a conscience.

"P.: Here you have introduced another word which
"has been mixed up with as much confusion of thought
"as duty—perhaps with more. But in the way you use
"it I presume you simply mean to express by it 'sense of
"'duty.'

"H.: We meant to express by it that inward feeling of
"which we are conscious, and of which we suppose almost
"all persons are conscious, which tells them when they are
"doing or intending to do right or wrong, or intending
"to avoid or not to avoid doing wrong, which tells them
"when they are doing or intending to do, or to neglect to
"do, their duty, or which encourages or reproves them
"according as either has been done. . . . Conscience
"admonishes us concerning our duty as we conceive it to
"be. Intelligence, that is, the teaching of observation, in-
"quiry, and reflection, can alone certify to us what duty is."

The concluding paper—on the "Desirable and the
"Practicable"—will be specially interesting. It draws the
main inferences on some of the subjects discussed in previous
papers, and suggests what thoughtful and well-intentioned
persons should do to attain the objects sought for. The
dialogues have discussed on more than one occasion what
seems to be an important thought sought to be elucidated
in the series—the effect of the hope of posthumous rewards,
and posthumous well-being, in comparison with the earthly
consequences of conduct. The following (vol. iv., page 296)
gives the conclusion :—

"P.: It may be worth considering whether, in guiding
"conduct by the best established rules for securing earthly
"well-being, individuals or nations can endanger their
"posthumous well-being, or fail to pursue the course most
"likely to obtain that in addition; or, whether it would be
"safer to reverse the process, holding out that if the means
"best adapted for securing posthumous well-being be
"taken, they must also be necessarily the best for attaining
"earthly well-being.

"H.: We have given consideration enough to those
"questions, and have no hesitation in pronouncing for the
"former course. . . . We do not prefer earthly to post-
"humous well-being, but we consider conduct shaped so as
"to attain earthly well-being is the best means of attaining
"posthumous well-being. We would fix our attention,
"therefore, to use your own words, upon the means of
"attaining earthly well-being, in order to secure that for
"which we long more—posthumous well-being.

"P.: Are you not presenting the question in a new point
"of view? Are you not making out that the means for
"attaining earthly and posthumous well-being are identical?

"H.: And so we think they are.

"P.: Why, then, did you express a preference for taking
"measures to procure the earthly rather than the post-
"humous?

"H.: Because we understand better what earthly well-
"being consists of, and can more readily form a judgment
"of the means by which it is to be obtained."

As we may naturally anticipate, we find in this paper, as
a sort of goal, the thought which, as will be seen by those
who have perused the present memoir, was the guiding
principle of Ellis's life. Nowhere, perhaps, has he put
it more clearly and concisely than at the end of this
paper. The Hindoos are led, by the guidance of their
teacher, to the following conclusions (vol. iv., pp. 289 and
303):—

"We will, therefore, put our finger at once upon two
"great blots in the method of instruction to be seen in all
"the schools with which we are acquainted—one of
"omission, and the other of commission. The first is, the
"absence of the larger part of the instruction indispen-
"sable for good self-guidance, and as a preparation for
"seeking and obtaining the additional instruction for the
"same purpose which can only be understood and appre-
"ciated after the school age; and the second is, the

"covering over and concealing the appearance of this
"vacuum, the allaying even the suspicion of it, by what is
"called religious teaching."

"We begin to see that there is no single obstacle in the
"way of increasing the general well-being so great as that
"of the tenacious adherence to practices in education
"derived from times when knowledge and its applications
"were far less advanced than they now are. When once
"attention, if only of a few, has been fixed upon this
"obstacle, the removal of it must be all but certain. The
"solitary doubt that can reasonably be felt is as to the
"time which will elapse before its removal can be accom-
"plished. However long that time is to be, of this you
"may feel assured, you leave us deeply convinced that
"there is no work to which we can devote ourselves more
"desirable, and at the same time more practicable, towards
"increasing the well-being of our countrymen, than the
"improvement of the character of prevailing education in
"the sense explained by you, and the bringing home
"education thus improved, as nearly as possible, to every
"child that is born."

There is little to record in these years of Ellis's doings,
except the production of *Philo-Socrates.* One or two letters
to Hodgson are of interest:—

"19th April, 1861.

"Your letter of yesterday seems to have shed a bright
"gleam of sunshine over my day's work. While striving
"to do our duty among the rank and file, toiling under
"the weights, almost beyond our strength, which we have
"to carry, crossed and disappointed in our expectations,
"and wounded in our family affections, we must seek for
"consolation in the manifest proofs of progress in our
"race. We must, in our advanced age, be content to
"forego the enjoyment pictured as the reward of the
"good and great men of old. The utmost that any of us

"can dare to expect to trace to himself of the improve-
"ments which he will leave behind him may be expressed
"by '*quorum pars parva fui.*'   And yet who would not
"rather have to act a small part well on the present stage
"than a great part among an inferior company?"

"7th December, 1861.

"I had resumed my weekly lessons at Mr. Rogers'
"school, but am now compelled to suspend them. I am
"now using my half holiday—a part of it at least, after a
"morning of discussion upon premiums in war risks, which
"it bewilders me to attempt to estimate—in soothing my
"ruffled spirits by writing a few lines to you.

"I cling to my unprofessional hobby for recreation and
"distraction, hoping meanwhile that common sense on the
"other side of the Atlantic will not be so entirely disre-
"garded as to add the horrors of a war with us to those of
"the fratricidal struggle in which they are already
"engaged.

"Mr. Shields' class at University College—I mean that
"of the schoolmasters—opened and proceeds successfully.
"I have not as yet missed one from the beginning, and he
"seems to be bearing up quite as well as we could have
"expected.   His own school is larger than ever."

"3rd February, 1862.

"If, after much self-communing, I had thought that the
"publication of my views upon the impropriety of mis-
"using the Bible by turning it into a school-book, and the
"rebutting of the objections, sometimes loudly expressed,
"sometimes whispered, against me for excluding the Bible
"from schools under my influence, would prevent the
"introduction of instruction in social science, I should
"have kept back my lucubrations. But I see no grounds
"for such apprehensions. The Privy Council and the
"training schools will not at all events be able to banish

"what they have never admitted. I believe I am telling
"great and important truths, which some cannot, some
"dare not from cowardice, and some prudently and wisely
"will not, tell. I am not a young man with a position to
"gain or hold, and am as well placed as it is possible to
"be to meet the howls of the ignorant and superstitious,
"and of those who simply cannot bear to be disturbed. I
"believe I am doing no more than my duty, and that the
"very agitation which may be produced will rather quicken
"than retard the improvements so urgently called for in
"education.

"As for the critical organs of opinion, *i.e.*, the periodical
"press—in that quarter I expect either silence or un-
"measured hostility, certainly no favour."

During this period, Ellis became acquainted with one or
two of the brave leaders of the movement for Italian freedom, who were at that time exiled from their country. One
of these was a Signor Avesani, a member of the Venetian
Government under Manin, which for a time held Venice
against the Austrians. Avesani was a gentleman of ability
and education, and often visited at Ellis's house. Another
Italian gentleman, whose acquaintance he made at this
time, was Signor Frisco, the educational inspector of the
Italian Government for the Naples district, then visiting
in England, who introduced to him Luigi d' Agostini, the
orphan son of Cesare d' Agostini, who was well known in
connection with the Roman struggle, and became an
exile upon the occupation of Rome by the forces of the
French Republic in 1849. The boy, left an orphan at nine
years of age, had found a friend in and been maintained by
a benevolent English lady, a relative of Sir John Franklin.
Ellis took him up, sent him to be trained under Shields, at
the Peckham Birkbeck Schools, so that he might assist in
introducing in Italy the improved method of education
which Ellis had sought to introduce in England. And
in respect to Italy, he was materially helped by a friend

with whom he and the ladies of his family became intimate
at this period. Madame Salis Schwabe, the widow of a
German gentleman, who had been the proprietor of large
print works at Rhodes, near Manchester, had, after her
husband's death, devoted much of her time and means to
the assistance of Italy and Italian patriots. She was the
friend of Garibaldi, to whom she sent aid and medical
comfort when he lay wounded after being taken prisoner
by Victor Emanuel. She had become an attached friend
and admirer of Ellis, and the strong impression which Ellis's
views had made upon her, in combination with her sympathy
with Italy, induced her to undertake the work of founding
schools in which Ellis's plans for teaching older children and
those of Froebel with respect to infant schools should be
practically carried out. Her schools, which were founded at
Naples about 1864, have become a great success, and been
in the end adopted by the Italian Government. But upon
this subject it will be well to let Madame Schwabe give her
own statement. She has kindly perused the manuscript of
the present memoir ; and the letter which she has written to
the author explaining how she was led to undertake the
foundation of her Naples School, and a few letters written
by Ellis during the years 1875–1878 to Signor Quarati,
the master—who had been trained in England under Mr.
Shields—are printed as an Appendix.[1] Their perusal will
be of much interest, as showing how easily a valuable
institution is developed from a small seed planted in suitable
ground.

The history of Signor Quarati, and the series of adven-
tures through which he passed before he became master of
the Naples School, are so romantic and interesting, and so
illustrative of Italian character, as to be worthy of record
here.

He was a Genoese and a devoted follower of Garibaldi—

---

[1] See Appendix A.

one of the many thousand Italians, noble, self-sacrificing patriots, who were ready to give their whole existence and, if necessary, to lay down their lives for the cause of Italy and liberty. He had, when almost a boy, joined Garibaldi, the leader who gave form and union to these aspirations, and was one of the first thousand who landed at Marsala and fought on with Garibaldi through Sicily and South Italy till Naples was free. Then he enlisted in the Italian army. But it happened that the accidents of history brought about a very unforeseen result. Quarati's regiment formed part of the army which soon afterwards—in obedience to political exigencies—was ordered to check Garibaldi's subsequent action in support of the freedom of Rome, and he found himself at Aspromonte opposed to and actually ordered to fight against the idol of Italian patriotism—the man who had devoted his life to the cause of Italian freedom. This was impossible to Quarati; he would rather have sacrificed his own life for Garibaldi. He deserted with a kindred spirit, a young Sicilian named St. Angelo.

Knowing that they would be proscribed by Italian laws and probably shot if taken, they sought, in despair of anything else, to make their way to Poland, there to fight in another country for liberty and against despotism, and they obtained money to pay their expenses. But another destiny was reserved for them. They found themselves unable to procure passports which would conduct them to Poland, but managed to find refuge in England. There they found out the Committee of sympathizers with Italian and Polish liberty, and among them Madame Schwabe, whose sympathy with and active help for these lads—for Quarati was then only nineteen—were at once engaged. She tried hard to obtain them a pardon, and meantime gave them a home under the care of her gardener. But the pardon was refused: desertion on the field of battle was too heinous a crime in the eyes of military authorities to be pardoned. So some other means of supporting themselves must be found for them.

Madame Schwabe deemed their lives too valuable to be sacrificed on the hopeless battlefields of Poland. St. Angelo was a trumpeter, and for him she first obtained an engagement in a band, and afterwards got him employment in the Manchester Mills which had formerly been her husband's and now belonged to her sons. Quarati wished to become a schoolmaster, and Madame Schwabe sent him to Ellis. Miss Ellis taught him English; and he was sent to the Peckham Birkbeck Schools and trained for the office of a teacher under Shields. There he remained some years, and was reported by Shields to possess great capacity for the work. But in 1866, when the troubles which had led to collision between Victor Emanuel and Garibaldi had become matter of history, and Garibaldi was again treated by official Italy with the affectionate regard which her people had always felt towards him, Madame Schwabe renewed her exertions for Quarati. She wrote a letter to the King, telling him his history, and begging that he might be pardoned and allowed to return to devote his life to the cause of his country. She sent the letter to Garibaldi, by whom, personally, it was recommended to Victor Emanuel. But the answer was still not altogether favourable. The King replied that Italy was a constitutional country; that he, personally, could do nothing, and that Quarati must return and submit himself to the laws of his country.

He had faith in the loving heart of his king. He went and gave himself up, was tried, and sentenced by the Military Tribunal to two years' imprisonment. But at this stage the King's prerogative came into force; in six days Quarati received a full and complete pardon. He at once returned to the army, fought in the campaign of 1866 against Austria, and after that was over, and the union of Italy had been accomplished by the cession of Venice, he was required to remain and complete his term of service in the army. But his friend, Madame Schwabe, had not lost sight of him. Italy needed a man with the capabilities which Quarati had shown he possessed for other work than the army had now to do. In 1870, Madame Schwabe again applied to the Italian Government, and by the interest she was able to make with Signor Correnti, the then Minister of Public Instruction, she obtained his discharge. She sent him to Milan for six months; then he went again for a short time to his old friends at Peckham; and then to Ancona, where he passed his examination and obtained his diploma as a school-master. For some time he was employed as an assistant in another school, but in 1873, he became head master of the school which Madame Schwabe had founded at Naples and which bore the name—from the building in which it was carried on—of the Ex-Collegio-Medico.

The only other production of Ellis's pen which was published during the time when he was engaged on *Philo-Socrates* was a lecture upon "Instruction in Elementary "Social Science, what it is, and why and how it ought to be "given in all schools," which he delivered on 29th October, 1863, at University College, Gower Street, on the opening of a course of lectures to a class of teachers formed for its study, and conducted by Mr. Shields. The only passage to which we need refer is an account of an interview with a political economist of some note—but it is presumed of the ancient school—who had met Ellis's approaches "with ex-"pressions of doubt about the possibility of making the "abstruse subjects with which the political economist has to "deal either interesting or intelligible to children," and even when Ellis pointed out the importance of the subject of wages met him by the dry remark that "the subject of "wages was one of the most difficult, complicated, and "unsettled within the whole province of political economy." The main object of the lecture was to show the utter mistake of such an idea. Ellis, knowing as he did from long and conclusive experience, that such teaching might be made not only the most interesting of all school lessons, but a valuable instrument for the formation of character, was specially desirous, and exerted himself in this address, to bring home to the minds of the teachers who attended his lectures the misconception involved in such an idea, and to prevent their being led away by it.

Chapter X.

1864—1874.

THE ten years succeeding the completion of *Philo-Socrates* were productive of great changes in Ellis's domestic circle. Some twenty years previously he had lost his elder son, William Henry—a most promising young man—at the age of nineteen, from typhoid fever, caught during a holiday excursion, to which he succumbed at a hotel on the Rhine, being unable to reach England. In 1855, his younger son, Edward, had married happily, and was now the father of a young family; and from the time of the loss of his elder son Ellis's family life had passed un-eventfully and happily. His wife and two daughters were all devotedly attached to him, and earnestly sympathized with and assisted him in his self-sacrificing work for the social improvement of humanity. But in 1865 he suffered one of the severest griefs of his life by the loss of his younger son, Edward, who died from a painful internal malady on the 16th February of that year, after a very short illness. It was in two ways a heavy blow to him. Edward was his only remaining son, who had fulfilled the promise of his boyhood, and to whom he looked for support and comfort in his declining years. He had been introduced by his father into the Indemnity Marine Assurance Company, where he had risen to the position of assistant underwriter. It will be remembered that Ellis had at this date been working for forty years at the Indemnity as its principal underwriter. It had under his auspices and by the help of his remarkable ability emerged from adversity, and become the leading company for marine insurance as well as one of the most conspicuous instances of commercial success in the city of London. He was naturally proud of it, and was looking forward to the time when he could resign his position at the head of the underwriting department of the office in favour of his son, whose election by the directors would have been practically certain. It will be realised from this what a loss that of his son was to him; but none, except those who were intimate with him, are aware how severe was his suffering, and yet how perfectly he controlled his feelings and continued steadily in the performance of his duty. The present writer, who had acquired his friendship some eight or ten years previously, and had for three or four years been assisting him in the building and subsequent management of the Gospel Oak Schools, has a vivid recollection of the interview when Ellis told him that all hope was given up. They were travelling to the city by the same morning train—a custom which lasted many years, and which obtained for the writer the advantage of conversations which he can never forget—and he remembers that he himself (who knew Edward well and was much attached to him) was less able to control his feelings at the sad intelligence than the father whose hopes and anticipations for the future were crushed by it.

Three years before the death of his son, his younger daughter, Mary, had married Arthur E. Durham, Esq. (now F.R.C.S.), and in 1866 his elder daughter, Lucy, married M. Albin Ducamp, a French gentleman residing in the south of France—curiously enough, in the same province from which his own Huguenot forefathers, the De Vezians of Languedoc, came. Thus all his family had left the home of their childhood; and in January, 1870, he suffered the severest loss which can fall on any man by the death of his devoted wife, after a married life of forty-five years, a loss borne with the same calm self-control which was a special feature of his character, though those who knew him intimately were all well aware how deeply he felt his bereavement.

His own health also began during this period to show signs of failure. In the summer of 1867, and again in the summer of 1868, he had an attack of sciatica, which seriously interfered with his walking powers, and compelled him to discontinue the long pedestrian rambles of which he was so fond. Another ailment, which had been gradually growing upon him, and which, though not dangerous, was troublesome and compelled him to resort to surgical aid, tended to interfere with his bodily activity, and from that time he became gradually more and more feeble. After his wife's death his elder daughter, Madame Ducamp, made arrangements, at much personal sacrifice, to spend most of her time with him in London, generally accompanied by M. Ducamp, though often separated from him for long intervals when the care of his estate at Cauviac (in the Department of Gard, where he resided) needed his presence. M. Ducamp warmly sympathized in the views of his father-in-law, and helped to spread them by translating one or two of his works into French, and publishing them at Paris. In 1871, Ellis was able to accompany M. and Madame Ducamp to Cauviac, where he spent two months, and derived much benefit from the beautiful climate of that lovely region, among the spurs of the Cevennes Mountains, where M. Ducamp resided.

After his granddaughter, Miss Ethel Ellen Ellis, the only daughter of his son Edward, grew up, she began to share with her aunt the care of her grandfather. She, as well as the rest of his family, was strongly impressed with the importance of his work, and has devoted herself with energy

R

to carry it on. She has written a series of reading lessons adapted for use in Board Schools, the London School Board having, though after much opposition, been induced, on the motion of Mrs. Fenwick Miller, to make lessons in conduct an optional—not a necessary—subject in the schools under their management. She has also conducted several voluntary classes of teachers, in which the lessons of the *Religion in Common Life*, formerly impressed by her grandfather upon his Royal pupils, were repeated to teachers of the London School Board.

But, though his bodily powers began at this period of his life to show symptoms of failing, the activity of his mind was unabated, and he never omitted an opportunity of trying to draw public attention to the great cause to which he had devoted his life. But none of his subsequent works were of the comprehensive nature of some of his previous ones— especially *Philo-Socrates*—and they generally comprised the same course of necessary knowledge, which he had often given, either furnished with a new dress or framed in such a manner as to attract the attention of a different class of readers from those whom he thought it possible to reach by his former works.

In February and May, 1865, two articles from his pen appeared in the *Museum and English Journal of Education:* the former on " Middle Class Education, what to aim at " and how to aim," and the latter on " Combinations and " Strikes, from the Teacher's point of view." The former was written in view of an expected commission to inquire into the subject of middle class schools. The latter was an interesting essay on a much-misunderstood subject, and a masterly exposure of the fallacy involved in the phrase " antagonism between capital and labour," an expression which, he says, " must have been invented to foster a pre- "judice rather than to recommend a truth." It is needless to trace the arguments of these articles. The conclusions of the former, dealing with a class of schools which had been

less the object of Ellis's exertions than those for the poor,
will however be interesting.   They are as follows :—

"Up to a certain age, the teaching and training best for
"the children of the poor, is also best for the children of
"the rich.   Beyond that age, the wealth of the parents
"determines the length of time for which the children can
"be detained from work to carry on further schooling. If,
"however, our own judgment in this matter were over-
"ruled, and we were driven to decide upon the merits of
"schools for the children of the poor and the children of
"the rich, by different standards, we should be disposed to
"judge somewhat in this way.

"Those schools for the children of the poorer classes
"are the best which are most successful in fitting them
"and in preparing them to become fit to preserve them-
"selves from destitution.

"Those schools for the children of the richer classes are
"the best which are most successful in fitting them and in
"preparing them to become fit to preserve themselves, in
"the expenditure of the wealth which they will have no
"occasion to earn, from frivolity, profligacy, and in-
"difference to the sufferings and helplessness of others."

The paper contains so interesting and characteristic an
anecdote that it will be interesting to quote it.   Those who
remember Ellis's peculiarly incisive method of interrogation
will have no difficulty in identifying the "silent listener":—

"Some years ago I happened to be among a numerous
"party dining together, previous to a visit of inspection to
"an evening school attached to a large industrial estab-
"lishment in this metropolis.   The conversation naturally
"turned upon subjects connected with education, and as
"will happen, fortunately in these days, doubts were
"expressed whether the character of the education
"generally provided was as good as it might be.   One of
"the guests grew warm and excited at some of the
"criticisms made upon what he evidently held to be above

"criticism. He was a thriving merchant. He had three
"sons—one in his own business, one at a university, and
"the third in the army. He was the sublime of soaring
"middleclassism. The climax of his justification of
"education as it is, and for leaving it undisturbed, was
"that the classics were the best basis for the education of
"the upper classes and the Bible for that of the lower.
"Another of the company, who had been a silent listener
"to the conversation, here asked diagonally across the
"table whether it was meant, in thus reserving the classics
"for the rich and surrendering the Bible to the poor, to
"convey an impression of the respective merits of profane
"and sacred literature. This question, as may be supposed,
"caused no little confusion to a man who evidently spoke
"as if in authority. Of course, he meant nothing of the
"kind. In fact he made us believe that he meant nothing
"at all."

After describing an address by the "silent listener" to
the boys upon the subject of provision for the future, and
the building up of the disposition and character upon which
their future happiness depended, he concludes:—

"It was gratifying to hear the warm expression of
"thanks, which, on the impulse of the moment, our admirer
"of classical and biblical education proffered to his
"troublesome interrogator. He seemed to feel for the time
"that something more might be done towards forming
"the intelligence and dispositions of the young than to
"cram them with words and phrases, whether extracted
"from the classics or from the Bible. It was sad to think
"how transient the favourable impression made upon him
"was likely to be."

It was about this time that Ellis became acquainted with
two eminent English clergymen—the Bishop of Natal and
the Rev. Charles Voysey—who rendered themselves, by
their courageous and outspoken search after truth, the
objects of public prosecution, and roused the bigotry of

such men as Bishop Wilberforce and Bishop Gray (of Capetown) to public legal prosecutions. It is needless to say, after what Ellis had written in *Philo-Socrates* upon "Truthfulness," and the "Theologico-Intelligence and Theologico-Morality" of that party in the Church who sought to suppress truthseeking by authority, that he cordially sympathized with these victims of modern intolerance and rancour—the same rancour which in the middle ages had resulted in the faggot and stake. He had been introduced to Bishop Colenso by Rev. William Rogers, and we learn from one of Mrs. Ellis's letters that in June, 1863, he dined with Rogers to meet Bishop Colenso, Rev. Benjamin Jowett, and Dean Stanley. The Bishop afterwards dined several times with Ellis, and visited, on his invitation, Mr. Shields's school. The following two or three letters to Hodgson give small glimpses of this friendship and of Ellis's doings in these years :—

"11th June, 1863.

"The weather has been unsettled and wet since we "parted at Peckham. We spent a most agreeable hour "at luncheon, at Mr. Shields'. The Bishop came out "manfully, and evinced complete tolerance of the secular "system in the school, and did not flinch from the dis-"cussion which arose out of my justification for not "intruding upon children the stuff which goes by the "name of religion."

"28th December, 1864.

"I do not doubt, and you ought not to doubt, that you "must be making a useful impression through your present "labours, even if you did not receive such gratifying "proofs as the one which I now return.

"Mr. Scott[1] has sent me a parcel similar to the one, I "daresay, sent to you. *Eternal Punishment* I gave to

---

[1] Mr. Thomas Scott, of Ramsgate, publisher of a number of pamphlets containing advanced thought on theological subjects.

"Mr. Rogers, unread however by me, and I recommended
"him to communicate with Mr. Scott, who would supply
"him with abundant material for reflection.

"I cannot encourage the *Truthseeker*, with a table of
"contents so exclusively controversial and theological;
"and, I fear, we should be too sanguine to expect that its
"editor may be either capable or willing to embrace a
"wider range of matter.   But if he were, co-operation with
"him would be useful.   We want more than truthseeking.
"As fast as it is found, we want to see it exemplified in
"conduct as well as pronounced in words.   They who
"seek truth, keeping this end in view, will be preserved
"from that interminable war of words, which has caused
"the school-men to lose their influence here and parlia-
"mentarians to tire out the French.

"I am as stout as ever in my wish to devise some plan
"with you by which principles and doctrines may be
"expounded and presented so as to influence conduct
"and mitigate the evils daily paraded before our eyes, to
"be nursed but not to be cured."

"5th May, 1865.

"I have profited by your kindness in drawing my
"attention to the speeches of Mr. Lowe and Lord Elcho"
(on the Reform Bill of that year).   "They are very suggestive
"and admirable up to a certain point.   They hit the
"weak point of those who claim an extension of the
"suffrage—the ignorance and bad habits of those who are
"not now qualified to vote—and then are as silent about
"a remedy as if those disqualifications were irremediable
"in the future—Mr. Lowe, who is obviously the deeper
"thinker of the two, not being altogether free from the
"suspicion of having assisted to prevent education being
"made as efficient in elevating the people as even the
"present low state of feeling on the subject would
"admit."

"22nd August, 1865.

"The 'Verulam,' with her episcopal freight" (the Bishop
of Natal) "went through the Downs yesterday. The blessing
"of God seems to be on the Bishop, so far as we may
"judge by the weather with which he begins his voyage.
"If the weather were bad, however, some of his
"inspired friends would no doubt remark that 'the Lord
"'chasteneth those whom he loveth,' while his spiritual
"enemies will be equally capable of turning either
"alternative to his eventual disadvantage."

In December of that year (1865) we find him giving a
series of lessons at the City of London School, Cowper
Street, City, of which the Reverend William Jowitt was
then head master. Mr. Jowitt was an able, clear-minded
clergyman, for whom Ellis formed a strong friendship. Both
he and his successor, Dr. Wormell, entered warmly into his
views as to education, and lessons upon conduct have
always formed part of the curriculum of that school.

In the year 1866, Ellis published a volume entitled
Thoughts on the Future of the Human Race, intended to
bring before the public in a single volume the same thoughts
which had formed the subject of the paper in *Philo-Socrates*,
entitled "On the Past, the Present, and the Future." It was
intended for the general reader, and to try and attract some
attention from the general public to the questions which
occupied his mind then, as they had done through life—
namely, the means by which progressive improvement might
be brought about and mankind made better and happier.
He begins by investigating, in his usual thorough way, the
knowledge we possess of the development of humanity in
the past, from barbarism to the present state of civilisation.
He then examines what special kinds of knowledge have,
more than others, assisted in this development, and the
utilization of that knowledge as a means of judging what
further advance in well-being may be anticipated—the new

or intensified causes in action for future progress, and, on the other hand, the obstacles which retard it. Human conduct as a cause of improvement, and knowledge and habits as a cause of conduct, lead up to the conclusion that we may with certainty expect in the future progressive improvement, meaning by that phrase (p. 252)—

" A steadily increasing preponderance (subject, may be,
" to occasional and temporary interruptions) of pleasurable
" over painful sensations in the lot of man, the more
" regular satisfaction of his physical wants and consequent
" absence of apprehension and anxiety concerning the
" sufficiency of future supplies, greater immunity from
" superstitious fears, and a growing disposition to derive
" enjoyment from intellectual and moral sources, which,
" besides the direct enjoyment, also provide an indirect but
" effective defence against excess in sensual indulgence."

The next portion of the book illustrates a peculiar trait of Ellis's character, his severity upon persons—generally those who assume a tone of literary superiority—who treat extensive improvement of the whole people as Utopian. An article in the *Saturday Review* (3rd June, 1865) had recently appeared, the writer of which combated what he considered "wild dreams" under the name of "the elevation of the "masses." His conclusion rested upon the following argument (p. 254):—

" There will, so far as we can see, always be in old
" countries poor, ignorant, coarse people. Occupations
" must go on which we cannot conceive a superior creature
" filling. As long as pork is eaten, pigs must be killed;
" and as long as pigs are killed, there must be pork
" butchers. Now, there is just as much apparent chance
" of the sky turning permanently a bright chocolate colour,
" as of a pork butcher being ordinarily a wise, learned,
" elegant, holy man."

A contemptuous sneer at a necessary, though repulsive, occupation as such could not be passed over. Ellis brings forward, for comparison, a similar instance of episcopal conduct which had recently occurred. A clergyman had, necessarily, surrendered a living of £5,000 a year on being appointed to a bishopric. But by an arrangement made with the patron, a parson was presented to the rectory in his place who happened to be a prebend and vacated his stall, worth £3,500 a year. This prebendal stall the bishop, being able to hold it with his bishopric, accepted in place of the rectory which he could not hold. And Ellis wonders (page 262) whether "pork butchers, faithfully performing "the duty of pig-killing, were much further removed from "piety and holiness than shepherds, who neglect their "flocks and squander the funds meant to secure the services "of faithful shepherds." He says (page 258): "We are quite "as hopeful of future pork butchers as we are of future pro- "prietors of redundant incomes. There are causes quite as "potent at work to diminish the ignorance and coarseness "of future pork butchers as to diminish the indifference of "the rich to the want and suffering of others in the midst "of their own luxury and profusion."

There is one other point in this book which will be worthy of observation. We have seen that at one time the word religion had an attraction for Ellis. He adopted it himself in 1856, after Mr. Caird's sermon, as the title of his own book, *A Layman's Contribution to the Knowledge and Practice of Religion in Common Life.* But in the work we are now considering, he decided not to use it, and gives his reason for the omission (page 176), which was to avoid confusion of thought and language. He points out that the name religion has been used in very different senses— sometimes as the declaration and sanctification of doctrines and rules of conduct specially designed to promote the well-being of mankind—sometimes to express and sanction conduct wholly opposed to human well-being as being grateful to God. Further, it cannot be denied that a large part of what has passed and now passes by the name of religion has been

and is in practice very different from what it is conceived to
be by those who accept it as the most powerful of agencies
in the promotion of man's welfare.   Many of the horrible
acts of the past, which are now clearly traceable to superstition, and are seen to have been the consequences of misdirected
passion, were reputed at the time to be sanctioned, if not
ordered, by religion.   And as there is a growing tendency to
make "religious doctrines and conduct" and "doctrines and
"conduct favourable to well-being" convertible terms, Ellis
decides, although agreeing that many persons prefer the
former phrase, that he will adopt the latter in the present
work.   Those who do prefer to use the word religion will
admit that in its highest, truest, and best sense it pervaded
both his writings, his work, and his entire life.

In 1866, a school for boys of the wealthier classes was
opened at Spring Grove, Isleworth, under the name of the
London International College, to which Ellis rendered considerable assistance, advancing a very large portion of the
money required for the purchase of the site and erection of
the buildings.   The original plan was due to Richard Cobden,
who desired to found a school of an advanced modern type,
having branches in different foreign countries, and to which
the pupils might, if desired, be transferred.   Unfortunately,
Cobden died before its opening, and his attached friend and
adherent, A. W. Paulton, Esq., took his place as chairman.
The first board of directors included Professors Tyndall and
Huxley, the eminent classical scholar, Dr. William Smith,
and also Ellis's friend, Dr. Hodgson, to whose influence
Ellis's help was due.   The first head master was Dr. Leonard
Schmitz, formerly head master of the High School, Edinburgh, and the school was opened by Ellis's old pupil, the
Prince of Wales.   The school became a valuable and useful
institution, Dr. Schmitz being succeeded as head master in
1874 by H. R. Ladell, Esq., M.A.

Two years later, in 1868, Ellis published another work,
entitled *What stops the Way? or our two great difficulties,*

with some hints concerning the way. This was an attempt to draw the attention of men of influence and position to the improvement of education. It is prefaced by an address "To Statesmen, Legislators, and Philanthropists," in which, after referring to the recent appeals in support of the gradual reduction of the National Debt and of the duty to have some regard in our consumption of coal to its limited quantity, he points out that the advancement of the well-being of posterity, which such appeals assume to be our duty, would be but inadequately cared for without attention to the advancement of the welfare of our posterity in other ways.

" To secure a provision of coal," he says (page v), "while " neglecting to secure a provision of those other essentials " of well-being, would be a scant performance of the duty " owed to posterity. And to me there is known but one " method of performing this duty satisfactorily, and that " is by being at the pains to gift posterity with intelligence, " industry, skill, economy, and trustworthiness. With " these qualities there will be no lack of the other essentials " of well-being."

The " two great difficulties " are thus stated (p. 10):—

" It may be reasonably inquired, why the education " admitted to be indispensable is so inadequately pro- " vided. And, if we do not mistake, there are two " circumstances which will nearly, if not entirely, account " for this omission, without imputing any intentional dis- " regard of duty:—

" 1st. The imperfect and mistaken notions which prevail " concerning the education desirable for the young, causing " education to be partly, if not wholly, withheld, while it is " given in words or appearance: the very schools and " teachers helping to conceal the void which would other- " wise be unendurable. This class of obstacles to real " education may be designated as 'verbal illusions.'"

" 2nd. The impediments placed in the way of education, " thus imperfectly conceived, by persons under the

"influence of those peculiar views of religion which give
"rise to so-called 'religious difficulties.'   Using the word
"'religion' in this peculiar sense, these may be called
"'religious illusions.'"

Both these are discussed in turn, in arguments which we
need not repeat.   But the consideration of the religious
illusions, brings in a discussion of the subject which—being
the last we shall have an opportunity of quoting—gives the
latest thoughts of the earnest and devoted thinker and
worker upon the "religious difficulty" and the use of the
word religion.   After pointing out the difficulties that would
arise, having regard to the number of denominations existing
in the country, if education were solely conducted in sectarian
schools, each denomination insisting that its own particular
views of religion should be embodied with the other instruction indispensable for forming capable and well-conducted
labourers, he points out the practicability, and urges the
adoption, of a plan for eliminating from each sect's religion
that which is peculiar to it, and for all to unite to teach that
portion which is common to all.   He says (p. 63):—

"In the great struggle, the beginning of which was
"probably the beginning of society itself, but never,
"perhaps, so intense as it now is, not for mere existence,
"but for enjoyable existence, it has been at last discovered
"that such existence is unattainable without education.
"Is there any difficulty in the way of this education which
"can be properly characterised as 'religious?' Can the
"luxurious expenditure of a few and a dearth of educa-
"tional means co-exist in a religious community?   And
"if so, what is the religion which entitles such a community
"to be considered 'religious?'

"The more a word appeals to the feelings of reverence
"and benevolence—the mainsprings of our best conduct
"when controlled and guided by intelligence—the more
"careful should we be not to allow ourselves to be drawn
"into vile, cruel, or debasing courses by those who use it

"ignorantly or dishonestly. If 'religion' rightly under-
"stood mean anything, it means something which inspires
"us to make greater efforts than we should make without it
"to improve the condition of our fellow-men. People tell
"us that it means much more. Be it so. Let us not,
"however, neglect to repeat what your high-flying, all-
"embracing, verbal-religionists seem disposed to over-
"look. 'Don't forget that it does mean—Tender care for
"'little children.'"

The *What stops the Way?* did not meet with much favour
from the reviewers. The literary mind failed to understand
the intense and earnest benevolence contained in Ellis's
appeals for energetic action in contending with poverty, vice,
and misery, and criticised his work merely as a literary
composition. The following letter to Hodgson refers to these
criticisms :—

"27th May, 1868.

"The notice of my last little book in the *Athenæum*
"was, as you say, pitiful enough. But what ought we to
"think of that in the *Spectator?* That my short-comings
"must be numerous I make no doubt. I might do nothing,
"and incur no blame and meet with no sneers, no ridicule,
"and no imputations. But I have some notion, well or ill
"grounded, that there is a great duty, which is very im-
"perfectly performed, partly through ignorance and partly
"through apathy. I am trying to do the little which I
"think I can do to the best of my ability, and within the
"measure of my means. How I rejoice to unite with
"others who, like you, think I am not altogether mistaken,
"visionary, or deluded, you know full well; and I shall
"persevere through good report and bad report, welcoming
"assistance, corrections, and suggestions, come from what
"quarter they may—even from the *Spectator.*"

We have seen that Ellis strongly discouraged the inculcation of lessons in conduct by means of a book; his

experience had shown him that teaching by a thoroughly competent teacher was the only safe method of leading the children to find out by their reasoning powers and then solve their difficulties for themselves. But, although no book could be an adequate substitute for such teaching, he was by no means insensible to the use of a book adapted to young minds, whereby they could recall the important lessons of the schoolroom. In 1872, he published an interesting little work, adapted for the reading of young children, entitled *Helps to the Young in their Efforts at Self-guidance.*

It sprang to some extent out of his experience in giving lessons to the boys at the City of London Middle Class School; and, with the experience he had of the prejudice entertained by the clergy of all orthodox sects against his method, he asked his friend Rev. William Jowitt, the head master of that school, to edit it and give it the sanction of his name—a request with which Mr. Jowitt willingly complied. The book deals with the elementary qualities of obedience and application—the implicit obedience to the matured experience of their parents which is the duty of children—then gives in simple language, adapted to juvenile comprehension, the thoughts which should be impressed on their minds on the fundamental qualities necessary to well-being. It then treats, but with less detail than in his larger works, the subject of wages, profits, money, &c. But there are one or two innovations of detail which it is interesting to note. In part i., which treats of the elementary qualities, a special chapter on " Kindliness and Generosity " is for the first time interposed between the chapter on " Intelligence and Skill " and that on " Economy or Thrift." After pointing out the various methods which civilized society has adopted for the care of the poor, the sick, and the young, and the feeling, implanted in man, of inability to allow his fellow creatures to starve or die for want of food, care, and tending, resulting in the establishment of poor laws, hospitals, infirmaries, schools, and other charitable institutions, he says (p. 17):—

"That most people should work intelligently and skil-
"fully, and should long have struggled to acquire habits
"of industry with knowledge and skill, is only what we
"might expect when man had once risen to the perception
"that a large store of the fruits of industry is indispen-
"sable for a state of existence that can be considered at
"all worth having. No less indispensable for such a state
"of existence is the prevalence of those feelings of sym-
"pathy, kindliness, pity, friendship, and love, which
"inspire us with the courage, determination, and self-devo-
"tion to face danger, suffer privation, endure hardship,
"and meet wounds and death with resignation, for the
"benefit of others, at the call of duty properly understood.
"Readiness to die for one's country has been held to be a
"sign of nobility of disposition. A better sign of such
"nobility would be readiness to die for mankind—a
"readiness only to be acquired by that self-discipline
"which brings with it the desire so to live as in all our
"thoughts and deeds not to disturb, but where possible
"to promote, the general well-being. To deserve and
"enjoy the consciousness that we live in the midst of
"those who are animated with such feelings towards our-
"selves, we must cherish the like towards them."

Surely we are not wrong in designating such lessons as this—the inculcation in their highest and noblest form of the principles which pervade the life of Jesus Christ, as told in the Gospels, and which manifested themselves in his death upon the cross—as being sufficiently religious to satisfy even the most exigent of its champions.

The last literary work extending to the limits of a book which emanated from Ellis's pen was an anonymous one, published in 1874, entitled *Studies of Man, by a Japanese,* which bears on the title page the motto:—

"The proper study of mankind is man. That study

"by all will enable each to judge what besides he ought
"to study specially."

Meditating in his quiet evenings at home upon the great
problem of social improvement, it occurred to him to put his
thoughts into a book, which should appear to look down
upon and criticise the anomalies, the defects, and the wants
of society as from a sort of bird's-eye point of view. It was
a similar idea to that which had led him to lay the conversations on moral principles of vol. iv. of *Philo-Socrates*
among the Hindoos. But on the present occasion he published his volume anonymously, and assumed for his view
of social life a Japanese standpoint. In his preface, he refers
to the practices of the foreigners who visited Japan, to what
the imaginary Japanese writer had read of their doings
throughout the world, and to what he had seen during a
visit to Europe of what prevailed in European countries.
He draws attention to the unblushing effrontery with which,
in the name of religion, Europeans continued to preach
doctrines utterly at variance with their daily practice—to
the large admixture of the ill-fed, ill-clad, and ill-lodged,
more or less dependent on the charity of the other classes
for the few comforts which ever came to them—to the
confession of incapacity to utilize the abundant means of
well-being and facilities of producing them existing in both
those countries, so as to secure well-being—to the enormous
extent to which instruments of destruction were manufactured,
and the fact that two millions of men in Europe were ready
prepared and drilled to make use of them—to the embarka-
tion of Chinese labourers for California, Peru, and Cuba,
and the inhospitable and cruel treatment which these docile,
industrious, and parsimonious people have met with from
labourers envious of the prosperity which they had earned
by industry and frugality—and to the condition of the
natives of Australia and the Caffres of South Africa side by
side with the more powerful races which are dispossessing
them of their land.

Those who are acquainted with Ellis's other works will easily form an idea of how he treats such an investigation as this. Tracing up the development of social life from barbarism to the present state of civilisation, he shows the practices of human beings at different states of social growth. How (page 17), in an early stage of development, men, peopling the world with invisible spirits out of their own imaginations, built temples, erected altars, and upon them slaughtered the choicest of their flocks and herds, and even human beings—sometimes their prisoners—sometimes even their sons and daughters. And how, even after men have risen to the conception of one God, the ruler of the universe, He is too often thought, if not spoken, of as an angry and vindictive being, disposed to afflict and torment them, and even providing for his creatures, after death, a continuance of existence of the most horrible kind, from which there is no escape, except for the small number of those who join in a particular form of belief, while even of these a few only are saved. He points out how this has led to imprisonments, persecutions, tortures, massacres, and crusades, which have brought discord and desolation where love and plenty might have prevailed; and how—even when torture and massacre have become prohibited by the growth of common sense and the more active exercise of the reasoning faculties—men brand each other with such epithets as unbelievers, heretics, infidels, and atheists, meant, by those who use them, to imply something worse than murderers and assassins. How, again, modern armies, going forth for aggression, have invariably been accompanied by the blessings of priests, and on returning home from their bloody triumphs have publicly returned thanks to the so-called " God of battles " for his goodness and mercy.

By what influences such a state of things as this is to be put an end to is the problem our Japanese sets himself. The study of rules of conduct in harmony with human well-being—or, as it is sometimes called, the study of

S

morals—is, we need hardly say, the remedy suggested, and extension of that study and teaching and training in these principles is shown to be the only possible cure for the evils which he has painted in vivid colours. But our Japanese fails to see the possibility of the teaching of true morals—or, as we may call it, true and real religion—in conjunction with other so-called religions which inculcate such strange delusions.

"What morals are taught," he says (page 28), "or can "be taught, in combination with such religions? one "would not think of denying that morals and rules of "conduct (that is, of conduct conducive to well-being) "may be taught in conjunction with a religion of which, "as interpreted by its ministers and not yet given to the "world, we have had no experience."

One very interesting passage of this work deals with the different action of the students of science and the students of religion. Our Japanese says (page 72):—

"A student of science, after having made himself master "of all former discoveries and attainments and their appli-"cations, is bent upon so using his powers of observation "and experiment as to become a discoverer in his turn. "The fixed idea with him is that there is something more "to be discovered and learned. Society interests itself in "his success. Patents and copyrights are meant to secure "to him some of the benefit which it derives from his "discoveries and inventions, and the beautiful creations of "his genius and art.

"The student of religion stops where his brother in "science begins. He masters the contents of books said "to be inspired and held to be sacred. His business is to "interpret them. He is pledged not to question their "authority. The scientific attainments of the day, "described in plain and accurate language, are irrecon-"cilable with many of the statements in the sacred books. "This cannot be hidden from the student of religion.

" And an essential part of his intellectual training is to
" make him expert in so manipulating language as to
" show that the words in the sacred books were intended
" to express something very different from the meanings
" originally attached to them. To the words in daily
" use a well-understood meaning is attached. We hardly
" know how we could otherwise live as we do. We call
" these their natural meanings. Divines who guide the
" studies of their pupils in religion teach them how to use
" the words of the sacred books in a non-natural sense.
" Teachers of science use no such subterfuges. As new
" truths dawn upon them, they correct their mistakes and
" alter their language. They do not pretend that the
" same word means first one thing and then another.
" When they thought that the earth stood still they said
" so. They afterwards discovered that the earth moved,
" and they said it moved; but admitted that they did not
" mean that it moved when they said it stood still."

And the conclusion to which the work leads up is
embodied in the following passage (p. 106):—

" An enlightened state of public opinion is only to be
" approached and eventually arrived at by general and
" judicious teaching and training. To accomplish this,
" the precious hours of childhood must neither be wasted
" nor misused. As the intelligent and skilful building,
" equipment, and the manning of a ship are necessary
" antecedents to a prosperous voyage, so the intelligent
" teaching and training of the young are necessary ante-
" cedents to a prosperous journey through life, and to
" the existence of a happy and progressive state of society.
" To intelligent lovers of their kind over the whole earth
" it may, therefore, safely be said, 'Educate! Educate!
" 'Educate!'"

It is somewhat amusing to read the reviews of this work.
Two which we have now before us both concur in accepting
the work as a genuine Japanese production, though one of

them refers to Goldsmith's *Citizen of the World* and the *Persian Letters* of Montesquieu, and the other to Voltaire's imaginary conversations as instances of the personation of Orientals by European writers.

Both deal largely with the literary style, and both fail to see the great and moving thought which actuates the work— the method of preventing and putting an end to the distressing facts from which the Japanese starts. One, while telling us that there is no reason to doubt the truth of the statement that it is written by a veritable Oriental, finds nothing better than that "the work is to a large extent "composed of propositions, true, but about as original as "that two and two make four, or that A is A," and the investigation by a Japanese of the disastrous effects which in all history have flowed from so-called religions only suggests to the reviewer the vague and unmeaning thought that "it does not apparently occur to him that there must "be some deep meaning in a sentiment which has been "displayed in some form or other by every people in all "ages."

The other review curiously enough finds internal evidence in the work of its foreign authorship. "The principal mark "(apart from the thought), by which one could recognise a "foreign hand, is an occasional meagreness of expression, "which is, perhaps, as likely to be due to natural over- "caution as to any actual failure to command words. It is "like what one would expect from a clever English boy "taking unusual pains to write clearly and correctly." The review is almost entirely literary.

"In the Japanese traveller's *Studies of Man*, as in a "Japanese artist's studies of nature," the critic tells us, "the outlines are correctly drawn, but the distance and "atmospheric colouring are omitted. At the same time, we "are so much accustomed to soften down everything, that it "may be no bad thing for us to have our attention called to "the bare outlines now and then."

However, he does not treat the substance of the work quite with the supercilious tone of the former reviewer. He concludes with the remark, " He shows that he has made " use of his western culture so as to master a respectable " amount of sound learning in political economy, social " ethics, and the principles of government. But any readers " who find his statements and conclusions wholly distasteful, " even after making the allowances we have pointed out as " proper to be made, are, of course, free to console them- " selves with the reflection that he is only a heathen " Japanese."

The *Scotsman* reviewed it in a more friendly style, though finding in it an attack on dogmatic religion. We have not seen the review, but the following letters to Hodgson refer in an interesting way to the work, retaining nominally (though Hodgson, of course, knew the writer) the position of anonymity:—

" 20th January, 1874.

" I do not deny that the MS. of *Studies of Man* " passed through my hands to Messrs. Trübner and Co., " that I am responsible to them, and that they have been " authorised by me to distribute and advertise as they may " think most judicious, in order to secure notice and circu- " lation. More than this I shall neither deny nor affirm.

" From time to time I have met several Japanese, and I " think you take a rather humiliating view of our influence " over them in assuming that no one among them should " be sufficiently inspired by us to be capable of expressing " such common sense views of human conduct as are " contained in the *Studies of Man.* It is a pity that the " author should have fallen into some of my crudities of " language and style, and thus prevented some readers " from doing justice to his narrative and reason. Some, " perhaps, will deplore that he should have been unable to " grasp the great truths of Christianity. The missionaries " must be at work upon him.

" I return your excerpt from the *Pall Mall*, and enclose
"two letters which have been received by Trübner and
"forwarded to me.   I shall, of course, be glad if these be
"favourable omens of the impression likely to be made by
"the Japanese in other quarters.

" I trust that he will be read in the same spirit by
"others as I read him.   He is striving to learn (and to
"record what he has learned) by what means the lot of
"mankind may be ameliorated.   In his studies he
"stumbles against the impediments which oppose him in
"the name of religion in all its various forms, and no
"choice is left to him but to sweep them out of his way."

"8th February, 1874.

" I thank you most heartily for your kindness in sending
"me the notice of the *Studies of Man* extracted from the
"*Scotsman*.   Its appearance in the columns of that paper
"is owing to your influence, if not to your pen, and the
"author ought to be proud of both or either.

"As far as I can guess at his intention, I should say, a
"little in opposition to the comment in the *Scotsman*, that
"his purpose was not to make a smart attack upon
"dogmatic religion, but to sweep away all superstitions
"and other obstructions which stand in the way of an
"education calculated to prevent human misery.   He
"was compelled to notice and expose some of those which
"prevail under the name of religion in the most advanced
"countries, in which the purest religion is supposed to
"influence conduct.

"What a strange exposure of an oscillation of public
"opinion is being made before us!   I have given three
"votes,[1] and on Tuesday shall give a fourth in vain.   But
"my faith in the future is unshaken.   Labours such as
"yours cannot fail to yield their fruit in due season, and

---

[1] The election of 1874 was then pending.

"happily for the labourers there is as much enjoyment in
"cultivating the ground with faith as in gathering the
"crop."

In addition to the four principal works which appeared
during this period, three or four smaller publications—
pamplets, letters, or lectures—gave evidence of Ellis's restless
activity. The first of these was a little pamphlet published
shortly after the commercial crisis of 1866, which began with
the failure of Overend, Gurney, and Co. It was intended as
a contribution towards the enlightenment of the large number
of people in the city who believed that the crisis was due to a
"drain of gold," to some defect in the currency laws, or the like,
and appealed to the Government to relax them. His pamphlet
was entitled " Three Letters from a London Merchant to a
"Country Friend on the late Monetary Crisis," and in it he
shows clearly that the crisis might be described as " a large
" number of individuals and companies unable to obtain
" payment of what is owed to them, and among them many
" who are thereby incapacitated from paying what they owe
" to others," and that it was fully accounted for by the
ignorance and recklessness of a number of merchants and
others in using the credit offered to them, and by the lack
of vigilance and sagacity in those that gave credit.

The next of his little publications was a small pamphlet
or tract, published in 1869, and entitled " A Chart of In-
"dustrial Life, with some instructions for its use." It was a
concise *resumé* of the series of lessons which he had so often
given, and which those who had received it had so highly
valued. This was the first time that he had condensed the
full story of the *Phenomena of Industrial Life* into so small
a compass and at so low a price. Although it contained
thirty-three pages, it was published at a penny, ninepence
per dozen, or five shillings per hundred, for the use of schools.

A course of four lectures, delivered by permission of the
Education Department at the Lecture Theatre of the Royal
School of Mines in Jermyn Street, on " The Laws of

"Conduct in Industrial Life and on the method of imparting "instruction therein in our primary schools," was the next work which we find him engaged in. The first lecture only was published. It was an interesting address, and we find him quoting and applying to the teachers' work an eloquent passage from his old correspondent (if we may so term him) Bishop Temple, formerly head master of Rugby:—

"There can be no greater improvement to any one's "mind than that he should thoroughly master the "principles of his own work; that by which he is to live, "that which is to occupy his time and his thought, that to "which he is to give all the desires of his heart, the "employment to which, if he is a thoroughly good "workman, he would really wish to give a good and hearty "service. Now there is nothing, I say, which does so "much for man as that he should thoroughly master "principles—as that when he is at work he should know "not only what to do, but why it is done; that he should "understand the reason for everything he is doing; that "he should be able, if new circumstances require him to "learn something quite new, to pass, without any great "difficulty, from one branch of his own particular employ-"ment to a kindred branch. All that really cultivates the "man more almost than anything else you can teach "him."

Ellis seems to have been feeling somewhat feeble—he was now seventy,—for we find him writing to Hodgson about these lectures at Jermyn Street:—

"17th May, 1870.
"I am a little nervous at what I have undertaken, but I "feel that the opportunity ought not to be lost, and I "must do my best. It is to be hoped that younger and "more vigorous men will come forward and take up the "work."

During this period, Ellis was invited to give evidence

upon the method of imparting instruction in elementary schools on the laws of conduct in industrial life before two Royal Commissions, one being the Schools Inquiry Commission of 1866, of which Lord Taunton was chairman, the other the Commission on Scientific Instruction and the Advancement of Science, of which the Duke of Devonshire was chairman. An anecdote which he related to the Commissioners, and which he has recorded in one of his books already noticed (*What stops the Way?* page 70), will be of interest:—

"One of Her Majesty's Inspectors of Schools in con-
"nexion with the Church of England, fifteen years ago,
"was listening to a lesson of mine. When it was done, he
"came and asked me questions about what I was doing,
"and, after I had answered all his questions, he asked me
"as to what was left out—that kind of thing which you
"might suppose a clergyman's attention would be drawn
"to—and he said, 'Mr. Ellis, if you will allow me to say
"'so, I should say you taught worldly wisdom.' I said,
"'Granted, I will accept your expression, and now,' I
"said, 'will you be so kind as to tell me wherein worldly
"'wisdom is opposed to heavenly wisdom?' He said,
"'Well, properly taught, I do not see any opposition.'
"'But,' I said, 'I intend to teach it properly, and if I am
"'not teaching it properly I will be grateful to you if you
"'will show me where I can improve my teaching. If I
"'understand you aright, properly taught, the first is not
"'opposed to the second?' and he said 'No.' 'May I
"'push it a little further,' I said, 'and ask you whether,
"'properly taught, it is not absolutely necessary to assist
"'the other?' He could not help himself."

A few letters to Hodgson, written during this period, will best conclude the record of Ellis's last ten years of active exertion. Many of them contain remarks upon the progress of educational work, and thoughts upon the events of that important epoch, which included, amongst other important events, the Franco-German War of 1870–1871, and the consolidation of Germany into a united nation.

"29th June, 1867.

"I am sorry, as you are, that the theological question "has risen up to disturb the quiet progress of our schools; "we must meet it as well as we can. We are in a position "in which the slightest indiscretion of friends is sure to be "taken advantage of by enemies. Improved education, "like political improvement, is not to be gained by 'rose "'water.' A steady purpose, with a determination to be "nerved by opposition to greater exertion, will, it is to be "hoped, carry us through."

"27th June, 1870.

"Don't despond, and don't underrate the good that you "are doing, because you cannot trace the influence exer- "cised by yourself, mixed up as it is and sometimes "counteracted by the influence of others. All my life I "have been working with a minority—an apparently "insignificant minority—and I would not venture to "say that the present state of society would be in any "respect less advanced than it is had I never existed. "But I have worked, and shall continue to work, as if the "progress of society depended entirely upon me. The "ranks in which I have fought have gained many a battle, "and will gain more. I am not expecting to be distin- "guished as a hero, and hope not to be branded as a "traitor, a coward, or a sneak.

"Locke, Adam Smith, David Hume, and Bentham were "great men and could abide the neglect and aversion of "their own generation, strong in the faith that their "expositions would prevail in the end. Let us share in "the faith of these great men, although we cannot aspire "to their fame. It is men like them and their humble, "unknown, but devoted followers, who have raised society "to what it is and to what it will surely be."

" 14th August, 1870.

"Although I have put off till now to thank you for
"your *Life of Turgot*" (which Hodgson had recently
published), "I have not delayed so long to read it. For
" three consecutive evenings it has served before retiring to
" bed as a tonic, a sedative, and an alterative—to strengthen,
"to compose, and to distract my thoughts from the sad
"and exciting topics which force themselves upon one's
"attention during the day. Among your many readers,
"I have no doubt that some will be inspired to walk in
"Turgot's steps, and that some who turn to your little
"book from mere curiosity will only close it after thoughts
"have been awakened which will influence for the better
"their future lives. Turgot's opinions and doings have
"survived the French Revolution, and, in like manner,
"yours and those of others who are striving for general
"improvement, irrespective of creed and race, will survive
"the infliction under which we are suffering and others
"yet to come.

"The enclosed may give you a few moments' amuse-
"ment. The 'Union'[1] seems to be beating up for funds.
"Mr. Stayner sent me a volume of reports and other
"papers specially meant to enforce the importance of
"including religion in, and excluding infidelity from, our
"schools. As you will see, I have been more generous to
"the 'Union' than to the 'League.' I never gave anything
"to the 'League,' but I have given to the 'Union' my
"last lecture and a copy of the Chart. I fear that the
"'Union,' however, will not be very grateful, for I have
"sent it no money."

---

[1] The National Education Union for the teaching of orthodox religion in
schools. The National Education League was formed for the promotion of
unsectarian education.

The following relates to the Franco-German War, then
pending:—

"13th February, 1871.

"Let us hope that order and prosperity will rise out of
"chaos, a better seed bed than that sink of iniquity,
"hidden by glare and glitter—the second empire. The
"captive Emperor's proclamation in to-day's paper shows
"that he is true to his colours to the end. Poor worried
"man! He has been cheated and deceived! He who
"never deceived anybody! I dare not say that the French
"nation did not require a severe lesson to bring them to a
"willingness to listen to words of wisdom and to open
"their eyes to facts and probabilities.

"I am attending Huxley's lectures at the· London
"Institution, Finsbury Circus, at four p.m., on Monday.
"Admirable as he ever is as a lecturer!

"I see Voysey's trial has ended as I fancy everybody
"expected. He will perhaps hardly have settled yet what
"he intends to do for the maintenance of his family, so
"that we may know how best to assist him."

"12th March, 1871.

"I am reading Darwin's *Descent of Man.* He seems to
"rebuke one's impatience at the slow progress of education.
"For, if man's evolution from some primeval type has
"been the work of countless ages, his further evolution
"into a rational being may require many more years—
"not to say ages.

"Do you hear anything of Voysey and what he intends
"to do? We called upon Domville yesterday, but only
"saw Mrs. Domville, and she did not seem to know more
"than that he had not left Healaugh" [Mr. Voysey's then
vicarage]. "I should like to hear that there was some
"prospect of his obtaining employment, both useful to
"others and remunerative to himself."

"15th April, 1871.

"In regard to the opening for extended usefulness,
"which you kindly suggest, I will not plead that I am
"'done up,' which might sound like repining; but I must
"confess that declining powers compel me to give up
"much that I would otherwise gladly undertake.

"Henceforward I am a 'retired' teacher, and I will not
"venture to claim that title except from those who admit
"that I ever deserved to rank as a teacher at all. One
"trifling suspension of my retirement I am now making
"in favour of my two eldest grandsons and their school-
"fellows. Perchance I may make some impression upon
"Mr. Munro, their master, at the same time, since he and
"Mrs. Munro both attend my lessons.

"It is now more than twelve months since I last visited
"the Gospel Oak Schools, and five years since I was
"inside any of the others. In fact, I am more indolent
"than even you would imagine. I cling to my 'faith' and
"leave 'work' to my successors, whoever they may be."

"8th May, 1871.

"'Religious' education (even if it be called sectarian
"and denominational), which embraces the social elements
"insisted upon by the writer, has far greater attractions
"for me than a 'secular' education (bepraised though |it
"be as liberal, unsectarian, and undenominational) which
"ignores or excludes them. Thorough teaching and
"training in the *duties* of common life will eventually
"throw off or neutralise all that is vicious, superstitious,
"or deleterious, if there be any such palmed off upon the
"young under the name of 'religion.'"

"13th July, 1871.

"I am greatly obliged to you for the opportunity of
"reading Mr. Dunoyer's letters" [on the state of the

working classes of Paris]. "As you say that you have
"another copy, I don't return them. I shall put them in
"the envelope to keep company* with the proof of my
"evidence and letter to the Commissioners of Scientific
"Instruction in Elementary Schools.

"It is as dangerous for us to shut our eyes to the state-
"ment of facts and descriptions of Mr. Dunoyer as it was
"for Napoleon and his advisers to shut theirs to the report
"of Baron Stoffel from Berlin. I am one of those who
"accept the truthfulness in the main of what Mr. D.
"narrates, and of much more that it is painful to
"think of.

"The question with which I follow up such statements
"is 'What is to be done?' A large and increasing number
"of our fellow creatures is complaining, and not unreason-
"ably, that their condition is miserable. When told to be
"resigned, because there is no help for them and that they
"are in the state in which it has pleased God to place
"them, they declare that they will not.

"'You can't help us,' they say to their well-fed and
"learned brothers, 'and, therefore, we will endeavour to
"'help ourselves, and we will begin by inquiring why a
"'few should consume so profusely while many have a
"'bare subsistence. At birth we are much alike; why
"'should some inherit largely and others have no inheri-
"'tance? Why should some be helped to the knowledge
"'which brings within their reach enjoyments innumerable,
"'while others are condemned to ignorance and its conse-
"'quences, want and suffering?'

"Many years ago, Bentham said that the oppressed
"many could hope to obtain relief only by 'making the
"'ruling few uncomfortable.' The prolétaires seem to be
"tired of 'rolling in the ditch,' and they present this
"alternative to those who are more comfortably placed,
"'help us out, or we will force you to share our mud.'

"Who ought to be most severely condemned—the

"ignorant, brutal, dirty, 'prolétaires,' or the instructed,
"cultured (that is the word), well-washed, and religious
"'propriétaires?'

"I am idle, hence this letter; perhaps you will say that
"I am cynical also."

"31st July, 1871.

"The contents of your letter of yesterday" (announcing
his election to the professorship of Political Economy and
Mercantile Law at Edinburgh) "are most gratifying in all
"respects.   I don't know that I ought to congratulate you;
"but I am quite sure that I may congratulate the gentle-
"men who have been most active in securing your
"appointment after having recognised your rare fitness for
"the chair, the University, and the public at large.   It is
"true that there is a wide field for usefulness opened to
"you, and that to make every effort to turn it to account
"will be a self-rewarding labour, but you have to sacrifice
"much domestic comfort.   But if you succeed in presenting
"political economy—that science which so many suppose
"to be cold, unfeeling, and corpse-like—in its true colours
"as a body of principles and rules of conduct for the peasant
"and artisan, as well as for capitalist, philanthropist, and
"statesman, you will do great service at this turning point
"of our destinies, and will be amply rewarded for all your
"self-devotion.   May you and Mrs. Hodgson and your
"children live to look back upon and enjoy the past trials
"endured while contemplating the evidences of success
"everywhere around!"

"16th August, 1871.

"People are astir, if not at all times stirring judiciously.
"And this is more satisfactory to the reflecting man than
"torpid submission, even if blandly represented as pious
"resignation.   But you have been working and are about
"to work with greater power, at the right end—to rouse
"and at the same time to instruct and direct the young

"how to make society what it ought to be and themselves
"worthy members of it.

"When we return in October" [from Cauviac, whither
he was going with Madame Ducamp] "your Edinburgh
"campaign will be about to open, and, however successful,
"you will not take rank with Bismarck or Moltke or the
"Red Prince or the Hero of Solferino. Nevertheless, the
"grand effects of your unseen and ill-appreciated labours
"will be more enduring than the effects of Gravelotte,
"Sedan, and Paris. Although unable to do much, I still
"hope not to be quite idle, and shall enjoy if I cannot
"share your triumphs."

"6th November, 1871.

"Although I am not yet informed of your private
"address, I must write to thank you for the copies of two
"numbers of the *Scotsman*.

"The latter of the two, which reached me this morning,
"I brought on here" (his office in the city) "in case I
"should have a leisure hour to read your inaugural
"address" [as professor at the Edinburgh University]
"by daylight. I have had it, and never did I spend an
"hour more delightfully, ending, I trust, with right feelings
"vivified, and good resolutions strengthened.

"Able, sensible, practical, and most opportune. These
"are the words which express the impressions left upon
"my mind by the perusal of your address I hope the
"lecture-room was crammed. I should like to have been
"a listener, and to have witnessed the effect which it
"must have produced upon the audience.

"I will only now add that I take for granted your
"address will be printed forthwith in another form and
"that I bespeak a thousand copies. I can hardly
"conceive any form of appeal to those who can influence
"educational improvement better adapted to inspire them
"with right thoughts and the desire to diffuse them.,

"Congratulating you most heartily upon your great
"triumph, for such it must be considered by all thoughtful
"people, among whom I comprise the dignitaries and
"others who had the gratification of hearing you, I
"remain, my dear friend, yours admiringly,

"WILLIAM ELLIS."

"16th November, 1871.

"When the inaugural address inspired me, as it did,
"with enthusiastic admiration, I fully expected that my
"feelings would be shared by numbers, and among them
"many likely to influence others by their intelligence and
"activity, and so far my expectations seem to have been
"warranted.   I shall be glad when some copies of it pass
"from the printer's hands into mine."

"22nd November, 1871.

"I intrude this small slip of my own merely to express
"how greatly I rejoice that your thoughts are necessarily
"much absorbed in the glorious work to which you are
"devoting mind and body.   The rich inheritance which
"you are thereby providing for yourself and yours can be
"taken from you by no one, whether he be base or
"capricious.

"What with political economists, who (to use Mr.
"Robson's words) seem to lose sight of the 'human aspect
"'of economics,' and with Lord Russell and Dixon, who
"would teach capacity of self-guidance by readings in the
"Bible free from sectarianism or denominationalism, I
"must say of you in Scotland, as I have often said of
"Shields in England, you are indispensable, for no one
"else *at this time* could do what you are doing.

"I hope the teachers of all the great schools will attend
"the evening class alluded to by Mr. Blair.   It will be
"the climax of your triumph if you rear up a number of
"teachers inspired with your sentiments, and intent upon

T

"acquiring the knowledge to which you can help them,
"with a view to impart it to the young, who in their turn
"look to them for instruction and example."

" 5th February, 1873.

"On all sides people are beginning to appeal to educa-
"tion as the one means indispensable for lifting the
"masses out of their present unsatisfactory state—not
"more unsatisfactory than it ever has been, but less
"satisfactory than it is vaguely felt it might be. How
"extraordinary it appears to me that one never meets
"with a word, from those who habitually address the
"public, to explain in what manner education is to
"achieve the good expected from it. And, in the mean-
"time, we see great efforts to extend education such as
"we have been accustomed to, and none to ascertain how
"far it is adapted to its purpose or to introduce the im-
"provements which will make it efficient.

" 26th May, 1873.

"Although your two last notes have remained long
"unanswered, they have not been unheeded. The fact is,
"that we had not been able to procure the May number
"of *Fraser* till Saturday.

"Miss Nightingale's is, as you say, a remarkable paper.
"I hope her name will attract readers, and the matter can
"scarcely fail to set some of them thinking. Once, before
"the Crimean War, she was at Champion Hill, and she
"was present at one or two of my lessons at the National
"Hall in those days.[1] She is one of those persons, the
"salt of the earth, who, unable to rest quietly enjoying
"themselves with so much misery around them, are
"determined to set to work, according to their opportu-
"nities, to diminish if possible, and at all events to relieve.

---

[1] See Miss Nightingale's memory of these lessons, and of Ellis, *ante*, page 98.

" She has done much in both ways, and evidently would
" have done more if she had known how, or if the social
" forces around her had not prevented.

" Professor Newman differs from Miss Nightingale,
" inasmuch as he is a speculative not a practical thinker.
" He would regenerate Sunday. She would regenerate
" mankind. I was well prepared to read the 'Note of
" 'Interrogation,' for I took it up on my return from a
" visit near Lowndes Square, and had to cross the gay,
" luxurious, ennui-evading crowd on my way to and fro.
" If this crowd be Christian and they worship a God, Miss
" Nightingale and others may well be anxious to learn
" what are characteristics of Christians and of the God
" whom they worship.

" The process of regeneration or (as I prefer to call it)
" evolution is slow. One of these days we shall have a
" thinking generation. To hasten this day is our aim; it
" will come, but with all our efforts it will not come in our
" time, and I agree with Herbert Spencer, we have no
" grounds for expecting it thus early.

" I paid Shields a visit last Saturday week; he still
" holds out, and his schools continue to be well filled.
" Mr. Teather[1] announces that he has reached a higher
" number than he had ever had—five hundred and twenty-
" three. With your seven hundred we may hope that
" some good will silently come out of our efforts."

" 15th July, 1873.

" Sometimes, mentally, I put this question to myself,
" 'Are you satisfied with what you have done and are
" 'doing towards the improvement of yourself and of
" 'the society to which you belong?' and my answer,
" unhappily, is in the negative. In palliation, for I have
" no wish to be over severe with myself, I admit that in

---

[1] Head master of the Gospel Oak Schools.

"many of my attempts I have been foiled and mistaken, and
"let into grievous disappointments. While, therefore, I
"would continue the good fight and bring forward reserves,
"I feel somewhat like a wounded or beaten man, less
"confident in myself, although unshaken in my con-
"fidence for the future with or without my co-operation.

"While I make such reflections upon myself, it can
"hardly be expected that I should not extend them to
"my friends, especially those whom I most esteem. It is
"the old old question. How can people in comfortable,
"circumstances (not to say luxurious) justify their style
"of living in the midst of destitution, without humbug?"

"26th November, 1873.

"I have been reading Robert Dale Owen's *Threading*
"*my Way*. It opens with the early days of his father
"Robert Owen. What an instructive and interesting
"record of opinions and events during the larger part of
"a century. How little have we to regret in what has
"passed away, and how much there is to encourage those
"who in their turn are forwarding the work of the further
"improvement still so urgently called for and so plainly
"obtainable."

"10th January, 1874.

"I had already seen the notice of the *Autobiography*"
[of John Stuart Mill—then just published]. "I agree
"entirely with your observations. Mill's bequest is one of
"the most remarkable ever made to society—melancholy
"and yet highly instructive. Although it will not add to
"his fame, it may be considered as a species of self-sacrifice
"made '*pro bono publico.*' We may all reflect how few of
"us could stand such a thorough 'turning inside out' as he
"has subjected himself to in so unsparing a manner. He
'may in his great work on *Logic* be said to have made
"his name famous while benefiting society, and afterwards
"to have conferred an equally great benefit to society by

"submitting his whole mental and moral growth and con-
"stitution with its weaknesses as well as his strong points
"to be dissected and criticised by foes as well as friends.
"It will, if I mistake not, be invaluable to seriously dis-
"posed young men in helping them to cultivate manliness
"of thought, and in awakening them to take an interest
"in problems as a rule glossed over and turned aside from
"ignobly and disingenuously."

1874—1881.

THE last few years of Ellis's life are full of pathetic interest. His bodily powers became slowly weaker, and year by year he became less and less able to work for the cause to which his life had been devoted. But the gradual failure of his strength was borne cheerfully and without repining, and his mind remained bright and active to the last. The intense devotion to the cause of the improvement of the welfare of humanity, which had ever been his ruling motive of action, remained unaltered, and from time to time he gave utterance, in such manner as his feeble powers permitted, to the thoughts which still held possession of his mind, while he continued to try to disseminate the knowledge which he thought should be the common property of every human being as a guide to right conduct. His correspondence with Hodgson was one of his greatest pleasures, especially during these years, when he was unable from feebleness either to go to the city for more than a short and gradually diminishing number of hours in the day, or to leave home in the evening. His growing weakness caused him to spend many solitary hours on the sofa, in which his thoughts, like those of the old warrior, reverted to the life-long struggle with ignorance and destitution in which he had been engaged, and he "fought his battles o'er again" in conversation with those of his intimate friends who from time to time called to see him, with undiminished energy and will, though with less physical vigour than during the maturity of his powers. One relaxation and change of thought was specially enjoyed by him. He was very fond of whist, and played a very good rubber; and the keen zest with which he watched the progress of the game, leaning closely down on the table, in consequence of his very short sight, and the pleasure he had in snatching a victory in an evenly-balanced contest, by a bit of bold and judicious play, will never be forgotten by those who took part with him in the game or watched its progress. The present writer, who, as has been before stated, began to assist him in managing the Birkbeck Schools in 1862, and continued the superintendence of them under Ellis's direction during the remainder of his life, was always received when he called in an evening with a cordial and affectionate welcome, and remembers well the delight with which, after an hour's chat about the affairs of the day, and reporting and consulting upon any matters relating to the progress of his schools, he would conclude with, " And now, what do you say to a game of whist ?"

A selection from Ellis's letters to Hodgson, which were pretty frequent during these last years, will be the best means of telling the story of the sunset of his life. They contain interesting remarks, not only on his own special ideas, but also on the events of the time, especially on the progress of France, in which country, as the home of his ancestors, he always felt great interest, and still more after the marriage of his daughter to a French gentleman. The first of them is curiously illustrative of one of his special characteristics—his extreme modesty. It was that which led him to withhold his name from the title page of many of his earlier works, although, after he found it necessary to publish in his own name, he always added a list of them, with an acknowledgment of his authorship, in the advertisement of his works which formed the fly sheet of his later books:—

" 10th February, 1875.

" I am deeply convinced of my incapacity to interest " the public. Whether the fault be in me or in the public " I will not venture to judge. Vanity would lead me to " lay the blame on the public. Wherever it be, the effect " is absence of demand.

" Five hundred copies of the last edition of *Progressive* " *Lessons* remain unsold. It is a work specially intended " for teachers, and teachers do not care for it or for the " subjects which it deals with. I have never parted nor even " thought of parting with the copyright of any of my " works. I have many sources of expenditure besides the " household, and these have been among them.

" If anybody could show me that I am one of the " lights of the age, but that there is a dark screen between " me and a public pining for light, I could but rejoice " (modestly, of course) in my projected elevation, and " assist the friendly hand capable of removing the screen, " diffusing my light, and enlightening the public darkness."

" 14th February, 1875.

" I will not delay even a day in answering your last " note, because I cannot imagine how I can have expressed " myself so badly as to lead you to think that I might be " fearful of your 'involving me in expense.' Expense would, " indeed, be a secondary consideration with me if I could " see my way to do more than I have done towards " making education the means of developing in the young, " through good teaching and training, a capacity for self- " guidance. The enemy who would open to me some new " channel leading in that direction should be forgiven, but " the friend who would do so should be cherished more " dearly, if possible, than heretofore.

" You may be quite sure that I shall be ready to offer

"every assistance to anybody who can obtain a wider
"circulation for the *Progressive Lessons*, and still more to
"anybody who can enable teachers to use them.

"What you say of most teachers is quite true, 'they are
"'to be pitied more than blamed.' But how many would
"put up with the expression of the pity which you feel?
"Would they not rather be disposed to pity or despise
"your efforts to recommend such teaching to them?
"Meanwhile we must have some compassion for the
"children. In industrial life the ignoring of important
"improvements causes subordinates to be discharged or
"cashiered, and principals to take refuge in the *Gazette*.

"Your answer to the Tailor question" (how a tailor
contributes to the management of a railway) "is all-sufficient.
"The learner is meant to have a vivid apprehension of the
"quantity and perfection of work which railway officials can
"perform by being relieved from the necessity of making
"their own clothes, &c., &c., &c. The learner, step by
"step, may rise to the apprehension that with the aid of
"division of labour and interchange, the industrial world
"becomes one vast co-operative society, in which the
"*tendency* of the efforts of each partner is to give him a
"share of the whole proportioned to his success in con-
"tributing to the wealth of all, and to prevent others from
"getting more than their share.

"The leading thought in my teaching has always been
"to bring my scholars to see, observe, think, and express
"for themselves; and, with skilful teaching in social
"science, there is really little need to forestall what the
"scholars can gather for themselves, stimulated, interested,
"roused, and awakened, of course, by their teachers. My
"first *approach* to success in realising my own wishes was
"in the Dean's book, and my second is the edition of
"*Progressive Lessons* from which you quote. But I am
"frightfully distant from the bull's eye at which I have
"been so long aiming. I believe, however, I am to be seen

" at less disadvantage as a teacher (with all my deficiency
" of sight and hearing) than as a writer. After all,
" teachers are not to be formed by books alone, any more
" than riflemen who, before they are led to face the enemy,
" get practice in the school of musketry. How enviable
" is the lot of the young soldier (granting the need of his
" ultimate services) compared with that of the young
" teacher. His instructor knows not only how to aim, but
" what to aim at.

"Coals are cheaper, as you perceive; I am sending
" some to Newcastle."

In April, 1875, Ellis published a short pamphlet, entitled
" A few words on Board Schools; what may be done in them,
" and the least that ought to be done in them," with an introduction by Rev. Lewis W. Wood. Mr. Wood was an able
and enlightened clergyman, vicar of Dunton Bassett,
Lutterworth, and chairman of his School Board. He had
made Ellis's acquaintance some ten years previously, and
had himself originated a system of moral teaching before
he knew him. He had consequently sympathized warmly
with Ellis's views when he came to know him. He was
struck with the value of his method of teaching the ordinary
facts of social life, and agreed with him as to the improvements needed in the system of education prevailing throughout the country. He, therefore, willingly consented to
become foster-parent to Ellis's pamphlet, and wrote a short
but instructive introduction to it. The pamphlet bears on
its title page as a motto the words, " Education is still in its
" infancy. Already it has done much for classes; and who
" can tell what wonders it may not, in its maturity, accom-
" plish for the masses?" It shortly sketches and explains
the series of lessons on the duties of social life already
described in these pages, and which are necessary to mould
children into " worthy members of a well-conducted and
" flourishing community," and gives examples of the kind of
lessons with which they should be preceded and accom-

panied, and which, in conjunction with reading, writing, and arithmetic, should be taught in all Board Schools. The description of this kind of lessons—the character of which will be in some measure given if we denominate them "world-object-lessons"—is as follows:—

"The subjects for the lessons are to be drawn from the "surroundings of children, and, where within reach, to be "illustrated by objects, drawings, models, diagrams, and "maps. Examples of what they are proposed to be may "be classed somewhat as follows:—

"The food, clothing, fuel, furniture, and utensils, and "the materials out of which they are made, shaped, and "adapted for use.

"The birds, beasts, and fishes, and domestic animals, "and how and why they are fed and cared for.

"The gardens and fields; and the trees, shrubs, and "plants, and how and why some are selected and culti-"vated, and others are rejected and destroyed.

"The houses, streets, roads, and towns, and the mate-"rials with which they are built and kept in repair.

"The vehicles, locomotives, ships, and the materials "used for their construction, maintenance, and employ-"ment.

"Places of residence, the street, the parish, the town, "the county; the country in which they are situated, "neighbouring countries, and other parts of the earth; "the whole earth and its shape, size, and movements.

"The sun, moon, stars, and planets.

"The succession of day and night, and of the seasons, "and the changes of weather: the regularity of the first, "and the vicissitudes of the last.

"Clocks and watches, and other contrivances for "measuring and marking time.

"The contrivances for procuring and distributing light, "heat, and water, and for regulating them to supply those "comforts safely and conveniently.

"The atmosphere which we live in, and which we
"breathe, the functions of our lungs in regard to it, its
"weight, the barometer, the thermometer, the common or
"drawing pump, the forcing pump, and other instruments
"and machines in daily use."

Mr. Wood's testimony, as a teacher who had adopted
this teaching in his schools (which, it will be remembered,
were village schools, in which the children were of the
humblest class), is valuable both as to its efficiency and the
practicability of giving it to such children. He says in his
introduction:—

"As a parochial clergyman, as a practical teacher, and
"also as chairman of a village School Board, I can bear
"witness to the good effects which result from the teaching
"described in the following pages, and which I venture to
"advocate so strongly. For I can conceive no greater
"crime towards a child than to allow it to face life without
"that knowledge beforehand, which will prevent delusions
"from captivating, incorrect ideas from warping, and
"unstable conduct from vitiating, its mind, its judgment,
"and its life.

"If Board Schools are effectually to benefit the masses,
"it must be by establishing an order of education very
"much in advance of that hitherto attempted. The intelli-
"gent application, as well as the mechanical processes of
"education, must be made of paramount importance."

In the Autumn of 1875 Ellis accompanied his daughter,
Madame Ducamp, to Cauviac, where he spent two months.
Before leaving he wrote to Hodgson:—

"19th August, 1875.

"We start to-morrow morning. In many respects I go
"with regret, and sorry to think that you are suffering
"and in bed. You would like, I daresay, to be on the
"move, while I rather long for repose. The only *vis* that
"I feel much of now is the *vis inertiæ*, and that explains

"why I seem to neglect my friends. But it is in appear-
"ance only, for their intentions and doings are not absent
"from my mind. My own doings (out of business) being
"*nil* and my sentiments and opinions being by this time
"familiar to you offer no food for the pen even if the brain
"were not at fault.

"I trust you will have conquered your indisposition
"before this reaches you, and since my tone and style can
"hardly be suitable for an invalid, even if tolerable to a
"convalescent, I must throw myself upon your indulgence
"to accept my leave-taking, such as it is, because I cannot
"go away without leaving on record some expression of
"my continued attachment to, and lively interest, in you
"and yours."

He seems to have derived much benefit from his visit to
Cauviac, for his *vis inertiæ* was so far conquered during his
visit as to give way to the impulse to write a paper, rather
more in the nature of a magazine article than his previous
writings, by which he wished to attract the attention of a
new class of readers, and which he desired, if possible, to get
published in *Blackwood's Magazine*. The following two
letters to Hodgson tell the story of it:—

"30th November, 1875.
"Do you know anybody through whom one might
"obtain an unprejudiced reading of an anonymous paper
"offered for *Blackwood's Magazine?* My reason for
"asking this question is that, a few days before quitting
"Cauviac, it occurred to me I would write a paper, so I
"began it at once and finished it a week ago.

"The title is 'The pressing want of our times.' Except
"for the frightful deficiency of literary merit, I think
"Professor Blackie would not judge ill of it. Of course
"to you and me it is but the oft-told tale, and with
"my name to it the observation would be sure to follow,
"'there he is repeating himself again.' I need hardly say

" that I have endeavoured to avoid wounding any religious
" susceptibilities, and it would be some gain to have such
" views countenanced by *Blackwood*."

" 4th December, 1875.

" The only thing that made me think of *Blackwood* was
" the desire to obtain a hearing from a different class of
" readers.   There is a movement just now which ought to
" prevent one's entirely despairing of gaining admission of
" practical common sense into schools.   I have been some-
" what amused within these few days with the letters of
" Auberon Herbert and John Morley and the comments
" upon them in the *Times*.   They both pass by, as if on
" purpose, but in reality unconsciously, what secular
" instruction must include if religion, sectarian or unsec-
" tarian, is to be excluded.

" Taking advantage of your kind offer, I send my MS.
" herewith.   Use it in any way you think most advisable,
" even to leaving it unused.   In whatever you decide I
" shall feel assured that *we* have but one end in view—the
" furtherance of the good cause.   I would do more and
" better if I could, and perhaps I ought to resign myself
" to do less, or nothing, and if you should be of Gil Blas'
" opinion, I will not be like the Archbishop; you shall still
" retain my confidence and friendship.

" Your account of Smiles does not surprise me.   Nearly
" twenty years ago I concocted a lecture on the early life
" of George Stephenson out of his very interesting book,
" and I have read parts of his other books.   He is a pleasing
" popular writer, with a plentiful flow of words and ideas
" *currente calamo*—a good reporter and narrator, and
" probably a good advocate, but not a good judge—*i.e.*,
" incapable of comprehensive summing up.   Shall I make
" you laugh, even if in a melancholy mood, when I say
" somewhat the same of a number of highly-gifted and
" variously-gifted men, such as Carlyle, Blackie, Ruskin.

" They surprise, fascinate, overwhelm—but do not convince
" you. *Satis eloquentiæ, sapientiæ parum.* There is
" absence of coherence and consistency in the reflections
" to which they give utterance, not only in different times,
" places, and books, but in different pages of the same
" book. They can misrepresent, denounce, and sneer
" at the principles of social science, which they do not
" understand, and perhaps never studied. Hence, like that
" famous divine whose epitaph, as given by you, amused me
" so much at the time, they are 'waiting for judgment.'

" Let us hope that, by better scientific training, the
" littérateurs of succeeding generations will be able to
" keep free from inconsistencies and distortions of truth,
" without any diminution of their verve and fertility."

Hodgson did not pass a similar comment upon the manuscript sent him to that of Gil Blas on the Archbishop's
sermons. He admired and agreed with it; but he suggested
a different method of obtaining publicity for it. An Educational Congress was to be held at Glasgow, on the 28th
and 29th December, under the auspices of the Educational
Institute of Scotland and the Association of Higher Class
Schoolmasters. Hodgson proposed to Ellis to read it in his
name and on his behalf at this congress, which would secure
its publication in full in the columns of some of the educational papers. It will be seen by the following letters to him
that Ellis agreed to this course, and the paper was so read
by Hodgson, and printed in the *Educational News* of 1st
January, 1876, the first number of that publication:—

" 7th December, 1875.
" Your offer to read my paper and to throw your shield
" over it is far too tempting for me to hesitate in accepting.
" I think you have my mind before you turned inside out.
" You and I desire to make known and gain acceptance
" for certain views in education, and would be sorry to do
" anything in our zeal to create aversion or disgust—to

"repel where we wish to attract; and if you think my
"name had better appear, I give my consent without
"reluctance."

"25th December, 1875.

"If I am striving 'to do good by stealth,' you are cer-
"tainly doing your best to make me 'blush to find it fame.'
"I am deeply sensible of your kindness, and trust that you
"will not damage your reputation for judgment by your
"attempt to lift into notoriety one who can scarcely stand
"public and critical inspection.

"Have you no fear, besides, that you may be assisting
"to develop unduly what our late much-revered friend
"George Combe would have called my organ of self-
"esteem?

"In bringing me before the Scottish Educational public
"with such a flourish of trumpets, I beg that you will, like
"a good godfather or judicious bottle-holder, add to, excise,
"or rub down any of the more palpable omissions and
"faulty and imperfect expressions that cannot fail to
"strike you and which would offend literary taste and
"prepossess listeners and readers against what they might
"otherwise be led to acknowledge as sound doctrine.

"I am very sorry to learn that you are likely to lose
"your friend Mr. Payne" [an eminent and well-known
Educationist]. "You are not yet quite old enough to be
"left like me almost isolated. In nautical language, I am
"over-due. In the company which I have served for more
"than fifty years, I have not one original master, and am
"the only original servant, and yet even now one of my
"later masters has just been killed by a fall from his
"horse, and another, whom I greatly esteem, and whom I
"think you must have met (Mr. Berger), is I fear dying.[1]

---

[1] Mr. Berger was a merchant (of the firm of Daniel Taylor and Sons)
who had cordially adopted Ellis's views, and used to give lessons on Social
Economy at one of the Birkbeck Schools. He was one of the trustees nomi-
nated by him when he formed a trust for carrying on the Schools.

"Although Professor Jevons' name is not strange to me,
"I am not sufficiently familiar with his works to be quite
"sure that I catch your meaning when you say that he is *no*
"disciple of J. S. Mill. Is he diametrically opposed to
"his principles, or does he merely disagree with some of
"his deductions and inferences? I am more indebted to
"the two Mills, father and son, than to anybody with
"whom I ever came in contact. I have been their disciple
"but certainly not their blind follower. Or, if I have missed
"the path in which they would have led me, those who
"do not form so high an estimate as I may of my own
"judgment might say that I have missed it through
"blindness."

"4th January, 1876.

"I hope that by this time you are again safe at home
"and none the worse for the exertions, bad air, and
"excitement of Glasgow, with fair reason, besides, to
"believe that some good has been done by your inter-
"course with the teachers from so many parts of Scotland.

"The six copies of the *Educational News*, for which I
"am a regular subscriber, reached me on Saturday. The
"thousand of No. 1" [which he had ordered for the
purpose of circulating his paper] "will, I dare say, be sent by
"some cheaper and therefore slower conveyance. But I
"will not wait to thank you for all the trouble that you
"have taken.

"If this new publication should at all correspond to our
"wishes, and occupy itself with something more than the
"routine of school work as hitherto done, you will be
"amply rewarded for your long-continued efforts to intro-
"duce light and common sense among teachers, and I
"shall rejoice to have had the opportunity of lending a
"hand, however feeble when it grasps the pen.

"Despite the good that you have been doing at Glasgow,
"I am not quite reconciled to the loss of your society, and
"I hope that the very first time you can be temporarily

U

"relieved from your regular engagements, you will con-
"sider yourself bound to compensate us for our dis-
"appointment.

"We have reached another turning point in the future
"of France, and I am hopeful. The decisions of the late
"Chamber, with all its shortcomings, have been respected.
"I shall rejoice if the members returned are liberal and
"thoughtful, but, whatever they may be, my principal
"anxiety is that there should be a cessation of *coups d'état*
"by governors, and of violent resistance to laws by the
"governed.

"What progress has been made in this country since
"the days of Adam Smith (mentioned lately by you)
"through the influence of the 'schoolmaster abroad,' and
"how much more may be expected from the influence of
"the improved schoolmaster?"

The paper itself is an interesting investigation of the
methods in education most likely to produce its main
object—the conversion of children into intelligent and well-
conducted members of society—and the main thought of it
is given in the following passage. After pointing out the
methods adopted by the farmer and manufacturer to produce
the precise article required by the needs of society, and, a
little more fully, how the nurseryman watches over infant
seeds and seedlings, utilises successive advances in knowledge as to the treatment of them, is constantly on the watch
to avail himself of any improved process, and applies to
them the precise treatment necessary to develop them into
the plants, trees, and fruits needed, he says:—

"Pursuing the train of thought suggested by the pro-
"ceedings of the intelligent farmer, manufacturer, and
"nurseryman, let us consider what has to be done by the
"educator who wishes to assist in transforming ignorant
"incapable children into intelligent capable men and
"women. We have to extend our inquiry into the methods
"for developing and perfecting the dispositions and attain-

" ments of men, as a means of securing conduct favourable
"to the well-being of each and all. Have we hitherto
"pursued the same course in conducting education that we
"have pursued in all other departments of human effort?
" Do we avail ourselves of all the lights thrown upon the
"subject by the best and latest researches, and are we
"working in the hope and expectation of yet receiving
"new lights from the same quarter?"

It will be hardly worth while to recapitulate the method
of solution of this problem, which would be—as Ellis said
to Hodgson—an oft-told tale. There is, however, one
passage which may be quoted with interest. He specially
points out the importance of a thorough grounding in the
elementary principles on which all social economy rests,
preliminary to embarking in a study of the more abstruse
questions. This very speciality had been matter of critical
remark by his reviewers. They found their self love, as
men who were criticising what they deemed complicated
problems of political economy, rather wounded by having
to read chapters in which the elementary qualities of industry, intelligence, skill, honesty, economy, and parental
forethought were fully and carefully examined in all their
details and consequences; and they failed to realise that the
more difficult problems of social life are only difficult if
discussed without proper grounding, but become simple—so
simple as to be easily taught to children at school—if a
proper preparation be laid for them by approaching them
with a thorough mastery of the more elementary principles.
We have seen how a reviewer of one of Ellis's works came
to the conclusion that there was nothing more novel in his
writings than "that two and two made four, or that A is A."
The comment reminds us a little of the old anecdote of
Columbus and the egg. The solution of a social problem is
provokingly easy when properly approached from first
principles; but the same problem seems difficult if the
simple method of solving it from the base be not adopted.

This was one speciality of Ellis's method, and he says of it in this paper:—

> "There is this advantage in a thorough acquaintance with
> "rudimental principles. It acts as a safeguard and warn-
> "ing against the offhand acceptance of doctrines opposed
> "to them, even where the fallacies cannot be detected. It
> "assumes the form of common sense, which, when it
> "guides conduct, makes its possessor a wiser man, though
> "illiterate, than the learned man whose attention has
> "never been drawn to it."

We proceed with a selection from the letters to Hodgson, which, during this and the ensuing year, are frequent and interesting. The first arose out of the following incident. A correspondent of the *Scotsman*, under the initials " T. S. C.," had written a letter, remarking in strong terms on the general ignorance of the laws of Political Economy which prevailed, and adding that such knowledge was not considered in business circles to be necessary or desirable, and that a man's reputation would suffer if he were supposed to be a student of it. As a remedy for this state of things he continued: " I would propose that a few of the leading "maxims of Political Economy should be thrown into the "form of a catechism and learned by heart in our schools. "Granted that the children would not thoroughly understand "them, do they understand the shorter catechism?" Hodgson had replied to this proposal by a letter deprecating the adoption of the "parrot-rote" system in lieu of really intelligent teaching, explaining how such knowledge might be properly taught, referring to the experience of the Birkbeck Schools and comparing the above plan to the practice of some Mahomedan tribes in Africa who literally imbibe the precepts of the Koran by washing off sacred sentences written for them on a board and then drinking the water. " T. S. C." had responded, failing to understand how such principles could be taught to children and defending his own plan of learning by rote.   Hodgson sent the correspondence to Ellis, from whom he received the following reply:—

"23rd January, 1876.

"The terms 'clever and narrow-minded,' with which "you characterise 'T. S. C.,' how applicable they are to "most of our cultivated men! Our scientific men, mean-"ing thereby men distinguished for their attainments in "*physical* science, are no exceptions. And the reason for "this appears to me to be that they are not trained to form "their judgments upon evidence. Even when that "malpractice is departed from with students of physical "science it is still persisted in in everything outside "physical science.

"I return the two letters of 'T. S. C.' and the copy of "your excellent answer to the first, in case you should "wish to keep them, or pass them on in quarters where "they might be useful. But unless it be to keep yourself "in practice, your powder and shot would be wasted "against such a target.

"I have just been reading in the last number of the "*Revue des deux Mondes* a tale by Cherbuliet, from which "I am tempted to make an extract for your delectation. "In explanation it must be premised that there are two "brothers, Geoffroy and Maurice. The first has made his "position, and is a clever man of the world, not over-"burdened with scruples, and, being by far the elder, acts "as queror and mentor to the other, who is unsettled and "has scruples:—

"'Maurice eut peine à ne pas sourire en l'entendant "'déclarer que toute saine politique doit s'appuyer sur le "'clergé. Il connaissait son frère pour un mécréant "'endurci, pour un libre-penseur si absolu, si affirmatif, "'qu'il l'avait surnommé jadis un Voltairien de Sacristie. "'Geoffroy, qui voyait courir le vent, devina l'impression "'que ses palinodies produisaient sur son frère. Que

"'veux tu, jeune homme? lui dit-il, en lui frappant sur
"'l'épaule, il n'y a que Dieu et les imbéciles qui ne
"'changent pas.'

" How long teachers will persist in classing themselves
"among those 'qui ne changent pas,' I will not pretend
"to guess. I would gladly assist them to something
"better."

                                 " 3rd March, 1876.

" We almost always see the *Contemporary*, but I was not
"even tempted to read the 'Buddhist Sermon.' From
"certain vague recollections of former readings, your
"quotations do not take me by surprise. The records of
"ancient religions and revelations and inspired teachings
"preserved to us from ignorant, barbarous, and supersti-
"tious peoples, all contain some remarkable, excellent
"aphorisms and injunctions, interspersed with others of a
"very different character; and a modern moralist who
"picks and chooses among them can generally find
"passages in support of whatever theory or system
"of morals he is disposed to favour. I think it has some-
"where been said that the student of sacred books will
"never fail to draw forth from them what he has taken in.

" Last night I read Mr. Martineau's[1] second article in
"this month's *Contemporary*, having previously read his
"first; and greatly struck am I by the wide range of his
"attainments, his beautiful style, his controversial skill,
"and his fertility of illustration. But he appears to me,
"in my ignorance, to have stretched his encampment into
"the 'Unknowable,' and to be rather intolerant of those
"who cannot find shelter under his tents.

" Professor Tyndall, who now confines himself almost
"exclusively to original research, and is striving to add to
"the 'known' what has hitherto been 'unknown,' has
"come into collision with some who consider themselves

---

[1] Dr. James Martineau.

"authorised expounders both of the unknown and un-
"knowable. They remind me of squatters, who are ex-
"ceedingly indignant when the progress of civilisation
"brings the rightful claimants to call upon them to yield
"up what they are not legally possessed of."

"21st June, 1876.

"It was quite refreshing to have a number of the
"*Educational News* containing something likely to
"interest anybody who is not a Scotch schoolmaster. I
"guessed that the leading article was yours, and Huxley
"never fails to interest, while he is sure to teach. What
"Huxley says of physical is equally true of moral science.
"Art precedes science. Man's existence has ever depended
"upon 'work.' He cannot defer his work till he has
"grounded it upon a scientific basis. The choice is not
"given to him, if he intends to live, 'to do or not to do.'
"He must do, well or ill as it may be. But, to encourage
"him in his efforts as he advances in knowledge, he finds
"that he is continually doing better and better, in spite of
"the obstructions thrown in his way under the pretence of
"giving him religious instruction.

"I should almost be tempted (think of my presump-
"tion) to suggest an improvement, merely verbal, upon
"Mr. Huxley's precedence to art over science. I would
"say practice or work (*ex necessitate*) precedes science, and
"then art (or work directed by science) follows. Other-
"wise we seem to require another word for 'art,' or drift
"into the use of the word 'art' in two senses."

"9th August, 1876.

"There is only one way in which I can now be amused
"by my friends, and that is by visits such as you kindly
"indulge me with from time to time. I have ceased to
"be a locomotive. I am a stationary engine on an old
"pattern, but although I give out little heat and little light
"and do but little work, I try to consume my own smoke."

The School Board election of November, 1876, was an event which attracted much attention from Ellis. The School Boards had done good work, but he desired that they should do still better, and should introduce into their curriculum education really adapted to mould the characters of their pupils. Early in the period when the contest was proceeding, he wrote a letter of more than a column in length to the *Times*, which appeared in that journal on the 2nd September, under the signature "Senex," and contains much earnest thought. He points out that " education is not and cannot be a thing of vocables " (or vague general terms). " It is a thing of earnest facts; of " capabilities developed, of habits established, of dispositions " dealt with, of tendencies confirmed, and tendencies re- " pressed," and he proceeds to draw attention to what has been attempted and omitted under the head of " Moral and " Religious Instruction." Quoting the School Board rules to the effect that " the Bible shall be read, and there shall be " given such explanations and such instruction therefrom in " the principles of morality and religion as are suited to the " capacities of children," he shows that no indication is given as to what is meant by "instruction in the principles of " morality and religion," a defect which he proceeds to supply by a careful explanation of the kind of teaching which children ought to receive for the formation of their character in future life, and concludes—

" Let us then by no means fail to include 'moral and " 'religious instruction' in our school teaching. Equally " let us be careful not to mislead our children by false " lights, or to impose upon them with vocables."

We proceed with the extracts from the letters to Professor Hodgson, which at this period give the best account of the gradual sinking to rest of his life and activity.

" 13th October, 1876.
" As you like new sensations, think of me attending a

"course of lectures on Political Economy. I am doing so
"for the sake of escorting Ethel. She wishes, by the
"advice of her G.F." [grandfather], "to have an opportunity
"of comparing his common-place method with that of a
"Fellow of Balliol College. Each lecture is followed by a
"conversational class. The lectures put me a little in
"mind of those which I delivered fifty years ago" [at the
London Mechanics' Institution, afterwards redelivered under
the auspices of Lord Brougham in other parts of the country].

" 10th November, 1876.

" Miss Helen Taylor" [stepdaughter of his friend John
Stuart Mill] "called upon me last Sunday week. She had
"been speaking at Southwark and had been very well
"received. She seems afraid neither of work nor excite-
"ment, and will, I expect, be able to forward the good
"cause side by side with Mrs. Westlake and others.

"I have been making another submission to time and
"destiny. I have given in my resignation of the post
"which I have held here for fifty years. The reasonable-
"ness of this step has not been questioned by my em-
"ployers, and they are proposing to elect me to a vacant
"seat at the Board. I resign my present duties on the 1st
"January next."

This election took place; and for the next year or two—
in fact so long as his failing powers enabled him to get to
the city—he went down to the office of the Company, where
his successors and the Board gladly availed themselves of
his experience and judgment in reference to any special
matters which arose.

We proceed with the letters:—

" 7th December, 1876.

"I have got Mr. Zincke's address, but as yet have done
"no more than glance through its contents. I confess that
"but for your recommendation I should not have sent for
"it. Twenty-five years ago I wrote a short notice of a

"pamphlet of his[1] in conjunction with Bastiat's Baccalauréat "and Socialism in the *Westminster Review*, and I met " him at Buckingham Palace and at Sir James Clark's.

" I agree with you that the address is to be welcomed "as coming from a chaplain to the Queen, and shall " be curious to see what practical good results from it "in the proceedings of the 'Society for the development " of the science of education.' '*Error*,' or as a lawyer said, "correcting me, '*Dolus latet in generalibus*.' I fear I shall "get bewildered in Mr. Zincke's vocables, and I am not "quite sure that he is quite free from self-bewilderment. " I agree with him that to make education efficient for its "purpose, the teaching of systematic or scientific morality "must be provided in *all* our schools. But what is scientific "morality? I will not venture into the doctrine of "Utility, for fear, like Mr. Zincke, I should not be able to "disentangle myself.

" More humbly and more cautiously I claim this for the "young—educators should *aim* at satisfying this claim— "that they should be sent forth from school prepared as "well as possible at their age to feed, clothe, lodge, and "enjoy themselves. No teacher who has given intelligent "attention to his vocation, thus understood, can fail to "recognise that instruction in the social duties—in what "each individual ought to strive for in regard to his "fellows and to society, and in all the amiabilities and "refinements of life—must not be omitted.

"Where are the schools in which such instruction is "systematically aimed at? Where are the societies, " colleges, and training schools, and school boards in which " the providing of teachers qualified in this sense is even " thought of ?

---

[1] The Reviews were separate. That of Bastiat's " Baccalauréat et "Socialisme" was in the *Westminster Review* of July, 1850 (Classical Education). That of Rev. Foster Barham Zincke's pamphlet, which was entitled " Why "must we educate the whole people, and what prevents our doing it?" was in the same Review of January, 1851 (Educational Movements).

"All hail to the new association and its president if
"they will even commence—still more if they will give
"hope of accomplishing—this easy work."

"27th February, 1877.

"I am a little ashamed that I should have expressed
"myself so unguardedly or loosely as to lead you to think
"that I disparage Mr. Zincke. Granting that he, like
"Dean Stanley and Professor Mark Pattison, is a philo-
"sophical divine, it does not follow that he is a divine
"philosopher. While I respect and admire them all, with
"your friend James Martineau, may I not say, because so
"I think, and with regret, that they have not been able to
"shake themselves free from the theological mire in which
"they were originally immersed without, if not against,
"their will?

"I have yielded to the persuasions of some of my lady
"friends, who think, proving thereby perhaps their intel-
"lectual inferiority, that I am not quite worn out, to
"preside at a class meeting here every Saturday at 3-30.
"Last Saturday was our second, and we mustered more
"than thirty, as many as our dining-room will accom-
"modate. I will give you the announcement under
"which we came together, and, from what you know of
"me, you can guess what must follow.

"'Class meetings, principally of teachers, for the pur-
"'pose of inquiring, examining, and learning how educa-
"'tion may be made as efficient as possible in directing
"'and influencing conduct.'

"Miss Helen Taylor and the Dowager Lady Stanley
"sent several ladies, and our old friend Madame Bodichon,
"whom I have not seen for more than ten years, wrote
"me an exceedingly friendly note, begging to introduce
"a young friend.

"All this occupies me a little, and I hope some good
"may come from it to others."

The class for ladies lasted, on Saturday afternoons, through the summer; and was deeply interesting to the ladies who attended it. It was so successful that, finding himself still able to do so, he repeated it to another class in the ensuing year.

We proceed with the correspondence :—

" 11th March, 1877.

" I am reading Harriet Martineau's *Autobiography* with "intense interest. What a life of labour! and yet, sus-"tained as that labour was by a purpose, we may truly "say *labor ipse voluptas*. Running nearly over the same "years, what a curious coincidence mixed with contrasts "is afforded by her autobiography and that of John "Stuart Mill. They may both be accepted as manifes-"tations of much that has been and is still going on for "the improvement and elevation of our race, and is an "encouragement to us and those who are to come after "us to strive for self-improvement as a means of im-"proving others."

" 19th April, 1877.

" Your active habits and comparative youth prevent "your understanding how I pass my time. I am gra-"dually breaking myself into idleness, not so much "passing time as allowing time to pass me. I continue "to take an interest in all good works, but I attempt to "do little besides, lest I might hinder and annoy rather "than assist."

" 8th October, 1877.

" I return Professor Newman's letter. I confess I see "no reason for his mourning nor for your desponding "views. My optimism, as you call it, consists of a firm "belief, based upon what appears to me most indis-"putable evidence, that we are slowly developing into a "better state of earthly existence, the result of man's "advancing intelligence and wiser conduct. This process

" of development is not uninterrupted.   But age after age
" we may see how much worse off we should be were we
" thrown back to any former state.

   " These opinions do not blind me to the necessity of
" continued and strenuous exertions for exposing econo-
" mical fallacies and discountenancing superstitions, under
" whatever form they may be presented.   I now seek
" repose, being nearly worn out, but I do not the less
" sympathize with you and others who still work, only
" more ably, in the same direction.   I would do much
" more than sympathize if I could see my way how to do it.

   " More than fifty years have elapsed since the truths of
" economic science were first brought to my notice: they
" made an indelible impression upon me.   After a time
" they inspired me with the desire of obtaining the intro-
" duction of the teaching of them into our schools, even
" into the humblest, and I have worked at this as well as
" my lights and means would admit.   During the former
" years of this period I have been spoken of as a mere
" economist, and now I am almost suspected of under-
" valuing those who are expounding economic truth and
" combating the illusions which overshadow them.

   " No sensible man dare say that the decay or collapse
" which you seem to dread is impossible, but, according to
" my interpretation of the past and present, it is exceed-
" ingly improbable.   In the same way, Broglie and his
" puppet may over-ride public opinion and France, but
" they cannot make me despair of her future."

                              " 26th October, 1877.

   " When I read such lectures as Mr. Hanson's, and the
" programme of lectures prepared by our friend, Mr.
" Domville,[1] and think besides of what you and others,

---

[1] William Domville, Esq., a strong supporter of the Sunday Lecture Society,
a society providing Sunday afternoon lectures for the people on scientific
subjects.

"my little self included, have been doing, I cannot but
"ask myself somewhat mournfully, yet not despondingly,
"whither does it tend and when?

"Not to travel beyond our own island, one-tenth of our
"countrymen are living in a state which it is distressing
"to contemplate, and perhaps more than one-half in a
"state of which we have no reason to be proud, with all
"our improvements. Can we feel satisfied that we are
"doing all that might be done, and that we may not be
"missing the right direction in our efforts to amend what
"is so palpably wrong? May some resources, as yet un-
"known, be some day placed at our disposal for elevating
"the lot of the masses. Less than a century ago, our
"forefathers longed for greater rapidity and safety of
"communication, for more light, more relief from pain,
"and better safeguards against fevers and disease, and we
"have now got the enjoyment of what our forefathers
"longed for. When may our descendants hope to enjoy
"that freedom from destitution, vice, and misery, which
"we are longing for? Are we striving in the right direc-
"tion and with all earnestness? I wish I could clear up
"my own doubts on this head."

"20th November, 1877.

"I suppose it would be difficult to find an English
"newspaper which justifies the doings of Broglie and Co.
"Our hopes rest upon the good sense of the mass of the
"French people and their trusted leaders, and upon the
"patriotism of the French army, composed of soldiers who
"have not ceased to be citizens.

"I read Smiles' *Life of Edward*" (Thomas Edward, the
Banff naturalist) "some time ago. One could but admire
"his wonderful powers of observation and his power of en-
"durance, and devotion to natural history. But altogether
"the book left a mournful impression upon my mind. I
"was shocked at the treatment to which he was subjected
"in the name of education, and pitied him and his wife

"for the mistaken views with which he started in life.   It
"was almost a miracle that he escaped ruin in its very
"worst forms.

   "While feeding on the crumbs of comfort which come
"to me from time to time, I solace myself while digesting
"them with attempts to forecast how much nearer a state
"of perfection mankind will be in the year 2000.   I try
"not to be impatient."

"28th January, 1878.

   "I have long been troubled with a complaint rather
"annoying and incapacitating me for exertion than pain-
"ful or dangerous.   It has gained upon me of late and
"has demanded more active treatment.   Hence my being
"confined to bed for a few days, and much more than
"before to the couch and the house.   But I try not to
"fret, and bear in mind the many years I have lived with
"immunity from physical suffering, for I have just entered
"upon my seventy-ninth year.   I still am able to go into
"the city two or three times a week for a couple of hours
"and thus obtain a little variety of occupation without
"strain or fatigue.

   "I am in great hopes that we shall soon hear of the
"cessation of the horrible doings in Turkey. But what
"principally cheers me is the steady progress that the
"parliamentary party seems to be making in France.
"The current of events there since 1871 has been more
"favourable than I ventured to anticipate.   There, as
"here, education is relied upon as one of the means by
"which political gains may be made permanent and
"secure.   What a pity it is that in both countries, with
"such excellent intentions, thoughts are so confused as to
"what education ought to aim at in order to accomplish
"the good sought for."

"14th March, 1878.

   "Your letter of yesterday has so far overcome my *vis*
"*inertiæ* that here I am, pen in hand, with the purpose of

"congratulating you on the success of your labours during
"the session now about to close. The power to work
"which has departed from me leaves my interest and
"sympathy in the good works of others undiminished.

"Professor Jevons sent me a copy of his Primer. I
"hope it will do all the good you anticipate. You know
"my opinion of old about the comparative use of books
"and teachers in schools. One would be sorry to deprive
"a teacher of the assistance of good books, but no book,
"however good, can compensate for the want of a compe-
"tent teacher.

"You may dismiss from your mind any fears that I
"have been or am suffering any pain. I am disinclined
"to work, am soon tired, cannot sustain my attention
"long, and find deafness creeping upon me as well as
"weakness of sight. This list of my infirmities, while it
"allays all your graver apprehensions, will, I trust, lead
"you to believe that my long silences do not arise from
"any diminution of regard for such friends as yourself, or
"interest in their doings."

"27th January, 1879.

"This day I enter upon my eightieth year. I report
"this event in my shaky hand for two reasons—first,
"because I use it as an occasion for suspending self-
"reproaches for my continued remissness in writing to
"you, and second, because it may suggest to you some
"reasons for judging my faults with indulgence. You
"will not, I am sure, suspect that because I have long
"been silent, I have ceased to think of you and those who
"are dear to you, and of the good works in which you are
"engaged.

"My meditations turn as much as ever upon 'Human
"'conduct as a cause and means of human well-being'
"and upon education as a means of inducing conduct
"indispensable for well-being. I need not enumerate to
"you the kinds of conduct which I refer to, neither will I

"omit to refer to parental forethought as one of them, as one
"indeed which neglected, all others will be deprived of much
"of their efficacy. And in looking to education as a means
"of inducing desirable conduct, I have something more in
"my mind than what passes current under that name.

"While absorbed in this one idea, or rather series of
"ideas, you will not be surprised to learn that I bestow
"little time upon schemes for Co-operation, Combinations
"and Strikes, Reciprocity or Protection in a fancy dress,
"Protection in its naked deformity, Cycles, Epicycles, and
"Spots in the Sun. When ignorance and dishonesty are
"swept out of industrial concerns, a microscope may be
"usefully employed to examine the meteoric dust which
"may be the cause of still subsisting 'Crises,' should any
"survive. Meanwhile, let us protect our eyes from dust.

"With kindest regards to Mrs. Hodgson, I remain, your
"sincere but eccentric and incorrigible friend,

"WILLIAM ELLIS."

"24th February, 1879.

"I fear one of your letters must have gone astray. My
"last was written 27th January, the day on which I
"entered my eightieth year. I made that day an excuse
"for pleading 'extenuating circumstances,' while admit-
"ting my remissness as a correspondent. I must confess
"that there was nothing in that letter calling for or de-
"serving notice; still I am uncomfortable at the thought
"that you may be throwing me off as not entitled to an
"occasional recognition.

"There is one comfort in the midst of surrounding
"gloom—the favourable current of events in France. It
"makes me more hopeful of the future, not only of
"France, but of all Europe."

"26th March, 1879.

"I have read Mr. Smith's pamphlet which you were so
"kind as to send me.

V

"He does not appear to me to throw much light upon
"the subject, nor to introduce more order into the late
"discussions.

"Where ignorance (and, combined with it, misty notions
"in regard to honesty) is banished or largely eliminated
"from the use of credit, will there be any reason for
"investigating any further into the hypothesis of cycles?

"The narrative of Sir J. Walmsley's early struggles[1] is
"very interesting. He is a type of the men who in the
"last generation assisted us on to our present advanced
"state—the grandfather, let us hope, of those who will
"help us on to the further advancement so urgently called
"for and only waiting the men and the hours.

"From grave to gay—from clouds to sunshine. Last
"Wednesday at midday I received a visit from Her
"Imperial Highness the Crown Princess of Germany, in
"remembrance of the benefit which she said she had
"derived from my lessons at Buckingham Palace twenty-
"five years ago. She was very affable and unceremonious,
"and asked me to add my autograph to her collection,
"and of course I did so."

After this date the letters to Dr. Hodgson become more
rare. The gradually failing powers were unequal to the task
of putting into writing consecutive thoughts, although he
still enjoyed visits from his friends.

"11th June, 1879.

"I shall be most grateful for any spare time you can
"bestow upon me when you come to town. I am always
"at home, except for an hour between eleven a.m. and
"two p.m., and would, if needful, fix that hour more
"definitely for any special purpose.

"I read the papers which you were so kind as to send
"me, and shall be glad to talk over the subject matter of

---

[1] Sir Joshua Walmsley was Professor Hodgson's father-in-law, and his life,
by his son, Colonel H. M. Walmsley, had recently been published.

"them when we meet. I am quite unequal to long and
"sustained attention, especially with a pen in my hand.
"One advantage results from this to my indulgent friends;
"they are spared the task of reading my writing, which
"has become nearly illegible. My tongue seems now to
"be my only efficient organ of communication.

"4th July, 1879.

"It is almost superfluous for me to tell you that I rejoice
"to learn that you have decided upon holding on to your
"chair for another year,[1] to be followed, let us hope, for
"another and another.

"The conviction of the importance of a knowledge of
"'Economic Science,' and of the blindness of a large por-
"tion of the public, makes it necessary to defer somewhat
"to that blindness in order to court attention.

"A day will come, perhaps at no great distance, when
"it will be acknowledged that an appreciation of the facts
"and phenomena of life, upon which economic science is
"based, is essential to right conduct, and hence to well-
"being. We may be disappointed, but at least we have
"the satisfaction of knowing that *we* have done, and *you*
"are doing, your best to hasten the coming of that day."

A few months after this—in April, 1880—Ellis published
another little pamphlet, under the auspices of, and with an
introduction by, his friend Rev. Lewis W. Wood. It is
described by the latter as intended to supplement the "Few
"words on School Boards," published five years previously:
and it is entitled, *A short statement of some matters which
ought to be known by all teachers and taught to all children
before their schooldays are ended.* It is an outline of the

---

[1] Professor Hodgson's appointment to the chair of political and commercial
economy and mercantile law at Edinburgh was originally for seven years only.
On its expiration Hodgson strongly objected to its being only renewed for
another term, all the other chairs being for life. He had, however, consented
to hold it for another year pending reconsideration of the matter.

various subjects dealt with by his previous works and which had been shortly sketched in his previous pamphlet of 1875 on Board Schools. The conclusions with which he sums up the pamphlet, containing as they do the last words of the veteran reformer upon the method by which only mankind can be made better and happier, are of interest, especially the following passage upon education and parental duty. After referring to the existing social defects—to poverty, vice, and mistaken judgment as to the distinctions between good and evil, wise and foolish conduct—he says:—

"Our reliance for the ultimate, though gradual, dis-
"appearance of social sores, is in education—an education
"which will impart to every human being, as far as
"possible, the knowledge indispensable for his good
"self-guidance, and the disposition to act upon that
"knowledge.

"To guard against misapprehension, let it be understood
"that nothing is to be excluded from the education thus
"relied upon that bears upon the health, attainments, and
"dispositions of the young. The participations of parents
"in such an education is indispensable. Children must be
"housed, clothed, fed, and that can only be done, with
"exceptions to be specially cared for, by parents—by
"parents who, previous to the birth of their children, were
"provided with the means of performing their duties. A
"scheme of education intended to prepare the way for an
"improved state of existence, which ignores the necessity
"of parental co-operation, is 'a mockery, a delusion, and
"'a snare.' And parents, unprepared to do their part
"efficiently, supposing them to be possessed of ordinary
"intelligence, are malefactors of the very worst description.
"For they have made a contract with their feeble and
"ignorant offspring in their absence to secure to them the
"fair chance of an enjoyable existence, knowing that they
"had not the means of performing their contract."

The introduction by Mr. Wood contains several valuable and eloquent passages, one of which we may quote:—

"'Efficient instruction' then, it is hoped, may be made
"the nation's clue to the nation's future well-being. Still
"the question remains—what is meant by 'efficient
"'instruction?' How shall the law's best intentions in this
"respect be satisfied? 'Elementary education' is only the
"scaffolding by which the moral being is ultimately built
"up. Reading, writing, and arithmetic are no more the
"grand result to be achieved, called education, than the
"knife and fork we use to convey food to our mouths is
"the slowly-developed system of physical processes and
"conditions we call the human frame. Education, to be
"really efficient, therefore, must sow the seeds of reasonable
"convictions with regard to the provisions and demands
"of human life in the minds of children, which may, after
"cultivation in the future, aid adults in the formation of
"habits which result in personal usefulness; and no
"instruction can be called good which does not also teach
"rules for good self-guidance, and thus deter men from
"actions which are not only hurtful to themselves, but to
"others also."

Little remains to tell of the gradual sinking to rest of the energetic worker. After this date, Ellis's power of wielding the pen became weaker and weaker, though he watched with interest the social events of the time. For the two or three letters to Professor Hodgson, which we have yet to quote, in one of which he sends him the "Short Statement," he was fain to avail himself of the help, as amanuensis, of his granddaughter, Miss Ethel E. Ellis, who was taking care of him during the absence of his daughter at her French home.

"April 25th, 1880.
"I am catching at an excuse to break my long silence,
"and Ethel is helping me with her pen; she also fur-

"nishes me with my excuse, for it was at her recommen-
"dation that I read an article by W. Bence Jones, entitled
"'Ireland, 1840—1880,' in the present number of Mac-
"millan. It has given me great pleasure, which I wish
"you to share; I therefore call your attention to the
"article, in case it should not yet have been brought to
"your notice. I am passably well. Ethel is doing her
"best to keep me out of a state of torpor."

"23rd May, 1880.

"Your favourable reception of Mr. Bence Jones' paper,
"induces me to call your attention to an article in the pre-
"sent number (May 15th) of the *Revue des Deux Mondes*,
"entitled '*La réforme de l'enseignement philosophique et
"'moral*,' par M. Alfred Fouillée. Fresh from the reading
"of this excellent article, I make bold to send you the
"accompanying 'Short Statement.' It is little more than
"an attempt to carry out a very small part of his sug-
"gestions; as you would perceive, the word Science is
"not to be found in it, and yet, if I am not mistaken, it
"contains matters which form the very foundations (small
"part may be) upon which anything which deserves to be
"called Social Science, Moral Science, or Science of
"Conduct must rest."

"June 20th, 1880.

"I am glad that you so far approved of my judgment
"as to find the paper in the *Revue des Deux Mondes*
"worth reading. What you say about our relative
"admiration may be true, but I don't think you have hit
"upon the right explanation of the difference between us.
"You do a dozen things while I have done but three.
"And I am gratified and encouraged. If I do not admire
"more than the half of what you do, it is because I am
"incompetent by my ignorance to appreciate them; and
"it would be presumption in me as well as bad taste to
"pretend to admire what I don't understand. It is a

"comfort for us to be able to think, as we may, that we
"are honestly working towards the same end—the im-
"provement and better position of our race."

Two months after this Professor Hodgson died of angina
pectoris at an international conference upon education at
Brussels. The sad event, which was sudden and wholly
unexpected, caused Ellis great sorrow, not only from his
warm personal attachment to the Professor, and his high
estimate of his mental powers, but because he was only
sixty-four at the time of his death, and Ellis hoped for
much further service from him to the great cause of the
advancement of humanity and the diminution of poverty
and destitution. Ellis survived him about six months, but
even during this period, and within a few weeks of his own
death, he wrote—or rather dictated—a short article in a
little monthly journal called *The Malthusian*, published by
a society denominated the Malthusian League, existing for
the purpose of carrying on a crusade against poverty and
destitution by means of the inculcation of the doctrines of
Malthus in favour of frugality, providence, and, above all,
parental forethought. This article concludes with the quotation of the following passage which Ellis adopts and
emphasizes. We may well accept it as his last words
addressed not only to the poor and needy—the class to
whom the best energies of his long life had been devoted—
but to all those members of society, high and low, who can
exert themselves to improve their welfare.

"The gradual diminution and possible extinction of
"poverty depends upon human conduct, and to make an
"impression on that, to teach the whole of mankind what
"good conduct is, and to inspire them with a sense of what
"they owe to themselves, to their families, and to society,
"we look more to our moralists than to any other class.
"The increase of our numbers always has been, must,
"and will be checked. The only alternative presented to

"us is, whether that increase shall be adequately prevented
"beforehand by parental care, or later and inadequately by
"poverty and its ghastly attendants. What choice will
"be made by those to whom the alternative is presented
"will depend upon whether they be instructed and
"thoughtful, or ignorant and reckless. It is not given to
"man to fix or alter the conditions in which he is born;
"but it is given to him so to shape his own conduct as to
"achieve for himself the highest state of happiness com-
"patible with those conditions. Teachers and moralists
"ought to explain to us what that conduct should be, its
"direction, and the limits within which it should be con-
"fined. They should also show us how to incline each
"individual to look for his own happiness in that direction
"and within those limits."

On the 18th February, 1881, William Ellis died. The
gradual failure of his powers had continued, and he had
become daily weaker. But the same cheerfulness which
had distinguished him throughout life remained to the end,
and the present writer, who saw him the Sunday before his
death, when he was unable from weakness to be dressed,
was received with the same calm and gentle cordiality as
ever. To the last he showed constant thought for the comfort of those around him, interest in the welfare of the
institutions he had founded, perfect resignation, and a sense
of duty faithfully and devotedly performed.

The Directors of the Company, for which he had worked
so long and which he had served so faithfully and ably,
passed a resolution expressing in cordial terms their recognition of the value of his services. The following is a copy
of the communication addressed to his family :—

" Indemnity Mutual Marine Assurance Company,
     " 13, Great Winchester Street, Old Broad Street,
          " London, 24th February, 1881.
"On the announcement of the death on the 18th

"February of Mr. William Ellis, the Directors of the
"Indemnity Mutual Marine Assurance Company, at a
"meeting of the Board on the 24th instant, unanimously
"resolved:—

"'That the Directors of this Company deeply and
"'sincerely sympathize with the family of their late
"'colleague, Mr. William Ellis, who, from the establish-
"'ment of the Company in 1824 till the day of his death,
"'was connected with it as underwriter, manager, and
"'director, and to whom, by his honourable conduct, un-
"'failing energy, untiring devotion, unflinching courage,
"'and wise counsel, the Company is indebted for its great
"'position of success and prosperity.

"'CHARLES CORKE, Secretary."

It now only remains to describe the personality of the
man the incidents of whose life we have sought to portray
in these pages. He was rather below the middle height,
very sparely built, and of a lithe and active habit of body.
His features were clearly cut and his eyes small but expres-
sive, with, frequently, a humorous twinkle when animated
by conversation. To the end of his life he continued the
old-fashioned custom of wearing a rather stiff white cravat,
which gave him a somewhat clerical appearance. From his
earliest years he had been a great pedestrian, and walking
was his chief exercise, for his extremely short sight rendered
it impossible for him to share in cricket and other games
which most young Englishmen love. But spite of his
defective vision, he had a thorough enjoyment of a beautiful
landscape, and could appreciate the charms of mountain
scenery as well as those of the commons and lanes of Surrey
and Kent, among which so large a portion of his life was spent
and in which, after he came to reside in the Regent's Park, he
was fond of passing the two autumn months when hard-
worked Londoners generally take their holiday. It should,
however, be remembered that a holiday, in the sense of a

complete absence from business of six weeks or two months, was never taken by Ellis until nearly the end of his life. His sense of the responsibility he was under to the large associated body of capitalists who had entrusted the management of their business and the care of their capital to him, led him to feel it his duty to receive and consider, as far as possible, personally the various risks and the many nice and intricate questions which were constantly arising in his daily work in the city, and to form his own judgment upon them.   Up to the year 1854 he had scarcely taken a holiday at all; in that year, as we have seen, he visited the Isle of Wight for three or four days at a time, "at the week's end," while his family were there.   After that time, and probably in consequence of the medical advice he then received, he relaxed his extremely close attention to business a little, and entrusted somewhat more responsibility to his assistants. But the longest absence we find him taking is for a fortnight or so, such as his visit to Dr. Hodgson at Fronfelen. His habit was to take a furnished house in some beautiful scenery in Surrey or Kent, such as Reigate, Shirley, Esher, Bexley Heath, or Tunbridge Wells, within reach by rail of London, and to come up to town four or five days in the week, taking long walks on the days when he was absent, and on Sundays, over the lovely heaths and commons of those specially beautiful English counties.   On these occasions he frequently invited his friends to visit him for a day or two, and all such visitors bore away with them specially pleasant memories of walks in his company, enlivened by interesting conversations.

As an underwriter he held, for a long series of years, the highest position in the city, and was the unquestioned head of the profession. The writer remembers once, before he knew him, asking a young underwriter at Lloyds whom he considered to be the leading underwriter, and receiving the prompt answer, "Oh! Mr. Ellis, without a doubt." His impartiality and honour were so thoroughly trusted that both underwriters and shipowners were perfectly satisfied to abide by his judgment; and many complicated questions which might have given rise to long and expensive litigation were settled by the papers being laid before Ellis. His occupation out of business hours and the objects to which his energies and his private time were devoted were not intruded upon his business connections. The following article from a weekly journal called *The Review*, devoted to insurance matters and written by a person who only knew Ellis as an underwriter, gives an account of the estimate formed of him by his business connections in the city. The paper referred to in it as having appeared in *Good Words* was written by Mr. William Jolly, one of Her Majesty's Inspectors of Schools, who knew and respected him highly. It gave an interesting sketch of his work out of business, which seems to have been almost unknown to the city world in which he moved. *The Review* says:—

"The August number of *Good Words* contains a short "biography of William Ellis, for many years underwriter "of the Indemnity Insurance Company. In that article is "shown a phase of his life to the insurance world almost "a revelation. True, now and again, it was whispered in "the city that a man of such business ability had a "weakness (as it was called) for education, and showed it "in a practical sense by purse as well as person, but Mr. "Ellis was known best in insurance circles as the very first "man in his profession. Added to good judgment and "acuteness, he possessed a gentle manner and perfect "politeness; but when he refused the risk which was "offered him with so much eloquence, the broker knew by "that quiet smile and almost merry twinkle of the eye "that in one moment he had appreciated the conditions "and judged the value of the risk. Mr. Ellis was in some "respects old fashioned, but that in a noble manner. "There was no necessity to ask him to initial a 'subject to "'approval' slip. His word was sufficient. In a word he

"was a man of the strictest probity and of generous
" instincts, yet he would have his premium, and the present
" position of the Indemnity is the best evidence to his
" ability.

" Amongst many incidents that show the man is one,
" perhaps well known, we cannot resist repeating. A
" shipowner, who had insured his vessels for some years
" in the Indemnity, called at the office to effect sundry
" insurances, and mentioned that owing to his absence
" from town his clerk had omitted to renew the policy
" upon one of his vessels, and that she had been unfor-
" tunately lost uninsured. Mr. Ellis only asked one
" question : ' Did you intend to offer me the renewal ? '
" ' Yes,' was the reply ; and before that shipowner left
" the office, a policy for the amount was executed and
" endorsed for a total loss, which was immediately paid.
" We know of a recent and similar act on the part of the
" Globe Marine. Insurance Company, but faith in these
" days between insurers and insured is a scarce article,
" and Mr. William Ellis and his doings are, we fear,
" purely historical."

This interesting notice shows both sides of his character
as an underwriter. In judging of a risk—whether or not to
accept it, and what was the proper rate to charge for it—he
showed the utmost care and caution, and never allowed persuasion or a false sense of generosity to influence him, with the
result that, of the whole fifty years, during which he
managed the business of the Indemnity Company, only
one showed an account on the wrong side. He always
decided for himself and acted on his judgment when formed.
The argument by a proposing insurer, " They have taken
" a similar risk elsewhere at the price I offer," was absolutely
useless. The answer was promptly given, " You are perfectly
" at liberty to insure elsewhere—the rate does not suit me."

If urgently pressed by a shipowner to do some act which
he disapproved of, he would consent to refer the matter to

the Board, thereby avoiding any personal friction with his customer. But the directors, when once they knew Ellis's views upon the advisability of a transaction, rarely, if ever, over-ruled him. This was the subject of one of his characteristic jokes: "Boards," he would say, "are excellent things "to make screens of."

On the other hand, in carrying out his contracts he always acted in accordance with the spirit rather than the letter of them, even to the fullest and most generous construction, frequently doing voluntarily what the law would admittedly not have required of him. One instance of this appears in the article we have already quoted. Another, which drew some attention at the time, and in which Ellis led the whole underwriting profession and practically compelled them to follow him, ought to be recorded. At the great fire which took place at Memel in the year 1854, not only a large part of the town but the ships lying in the port were destroyed. Several of them which were insured by the Indemnity Company against the usual sea risks were burnt. It was then a very doubtful question whether such policies would include the burning of a ship at her moorings in port, and the numerous other underwriters and insurance companies affected differed widely in their views, many of them proposing to resist the claims. But Ellis never hesitated for a moment. He at once announced that every loss would be paid in full, and the course which he took practically compelled every other underwriter and insurance company to follow his example. The shipowners of London were so sensible of the important service rendered by Ellis to the cause of honour and good faith, that they recognised it by subscribing to present him with a silver salver on which the circumstances we have mentioned were recorded.

The editor of the *Review* has recorded his "gentle manner "and perfect politeness," traits which were well known to his friends. An eminent city merchant, who had for a long series of years been in the habit of effecting insurances with him, gives the following account of the interview when he went to bid him adieu on his retirement, which illustrates the same trait of his character: " Mr. Ellis," he said, " I used " to come in to see you when I was a junior clerk at £30 a " year. I have been in the habit of coming to you for " twenty-five years and am now a leading partner in my firm, " and I wish to acknowledge that you treated me with the " same kindness and courtesy then as now." " You could " not, sir, have said anything which would have given me " greater pleasure." Sometimes it happened that his firmness in adhering to his own view and declining to give way to arguments in favour of a different course excited the anger of gentlemen possessed of less calmness and self-command. On one occasion an irascible shipowner lost his temper and became rude and offensive without being able to ruffle Ellis's manner or to make him show signs of anger. The next visitor, who, waiting his turn in the room at the Indemnity office which Ellis in company with his two assistants occupied, and which was open without any waiting room or outer office to the public, asked him how he managed so admirably to control his temper. " It is the " easiest thing in the world," he replied; " I said to myself— " there's a fool in the room, shall I double the number?"

His consideration for his subordinates in the office was most remarkable. Often he would curtail or deprive himself of his own holiday to enable a junior officer to enjoy one. And another incident in relation to the bonuses voted by the Directors illustrates this trait of his character. His own fixed salary was £2,000 per annum. But the company, when in successful years they divided the large profits earned in the course of their business, which were mainly due to the knowledge, skill, and sound judgment of their senior underwriter, and sometimes amounted to hundreds of thousands of pounds, felt it due to him to recognise his services more highly, and voted him a bonus, in addition to his salary, which for many consecutive years amounted to the sum of £10,000. But Ellis intimated to the Board that he should decline to receive any bonus unless the other officers and clerks in their employ shared in the prosperity of the company, and in consequence of this a bonus proportioned to his services and position in the office was always voted to each of them at the same time.

In private life his habits were simple and frugal, though he never denied himself or his family any reasonable gratification. One instance of this was that until late in life, after he had received the advice of his physicians to take greater care of himself, he always travelled to business by railway second class, and in this wise the writer used to travel with him to town for many consecutive years, even when they were holding their daily consultations upon the building and management of the Gospel Oak Schools, on which Ellis was expending thousands of pounds. He always, until compelled by failing health to abandon the custom, walked home from the office, a distance of about five miles.

Until long after he could well have afforded it he did not keep a carriage, and when he did so it was mainly for the use of his wife and daughters. He used to say that "he "only wished for one luxury—the luxury of keeping a con-"science," or, as another friend reports the same saying, "others may keep a carriage—I prefer to keep a conscience."

He was simply and unaffectedly hospitable, and had always a spare room and a warm welcome for friends from the country, or, when he was staying in the country, for visitors from town. And on Sunday evenings he was always at home and generally visited by some of his many friends, with whom, especially those who sympathized with him or assisted him in the great work of his life, he delighted in conversation and talked freely over not only the passing events of the times, but their own private affairs, if—and only if—they wished to consult him. His advice and help, and often aid of a more substantial form, were always open to those for whom he had an esteem and regard. His wife was a great lover of music, and his children were good amateur musicians, his daughters being excellent soprano singers, and his son Edward playing the violoncello. Consequently performances of high class music frequently took place at his house.   For many years after he moved to Lancaster Terrace, Regent's Park, Mrs. Ellis arranged a series of amateur musical performances at her own residence, at which the beautiful masses of Mozart, Beethoven, Haydn, Cherubini, and other great composers, and selections from the principal oratorios of Handel and Haydn, and the operas of Mozart, Gluck, and Rossini, were performed by a chosen party of about twenty vocal amateurs, with an accompaniment of a quartett of stringed instruments, conducted by an experienced pianist.   For some years, and down to the time of his death, these performances were conducted by Mr. Edward Holmes, the well-known author of the life of Mozart.   At these evenings Ellis, who had not any strong musical tendency, was always present to welcome his guests, and glad to chat to them during the intervals of the performances.

For his friends his conversation had a very great charm. From the records preserved by Plato of the conversations of Socrates, in which there is much of dramatic interest, there must have been great similarity of style in them to those of Ellis's; in addition to which the subjects which Ellis was fondest of discussing—the discovery of what was right or wrong under any state of circumstances which might be brought forward for consideration, and the further discussion of how influence might be brought to bear on humanity to adopt the right course, are precisely those which form the staple of the Socratic dialogues.   Like Socrates, he often said, "I can only claim one kind of knowledge—I know "when I do not know."   Mrs. Fenwick Miller, one of his attached pupils, says of him[1]:—"I knew him only in his old

---

[1] *Readings in Social Economy*, Preface, page x.

"age; nevertheless, his mind was the most acute, vigorous,
"and truthful, the most capable of piercing to the centre,
"and declaring the nature of things, and the most vivifying
"and strengthening in its influence upon another, that it has
"been my privilege to know." He was in the habit of
passing almost imperceptibly from conversation to interrogation. The custom of leading his boys by questions to a
solution of their difficulties introduced itself into his conversations with his friends, and the method of coming to a
conclusion in conversations on general subjects often took
the same course. To the value of that method all teachers
who have ever tried it bear testimony. Professor Hodgson,
a very able teacher, says of it in a letter to one of his
friends:—"The Socratic method is the true one, especially
"with the young. They must not only *hear* but *speak* and
"think that they may speak. An eloquent description of
"a landscape may be very charming and even impressive,
"but what is that compared with a view of the whole scene
"*through one's own eyes.* It is climbing step by step, in
"good company, the hill before whose top it is seen in all
"the harmony of its component parts. What we hear we
"may forget; what we think out for ourselves we remember
"through life, and what is far more, it is vital for good in
"action."

How highly Professor Hodgson—himself one of the most
brilliant conversationalists and eloquent speakers of his
time—thought of Ellis's powers in conversation may be
gathered from the following extract from a letter to his
wife, containing an account of an evening spent at the
house of Dr. Chapman, whose secretary was then Miss
Marian Evans, better known as George Eliot. He says:—

"   30th December, 1850.
"About eight, we" (he and Ellis) "walked down to
"Chapman's, in the Strand, and spent three hours there
"very pleasantly. Mr. R. W. Mackay, author of the

w

"*Progress of the Intellect;* the Rev. Phillips Potter, author
"of the *Characteristics of Socrates and Plato;* Dr. Travis,
"an independent gentleman ; Mr. Spencer, sub-editor of
"the *Economist;* a Mr. Day, who was for eleven years a
"monk, and who, like Dr. T., writes in the Open Council
"of the Leader; Mr. Woodfall, son of Junius' famous
"publisher, and two or three ladies were there.   Dr. T. is
"a young man with a very fine countenance, beaming
"with benevolence, and which, when once seen, it is
"difficult to forget ; but he is obviously an impracticable
"dreamer, bound in verbal formulas, and rotating darkly
"in a vortex of insane speculation.   He and Mr.
"Spencer were sparring away with the gloves of polite
"controversy, when Mr. Ellis pricked up his ears at some
"sound of ' re-organization of society,' and was all atten-
"tion in a moment.   I kept strict silence on purpose, and
"left all open for Mr. E., who, by and by, struck in with
"a very pertinent remark which compelled Dr. T. to un-
"fold his social scheme at some length.   I will not trouble
"you with this or with a sketch of the discussion itself.
"Mr. E., however, now with broadsword, and now with
"rapier, made very sharp and short work of it ; but it was
"like wounding a mist which closes in instantly, and
"leaves no trace of the disaster.   Dr. T. retired behind
"his verbal entrenchments and was not to be dislodged.
"It was a rich treat to hear the courteous irony—or ironic
"courtesy—with which Mr. E. disabled first Dr. T. and
"then the ex-monk, who was tempted in an evil hour to put
"in a word about 'antagonism between labour and capital.'"

And elsewhere[1] Professor Hodgson has paid this well-
deserved tribute to his power and influence :—

   "He has long and effectively vindicated, in all teaching
"of both sexes and of every rank, its true place for

---

[1] In the dedication to Ellis of his book on the *Education of Girls and the
Employment of Women.*

" economics as a branch of moral science, needful and fit
"to guide conduct, to train character, and to shape
"condition, as well as to develop intelligence. To him
"very many (the author being one) owe much for great
"personal kindness, but, above all, for a higher, wider,
"clearer, more definite, practical, consistent, and inspiriting
"view of education as it ought to be and will be."

It is impossible to record in this sketch of his life many of
the conversations which attracted his friends, and which
have left in them the memory of the great power with which
he grasped every question which he discussed; but a very
few instances will show the incisive clearness and logical
force of his style—especially the manner with which anything
unreal was met and dealt with. On one occasion a lady,
after boasting of the linguistic accomplishments of her
daughter—how she was already proficient in English,
French, Italian, and German, with a fair knowledge of Latin
as well—asked Ellis whether he could recommend her a
Spanish teacher, as she was anxious her daughter should
add that language to her accomplishments. "May I ask
"first, Madam," was the reply, "when is she going to learn
"something worth knowing in all these languages?"

For worldly fame or glory he had a great contempt. On
one occasion, during his life at Croydon, a fellow-passenger
by the coach to town was holding forth on the glories of the
first Napoleon, and turning to Ellis for corroboration said,
"Now that is what I call a great man, don't you?" At that
moment they happened to be passing some shops, and
pointing to a butcher who was standing by a large shop full
of meat, Ellis replied, "Well, I might call that man a great
"butcher, but I don't know that I should call him a great man."

Upon the assumption of superior virtue Ellis was always
severe. An anecdote which he tells of himself in his *Philo-
Socrates* (vol. ii., page 29) is a good illustration of this. He
says:—

"In the days of my youth it happened to me to be put

"upon my defence by one of your self-constituted saints. I
"had been invited on a Sunday to a friend's country house
"about ten miles from London. Glad of an opportunity
"for exercise and air free from smoke, the day being fine,
" I sauntered down with a pleasant companion, so as to
"arrive soon after morning service. We had not been
"long there, chatting over luncheon, before another visitor
"made his appearance. When he heard me say that I
"had walked from town, he remarked that I must have
"walked very fast. 'Quite the reverse,' I replied; 'I started
"'early on purpose to breathe the balmy air of this
"'glorious day at my leisure.' 'Then,' said he, 'you have
"'not been to church?' I readily admitted that I had not;
"and straightway he made known to me how greatly he
"disapproved my neglect of public worship. I knew that
"he had not come so great a distance as I had; but still it
"appeared to me that he could hardly have walked from
"his house since church-time; and a remark to this effect
"brought forth the explanation that he had ridden, not
"walked, over. 'Now,' said I, 'let us appeal to our
"'excellent host; let him be the judge which of us is the
"'greater sinner—I, who have disregarded no command-
"'ment, or you, who have made your horse labour on the
"'Sabbath day.' My reprover's countenance assumed an
"expression of mixed annoyance and anger at this
"unexpected retort, and I could not refrain from
"suggesting as a justification of what he had done, that
"perhaps it was a pleasure, rather than work, for his horse
"to carry so good a Christian."

But to children he was always gentle and friendly, and
his popularity among them was great. No corporal punishment was permitted in his schools ; moral influence, and
the interest excited by his able and well-trained masters in
the subjects taught, were sufficient to secure attention and
good conduct in the most numerous classes. He considered
that corporal punishment had a thoroughly bad effect, and

in reply to those who thought that it was needed in order to maintain discipline in schools, he always contended that if a master could not keep order without it, it must be the fault of the master himself; and pointed to his own schools as evidence of that proposition. In a letter to Mr. Mattieu Williams, he says :—

"9th June, 1851.

"I applaud your testimony in favour of the discon-
"tinuance of punishment—especially corporal punish-
"ment—as part of school discipline. All teachers will
"be of one mind with you when once they feel themselves
"competent to explain how suffering necessarily follows
"ill-conduct, either of itself or through the intervention
"demanded for the protection of others, and to conduct
"their training in accordance with what they teach."

An anecdote of Rüntz's method of influencing boys, which took place at the time of a visit by Ellis to his school and was approved by him, will illustrate this. A boy who was at the Birkbeck School, in Southampton Buildings, seemed to be incorrigibly idle, and would not do any of the exercises allotted to him. Rüntz asked him why he did so; and he replied that he did not like work, and wouldn't work. Rüntz placed the boy alone, having first emptied his pockets, in a gallery where he could see the other boys working, but had nothing to do. So he remained for the morning and again during the afternoon. Next day the boy wanted to return to his place in class; but Rüntz declined to allow it. He had taken a day's idleness for his own benefit; and now he could do so for Mr. Rüntz's satisfaction. On the second day he pleaded hard to be allowed to return to his class; Rūntz allowed it, and the boy never again tried the experiment of wilful idleness.

One act which shows Ellis's deep and intense sympathy for neglected children was his reprinting and circu-

lating in large numbers a song by Dr. Charles Mackay, which appeared in the *Illustrated London News* of January 29th, 1853. We reprint it here, and our readers will judge by the foregoing papers how entirely it appealed to his deepest and most earnest aspirations.

THE SOULS OF THE CHILDREN.

By Charles Mackay, LL.D.

"Who bids for the little children—
　Body and soul and brain?
Who bids for the little children—
　Young and without a stain?
Will no one bid," said England,
　"For their souls so pure and white,
And fit for all good or evil,
　The world on their page may write?"

"We bid," said Pest and Famine,
　"We bid for life and limb;
Fever and pain and squalor
　Their bright young eyes shall dim.
When the children grow too many,
　We'll nurse them as our own,
And hide them in secret places,
　Where none may hear their moan."

"I bid," said Beggary, howling,
　"I'll buy them, one and all,
I'll teach them a thousand lessons—
　To lie, to skulk, to crawl;
They shall sleep in my lair, like maggots,
　They shall rot in the fair sunshine;
And if they serve my purpose,
　I hope they'll answer thine."

"And I'll bid higher and higher,"
　Said Crime with wolfish grin,
"For I love to lead the children
　Through the pleasant paths of sin.

They shall swarm in the streets to pilfer,
  They shall plague the broad highway,
Till they grow too old for pity,
  And ripe for the law to slay.

Prison and hulk and gallows
  Are many in the land,
'Twere folly not to use them,
  So proudly as they stand.
Give *me* the little children,
  I'll take them as they're born;
And I'll feed their evil passions
  With misery and scorn.

Give *me* the little children,
  Ye good, ye rich, ye wise,
And let the busy world spin round,
  While ye shut your idle eyes;
And your judges shall have work,
  And your lawyers wag the tongue,
And the gaolers and policemen
  Shall be fathers to the young.

I and the Law, for pastime,
  Shall struggle day and night;
And the Law shall gain, but I shall win,-
  And we'll still renew the fight:
And ever and aye we'll wrestle,
  Till Law grow sick and sad,
And kill in its desperation
  The incorrigibly bad.

.I, and the Law, and Justice,
  Shall thwart each other still;
And hearts shall break to see it,
  And innocent blood shall spill:
So leave—oh, leave the children
  To Ignorance and Woe—
And I'll come in and teach them
  The way that they should go."

"Oh, shame!" said true Religion,
  "Oh, shame that this should be!
I'll take the little children,
  I'll take them all to me:
I'll raise them up with kindness
  From the mire in which they're trod;
I'll teach them words of blessing,
  I'll lead them up to God."

"You're *not* the true religion,"
  Said a Sect with flashing eyes;
"Nor thou," said another scowling,
  "Thou'rt heresy and lies."
"You shall not have the children,"
  Said a third with shout and yell;
"You're Antichrist and bigot—
  You'd train them up for hell."

And England, sorely puzzled
  To see such battle strong,
Exclaimed with voice of pity,
  "Oh, friends! you do me wrong!
Oh, cease your bitter wrangling;
  For till you all agree,
I fear the little children
  Will plague both you and me."

But all refused to listen;
  Quoth they—"We bide our time."
And the bidders seized the children—
  Beggary, Filth, and Crime;
And the prisons teemed with victims,
  And the gallows rocked on high;
And the thick abomination
  Spread reeking to the sky.

Summing up his character, it may be said that the whole
superstructure was built up on the foundation of a strong
sense of duty and an equally strong feeling of benevolence,
a feeling not limited to his immediate friends and relations,

nor even to his countrymen, but which extended to all mankind. We have seen, in many of his letters, how deeply and
personally he felt the misery, destitution, and vice which
exist around us. He was never weary of thinking how this
could best be put an end to, or what he could do to raise
the wretched victims of ignorance, indolence, and neglect.
But his consideration of the causes of, and remedies for, this
state of things showed him that mere charitable relief was
merely a slight palliation of, not a remedy for, the evil : it
left the source untouched. And, although he often gave
help to those who were suffering from misfortune not due
to their own misconduct, he saw that indiscriminate almsgiving was even worse than useless in its effect ; it demo-
ralised the recipients and interfered with the formation of
habits of industry and self-reliance. He never, therefore,
gave alms to strangers ; but seeing clearly, as he did, that
misery and destitution are the necessary result of bad conduct, he devoted his life and a very large part of his savings
to the method which seemed to him the best for removing
their cause, and bringing about right conduct among the poor
and also among the rich—among the poor by leading them to
the knowledge and habit of right self-guidance—among the
rich by further leading them to the study of what are the best
means to improve the welfare of the poor, and to the disposition to labour for that object, and so to advance the general
well-being of mankind. By such work as this, which he had
described as " the Knowledge and Practice of Religion in
" Common Life," he deemed that the truest happiness which
any human being can hope for might be attained—the
happiness of doing whatever good lies within the limit
of his powers to his friends, his fellow-countrymen, and
the world.

APPENDIX A.

CHAPTER IX., PAGE 250.

LETTER FROM MADAME SALIS SCHWABE.

DEAR Mr. Blyth,—In returning you with many thanks the manuscript of your memoirs of the late Mr. Ellis, which you kindly placed in my hands, I beg leave to express, however imperfectly, my appreciation of the masterly way in which you have brought into full light the salient points in the character and in the teaching of that eminent man.

To us who have sat at his feet, to learn, not abstruse formulas, but some of the life-bringing principles which ought to direct the conduct of man whilst sojourning on earth, the fact may well seem inexplicable that so few years after the close of William Ellis' career, his name—the name of John Stuart Mill's admired friend—is almost forgotten and, among the younger generation, utterly unknown. We all remember to what extent Ellis courted obscurity during life and oblivion after death. But it is surprising, nevertheless, that the nation should allow one of its patriarchal teachers of political economy as applied to the education of the people to be thus lost to memory.

There was a time when the leading journal of these islands[1] did not hesitate loudly to proclaim, in an article of consummate ability, that Mr. Ellis was "the founder of social science," and I am thankful to you for having drawn attention to this fact in chapter vii. of your delightful volume.

Alas! in 1887 all this had changed. I listened in vain, and

---

[1] *Times*, November 10th, 1873: Review of the *Autobiography of John Stuart Mill*.

possibly some others present may have done the same, for a word of acknowledgment of Mr. Ellis' transcendent merits in the speeches held at the Drapers' Hall on July 8th of that year in the interests of the Maria Grey Institution, when our Princess Royal, the then Crown Princess of Germany, formed part of the assembly, although I have reason to believe that among the motives which procured for that meeting her august presence was Her Imperial Highness' desire to do honour to the memory of Froebel and to one of the teachers of her youth, William Ellis, whose memory, as you well say, she has never ceased to cherish. When in 1869 I enjoyed the privilege of an audience, I remember Her Imperial Highness saying, in course of conversation, "*Der liebe gute Mr.* "*Ellis! Warum kommt er nicht einmal nach Berlin? Sie glauben* "*nicht wie viel ich von dem Manne gelernt! Mein Vater schätzte* "*ihn auch so hoch.*"[1]

Well, not one of the speakers had a word to say about Mr. Ellis, nor did any of the periodicals but one, so far as my observation extended, in their remarks on that brilliant assembly, so much as allude to Mr. Ellis, the pioneer of most of what is attempted in this country as regards middle class education. Allow me to say a word on that sole exception, viz., the article which appeared in the *Spectator* of July 16th, 1887, under the title of "Pedagogy." In it I found, to my greatest pleasure, a high appreciation of the work done by the "Froebel Institution" at Naples, now called "Istituto "Internazionale Vittorio Emanuele II." But when I read on I could not help observing that the able writer of that article, when speaking of the late William Ellis, was but slightly acquainted with the actual nature of his work. "In the Froebel Institution at "Naples," remarks the writer, "an almost unique attempt is made "to connect with a large infant school of the most approved modern "type upper departments in which the principles of Pestalozzi and "of Froebel are well carried out." Now it was William Ellis who first inspired and enabled me to become the humble means of establishing such an Institution. Twenty years ago, by his generosity, an Italian, Signor Quarati, was entirely trained during four years at the Birkbeck School at Peckham under Mr. W. A. Shields, and

---

[1] "Dear, good Mr. Ellis! Why does he never come to Berlin? I cannot tell "you how much I learnt from that man! My father also valued him so highly."

became, first, head master, and now, jointly with Madame de Portugall, director of the Froebel Institution at Naples. He now instructs all the classes above the Kindergarten in the principles of social economy and right conduct as taught by Mr. Ellis. Mr. Ellis never allowed a year to pass without writing to his former pupil; and Signor Quarati kindly sent, at my request, copies of these letters, of which I am happy to add at the close of this letter those written in his own handwriting (the later ones being written by his daughter, Madame Ducamp, in her father's name) as they exemplify the warm and lasting interest with which he regarded all who had in any way been associated with him. All who ever came under the influence of William Ellis testify to the purity and elevating character of his teaching, and I know many whom he has inspired to noble and unselfish work.

"A prophet is not without honour save in his own country." I have often felt most acutely the truth of this saying as regards Froebel and William Ellis, who, alas, are little known except by name in their own countries, even by many who speak as with authority on matters of education. It would be impossible in this short letter to say all I would of those remarkable men. Froebel and Ellis did not, as so many wrongly imagine, give to the world stereotyped mechanical systems, to be blindly followed by the unthinking and superficial, but they, each in his own way, taught the principles of eternal truth, and left it to each true-hearted and intelligent pedagogue to build on this foundation his own superstructure. Hence are their teachings adaptable to the needs of the day at all times and to all countries.—I am, dear Mr. Blyth, yours very truly,

8, Clarges Street, W.,   JULIE SALIS SCHWABE.
    31st August, 1888.

LETTERS FROM WILLIAM ELLIS TO SIGNOR QUARATI.

December 25th, 1875.

Dear Mr. Quarati,—Your letter of the 20th inst. has reached me in safety, as also did the one of last summer to which you refer. I need hardly assure you that I cannot but be pleased to hear anything affecting your happiness, as well as that of your wife, and you both have my best wishes for the success of your united works, professional and domestic.

The diminution of prejudice from day to day may, without vanity, be accepted as one result of your own good workmanship. People, however ill-disposed, cannot hold out against success. They may come to find fault, but are forced to bear witness to what they find well done. Happily, the schoolmaster of our day is beginning to be considered as the head of any other establishment. The farmer who gathers large crops from his land, the grazier who rears healthy herds and flocks, the captain who navigates his ships safely, the engine driver who drives the train with undeviating care and punctuality, and the engineer and architect who design and construct their works so as best to fit them for the service required—all by their success command the approbation of the best judges. In like manner so does (or will) the schoolmaster who receives into his school ignorant and incapable children and sends forth intelligent, capable, and well-conducted adults. It is not a matter of indifference to him whether they be Jew or Gentile, Catholic or Protestant, Christian or Mahomedan, orthodox or heretic, a bit more than it is whether they be dark or fair, tall or short, long or near sighted. He must be resigned to all this as being beyond his control, but whatever else they may be, it is his determination to spare no effort to send them forth *capable, intelligent,* and *well educated.*

8th January, 1876.

My dear Mr. Quarati,—I have delayed answering your friendly remembrance of me of the 22nd of last month, till I could send you the first number of a new educational periodical which contains the report of a paper from me read by Dr. Hodgson at a meeting of schoolmasters at Glasgow.

You will see that if I have nothing new or better expressed to deliver, my faith in what education can be made to do for the improvement of mankind and for bettering the condition of all classes remains unshaken. Indeed I may say it is stronger than ever. One caution is necessary—that teachers should not be misled as to what they ought to aim at under the name of education. With them it ought not to be a question between higher and lower, sectarian and unsectarian, but how best, according to the means and time at their command, to impart the knowledge, or as much of it as possible, essential for good self-guidance and, by example and discipline, to form dispositions and habits which will make knowledge lead on to conduct and acts, and not evaporate in words.

Nobody can be better prepared to hear of the difficulties and uncertainties which are attached to your present work. I am rather surprised that you have thus far got on so well. It will be a satisfaction to you at all events that whether the present school's existence be of long or short duration, you will have exerted all your powers for its stability and prosperity. If Naples be incapable, it is to be hoped that other parts of Italy will be capable, of appreciating and rewarding such services as you can render.[1]

———

4th January, 1877.

My dear Mr. Quarati,—I am very glad to learn from your letter of 29th December, 1876, just received, that the school continues to thrive and grow. By which I conclude, although you report nothing specially of yourselves, that you and Mrs. Quarati are thriving also.

We have, I think, arrived at this stage in education that good teachers with a little tact and discretion can keep aloof from party strife, let the party assume what name or colours it will. I do not say that good teachers may not be harassed and distracted, but intent upon their work, and with a clear perception of what they are aiming at on behalf of their children, they will bear with obstacles as part of the condition in which they are placed, from which there is no escape, but will trouble them much or little according as they control and guide themselves.

A good teacher occupies a vantage ground. He is relieved from the necessity of controversy. Teaching with him means assisting his pupils to learn to form their *own* conclusions and opinions, not to take the conclusions and experiences of others, even of their

---

[1] The institution which embodies those schools is now constituted by Royal Decree into a corporate body *(ente morale)* and placed on a permanent basis.

teachers. This is quite as true in moral as in physical matters, in rules of human conduct as in physical phenomena. The rules of conduct which lead to well-being, and guard against want and misery, are the very pith of all religion when separated from the dross, the ignorance, the superstition, and the barbarism with which it has too often been mixed up. The good teacher having made this separation in his own mind, gives the benefit of his enlightenment to his children—he invites their attention to religion pure and undefiled, and gradually opens their eyes to the consequences of such religion in conduct. With such teaching there will be little need of meddling with what, under the garb of religion, leads to bitterness of feeling and interminable contentions.

———

19th January, 1878.

Dear Mr. Quarati,—I am very much obliged to you for your letter of the 10th inst. I read with great pleasure all the details of your doings. I am now past work, and live in the recollection of my attempts, however insignificant, to promote and improve the education of the young, rejoicing, in what I learn from you and others, that the good work is persevered in by younger and abler teachers.

While education must be at the base of all social progress that can reasonably be expected, we must bear in mind that the fruits of education do not grow and ripen all at once. With the best of teachers and the best appliances the reward will be mostly in the future, and some in the far future.

No discouragement, therefore, ought to be felt because progress is slow with comparatively incompetent teachers—those who are conscious of their own imperfections and those who are blind to them. One of the most hopeful signs of the closing years of the nineteenth century is that public opinion has become alive to the duty owed by adults to the young, that education should be imparted to all, that is, that all, as nearly as possible, should start in life knowing what to do, and ready in disposition and habits to practice what they know.

APPENDIX B.

PART I.

LIST OF WILLIAM ELLIS'S WRITINGS

In order of date, including Pamphlets and Contributions to periodical literature and letters to journals.

1824 to 1826. Articles in the *Westminster Review*, viz.:—
   April, 1824. On West India Slavery.
   July, 1824. On Charitable Institutions.
   April, 1825. On Exportation of Machinery.
   July, 1825. On McCulloch's Political Economy. (By W. Ellis and J. Stuart Mill jointly.)
   Jan., 1826. On the Employment of Machinery.

1829. Conversations upon Knowledge, Happiness, and Education between a Mechanic and a Patron of the London Mechanics' Institution.   Baldwin and Cradock.

1832. The Parents' Cabinet of Amusement and Instruction. [Second edition, 1835. Third edition, 1859. Fourth edition, 1889.] [Edited by W. Ellis. Articles by many different writers, including both W. Ellis and Mrs. W. Ellis.]   Smith, Elder, and Co.

1846. Outlines of Social Economy. [Second edition, 1850. Third edition, 1860.]   Smith, Elder, and Co.
   Translated into French by M. C. Terrien, with an introduction by M. Barthélémy St. Hilaire, and published by Guillaumin and Co., Paris, 1850.

1847. Outlines of the History and Formation of the Understanding.   Smith, Elder, and Co.

1848. A few Questions on Secular Education, what it is, and what it ought to be, with an attempt to answer them. Preceded by an Appeal to Richard Cobden, Esq., M.P., and the members of the late Anti-Corn Law League. (Pamphlet.)
Smith, Elder, and Co.

Questions and Answers Suggested by a Consideration of some of the Arrangements and Relations of Social Life, being a Sequel to Outlines of Social Economy.
Smith, Elder, and Co.

Article in the *Westminster and Foreign Quarterly Review* for October on Causes of Poverty.

1849. Introduction to the Study of the Social Sciences.
Smith, Elder, and Co.

Articles in the *Westminster and Foreign Quarterly Review* :—
January, on Distressed Needlewomen.
April, Review of Mary Barton, by Mrs. Gaskell.
October, on The State of the Nation.

1850. Progressive Lessons in Social Science. [Second edition, 1862.]

First edition translated into French by M. C. Terrien, and published by Guillaumin and Co., Paris, 1851.

Second edition translated into French by M. Albin Ducamp, and published by Guillaumin and Co., 1873.

Articles in the *Westminster and Foreign Quarterly Review* :—
April, on Relief Measures.
July, on Classical Education.

1851. Education as a Means of Preventing Destitution.
Smith, Elder, and Co.

Translated into Dutch by Heer J. P. Bredius, with a preface and concluding address to Heer J. R. Thorbecke by the translator, and published by W. E. J. Tjeenk Willink, Te Zwolle, 1852.

Article in the *Westminster Review* for January, on Educational Movements.

Article in the *British Quarterly Review* for May, on The European Difficulty.

1852. Reminiscences and Reflections of an Old Operative. (Pamphlet.)
Smith, Elder, and Co.

X

What am I? Where am I? What ought I to do? How
am I to become qualified and disposed to do what I ought
to do?   Smith, Elder, and Co.

1853. February to June. Thirteen papers on Secular Education,
published in the *Hebrew Observer*.

1854. Lessons on the Phenomena of Industrial Life and the Con-
ditions of Industrial Success. Edited by Rev. Richard
Dawes, M.A., Dean of Hereford. [Second edition, 1858.
Third edition, 1861.]   Groombridge and Sons.

1857. A Layman's Contribution to the Knowledge and Practice of
Religion in Common Life.   Smith, Elder, and Co.
Where must we look for the further Prevention of Crime?
                                    Smith, Elder, and Co.

1858. Letters from Tom Brown to Rev. Frederick Temple, M.A.
(Head Master of Rugby), on the occasion of sending some
of the young Browns to Rugby School. Reprinted from
the *Manchester Examiner and Times*. (Pamphlet.)
                                    Dunnill and Palmer, and
                                    A. Ireland and Co., Manchester.

1859. An address to teachers, delivered 11th October, 1859, at
the South Kensington Museum, under the auspices of the
Science and Art Department of the Committee of Council
on Education, on The Importance of Imparting a Knowledge of the Principles of Social Science to Children.
Being the first of a course of Lectures on that subject.
(Pamphlet.)   Eyre and Spottiswoode.

1861 to 1864. Philo-Socrates. A series of papers wherein subjects
are investigated which, there is reason to believe, would
have interested Socrates, and in a manner that he would
not disapprove, were he among us now, gifted with the
knowledge and familiar with the habits and doings of our
times. 4 vols.   Smith, Elder, and Co.

1863. Instruction in Elementary Social Science, what it is, and
why and how it ought to be given in all schools. Being
the introductory lecture delivered at University College,
29th October, 1863, to the class formed for a course of
instruction in Social Science and the art of teaching the
subject in school. (Pamphlet.)   Smith, Elder, and Co.

1865. Middle-Class Education. What to aim at, as well as how
to aim. An article in the *Museum and English Journal of
Education* of 1st March. (Reprinted as a pamphlet.)
Nelson and Sons.

Combinations and Strikes from the Teacher's point of view.
An article in the same paper of 1st July. (Reprinted
as a pamphlet.) Nelson and Sons.

1866. Thoughts on the Future of the Human Race.
Smith, Elder, and Co.

Three letters from a London merchant to a country friend
on the late Monetary Crisis. James Gilbert.

1868. What stops the way? or, Our two great difficulties: with
some hints concerning the way. Smith, Elder, and Co.

1869. A Chart of Industrial Life, with some instructions for its
use. (Pamphlet.) Simpkin and Marshall, and
A. Ireland and Co., Manchester.

1870. An address to teachers on the Laws of Conduct in Industrial Life, and on the method of imparting instruction
therein in our primary schools; being the first of a course
of four lectures delivered by permission of the Lord President of the Committee of Council on Education at the
Lecture Theatre of the Royal School of Mines, Jermyn-
street, on 23rd May, 1870. (Pamphlet.)
Chapman and Hall.

1871. An appeal to the London School Board. (Pamphlet.)
Pardon and Son.

1872. Helps to the Young in their Efforts at Self-guidance. Edited
by the Rev. W. Jowitt, M.A., Headmaster of the Schools
of the Corporation for Middle Class Education, Cowper-
street, Finsbury.

Translated into French by M. Albin Ducamp, and published by Guillaumin and Co., Paris, 1873.

Article in the *Beehive* of October 26th. Hints to Parents.

Letter published in the *Leicester Chronicle and Mercury*
in October, on The Purpose of Education, signed
"Educator."

1873. Letter published in the *Times* of 10th November The
Founder of Social Science.

1874. Studies of Man, by a Japanese.   Trübner and Co.

1875. A few words on Board Schools; what may be done in them and the least that ought to be done in them, with an introduction by Rev. Lewis W. Wood, Chairman of Dunton Bassett School Board. (Pamphlet.)

            Ward and Sons, Leicester.

The Pressing Want of our Time: a paper read at the meeting of the Scottish Educational Congress at Glasgow on 30th December, 1875, by Professor Hodgson on behalf of W. Ellis, and printed in the *Educational News* of 1st January, 1876.

1876. Letter on practical education, published in the *Times* of 2nd September, and signed "Senex."

1880. A Short Statement of some matters which ought to be known by all teachers, and taught to all children, before their school days are ended, with an introduction by Rev. Lewis W. Wood. (Pamphlet.) W. Willson, Leicester.

The Struggle for Enjoyable Existence. (Tract.)

            The Malthusian League.

1881. A short article in the *Malthusian* for January, "An appeal to our friends and our opponents."

Part II.

The following works are either adaptations of Ellis's teaching for use as reading books in schools, or amplifications of portions of it written either by teachers who have studied under him or persons who have adopted his views:—

Reading Lessons in Social Economy for the use of Schools, by Benjamin Templar, Head Master of the Manchester Free School. [Second edition, 1862.] Jarrold and Sons.

The advanced Reading Book of Constable's Educational Series; contains (pp. 142-197) an excellent series of lessons by W. A. Shields, Head Master of the Birkbeck Schools, Peckham.

            Gordon, Edinburgh.

The Sixth English Reading Book of the same series contains (pp. 315-339) a continuation of the subject by other hands.

            Gordon, Edinburgh.

Readings in Social Economy, by Mrs. Florence Fenwick Miller, member of the London School Board (1883).

Longman, Green, and Co., London.

Lessons in Social Economy for the use of Teachers, by James Rüntz, Head Master of the Birkbeck Schools, Kingsland (1884). Educational Supply Association.

Introduction to Social Economy. Reading Books for Children, arranged by Ethel E. Ellis. (Book 1, 1885. Book 2, 1886. Book 3, 1888.) Educational Supply Association.

Suggestive Lessons in Practical Life, being Reading Books for School and Home; designed to train the young to thoughtfulness and intelligence, through observation of the facts of the world's industry and skill, by Alfred Jones. (First Series, 1886; second edition, 1888. Second series, 1886. Third series, 1886. Fourth series, 1887.) Smith, Elder, and Co.

———

The following books, addresses, and pamphlets are by friends of or fellow-workers with Ellis, in sympathy with or elucidation of his views:—

What should Secular Education embrace? by George Combe. (Pamphlet. Second edition, 1848.) Maclachlan, Edinburgh.
Simpkin, Marshall, and Co.

Remarks on National Education, by George Combe. (Pamphlet, 1848.) Maclachlan, Edin.
Simpkin, Marshall, and Co.

Suggestive Hints towards Improved Secular Education, making it bear upon practical life, by Rev. Richard Dawes, M.A., Dean of Hereford. [Eighth edition, 1861.] Groombridge and Sons.

Education: Its principles and practice as developed by George Combe. Compiled and edited by William Jolly, H.M. Inspector of Schools (1879). Macmillan and Co.

The Science of Conduct: its place in Education. A lecture delivered before the College of Preceptors, November 19th, 1879, by R. Wormell, D.Sc., M.A., Head Master of the School of the Corporation for Middle Class Education, Cowper-street, Finsbury. E. F. Hodgson and Son.

The following pamphlets and addresses by Professor William Ballantyne Hodgson, LL.D., viz.:—

Two lectures on the Conditions of Health and Wealth, educationally considered.　(Pamphlet, 1860.)

James Gordon, Edinburgh.
Hamilton, Adams, and Co.

The Education of Girls and the Employment of Women (1869).

Trübner and Co.

Inaugural address on his appointment as Professor of Commercial and Political Economy and Mercantile Law in the University of Edinburgh (1871).　　　　James Thin, Edinburgh.

A. Ireland and Co., Manchester.

Address on Education, delivered as Vice-President at the meeting of the Social Science Association, at Norwich, 4th October, 1873.

Address delivered at the Annual Meeting of the Educational Institute of Scotland, 18th September, 1875.

Murray and Gibb, Edinburgh.

The Instruction of the Community, especially the Wage-receiving Classes, in Economic Science.　A paper read at Aberdeen before the National Association for the Promotion of Social Science, 25th September, 1877.

Free Press Office, Aberdeen.